PRAISE FOR THE SCARLET ODYSSEY SERIES

"Wakanda meets *Warhammer 40,000* . . . Readers will enjoy the setting and the magic system."

—*Publishers Weekly*

"Rwizi's debut is noteworthy for its African-inspired setting."

—*Library Journal*

"Raised in Swaziland and Zimbabwe but now residing in South Africa, C. T. Rwizi is a remarkable new talent. He deftly juggles five very different protagonists; establishes a vast yet intricate new magical system unlike anything else I've ever seen; and unfolds stories scattered across the distant past, the chaotic present, and entirely different planes of existence."

—Tor.com

"C. T. Rwizi . . . builds a rich setting by combining recognizable aspects of his home with deft and fantastical world building."

—*Medium*

HOUSE OF GOLD

ALSO BY C. T. RWIZI

THE SCARLET ODYSSEY SERIES

Scarlet Odyssey

Requiem Moon

Primeval Fire

HOUSE OF GOLD

C. T. RWIZI

This is a work of fiction. Names, characters, organizations, places, events, and incidents are either products of the author's imagination or are used fictitiously. Otherwise, any resemblance to actual persons, living or dead, is purely coincidental.

Published by 47North, Seattle

www.apub.com

Amazon, the Amazon logo, and 47North are trademarks of Amazon.com, Inc., or its affiliates.

ISBN-13: 9781542037129 (paperback)
ISBN-13: 9781542037136 (digital)

Cover design by Richard Ljoenes Design LLC
Cover illustration by Natasha Cunningham
Cover image: © Bernd Vogel / Getty; © shunli zhao / Getty; © simonkr / Getty; © Tuul & Bruno Morandi / Getty; © antishock / Shutterstock

Printed in the United States of America

For Takunda. Sweet dreams, little brother.

Part 1: The Habitat

CHAPTER 1:
HONDO

Tick, tick, tick.

My eyes drift to one of my twenty-four siblings, who are waiting with me outside the War Room, and I'm reminded yet again of why I hate that word. *Sibling.* She and I are not genetically related. None of us are. I certainly don't like to think of her as a sister. But that is how we were raised: as equals, counterparts, rivals. Siblings.

She notices me staring, and a slight frown visits her face. I look away.

There's a clock ticking on the cement wall behind me, a curious anachronism the Custodians say once hung in the office of some consequential leader back on the Old World. I feel the movement of its little analog gears like a musical beat inside my head. A pleasant sound, even though each tick should remind me I'm a step closer to what I know will be the end.

Because a month from now, I will be recycled.

Tick, tick, tock.

I sneak another glance at Nandipa, my not-sibling. She has a look of deep concentration as she watches the simulation unfold on the other side of the glass windows separating us from the octagonal War

Room. I catch myself wishing I could brush the cloud of hair around her face, that I could make her smile at me the way I've seen her smile at Benjamin, that she would laugh as she watched me strangle Benjamin until his dead eyes bulged and . . .

And I should probably go see Counselor to find out exactly what's wrong with me. Something has been wrong with me for a while now, I think.

I look away again, and the clock keeps ticking. I would be afraid if the fear of endings had not been rigorously trained out of me. But people like me, people like my Prime—we were born for endings. Our existence is a temporary and carefully controlled deviation from the norm. *Expies*, they call us. As in *experimentals*. Our purpose is to stress test the durability and social cohesion of the more established genetic lines, and judging by the numbers on the all-important scoreboard inside the War Room, our usefulness is almost at an end.

My Prime, Jamal, is in session in the War Room with *his* two dozen siblings, seated at a round conference table where the hologram of a world map hovers at their center. Every year the Primes begin a fresh war game as leaders of their own geopolitical domains on a new hypothetical planet, a patchwork of colors spread out across the map. But as the game progresses, the colors bleed into each other, uniting, conquering, forming strategic alliances. These games are what the Primes were built for.

My siblings and me? We were built for the Primes.

As always, today we watch their game of empires from outside the glass War Room, keeping one eye on the players and the other eye on each other. A digital scoreboard in the room tallies the victories and losses accrued throughout the year, ranking the Primes from first to last.

I'm no dimwit, I don't think, but I understand what's going on in only the most basic sense. Sophisticated programs simulate the behavior of populations and armies, as well as individual generals, diplomats, politicians, and even assassins. Throughout the year the Primes pit their respective forces against one another in a scramble for influence. Send an assassin program to dispatch a rival general, and if you succeed, you earn influence. Get caught, and the game turns against you.

It's about getting the timing right; knowing where you're vulnerable, where to protect yourself, where to deploy your resources; knowing who to bribe, who to ally yourself with, who to betray.

And all the while, the scoreboard watches, keeping a tally that will doom whoever ultimately falls short.

Jamal's name has been sitting at the bottom of that tally for months now, and any hopes he might escape from that hole were squandered long ago.

I know what this means for the both of us. Jamal knows, too, but he's been more reckless than usual this year, bent on being contrary, thriving on the frustration of his siblings. While they were jockeying for influence, forming competing axes of power that grew to span the globe, he cornered a small but strategically vital patch of land and sealed it off from the rest of the map, nurturing an insular but self-sufficient population protected behind impenetrable defenses, firewalls, and the threat of mutually assured destruction.

No one has dared to attack him.

Unfortunately, seeing as the war games are about questing for influence, not hunkering down, the scoreboard has not been impressed. And now there's a stalemate between the two main coalitions, both of which need his cooperation to win.

"Give it up, Jamal," says Chairman David, the room's holograms casting a greenish film across his broad face. "I'll give you thirty points if you concede. Thirty points. Think about it. You'll have a fighting chance to save yourself."

David has been chair for the past three years, winning every game since the Custodians began the first simulation the year we all turned sixteen. He has the charisma and physique of a team captain from one of those soccer vids from the Old World. He smiles a lot. Likes the sound of his own voice. I heard his genetic profile came from a long-dead leader of the United Nations. His Proxy, Benjamin, is almost a carbon copy of him. He smiles a lot too. Likes to tell the rest of us what to do, and most of the other Proxies follow his lead.

Sanctimonious pricks, the both of them.

"Make it three hundred and I'll consider it," Jamal says in the War Room, getting a few snickers from his siblings and a few more from those of us watching outside.

I glance at the scoreboard. Three hundred extra points would put him halfway up the rankings, leaving the second-lowest score to take the fall. But the owner of that score happens to be a member of David's coalition, and knowing the chairman, he's not letting one of his own get recycled.

"No one sane would give you that much," David growls at Jamal. "No one has to give you anything, in fact. We could end the game now and we'd all be safe, except for you. I'm doing you a favor."

"How very thoughtful of you," Jamal ripostes. "But if you end the game now, you lose the chair." He grins lopsidedly, eyeing the scoreboard, where David's name is currently second from the top. The name holding the place of honor belongs to the leader of David's rival coalition, and she has been very quiet today. "Or," Jamal offers, "I could concede to you, and you could keep your winning streak, all for the low sum of three hundred points. I'd be doing *you* a favor."

David's eyes find Paul, the high-strung owner of that second-lowest score, whose shoulders stiffen. Paul looks up at the silent shadows watching from behind the windows on a second floor, our ever-present and often faceless Custodians, and a touch of fear makes his lips tremble. He shakes his head at David, his face almost pleading.

"You know I can't do that," David finally says, words spoken as a sigh.

"Then I guess I'll have to congratulate future Chairwoman Clarice." Jamal's cunning gaze latches on to the young woman across the round table. "I hope, future Chairwoman, as you celebrate your imminent victory, you'll make a toast in my name. To honor my memory."

Even in the standard-issue sky-blue jumpsuit we all wear every day, Clarice has the stature and bearing of royalty. I wouldn't be surprised if some genetic ancestor of hers was a queen.

She bares her teeth. "Don't address me, Rat. I have nothing to say to you."

Jamal stopped taking offense to that particular epithet years ago. In fact, the only thing it ever does is embolden him. His grin sharpens with cynical amusement. "A marvelous strategy. Keep me at arm's length. Don't look like you're cozying up to me too much. Otherwise people might start thinking we're working together. Or . . . are we?" He winks at David, which makes Clarice fume.

"Why are we tolerating this?" she demands, glaring at the rest of the room. "He's hijacked the simulation. He's been a constant source of division and disruption all our lives, and we finally have the chance to get rid of him. I say we take it. At this point his absence would be a greater good than any chair."

"Agreed," says a nervous Paul. "Jamal has the lowest score. He should be the one to take the fall."

I can't help but snort. How transparently desperate. Paul's Proxy hears me and throws me a dirty look. I grin at him until he looks away.

"Yes, Chairman David," drawls my Prime in the War Room. "Concede. Help future Chairwoman Clarice get rid of me. But of course, if she was so devoted to the greater good, she could simply concede herself and let you declare the game over."

"A fair point," David says thoughtfully. "Are you willing to concede, Clarice? For the greater good?"

"Go to hell, the both of you," Clarice throws back, and Jamal's eyes glitter with smugness.

"And thus we return to where we began," he says. "Three hundred points for the chair, David. No more, no less."

When the day's session ends, I wait outside the War Room for Jamal. Most of the Primes walk out in pairs or in groups, their Proxies falling in silently behind them. I keep my gaze studiously on the floor as Nandipa passes by with her Prime. Jamal is alone when he joins me, the look on his face the usual blend of pride and resentment.

He and I actually share genetic material, so in many ways, we are alike. We are both lean, long limbed, and sharp featured, though the people of the Old World might have thought him North African by the lightness of his skin and the slickness of his curly hair, whereas I am more strongly descended from the ancient Maasai and the rebel fighters of millennial Uganda.

I used to think Jamal was jealous of David and the other Legacies—the regal Clarice, the silently intelligent Adaolisa, the smooth and elegant Moussa, who are each, unlike us, the progeny of highly successful genetic lines refined by the Custodians over many generations. I used to think he hated existing solely to test them, living with the knowledge that his own line would not continue past him.

If only it were so simple. Jamal's resentment and discontent go well beyond his siblings to the very foundations of the Habitat, a dangerous mindset to have in a place where disobedience can make you vanish.

"I'm beginning to think being recycled would be preferable to another day of this bullshit," he mutters as he joins me.

By reflex I look around the hallway to check if anyone overheard him. "Be careful, Jamal," I say in a low voice. "The Custodians could be listening."

"You worry too much," he says dismissively, stretching the muscles of his neck. Then he frowns as he looks at me. "What's got you so worked up anyway? I've felt nothing but tension from you all day long."

How can he not know? I was built to care for him beyond anything else in the world, beyond even myself, and now I have to live with the knowledge that in a few weeks, he will die. How can he, of all people, not see it on my face? "It's nothing," I say.

He scowls but holds his tongue when we notice David approaching us with Benjamin in tow. We're of a similar height, but those two wear their jumpsuits like princely supermen, and unlike us, they are almost identical in appearance.

Benjamin eyes me the whole time. I watch him back. The way he's built, he could probably snap me in half. But I know I'd slit his throat before he ever got the chance.

"Stop being unreasonable, Jamal," David says. "Thirty points would put you just fifteen off from Paul. He's an ally, but I can't protect him if you beat him fairly, and I know you're smart enough to make up the difference with a little luck. It's your best chance."

"It's a shit chance, and you know it," Jamal replies. "No way in hell I'm closing that gap in less than a month. I've given you my terms. What happens next is up to you."

An ill-tempered sentiment crosses David's noble features. He glances at me, then back at Jamal. "So you'd let your Proxy face recycling just to spite me, is that it?"

"Oh, I'm sure he doesn't mind."

David's frown deepens. "You realize you'll be right next to him, don't you?"

"I don't mind either," Jamal says blithely. "It'll be a nice change of pace. I'm getting bored with these games, to be honest."

When David glances my way again, I smirk.

Disgusted, he tugs his Proxy away. "Let's go, Benjamin. These two are hopeless. Fucking expie rats," he adds under his breath, just loud enough for us to catch it.

"I could kill them both if you want," I suggest to Jamal as we watch them go, and I'm not completely sure I'm joking.

"I'll not have you waste a single breath on that hypocrite. He's not worth the dust on your shoes." Jamal considers me again. "But you're not actually worried, are you? About the Big R? Is that why you're so on edge?"

I could lie. He'd know, but he wouldn't push it. "I don't want you to die," I answer honestly.

"And I'm not going to die, you idiot! Neither will you. Do you really think I'd gamble your life away? We're getting those points, Hondo. Someone is taking the fall, but it won't be us."

"How?" I ask. "David wants the chair, but he's not the type to betray an alliance."

"Like I've told you before, what David wants is irrelevant. It's the person pulling his strings I'm counting on, and I know *she'll* do whatever it takes to win."

I still can't imagine David being under anyone's control, but the Primes were engineered for the War Room, and even though I can sometimes follow their choices and predict their moves, their games are ultimately beyond my ken. My sole purpose is to keep Jamal safe and let him do the thinking. I should trust him implicitly.

I nod. "As you say."

He pats me on the shoulder. "Good. Now, why don't we go release that tension I sense inside you? I'm sure you'll feel better after you hit something."

"If we spar today, I'll hurt you," I warn him. "I'm too wound up."

"I can take it. Just . . . go easy on me, okay?"

I nod, but we both know that I won't.

One side of the gymnasium is a thick layer of reinforced transparent polycarbonate. An ocean of pale-blue water presses up against the glass-like material, clear enough that the other sectors of the Habitat are visible as beehives of titanium, glass, and lights rising out of the seabed.

The story goes our ancestors left Africa on Old Earth centuries ago, crossing a long-range jump gate to a distant arm of the Milky Way and settling the habitable worlds scattered across what they called the

Tanganyika star cluster. They came to this world and named it Ile Wura, House of Gold, for its richness in natural resources. They settled on Tripoli V, the moon of a gas giant orbiting a gentle star. They settled on New KwaNdebele, Mawu-Lisa, Élysée Bleue, and several other planets and moons, building cities and nations that grew prosperous enough to compete with those on the older colonies closer to Sol.

But not even a century after their arrival to Tanganyika, their civilization fell prey to the spread of cybernetic technologies. Once-promising societies devolved into brutal and oppressive regimes run by cybernetically enhanced tyrants.

On some worlds, like ours, the blight of cybernetics was so vicious it manifested as an actual disease, turning anyone it infected into a mindless and dangerously violent beast. The Custodians, geneticists who'd settled on Ile Wura and despised all manner of cybernetic technology, found themselves the only people unaffected by the plague and soon became the last keepers of knowledge in an increasingly vicious and illiterate world.

As Ile Wura descended into further madness, the Custodians built a subaquatic refuge and retreated from the chaos on the surface, and it was there that they began the Program: a plan to breed leaders strong and capable enough to defeat the cybernetic plague and its tyrants and restore our lost society to its uncorrupted state.

Jamal and I were gestated together in the twenty-fifth tank of the conception ward, over in the children's sector of the Habitat. When we emerged from our glass-and-steel womb, Jamal was whisked away with all the other Primes who were born that day to live apart from me and my fellow Proxies, and we wouldn't see or even hear of each other for the next seven years.

During those years I went by the name Two-Five, the number given to me by my gestation tank, like all the other Proxies. It was probably done to make the job easier for the nurses who minded us. And so my early childhood was such that I shared sleeping quarters with One-Five and Zero-One, sat next to Two-Two during reading class, and stood between Zero-Four and One-Seven when we waited in a neat line to get our hair buzzed down to the roots.

When I look back at my life during those years, I often feel like I'm recalling a distant, gray dream that happened to someone else, and I suspect that this is by design. We wore collars that kept constant vigil over our brain chemistries; pills and other medications were quickly administered to keep us optimized. A nightmare would be interrupted by an expressionless nurse with a pill and a glass of water. The rare tantrum or even the thought of one would be preempted with a shot of a clear liquid injected into the shoulder. I was never unhappy. I felt the joy, love, and comfort necessary to rear up a healthy child, except none of those emotions felt like they came from within me. They'd been put there by the Custodians one deliberate neurochemical at a time. I was a tenant in a mind and body that did not belong to me.

It wasn't until I turned seven that the dour veil was lifted from my life and my world burst into color, and I remember that day, unlike much of my early childhood, with crystal clarity. A nurse brought me into a windowless room with two chairs and told me to sit down. Then she left, sliding the door closed behind her.

When the door slid open again, in walked a boy I'd never seen before, who in many ways looked just like me but was different in just as many ways. His smile was the brightest I'd ever seen. His eyes were full of intelligence, like he had so many secrets he couldn't wait to tell me.

He sat down on the other chair, and his smile grew as he studied my face, several milk teeth missing, just like me. I'd never wanted to smile at any of my siblings. I couldn't help but smile back at this strangely exciting boy.

"Hello," he said. "My name is Jamal. Do you want to know your name?"

"My name is Two-Five," I told him.

"No, silly. I mean your real name."

"I have a real name?"

"Yes. Your name is Hondo. It means *war*. Because you're a hero. Or you will be one day."

"I will?"

"Of course."

He sounded so sure of this, and I had no reason to doubt him. "Okay."

Jamal stood up and offered me his hand. "Come. I'll show you where I live. It's where you'll live from now on too. We'll be brothers. The best of friends."

That was the first time true joy bubbled out from within me, without chemical aid. Half of me had been missing from my life all along—I hadn't known it until right then—but here it was, restored to me, and I was complete.

I was sixteen when I first met someone from the surface. I remember waking up inside a glass room in nothing but my boxers and with no recollection of how I'd gotten there. Across the room lay a man dressed in filthy rags. His hair was unkempt, and he smelled like a beast. A feral strength coiled around his tensed muscles, and there was something synthetic and wild about the way his eyes shone. I knew immediately he was a savage from the surface.

He, too, was just rousing to consciousness, looking about himself with bewildered terror, and when those eyes of his locked on me, we both sprang up to our feet.

He was afraid. I could *feel* his fear like nothing I'd ever felt before. I swear I could *hear* it, but before I could grapple with what was going on, a clock began to tick above us, and the savage man attacked.

I knew I was being tested. I couldn't see who was behind the glass walls boxing us in, but I could sense their eyes on me, watching, assessing, and I knew the result of this test would be important. I would later find out that the three Proxies who'd failed the test had been removed from the program along with their Primes.

Removed, meaning recycled.

This was our trial of blood.

In the end, the savage was no match for my engineered strength and years of relentless training. I'd survived a thousand blows from our unsympathetic weapons masters. Battled combat mechs until I could read them five moves ahead. I'd broken every bone in my body, been resuscitated six times from the edge of death. He was hardly a challenge.

But as I choked the life out of him with my bare hands, I realized: He wasn't there to test my fighting skills. Taking his life was the test itself. To see if I had it in me to kill another human being. If I was cold blooded enough.

I still remember the look in his eyes in his last moments, the thrill that raced through my veins. He was a surfacer, little more than an animal, is what we were told. But I could see a thinking person somewhere inside him. Part of me wanted to release the hold on his neck and ask him why he was savage, but I had a trial to pass, and the violence had taken me, so I held on and watched as the life went out of him.

Three years later, and I could draw his face in vivid detail, down to the zigzag scar beneath his left eye and the shape of his blackened teeth.

I show Jamal little mercy as we kickbox in our exercise grays on the gymnasium's floor. He's quick on his feet, and he knows how to take a punch without whining about it, but just as I could never match his wits, he could never match the superior muscle density and bone tensile strength of a Proxy. That's my job, to make sure he never has to. The second man I killed was a Proxy who'd been sent to assassinate him, and the third was the Prime who'd ordered the hit.

His abrasive nature has made him many enemies and no friends in the Habitat, but that incident was the first and only attempt on his life. I think it scared a lot of people, what I did. I regret the way some of them look at me now, but an example had to be made.

A Custodian in a black combat uniform—one of the wardens on duty—watches us from the other side of the gymnasium, the ambient pale-blue light of the ocean dancing on the surface of his tactical helmet. Jamal lets his attention stray to the warden, and I punish him for it with a punch to the gut. He crumples to his knees in pain, winded, but I'm still too agitated to stop sparring just yet.

"Get up," I growl.

Still on his knees, he hugs his stomach, shaking his head. "No. Please. I've had enough."

"I said get up!" That gets me a few disapproving looks from the others using the gymnasium. I ignore them. "Get up, Jamal, or you'll be sleeping under anesthesia tonight."

He groans again, but he knows I'm lethally serious. "All right, all right! Just let me catch my breath, would you?"

The other Proxies disapprove of the way I treat him. I've sent him to the infirmary quite a few times. They think it's evidence of an inherent mental imbalance, a manifestation of my expieness. They might be right. I revere Jamal and never mean to hurt him, but sometimes the violence in me is like a flooding river: once it starts flowing, I'm caught in the currents, and I go where it takes me. Jamal can pull me out of it with a single command, but fool that he is, he likes to see how far he can bend before he breaks.

We keep sparring, and I work up a sweat putting him through his paces. He lands a few well-placed kicks and punches, but I never fail to pay him back for it.

"Enough!" he eventually snaps. "Cool off! Any more of this and you'll take off my face." He winces as he caresses the bruises I've put on his jaw. I suffer a sobering stirring of guilt.

Guilt that quickly pivots into annoyance. "You could have stopped me sooner, you know."

"I know," he admits. "I'm not blaming you."

I let out a breath and begin to undo my wrist wraps. "You're getting stronger," I tell him, which makes his face light up with delighted surprise. "But you're distracted. Your mind is elsewhere when it should be focused on the ass kicking I'm giving you."

He snorts, and then his gaze wanders back to the silent warden watching us from the window. Mysterious thoughts slither beneath the surface of his eyes. "Come," he says. "I think I've earned some time in the sauna."

Something rebellious is on his mind, I can feel it, and I've grown weary of the things he says to me when he's in a rebellious mood. I follow him anyway.

The days on Ile Wura are twenty-five hours and thirty minutes long, but the planet's calendar, with its leap weeks and leap months, was designed to hew as closely to the Earth standard year as possible.

When we were younger, we lived in a different sector of the Habitat, where our minders were nurses whose names we never learned. Then we turned sixteen and the trials of blood came and the war games began, and we were moved to a new sector with wardens for minders, whose faces we never see.

Years later and they still put me on edge. Shadows in black tactical gear and masks who guard the domes and tunnels, watching us in silence. I can never tell how many of them there are. And are they the same people each year, or do they come and go? Where do they even come from?

Could they be us in the future? I often wonder. Could they be former Proxies, here as silent guardians of the next generation?

"A good question, isn't it?" Jamal whispers to me as we stew in the humid heat of the gymnasium's sauna, black cotton towels wrapped around our waists. "What are they hiding behind those masks? Are they even people, Hondo?"

When you grow up around Primes, you learn to accept that your every breath, your every eye movement and twitch of the mouth, is a window into your mind, as though you had transparent glass for a skull. Jamal has taught me ways of insulating myself from the penetrating gazes of his siblings, but I cannot enjoy a single private thought without him reading it off my face.

I close my eyes, resting my head against the synthetic wood paneling behind me. "What else could they be if not people?"

"Androids. Reanimated corpses. Who the hell knows?"

I don't want to encourage him, so I keep my mouth shut and my eyes closed.

"Remember that data stick I told you about?" he says in a weird non sequitur. "The one Counselor keeps in the top drawer of his office desk?"

"The one that has a biometric lock you'll never crack? What about it?"

"I might have found a way to crack it."

This should be impossible, and I might have dismissed him immediately, but the mixture of fear and excitement I sense thrumming off him gets my attention. I look at him. "What are you talking about?"

"I got another message today," he quietly says.

"*What?* When?"

"This morning, just before session. It was almost identical to the last one. But . . . something else happened. Strange programs started popping up on my PCU. I tried deleting them, but they kept reinstalling themselves. So I took a look. Hondo, I couldn't believe my eyes."

The blood chills in my veins. "What kind of programs?"

"High-level decryption tools," Jamal almost whispers. "Exploits, programs that would eviscerate any security system in the Habitat. I've never seen anything so advanced. And it gets crazier. I was still looking at these programs when I received another message. Attached to it was a large file containing decrypted data. Guess what was in it."

I really don't want to hear it, but I ask anyway. "What?"

"The biometric templates of every Custodian," Jamal tells me. "Including Administrator and Counselor. At first I didn't understand what I was supposed to do with this data. Then I discovered that one of the programs can use templates to bypass biometric sensors. Someone has almost literally given me the keys to this whole place."

My fingers curl into each other, and suddenly I want to hit something again. "We need to report this to Administrator. Someone is trying to get you into trouble. To frame you for something. One of your siblings, no doubt. When I find out who it is . . ."

"There's no way it's one of them. No one has this kind of access."

"Then who does?"

Jamal gives me a silent stare. He's going to do something stupid, isn't he. Or more accurately, he's going to make *me* do something stupid. "What if it's the Custodians?" I suggest, trying to rein him back in. "Maybe it's a test. Maybe they want to see how you react."

"Unlikely. This reeks of subversion. Whoever it is, they're no friend to the Custodians, and I sense they're probably using me, but I want to play their game. That's why I need you to steal Counselor's data stick. It should be easy for you given your skills."

I hiss out a lengthy curse. "By the ancestors, do you even hear yourself? You're supposed to be the smart one here!"

"The Custodians are hiding something from us, Hondo. I can feel it in my bones, and I know you feel it too. Don't you want to find out what it is?"

"Not at the cost of your life! Legacies have vanished for lesser offenses. With you, they won't even hesitate."

"Then . . . don't get caught," he says.

I regard him for a long moment. He gave me my name on our seventh birthday. If I had failed my trial of blood, we would have both paid for it, just as we'll both pay when he fails his trial of the war games. We came out of our gestation tank on the same day, and if somehow he died before me, I would end myself. We are closer than brothers. We are the same soul in two bodies, and there are no secrets between us.

But sometimes I wish to the ancestors I had a Prime with a little more sense and a little less of a death wish.

"Is that an order, Prime?" I say.

"Oh, come on. Don't be like that." When I don't relent, he clenches his jaw and hardens his voice. "Yes, Proxy, that's an order. Are you happy?"

"No," I tell him, "but I want you to remember this moment when they recycle us for your stupidity."

"Expie rat," he says under his breath, shaking his head.

I give in to the urge and punch him in the side. As he gasps in pain, I close my eyes and return to the business of enjoying the sauna.

Chapter 2: Nandipa

Lights, camera, action.

I'm an actress in one of those old drama serials from Earth, and my role: the spunky heroine who makes the whole room stop and stare with her dramatic entrance.

Granted, the stage could be better. The dinnertime cafeteria doesn't exactly scream *glamorous*. And my talents are clearly wasted on the audience of Primes and Proxies dining in their eternally blue jumpsuits, since they barely notice me when I walk in. I might as well be performing for the fish outside the glass on the other side of the room.

No matter. A heroine cares only for the completion of her mission.

I spot Benjamin sitting at his usual table, poking at his boiled kelp with a fork and a detached look on his face. He's alone. *Perfect.*

I flash my smile. "Benjamin. There you are. I've been looking all over for you."

Benjamin. Broad and handsome in that leading man type of way. Hero complex. Vulnerable to flattery, just like his Prime, but today he sighs in exasperation as I settle down across from him.

Not at all the reaction I was expecting. "Wait," I say, eyeing him suspiciously. "Have you been avoiding me?"

"No." He rises, picks up his tray, and starts walking away.

"You have!" I get up to follow him. "Why?"

Benjamin drops his tray off at the designated counter and keeps walking, ignoring me like he's some big-shot celebrity and I'm a pesky reporter out for a scoop. And to think I prepared a whole performance for him.

"Benjamin!"

His long legs give him a fast stride, so I have to jog after him as he leaves the dining hall. I follow him out onto the Green, a square of grass and open air beneath the Habitat's largest dome. A lamp powerful enough to imitate a miniature sun is about to set in a clear sky simulated by the panes of the dome's color-changing glass. Well-tended trees and park benches lend to the illusion of a quaint little town square, and it's easy to forget that those towering snowcapped shapes behind the dome's blocky cement buildings aren't actual mountains in the distance but holograms.

"Benjamin, we need to talk!"

"No, we don't," he says, his footsteps crunching on the gravel path skirting the Green. "Prime David has decided to let Clarice win the chair. He will not betray Paul's trust. Besides, it's about time the Rat and his Dog bit the dust. We've been trying to get rid of them for years."

"Okay," I say. "I hear you, but the thing is—would you slow down for a second?"

Benjamin finally deigns to stop and look at me. Look down at me, rather. I'm not short by any means, but he and his Prime are at least a head taller. "I understand your perspective," I say in a low voice, looking around to make sure no one's listening, "but letting Clarice win the chair is not going to work for us. She's already powerful enough without it."

"We can handle her," Benjamin says firmly.

"Handle her? Have you actually thought this through? Who do you think she'll come for next year?"

"Who?" Benjamin says stupidly, to which I backhand him lightly on the chest.

"You, Benjamin! Your Prime! You're her biggest threat." *As far as she knows anyway.*

"We can handle her," Benjamin says again. "But we can't betray Paul."

"Paul made his own bed. If you'll remember, we wanted to work with Jamal, but Paul objected."

"Everyone objected!"

"Paul was the loudest," I say. "It was also his mistake that let Clarice gain a foothold in the first place. He's a weak link. We're sorry it's come to this, but we have to do what's best for ourselves. Tell David—"

"Prime David," Benjamin corrects me, and I almost vomit a little inside.

"Tell Prime David," I patiently say, "that losing the chair is not an option. There's eight in the alliance excluding Paul; if our Primes all chip in, they can raise Jamal's three hundred points. After he concedes, David's lead over Clarice will be insurmountable, and the game will be over."

"Then Paul takes the fall," Benjamin says.

"Unfortunate, but yes."

"So you'd choose the Rat over Paul."

"We're choosing the chair, Benjamin."

"Prime David won't agree to this."

"Then remind him of the terms of our agreement," I say, injecting acid into my words. "Win or lose, Clarice will come after you next year. Disobey us, and we'll stand by and watch her tear you apart."

Benjamin's face becomes stone. He's gotten so used to me being nice he forgot I'm not above playing the evil witch should the need arise.

"Is that all?" he demands.

Perhaps the witch came out too strongly. Time to bring back the heroine for some damage control.

I place a gentle hand on his arm. "I'm not your enemy, Benjamin, remember? I like you, and your Prime is good at people. Mine's good at the bigger picture. Tell David—Prime David—to do his part. The others might need a little convincing, but they'll ultimately follow his lead. This is the best outcome for you and the best for us. We need each other to survive, but we have to play to each other's strengths."

Benjamin gives me a moody glare. "I'll talk to him."

I smile, squeezing his arm for good measure. "Thank you. And maybe later you and I can—"

I stop talking, sensing a pair of eyes watching us from across the Green. An involuntary shiver takes me when I look and see the Rat's Proxy standing there with a blank expression.

He's the slicing edge of a butcher's knife personified: lank, sharp, and angular, restrained violence lurking perpetually in his gaze. He's also the only one among us to have spilled the blood of a sibling and, worse, a Prime. The Custodians decided he'd been justified in his actions, if a little too thorough, but still, I've never liked him. I've had no cause to be wary of him, either, but this is the third time I've caught him watching me just today. What's going on here?

"What the hell are you staring at, freak?" Benjamin barks at him.

The Rat's Proxy answers with an unreadable smile, and then he walks away without a word. I shiver again.

"What a creep," Benjamin remarks, and I silently agree.

I'm no longer in the mood for whatever I was about to suggest to Benjamin before we were interrupted. In fact, I suddenly need to check on my Prime and make sure she's all right.

"Talk to David tonight," I tell Benjamin. "We want this game wrapped up by tomorrow evening."

I don't wait around long enough for him to protest. I leave him on the Green and duck into a tunnel, heading toward the Habitat's residential sector at a brisk walk.

Adaolisa and I are Legacies, meaning we carry the burden of being the latest avatars of genetic lines that have been tweaked and refined since the Program began who knows how long ago. Unlike most of our brothers and sisters, whose lines are newer and still works in progress, or the much rarer expies, unfortunate human experiments destined for the rubbish bin, Legacies are supposed to be sure successes. Perfect. Without fault.

I don't feel like I'm any of these things—I know I'm not. My Prime, on the other hand, is probably the Program's greatest success.

We were halfway through the first war game the year we turned sixteen when she decided she didn't like the heat that came with being at the top of the scoreboard. She still wanted control of the chair, however, so she hatched a plan to address both problems.

She had me approach David—charming, handsome, popular David—who at the time was languishing dangerously close to the bottom of the scoreboard. They would be partners, I persuaded him. Adaolisa was good at the game and could guide his path, ensuring not only his survival but his victory. She would put him on the chair, and in exchange, he would make whatever moves she told him to make. He would be a front for her power, allowing her to rule the Habitat inconspicuously.

Knowing he was one step away from getting himself and Benjamin recycled, David accepted the offer. And there you have it, the biggest secret in the Habitat: David is flawed. Nothing's wrong with him on the surface, but whatever genetic traits were supposed to make him smart enough for the war games misfired, and my Prime was the first to identify this weakness and use it to her benefit.

She's wise enough not to keep his leash too tight, allowing him the illusion he's a self-made man, but sometimes he needs a reminder of why he's still around, and I'm the one who has to give it.

I find Adaolisa standing in our private living room, studying the map of this year's war game projected on the holo screen. It's not unusual for her to study that map; she'll be dissecting and analyzing it months after the game has ended. But the way she's gnawing at the tip of her thumb tells me something's off.

We both carry the genetic heritage of western and southern Africa within our blood, and with our engineered fine-boned features and radiant bronze skin, we could be Old World starlets, though there's nothing Adaolisa hates more than standing out. The only concession she makes for appearance's sake is a perm for her short hair. I, on the other hand, grew my curls into the best-looking Afro in the Habitat.

I pick up my semiacoustic guitar from its stand by the wall and plop down on a beige armchair, knowing Adaolisa hasn't noticed my arrival. She's so far away she doesn't react even as my calloused fingers begin to pluck the strings, sounding out the arrangement of a neo-Brazilian folk song I'm working on.

Counselor prescribed the instrument to me years ago to balance out what he thought was a restless temperament. I can usually entertain myself for hours while Adaolisa does her thing. Usually. Today her quiet unease makes me feel like I want to tear out of my own skin.

Tired of waiting to be noticed, I strum a single grating chord and speak loudly. "Please tell me you know I'm here and are simply too preoccupied to acknowledge me."

She startles at the sound of my voice, pressing a hand against her chest. On seeing me, she tries and fails to look casual. "What? Of course I knew you were there."

I kiss my teeth, shaking my head. I don't know how many times I've told her to pay more attention to her surroundings. "What am I going to do with you?"

She gives a perfunctory wave of the hand, looking back at the map. "I'll be fine. You'll always be there to watch over me."

"And if I'm not? What if something happens to me and I'm not there to protect you?"

Dry amusement seeps into her voice. "My love, if things get that far, I'm in trouble anyway. How did your talk with Benjamin go?"

I set the guitar aside and relax into my chair, remembering his sullen face with an inward sigh. I really do hate upsetting him. "He'll make sure David does the wise thing."

"Good. I'm sorry for Paul, but we can't afford to lose the chair." Her eyes become hooded, focused on the map, but distant, like she's trying to peer into the future itself. "One way or the other, we're getting out of here."

That's the promise, at least. Survive eight games, and we'll have proved ourselves worthy to leave the Habitat and join our predecessors in the war against Tanganyika's cybernetic tyrants. The world of Ile Wura might be too far gone, forever lost to a consuming and self-replicating cybernetic madness, but there are other worlds in the cluster that can still be liberated. Just last year, the colonies of Dar al Amal and Novo Paraíso held their first democratic elections in many decades after their despotic governments were brought down from within—the work of Habitat alumni.

The enemy is formidable, we've been told, clever and possessing inhuman strength and reflexes, and only the best of us can hope to contend with them. We must be smarter than they are, stronger and faster. We must be living proof that the technologies they use to defile their minds and bodies cannot triumph over what pure genetics have given us. We must prove we can infiltrate, persuade, seduce, and kill our way to peace.

To live under a sky; to feel the unfiltered light of the stars, the breath of the wind on our faces; to liberate a world from the clutches of tyranny: that is the promise of life beyond the Habitat.

I wish we could live down here forever. I get enough sky, stars, and wind from the Green and from Old World drama vids. Do I sometimes wish I could step into a scene and bask in the sunlight like the actors, or run through a field of flowers, or dive into a pristine lake while the sun shines high and hot above me?

Absolutely. But I've seen vids of what it looks like out there, cybernetically enhanced humans hunting and killing people for sport, infected people driven mad enough by their implants to bite and tear into each other with their teeth. I was forced to contend with such savagery during my trial of blood. I still dream about it sometimes, waking up in a glass box with a strange woman who attacked me the second she saw me, the hatred twisting her pockmarked face, the rage burning inside her unnatural eyes.

No. The surface can stay where it is as far as I'm concerned. Or at least, it would stay there if I made the rules. But I don't, so we can either get recycled or fight our way out.

Adaolisa decided long ago which path we'd be taking, and she's been doing a fine job of getting us there. Her concentration is still scattered today, though.

"Are you going to tell me what's wrong, or are you going to make me ask?" I say.

"Well, since you've asked." She fishes out her portable computing unit from its pocket on her right thigh, taps on the touch-screen interface a few times, then hands it over.

Frost touches my spine as I accept the PCU. Splashed in red across the skyline of a nighttime metropolis are these words: **They Are Lying to You**.

"Is this a new message or the same one from last time?" I know the answer even before I've finished asking the question. The city in this image is different, and the sky in the last picture was a shade lighter than dusk. That's four different messages now.

"I got it this morning," Adaolisa tells me, confirming my fears. "And it's not the only thing they sent this time. Several programs installed themselves onto the PCU. Incredibly dangerous programs that could get us recycled if the Custodians caught us using them."

Consciously restraining my fingers from crushing the device, I deactivate it and place it on my lap. "Did you delete these programs?"

"Not yet."

I'm not a violent person, I don't think, but my blood is already running hot in my veins. A cold-blooded sort of hot. Someone is playing games with my Prime. Whoever they are, I pity them should I ever learn their name. Not even Benjamin would know mercy from me if he turned out to be the one behind these shenanigans.

"Who is doing this?" I look up and find Adaolisa watching me with uncertainty. The same question has been bugging her all day. "Do you think it's Clarice? It has to be, right? Maybe she figured out your arrangement with David and is trying to rattle you."

"If Clarice knew, she'd confront me and expose us publicly. It's not her."

"Then maybe it's the Rat," I suggest. "His Proxy has been watching me."

"Really? Why?"

"I don't know. I caught him staring at me three times just today."

Adaolisa turns back to face her map on the holo screen, folding one arm across her chest and lifting the opposing hand to her chin—her favorite thinking pose. "Jamal thrives on chaos and division," she says. "And I'm convinced he's a lot smarter than he likes to let on. But whatever he'd gain from doing this . . . it cannot possibly justify the risk of angering the Custodians, especially when he's already fighting for his life."

I'm not so sure. As far as Jamal knows, he'll be taking the fall. I wouldn't put it past him to sow chaos and suspicion on his way out simply to spite the rest of us. He could be sending these messages to everyone for all we know.

I voice that thought and get a laugh out of Adaolisa.

"Then we'll never know, will we? Tough chance anyone shares that information. I certainly won't."

"Then I guess it's useless to worry about it right now," I say. "Not until we know more."

"Agreed." She waves the map away and brings her hands together. "So. Another episode of *The Brave and the Heartless*? I believe Regina's much older husband is about to learn that his youngest son is actually his grandson. Or is it nephew?"

I smile, though I have to force it a little. "I'll get the blankets," I say.

Watching old drama serials is one of my favorite pastimes, like looking through a window to an alternate dimension filled with sunshine, romance, pretty dresses, and heroines with interesting if somewhat frivolous lives. I find them all quite ridiculous, and yet I can't help but envy them as well, how they take their blessings for granted, like they can't even imagine a life confined to an undersea Habitat where they'd never see the sun.

It's pure escapism, demanding nothing from us save that we be amused, and every night Adaolisa and I curl up on the couch and spend our daily allotted hour of digital entertainment watching new episodes of our favorite serials. This hour is usually enough to cleanse my mind even if I've had a bad day, but tonight I remain preoccupied and pay little attention to Regina's flailing attempts to salvage her marriage to the family patriarch while trying to work out which of her three hunky stepsons or two brothers-in-law is the true father of her child.

My mood has not improved by the end of the episode.

Paul and his Proxy, Saul, are recycled two mornings later. As usual, our sleep that night is deeper than ordinary, thanks to whatever gas is pumped into the ventilators. None of us hear or see anything, but when we arrive at the assembly auditorium at exactly six in the morning, we find both young men on the stage, suspended in separate glass tanks filled with a transparent blue gel. Whether they are already dead or simply unconscious, I can't tell, but their eyes are closed and their limbs immobile.

Administrator and Counselor are there as well, two hefty men of middle age wearing dark suits with high collars. Administrator keeps himself clean shaven, while his counterpart cultivates a thick and full beard and always seems to peer down at the world from above the rims of his spectacles. Like the few other Custodians who show their faces, they are never without a pair of silver disks attached to their temples. I've never figured out what those disks are. The prevailing consensus is that they are communication devices.

We're all quiet today. The sight of Paul and Saul floating helplessly in those tanks fills me with a dread I cannot push away. I knew Saul as One-Three before we turned seven. My best memory of him is when he sided with me the day Two-Zero, who later became Charlotte, insisted I'd stolen one of her colored pencils, even though I hadn't. Saul and I didn't become friends after that, not inasmuch as anyone can have friends in the Habitat, but we developed a distant cordiality that continued even when our Primes started butting heads.

He's gone now. Never again shall we exchange polite greetings when our paths cross in the Habitat's hallways. Never again shall we smile at each other when our eyes meet in the cafeteria. He was never someone important to me, but seeing him and his Prime in those tanks breaks my heart all the same.

I think about Adaolisa suffering such a fate, and my eyes begin to sting. There is nothing I wouldn't do to stop that from happening.

Administrator stands in front of the tanks for a long minute, letting us take in the gravity of them, absorb the reality of what awaits those of us who fall short. Sorrow lines his face, but like with every other Custodian, I sense nothing from him even as he stands just a few yards away.

"They are empty where they should be full," Adaolisa once whispered to me. "Like husks with no souls."

She's not the only one who fears the Custodians. I'm not sure they're fully human myself.

"It gives me no pleasure to stand before you this morning," Administrator finally says. "For today we must bid farewell to two more members of our community, Paul and Saul." Holo photos of their smiling faces appear in front of their tanks, tinged blue by the gel inside the glass.

I feel a tug of emotion at the sight, but I remain largely numb. I think we all do.

"The loss of a sibling or a friend is never easy to bear," Administrator continues in his cavernous baritone. "Indeed, it may feel cruel. But I'd like to remind you this morning that the survival of the human race depends on the success of the work we do here and the sacrifices we make. Though Paul and Saul have proved unworthy for the challenges some of you will face off-world, their contributions have helped shape you, my children, and the essence of who they were will be fed back into the Program. One day they shall return in greater perfection, and one day all of us shall be celebrated as pioneers, the forerunners of a new enlightened society."

He hits all the usual notes with the rest of his speech. Congratulating us for surviving yet another year. Painting a hopeful picture for those of us who survive the next four years. Promising a feast to celebrate our success. I listen half-heartedly, impatient for this whole day to be over. I don't think I give anything away with my expression, but a few times I feel Counselor's assessing gaze sweeping over me and Adaolisa.

At the end of Administrator's speech, we're allowed one last look at our lost siblings, and then we're dismissed to spend the day however we like. We won't see it happening, but the tanks will be removed from the auditorium, and the gel will slowly dissolve the bodies inside, breaking them down to the atomic level. Whatever is done with the result is a mystery to us; some of the less savory speculations claim the recycled material is added to the Habitat's water-treatment plant.

No one goes to the promised feast in the cafeteria, an act of defiance Administrator seems to tolerate. Instead, it's become tradition to gather in the rec room above the gymnasium, where we allow ourselves to spend a day without scheming against each other and to commiserate on our hopelessly complicated feelings about surviving yet another year and what that survival has cost us.

White-petaled daisies grow in flower beds by the Green. Before Adaolisa and I head to the rec room, we each pick a daisy and place them at the door to Paul and Saul's quarters. The flowers won't stay there for long—a Custodian will vacuum them away when they wilt—but when you watch as many Earth serials as we do, you learn that placing flowers at the grave site of the deceased is the best way to honor the dead.

There is no grave site, but their door isn't far from one, I'd say. A cold, lifeless thing. No one will live on the other side until our generation has left the Habitat and a new one comes to replace us. And so long as we live here, that silent door will always be a reminder of Paul and Saul and what we stand to lose ourselves, as unnerving and indifferent as a grave.

Someone else has stuck a pair of sketches on the door with putty adhesive, smiling portraits of both young men rendered skillfully in the monochrome black of e-paper. Whoever drew them did the same thing last year, too, when Hope and Grace were recycled. I run my fingers over Saul's portrait, and in that moment a waterfall of grief almost claims me.

I'm not shortsighted enough to blame myself or Adaolisa for his death; in the Habitat, someone is always chosen to die. But I grew up with him. I knew him from before we met our Primes, from before they gave us names. This is yet another limb taken from me, the stump cauterized for the good of the human race.

Sometimes I wonder: If this is what it costs to save humanity, is humanity even worth saving at all?

"Farewell, brother," I say.

Adaolisa takes my hand and squeezes it. She has tears in her eyes, so I reach over to wipe them just as she does the same for me.

She named me Nandipa on the day we were brought together, meaning *a gift given by a higher power.* We had both just turned seven. As she later told me, I was the sister she'd been praying for all her life, though in retrospect I don't think *sister* adequately describes what we became to each other. I don't know if the word exists.

Arm in arm, we leave this particular door for the last time, knowing we will never return.

Moussa is on the piano when we arrive, playing an appropriately mellow and nostalgic melody. The rec room is a dome with the best and widest views of the Habitat; from here we can see all the way to our childhood sector, inaccessible to us ever since we were ferried to this side of the Habitat on submarines.

Sometimes it's possible to spot tiny little figures running past the windows, and sometimes they wave excitedly when they see us. I have memories of looking up to this same dome as a child, wondering who those distant shapes moving about inside could possibly be. Even today, as I stand where they stood back then, I wonder what happened to them and where they are now. *They are lying to you.*

No. I cannot let those messages get to me.

We make light conversation with some of our siblings, even Clarice and her Proxy, Charlotte. Clarice isn't especially antagonistic to my Prime—as far as she knows, David is her biggest rival—but they've always found themselves on opposing sides of any alliance. Today Adaolisa congratulates her on her success in this year's game, and Clarice wishes us better luck in the next one.

David broods on a couch, staring out the windows while Benjamin tries and fails to cheer him up. He rebuffs anyone who approaches him for conversation, but the second Jamal walks into the rec room, David's eyes go crazed with fury, and he gets up, moving to intercept.

"You dare show your face here?"

Moussa's melody falters, then fails. The Rat's Proxy doesn't make a move, but I see his pupils dilating. Benjamin must see it, too, given the instant change in his posture. I glance around the rec room; there aren't any wardens posted. If David does something stupid, someone is going to get hurt.

"We've come to pay our respects," Jamal says with surprising sincerity. "Just like you." I half expected him to smirk and say something incendiary.

But David isn't mollified. "Paul despised you," he spits. "We all do. He wouldn't want you here. Leave."

Jamal doesn't budge. "I don't like this any more than you do, David."

"He's gone because of you. You're a fucking expie. You're vermin. You aren't meant to survive . . ."

As David continues his litany of insults, I lean closer to Adaolisa to whisper into her ear. "If we don't get him under control, people are going to start asking questions."

"Let him grieve," she tells me. "All people will see is a man buckling under the weight of his own guilt."

". . . you should have been recycled a long time ago, you mongrel bastard," David shouts, trembling with so much emotion that some of those watching are agape. I've never seen him so unhinged. I think we might have broken him.

Jamal, usually caustic and full of vicious words, surprises yet again. "Hate me if it's easier for you," he says calmly, and I get the sense he's addressing the whole room. "I don't mind. But today isn't about us. It's about Paul and Saul, the brothers we lost for no reason any of us can understand. I swear I'm not here to cause trouble. I'll speak to no one if you wish."

"Leave them be, David," says Moussa from the piano. "Jamal is right. Today isn't about us."

Moussa is David's closest friend and ally, but now David whirls to face him, rage twisting his face. "They have no right to be here!"

"Will you just stop?" Moussa shouts. "Stop it, all right? *You're* the one who betrayed Paul! And we get it; you're upset about it. But *you* made your choice. Now leave Jamal alone, and let us all grieve in peace."

David seethes, sweeping his glare around the room as if to challenge someone else to speak up to him. I feel a wave of pure hatred from him when his eyes pass over me and Adaolisa, but he avoids singling us out. "Fine," he says. "Then *I'll* leave. Come, Benjamin. We're done here."

He walks out in anger, Mr. Habitat himself, his reputation tarnished perhaps beyond repair, a lamb sacrificed to protect my Prime's rule over the war games, no one the wiser to the true architect of Paul's demise.

I know we have no choice but to play these games, to act the parts we were given. We did not choose these roles for ourselves; they were chosen for us. I know this, but sometimes . . .

Sometimes I wish I could march into Administrator's office and dig the eyes right out of his skull with my bare hands.

Chapter 3: Hondo

I make an appointment to see Counselor first thing in the morning and knock on the door to his office before he's taken his usual dose of coffee. He welcomes me in with his dead, fixed smile, little silver disks shining on his temples, and immediately I almost decide to walk back out.

I don't think I'll ever get used to the deadness that surrounds a Custodian. Just being in the presence of one is unnerving to me. It feels like I've walked out of an air lock and straight into the crushing depths of the ocean. For some reason this oppressive emptiness is particularly strong around Administrator and Counselor. Maybe because they show us their faces? They feel like dead men wearing living bodies.

The furnishings of glass and white upholstery make Counselor's office feel more spacious than it actually is. It overlooks the Habitat's kelp farms, where aquatic mechs cultivate various genetically engineered pressure-tolerant seaweeds in neat rows. Round lamps attached on strings to the seabed bob up and down between the rows, each one a little orb of artificial sunlight.

I'm directed to sit on a white couch, which I do.

"Would you like a cup of coffee?" Counselor offers, just like I knew he would.

"Yes please," I accept with controlled casualness, but as soon as he turns his back on me to attend to his coffee machine, I burst into motion.

Theft is nothing new to me. With no allies in the Habitat, Jamal has relied heavily on artifice and subterfuge to collect information. I've pilfered many items for him over the years—notebooks, sketchbooks, day planners, PCUs—so slipping across the room and quietly lifting a data stick from Counselor's desk drawer while he distractedly makes coffee is rather trivial.

It's the part that comes immediately afterward that leaves me feeling clammy and light headed: selling my presence here. Whatever I say has to be the truth. One doesn't lie to a Custodian.

"There you go," Counselor says, placing a white mug on a coaster in front of me. The fragrance wafting out of the mug is heavenly.

As he settles down on the couch across the glass table with his own coffee mug, I lift mine and take a whiff. Everything we eat here is made from some type or another of cleverly processed kelp. From bread to dairy to the occasional slice of chocolate cake. I don't think this coffee is, though. This smells like soil and air and sunlight, or what I imagine they might smell like.

I take a sip and savor the pleasantly bitter taste. "This is really good," I remark, which gets me a chuckle from Counselor.

He crosses one leg over the other and says, "If I didn't have the best coffee in the Habitat, no one would come see me."

I'd like to lose myself in this rare delight—nothing else in the Habitat tastes this rich—but the deadness around Counselor and the way he's peering at me from above his spectacles keep me sober. Reluctantly, I place the mug back on the table and rest the palms of my hands on my knees.

"So what brings you here this morning?" he says, and I feel my mouth going dry.

I clear my throat and decide to push past my awkwardness. We're both adults here. "Counselor, I've been having certain . . . thoughts . . . lately. They're inappropriate and a hindrance to my duties. I was hoping you could help me get rid of them."

Counselor considers me, his synthetic contact lenses flashing with scrolling lines of data. I know he's probably monitoring my vitals, pulling up my records, going through all the conclusions he's ever come to about me.

Suddenly I feel foolish. What the hell was I thinking?

"What is the nature of these thoughts?" he calmly asks me.

"A girl," I mumble. "No, a woman. I guess? Another Proxy." I should leave. Apologize and walk out of here. This is a mistake.

"Can you describe these thoughts in more detail?"

I stare blankly at the man. "What?"

"I don't want to jump to conclusions, you see."

"I . . ." Speech fails me.

"Are these thoughts romantic? Are they hostile? Violent?"

"Violent?" I repeat. "No! Never. Not to her, anyway."

"So you like her."

"Yes," I say after a pause.

I could swear Counselor's smile widens, but the deadness around him remains thick, unyielding, like I'm trapped inside a coffin with a fresh corpse. "You are attracted to her," he says. "Sexually."

I stare at the hands on my knees. I nod.

"Proxy Hondo, are you sexually frustrated?"

When I look up, I find him contemplating the data stream being fed into his lenses. He's testing me, trying to see how quickly I lose control. The Custodians are always testing us. "What?" I ask.

"Have you tried . . . propositioning one of your peers?"

What the hell. "Proposition?" I repeat, disbelieving my ears.

"Yes. Have you approached someone and expressed your desire to—"

"Counselor," I say, stopping that sentence before it goes anywhere else. "No one will even speak to me. They either hate me or they're afraid of me. Proposition? They'd laugh in my face!"

Counselor clucks his tongue in disapproval. "Now, now. Self-pity is a pointless exercise. It will gain you nothing. You should know this."

I absolutely loathe everything about this conversation. "Can you help me or not?" I demand, losing my patience.

His gaze sharpens back on me, a grin parting his beard. "You're a young man, Proxy Hondo. Sexual desire is a natural part of your development. We do not forbid indulgence in such desires, and indeed, all safeguards against procreation have been deployed. You have nothing to fear. But you'd be wise to heed my warning: Whatever you do, keep your heart out of it. If you are not careful, pursuing a romantic relationship while you're still trying to earn passage off-world can be the end of you and your Prime. I've seen it happen many times. It's never pretty. Your loyalties become split. You become more susceptible to manipulation. Jealousy enters the picture. Resentment. Tears. Heartbreak, even murder. A truly ugly business."

When I say nothing, he asks, "Do you believe the young woman in question reciprocates your feelings?"

I burn with shame, my eyes falling to my lap. "I doubt it."

"Then be careful she doesn't catch wind of them, lest your desires be weaponized against you."

My face contorts into a frown. Does he think I'm stupid? "This is why I came here, Counselor. What can I do about it? I don't want anything to distract me from my duty to Jamal."

"Then don't let it," he says simply.

I could scream in frustration. "Counselor, isn't there a pill you could give me? Anything at all to suppress these thoughts?"

"Nothing that won't cause an unacceptable hormonal imbalance. I'm sorry, but this is a problem you'll have to resolve on your own."

"Resolve."

"Yes."

"How?"

Counselor knits his brow with sudden displeasure. "You have two hands, Proxy Hondo. Do not expect me to show you how to use them. Now off with you."

I let myself temporarily forget the data stick now sitting snugly inside my chest pocket. Jamal will be attending lectures all morning anyway, and I'm due in the Range in a few minutes, so that's where I go.

In the locker room, I don my training gear over my blue jumpsuit, including bulletproof armor pieces of ceramic and composite metal foam for the chest, arms, and knees.

Our Primes receive an education equal to their souped-up cognitive abilities, extensive in both breadth and depth, indoctrinating them in the theory and application of political power so they can stand against even the most cunning cybernetic masterminds. Us Proxies, though, receive an academic education limited to the basics. Reading. Writing. Mathematics. A broad but elementary cross section of the sciences. The five modern dialects.

We do receive extensive instruction in weapons engineering and learn the operation of various vehicles through simulations, but our true instruction occurs here, in the Range, where we hone our minds and bodies against mechanized enemies under the watchful eyes of our weapons masters. Because while our Primes are destined to fight the enemy with their minds, we exist to shield them from whatever physical dangers might rise against them, and we must be flawless in our duties.

I've been training with three other Proxies this month, so I'm surprised when I walk out of the locker room to find Nandipa there as well, waiting with the others in her training gear. Her pupils dilate as soon as she sees me, and I don't like the thing my heart does in my chest.

"What are you doing here?" I blurt out.

"I'm busy this afternoon," she says, "so I asked to join your group." The way she's watching me, I could almost think she expects me to bolt or attack. An unfriendly smile breaks on her face. "You don't mind, do you?"

I think she's mocking me. I also realize I've been staring like an imbecile. "Why would I?"

"You asked."

I don't respond, and I'm relieved when our weapons master joins us right then, a hulking woman in full tactical gear and a helmet that covers her whole face. We have a different master every year, all of them faceless, but I've noticed that the deadness around them is always weaker than usual, making their presence easier to tolerate.

The deadness is still there, though. I could hardly linger within three feet of it.

"I've been told to go easy on you this week," she says, "so you'll all do the maze a few times; then you're free to go. No enemy projectiles today—the mechs will attempt to engage you at close quarters. But if you're dumb enough to let one get close, you'll be wheeled out of here on a stretcher. First round is solo. Maximum time limit: five minutes. You know the drill. Who's first?"

I volunteer. The lights dim, the timer starts, and the humanoid combat mechs populating the maze come to life and start hunting. I've done this at least a thousand times before, so I move through the maze with purpose, even in the pitch dark, my submachine gun humming with readiness.

The mechs sweep the maze in search of me, and I pick them off one by one, mapping my way across to the other side. My gun fires only blanks, but sensors compute the theoretical trajectory of my bullets and deactivate a mech whenever I hit one. I'm through the maze in just under two and a half minutes.

Haroun, Moussa's Proxy, goes in after me and beats my time by a fraction of a second. We've both clocked faster times, but he comes out of the maze looking satisfied with himself. The next two to go in miss my time by about a tenth of a second and come out glowering.

I long ago learned that I'm the man to beat in the Range. Not because I'm especially capable—the Legacies almost always outdo me—but because the others consider it a great shame to be surpassed by a genetic experiment. Which I suppose is the purpose of me. To set the benchmark for my siblings. The absolute floor of their abilities.

I find it amusing, in truth. Most of the time.

Nandipa goes in last, and it's clear from the outset she has a point to prove. Infrared cameras display her progress on a screen. I watch it with the others, stunned by how quickly she blazes her way across the maze, shooting the mechs down like they've offended her.

A nervous thrill goes through me when she emerges from the maze a full twenty seconds faster than the rest of us, marking me with a look that would ordinarily raise my hackles and get me ready to fight. Today, I'm just confused.

"Impressive," says our weapons master, glancing at the timer above the screen. "I do believe that's your personal best, Nandipa. Great job."

"Thank you, madam," she says, but her eyes don't leave me.

I feel them on me throughout the rest of the training session. Even as we remove our gear in the locker room afterward, she watches me deliberately, and I think I'm getting annoyed with this. What the hell is her problem?

After packing up, I leave the Range, but just before I reach the tunnel to the Green, Nandipa falls into step beside me.

I stop to look at her, and I don't manage to keep a scowl off my face. "Can I help you?"

"I don't know," she says, defiant, combative. "Can you?"

I don't have time for this, whatever this is. "Excuse me. I have somewhere to be."

I enter the glass tunnel, but she follows me, keeping up with my stride. "It rankles, doesn't it?" she says. "Having someone watch you like a creep?"

I skid to a stop once again. "What? I wasn't—"

"Being a creep? Because you absolutely were. So what's your deal, Hondo? Why have you been watching me?"

I curse under my breath. I haven't told Jamal about . . . this. Maybe he already knows and is simply waiting for me to tell him myself, but I was hoping to ignore the whole thing altogether. Now I'll have to talk to him before Nandipa goes running her mouth and spreading rumors to the rest of the Habitat. I should have kept my damned eyes to myself.

"I apologize," I force myself to say. "It won't happen again, I swear." I don't mean to sound desperate, but it seems to sap some of the aggression from her, replacing it with something even worse: curiosity.

"Why did it happen to begin with?" she asks, tilting her head and sweeping her gaze over my jumpsuit.

Inside the glass tunnel, with the ocean pressing toward us on all sides, I realize that I've never been alone with her before. Opposing thrills tug at me, Counselor's warning ringing in my ear. *It's never pretty.* "Don't worry about it," I tell her. "Like I said, it won't happen again."

"Bullshit." She folds her arms, hostility returning to her face. "You owe me an explanation. What are you up to? What are you planning?"

"Nothing!"

"Bullshit."

She won't let this go, will she. Abruptly I know exactly how to solve this problem. What's that word Counselor used? Proposition? Yes. Let's try that. Might cost me my dignity, but what is that worth to an expie anyway?

I breathe in, then out. "I like you," I confess, "and I think you're nice to look at. I got carried away. Sorry."

Her eyes widen. She blinks at me several times, then laughs. "Wait, you're actually serious."

Problem solved, I guess. I expected her to react scornfully, but to actually see it proves Counselor right. This is definitely not pretty. "Whatever," I say. "Now you know. Maybe you can go laugh about it with Benjamin. I'm sure he'll find it hilarious too."

I walk away, my footsteps feeling heavy, my skin burning with something too close to shame. This time, she doesn't follow me.

Jamal has pictures of shirtless men on his bedroom wall. I didn't understand why until he explained to me in plain language that he finds men sexually attractive. That little revelation had me recalling his brief but puzzling friendship with Moussa in a new light. At the time it made little sense to me; as far as I knew, they disliked each other. So why were they suddenly sneaking around the Habitat like coconspirators?

Turns out they were "propositioning" each other, and I was probably the last person in the Habitat to understand what was going on. Ancestors, I'm probably the last person in the Habitat who still hasn't "propositioned." And at this rate, I'll probably get recycled before I ever get to.

Jamal is lounging on the couch when I walk into our living room, watching an old soccer match on the holo screen, as usual stripped down to only his gray boxers.

As soon as he sees me, he turns off the holo screen and shoots off the couch. "Did you get it?"

Reluctantly, I pull out the data stick from my pocket and present it to him.

He walks over and accepts it with a huge grin. "Ancestors, Hondo. Is there anything you can't do? You're my freaking hero."

"Whatever," I say, though we both know I enjoy the praise. "Let's just hope I didn't go through all that trouble for nothing."

"You fret too much." Jamal is already docking his PCU to our personal cyber workstation and its arrangement of three screens. Settling down by the station, he picks up the data stick and turns it over in his hands. "Fingerprint authentication, as I suspected. But that won't be a problem for us, will it."

He places the data stick next to the PCU, and I watch him use the mysterious hacking program to bypass the stick's fingerprint sensor, presumably using Counselor's template from the biometric database.

In addition to the simple mobile devices allowed to us Proxies, Primes are also issued PCUs, beefier handheld computers with superior processors, more sensors, more modules, and clever little retractable keyboards for increased utility. These devices are apparently so essential to Primes their jumpsuits come with a pocket on the right thigh made specifically to carry one.

Jamal keeps the keyboard folded away, using the workstation instead. He doesn't take long; less than five minutes after he fired up the program, a cascade of windows appears on the screens, displaying hundreds upon hundreds of files.

"Ha! We're in! Now let's see what game Counselor is playing. What are you hiding from us, hmm?"

I feel like an idiot for giving in to Jamal's foolish schemes, so I leave the room to go take a shower. I let the lukewarm water sluice down my body for a long while, trying and failing to wash off the shame I can still feel crawling all over my skin.

Of course she laughed. And soon they'll all be laughing. What else did I expect? She's a Legacy, and even if it weren't for my genetic flaws, I'm a killer, more so than anyone else in the Habitat. I don't doubt any other Proxy would have killed, too, in my position, but the violence claimed me that night, and maybe I went too far.

I barely remember the details. A mist of red settled over me when I saw someone trying to drown Jamal in the gymnasium's pool, and I reacted. By the time it was over, there was blood everywhere. One of the

Primes vomited when she saw what I'd done. Even Jamal was horrified, much as he tried to hide it.

Expie rat. A wild animal. Laughing was a mercy. She should have recoiled in disgust.

A collection of my own digital sketches covers the wall next to my bed, which I drew on discarded e-paper collected from the recycling center. Old World soccer stars. Aquatic mechs. Shato, the Habitat's octothon. I study three portraits in particular as I towel off. The subjects depicted can't speak for themselves any longer, but I'm sure if they could, they'd gloat over my humiliation.

Theirs are the faces of the three people I killed.

I don't think it's guilt that drove me to hang those portraits there, simply the need to honor the subjects. A demonstration that I regret having to do what I did even if I had to do it.

"Hondo!" Jamal calls from the living room. "Shit, Hondo, you have to see this."

I finish drying myself and pull on a pair of gray boxers before going to see just how much trouble Jamal has brought down on us.

Still seated by the workstation, he gives me a wide-eyed, almost fearful look. "I was definitely not supposed to see this."

"You think?" I mutter to myself, moving close enough to peer at the screens over his shoulders. There are multiple documents and files open, many with pictures of people I've never seen. I can't make immediate sense of it. "What is all this?"

"Birth certificates. Identity documents. Criminal records. Academic report cards. Court cases. Psych profiles. Residential addresses. Bank transactions. Extremely detailed information on hundreds of people at least," he babbles in a nervous stream.

None of the faces on the screens tickle my memory. "Who are they?" I ask.

"I think," Jamal says, "that these right here are the faces of the Custodians. The wardens, the cooks, the janitors. The people behind the masks. It seems they get paid to work here, in a currency called shillings. Some get paid a whole lot more than others, but that's probably the least interesting thing I can say about them."

"So they're real people, then," I tease. "Not androids or zombies?"

"I . . . can't say."

"What do you mean?"

Jamal shakes his head like he's completely mystified. "They were all sentenced to death, Hondo. Murder, fraud, trafficking. On paper, they *are* dead, and I think working here is a way out for them. Seems they get passage off-world once they've finished their contracts. But what's even more curious are the places they came from." He brings several identity documents to the foreground, all stamped with seals from governments I've never heard of. "SalisuCorp," Jamal reads. "ZimbaTech? Are these political entities or companies?"

They are lying to you, I remember. *Ancestors, we're dead men.* "Jamal, did you copy any of this information?"

"Not yet. Why?"

"You should let me put the stick back in Counselor's office. Today. Now. Then we should both forget that we ever saw what was on it."

He frowns like he wants to protest but ends up slumping in his chair. "I suppose you're right. None of this makes any sense, though."

I don't care about things making sense right now, only damage control. "I'm going to put on some clothes. Then I'll visit Counselor's office again and drop the stick somewhere on the floor or beneath an armchair while he's distracted. I suggest you stop poking around any further. We're in enough trouble as it is."

In the bedroom I pull out a clean jumpsuit from the closet and get dressed. I'm tightening the straps of my charcoal-black sneaker boots when Jamal calls me again.

"Hondo! Come see this! It's another message!"

I'm out the door and in the living room in the span of a breath. Jamal has undocked his PCU from the workstation, and he's pacing around as he stares at the screen. Waves of fear and excitement pulse off him like radiation from a heater.

"What does it say?" I ask, my heart racing.

"Here, look at it yourself."

On the screen, the towers of a city dominate a sunset sky. There have been four other messages very similar to this, except now, written in red letters across the image are the words **Mech bay, control room, five p.m. Don't be late.**

I look at Jamal, and I already know what he's decided. "This might be a trap," I say. "I don't like it."

"Then we walk in with our eyes open," he says. "I *have* to know what this is about, Hondo. Something is happening here. Don't tell me you can't see it."

Oh, I see it. Clearly. Someone has singled out Jamal. For what purpose, I cannot say, but there's little chance they mean him well.

He's right, though. We have to answer this summons. Right now it's our only chance to find out who's behind these messages and to hopefully put a stop to the whole business before it gets us killed.

I glance at the digital clock embedded in the left sleeve of my jumpsuit. "We have a few hours. For now, it's best I return the data stick before Counselor realizes it's missing. If he hasn't already."

I move to pick up the stick by the workstation, but Jamal puts himself in my way. "Wait. Why don't we hold on to it for a while longer? At least until after the meeting."

"What? Why?" That's when I notice the numerous progress bars on the screens, as well as the blue light flashing rapidly on the data stick. "What the hell are you doing? You're not making copies of the data, are you?"

He gives me a guilty look.

"Jamal!"

"We need insurance!" he says. "You don't just *return* something like this! We have to protect ourselves in case Counselor figures out who stole it."

"If that happens, we're dead. Our only chance now is to return the damned thing and hope Counselor never finds out we took it."

I move past Jamal to get the data stick, but he turns me back around and grabs me by the shoulders. "Hondo, look at me. You were right, okay? This was a bad idea. But now we've seen something we were never supposed to see, and I need to create insurance so that Counselor doesn't decide to vanish us because of it."

"And you think making copies of his sensitive information is how you stop him?"

"*If* he figures out we stole the stick, *then* I'll let it slip that I've uploaded an encrypted copy of his data and locked it behind a dead man's switch, and if I don't disarm it every evening: Boom. Everyone knows his dirty little secret. But that's only in the absolute worst-case scenario."

Despair weakens my knees. "Jamal . . ."

"Relax," he says, squeezing my shoulders. "It's just a precaution. We might never need it. Remember, Counselor was stupid enough to leave the stick practically out in the open. He might be stupid enough not to notice it's missing."

I am not Jamal's slave, nor am I his manservant. My purpose is to keep him alive, even if I must act against his wishes. He wouldn't be able to stop me if I decided to take the stick. I consider it.

"Please, my brother. Trust me."

Trusting him is what got us here in the first place, but it has always been difficult for me to say no to him. "After the meeting," I relent. "But this is the last time I steal anything from a Custodian, understood?"

He nods, relieved. "Perfectly."

The next few hours seem to crawl.

I alternate between pacing restlessly in the living room and hovering over Jamal's shoulder as he continues to sift through the contents of the data stick. He curses and shakes his head with each new discovery, though for now he keeps his conclusions to himself.

I don't stop him when he starts making annotations and typing out pages upon pages of notes, which he prefixes to the encrypted data. He also attaches the mysterious messages from his PCU.

"Why bother?" I ask. "The whole point of this is to threaten, not to actually release the data. If it's released, it'll mean we're already dead."

"I know," he says. "But I want whoever sees this to be able to follow my train of thought. It's all a lie, Hondo. Everything. Did you know the dead space we feel around them is some kind of field they generate deliberately? It's supposed to repel our minds or something."

It's like a bolt of lightning has gone through me. "What the fuck?"

"I know, right? It's some kind of tech they wear. There's an email exchange here between Counselor and someone else discussing a new design for the tech. Looks like they're thinking of making it stronger. And the way they talk about us . . . it's like we're barely human. We're test subjects."

He's in shock. I can practically feel the tremor in his hands, like current in a live wire. Not that I blame him. If any of what he's saying is true, I don't know if we'll be able to go back to normal after this.

I put a hand on his shoulder. "You need to forget everything you saw. Let it go."

"Forget?" He gazes up at me, liquid eyes shiny with light from the screens. "You don't understand, do you."

"Understand what?"

He seems to struggle to find the words, like he doesn't even know where to start. In the end he gives up, returning his attention to the workstation. "I'll tell you after the meeting."

I should have never agreed to steal that stick.

The appointed hour draws near eventually, and we leave our quarters together, cutting through the kelp-processing plant to get to the mech bay. Jamal inches closer to me whenever we come within visual contact of a Custodian, his fear amplifying my agitation and flooding me with so much adrenaline I can almost feel myself buzzing.

"Will you relax?" I tell him. "You're winding me up."

"Sorry," he says. "I can't help it." His eyes dart around the sector's brightly lit aisles of kelp-processing machines, taking in the various masked figures moving about as they work. "These are bad people, Hondo. Some of them have done things you wouldn't believe."

"Put it out of your mind," I say, though I know it's futile. What the hell am I supposed to do with him? I've never seen him so distressed.

We reach the mech bay with five minutes to spare. Much of the Habitat's fleet of aquatic mechs sits dormant on designated racks, their multiple articulated arms and freely rotating thrusters tucked into their sides. A pool of seawater takes up the far end of the building, where the mechs are launched and cycled out into the deep through pressurized chambers.

The control room on one side of the bay is vacant. I tell Jamal to wait by the door while I search the rest of the building. There'd normally be someone busy with repairs at this time of the day, but there's no one near the workbenches. I walk down the rows of mechs until I reach the pool. Nothing.

When I return to Jamal, he's inside the control room, standing in front of a large workstation tinged green by a layout of active camera feeds. Someone should be here, monitoring the mechs currently deployed through the feeds. The complete silence puts me on edge, but I don't voice my concerns to Jamal. He's nervous enough already.

The feeds have caught his interest, though. I watch as he leans forward, taking control of one of the mechs and its camera feed through a small joystick and a set of keys on the control panel.

"Stop that," I growl. "What are you doing?"

Under his control the mech rises over the kelp farms and their bobbing light orbs, swimming away from the Habitat. A massive hole in the seabed begins to resolve in the distance. “Ha! Is that Shato’s lair? I wonder if he’s in there right now. Let’s go take a look!”

Our neighborhood octothon, a tentacled seabeast native to this planet, rarely makes an appearance, though apparently he considers the Habitat his nest and is aggressively defensive of the aquatic mechs. I’ve always wondered where he disappeared to, so I’m intrigued despite myself. So intrigued that I fail to sense someone else entering the mech bay until they’re almost on top of us.

“Of course. Of fucking course. I *knew* it was them.”

Jamal startles, and I’m blocking the way into the control room before I can think, though my primal instincts to defend him soon have to contend with my surprise.

I came here prepared to kill whoever was playing mind games with my Prime. The fog of violence had already begun to mist my thoughts. But now I find myself, for the second time today, completely flummoxed.

“What are you doing here?” I say.

Chapter 4: Nandipa

I knew it. *Of course* it's the Rat and his lying Dog of a Proxy. *"I like you,"* he said. To think I spent a whole afternoon worrying about how the hell I was going to put him down gently.

Well, screw that.

My tech knife is already in my hand, an electrical weapon I borrowed from the Range a while ago, dispossessing it of its tracker so I wouldn't have to give it back. Hondo has put himself in front of the door to the control room; at the sight of my knife, his pupils expand to almost blacken his eyes.

They say he's psychotic, and I've caught glimpses of the rabid animal he keeps on a leash during training, like he's walking a tightrope between sanity and complete madness. I also saw what he did that night in the gymnasium's pool. I know what he's capable of. But I also know my own strength.

I step closer.

"Nandipa . . ."

Adaolisa is a tightly wound knot of concern behind me. She's a natural diplomat who considers violence a failing of shrewd planning. *"The first resort of the impolitic,"* she would say, so I know she'd rather we walked out of here and schemed our way to revenge. But I'm not leaving without answers.

"Explain yourselves," I demand, "or prepare to fight for your lives."

Smug behind his silent Dog, the Rat folds his arms and leans his back casually against a wall. "Feisty. *Very* intimidating. Not sure what you think we should explain, though. Hondo and I are just out for a stroll. What are *you* doing here?"

"I'm in no mood for games, Prime Jamal."

"Neither am I, Proxy Nandipa," he says, then slants his gaze at Adaolisa. "Besides, I'm not so stupid I'd do something to piss off the queen of the Habitat herself."

I don't react. Neither does she. "I have no idea what you're talking about," she says. "I'm not a queen."

"Oh, I beg to differ, Your Majesty. If I was wrong, I'd be melting in a tank right now." The little shit is actually gloating.

So they know. Is that what this is about? Some harebrained attempt to blackmail us?

I sense Adaolisa weighing her options. Do we walk away and let them expose us? Or do we appear to admit defeat and negotiate, only to turn around and plot their destruction?

"What do you want?" she says, deciding to play along.

But the Rat frowns like he's confused, then moves close enough to peer at us from behind his Proxy. His eyes dart back and forth between us before he says, "Have you perchance received any interesting messages of late? The last one might have said something like, *Mech bay, five p.m., don't be late.*"

I glance at Adaolisa, then scowl at the Rat. "Are you going to pretend you're not the one who sent it?"

"Why the hell would I?"

We stare at each other for a beat. Okay, so it seems I might have jumped to conclusions. *But if not him, then who?*

"I don't like this," Hondo mutters. "Jamal, we should leave."

"A fine idea." I pocket my knife and move to take Adaolisa by the arm. "Let's never do this again, shall we?"

We don't get far. A field of emptiness presses against us as Counselor steps into view, blocking the exit. Like the other Custodians, he's an active absence of living energy, a sucking void of thought and emotion, but I don't need to sense him to see the rage smoldering behind his spectacles.

"You've made a grave mistake, the four of you," he says with unsettling calm. "I expected this much from Jamal. You've never quite known your place, have you, Rat?" His spectacles reflect the room's lights as he looks back at me and my Prime. "But you, Adaolisa? What a waste."

The idea of facing off against a Custodian makes me tremble, but my knife is out again, my engineered endocrine system pumping me full of adrenaline and amphetamines.

I know Adaolisa is scared, but she keeps her cool. "Counselor, I'm not sure what you think is happening here, but all we did was answer a mysterious summons from an unknown sender."

"Same here," Jamal says, reaching into the pocket on his thigh. "I got a message on my PCU telling me to be here at five sharp. I can show it to you if you like."

Adaolisa takes out her PCU as well. "We received the same message. And it wasn't the first one they sent."

"How many did you get?" Jamal asks her, still hiding behind Hondo.

"Five. You?"

"Same."

Counselor came here furious. I think he still is, but he's also confused now. "Show me," he says, gesturing for the PCUs.

I stop Adaolisa from approaching, taking the device so I can hand it over myself. Hondo does the same thing, his concerned Prime remaining by the entrance to the control room. I sense Hondo glancing at me, but he averts his eyes as soon as I look back.

Counselor takes Adaolisa's PCU first and swipes through all her recent communications. With a deepening frown he accepts Jamal's device from Hondo and goes through it as well. I lean close enough to see that the messages are identical to the ones that were sent to us.

Counselor shakes his head, looking troubled. "This is a serious breach of security. The four of you, come with me immediately. I'm going to get to the bottom of this."

He has no sooner turned around than the ground shifts violently, shudders rippling up from the floor and through my whole body. The sound of a distant boom accompanies the quake, followed by the ear-splitting wail of the emergency alarms.

"What was that?" Counselor says, looking up at the ceiling like it might fall on us any second.

Which, I realize with dismay, isn't out of the realm of possibility. "It sounded like . . . an explosion," I say.

We wouldn't even feel it, if it happened. If the bay imploded, the sudden and immense pressure of the ocean would superheat the air around us long before the water rushed in, and we would be incinerated faster than the speed of thought.

An announcement rumbles across the bay, delivered over the alarms. *"Attention. This is not a drill. There has been a breach. Containment protocols are now in full effect. All sectors will be quarantined to contain structural damage. Exit all tunnels immediately. Proceed to the nearest bunker and await further instructions. Attention. This is not a drill . . ."*

"Is there a bunker in the mech bay?" Adaolisa asks me, visibly tense.

I shake my head, running through my mental map of the Habitat. "The nearest one is in the kelp-processing plant."

"She's right," Hondo says. "We must hurry. Jamal!"

"Wait, everyone. Come see this." The Rat is inside the control room, doing something on the terminal.

"Jamal, there's no time!" Hondo cries.

"It's not an accident! We're under attack. Shit, they're firing torpedoes at us!"

Explosions rock the building so hard one of the dormant mechs falls off its rack in a loud clatter. Counselor loses his balance, the PCUs slipping out of his hands. The ensuing boom supersedes the volume of the alarms.

Despite our better judgment, Adaolisa and I follow Hondo into the control room to see what's happening for ourselves.

"Look." With a trembling hand Jamal points at one of the screens. "The Green is already down."

I cover my mouth, but Adaolisa fails to hold in a gasp at the sight of what was once the Green. The dome has cracked open like an eggshell, everything within pulverized. Another screen shows a fleet of subaquatic vessels firing projectiles at the rest of the Habitat. Each hit causes an explosion we feel.

"My God, they've found us," Counselor whispers behind me. "How did they find us?"

I spin round to look at him. "You know who these people are?"

For an instant, pure fear, more emotion than I've ever seen on a Custodian, but then he masters it, fixing his face into a frown. "Get to a bunker. *Now.*" And he's out the door before I can say anything.

"Ada, let's go."

"Wait," she says. "Where's Counselor going?"

I thought he might have already left the bay, but he's halfway down the rows of mechs. "It doesn't matter. We need to leave before this bay is sealed off."

"There's an emergency submersible on the other side of the bay," Jamal tells us in a high-strung voice, tracking Counselor's retreating form. "I'd bet my nut sack he's planning on escaping."

Adaolisa gives him a sharp look. "What makes you say that?"

"Call it a hunch. Counselor obviously knows who's attacking us, and if he's escaping rather than running to a bunker . . ."

“He knows we won’t survive,” Adaolisa finishes for him. She looks at me. “Nandipa, we can’t let him leave without us.”

I’d rather we escaped to a pressurized bunker, but I nod. “Fine. Let’s go.”

Jamal picks up the discarded PCUs and hands one to Adaolisa, and then they all follow me as I race down the bay after Counselor. Hondo grabs a large torque wrench from one of the worktables and catches up to me just as I reach the edge of the bay’s pool. We find Counselor operating a terminal to lower the bullet-shaped emergency submersible from its hoist above the water. Its surface is a color-absorbing matte black, and the glazed compartment up front has seats enough for six people.

“What are you doing here?” he bellows when he sees us. “I told you to get to a bunker!”

The walls shake under the strain of constant bombardment. The bay could implode on us at any second. I make sure he sees my knife. “We’re coming with you.”

“Absolutely not. The protocols are clear. You must evacuate to a bunker and await further—”

He jumps when Hondo strikes a metal surface with the torque wrench. “How far do you think you’ll go with a hole in your skull?” Hondo says. “This isn’t a request. We’re coming.”

As the submersible completes its descent into the pool, Counselor eyes us darkly, a look I might have shied from ordinarily, but right now my blood is saturated with stimulants, and I’d kill every Custodian in the Habitat if that was what it took to get Adaolisa out of here.

Recognizing that we’re dead serious, Counselor utters a stream of passionate curses. “Fine! Get in. Quickly, before we all die.”

The Primes enter the submersible first, then Counselor, who takes the helm. I brave the emptiness around him to strap in next to him upfront, my knife in plain sight as a silent warning of what will happen if he tries anything I don’t agree with. I can hardly believe what I’m doing.

"We're all settled," Hondo says as soon as the door closes. "Get us the hell out of here, Counselor."

"Giving me orders now, are you?" Counselor gripes, but the submersible is already sinking into the pool.

The alarms become muffled as the water engulfs us, but the bombardments are strong enough to make our seats vibrate. Deep inside the pool, Counselor navigates the submersible through an open hatch into a pressure chamber. The lights on the closed hatch on the other side of the chamber remain red.

Powerful hydraulics hiss as we begin to cycle out of the Habitat. The hatch behind us closes, and more alarms blare, warning us that the chamber is pressurizing. But then there's a sudden and tremendous crashing sound, followed by the creaking of metal under severe stress.

"What the hell was that?" Jamal says from his seat two rows behind me.

"I think the bay has caved in," Adaolisa answers, radiating fear.

"The hatch should hold until the pressure equalizes," I say, projecting a sense of calm to her. I sense Hondo doing the same thing for his Prime.

It seems to take forever, but finally the lights in the chamber turn green, the hatch opens, and Counselor moves us forward, navigating a rather long tunnel before bringing us to a vertical shaft. The exterior lights reveal a smooth, metallic, circular wall; the submersible remains horizontal while we ascend the shaft. About thirty feet up another hatch irises open above us, letting us out of the seabed near the kelp farms, maybe a mile away from the nearest Habitat structure.

I numb myself to what I see ahead of us, inhibitory neurotransmitters reducing the effect of my shock, yet for all that, I'm still unable to believe my eyes.

The submarines that came from nowhere have pummeled my home into a ruin scattered on the ocean floor. A hive of buildings that withstood incredible pressure for hundreds of years, gone in minutes.

Is anyone still alive?

As we watch, the submarines continue their bombardment, like they know about the bunkers deeper below.

"Why are they doing this?" I hear Adaolisa say, and I can feel the brokenness inside her.

Counselor's shock is so palpable I could almost swear I can sense it even through the emptiness around him. "Centuries of work," he mutters. "All gone. How did this happen?"

"Move it, Counselor," Hondo barks. "They might see us."

When Counselor remains still, I reach over to shake him out of it. "We have to go!"

He curses loudly; then I'm pushed back into my seat as we accelerate up and away from the Habitat. The last thing I see before my now-ruined home is lost to me forever is a vast tentacled figure wrapping itself around one of the submarines, its full shape briefly flashing into view in the light of an exploding torpedo.

Conceptually, I know that leaving the Habitat is a thing that happens. Lots of people have done it before, and in fact, leaving the Habitat and saying goodbye to ocean dwelling forever is precisely what Adaolisa has been fighting for all our lives. I know this.

I still can't believe it's actually happening. Especially not with me all but holding a knife to Counselor's throat while the Rat and his Dog come along for the ride. My world has abruptly become unreal.

"What if they follow us?" Adaolisa says minutes into our ascent through the pitch-black ocean.

Counselor switched off all exterior and interior lights, perhaps to decrease our visibility to potential enemies, so we're all dark outlines against the blue LEDs lighting up the dashboard.

"I think Shato kept them busy for a while," Jamal says. "And this thing was built for speed. If we keep moving, they won't catch up."

"But where are we going?" she says. "And who were those people, Counselor? Why did they attack us? You owe us an explanation."

"I owe you nothing," Counselor fires back. "Bringing you was a mistake."

"Bringing us is the only reason you're still alive," I say, making my knife flash in the gloom. "Remember that."

"Thanks for the reminder," he replies with a snarl. "Now be quiet, all of you. There could be enemies listening for us."

I've never stayed this close to a Custodian for so long. The field of emptiness around him is making me dizzy. I'm not sure how much longer I can take it, but I keep it off my face, distracting myself by wondering what the hell is supposed to happen now.

I assume there'll be a spaceport somewhere on the surface. Will a ship be waiting for us, or does it only come once every several years to collect the Primes and Proxies who've beaten the war games? What will they do with us? *Dear ancestors, are we the only ones still alive?*

I nearly jump out of my skin when Hondo speaks into my ear a while later. "We should trade seats."

"I'm fine," I say automatically, though I have to cobble my thoughts together as if through a drunken fog.

"You're not," he says simply. "We can take turns until we get to the surface."

"A good idea, Nandipa. You should come rest."

Adaolisa's worry sobers me a little, so I accept the offer and move to the seat next to her while Hondo replaces me next to Counselor. Jamal watches us from his seat in the rear, his eyes wide and alert.

"Are you all right?" Adaolisa says, reaching over to feel my forehead like she's checking for a fever.

"Are you?"

Tears escape her eyes as she shakes her head. "I really don't know what's happening."

It strikes me for the first time how unusual that answer sounds coming from her lips. I've always trusted her to know what's going on. Few things ever take her by surprise, but now she's just as lost as I am, and I'm not sure what to do about it.

"If you ask me," Jamal pipes up, "those were people from the surface."

We both look at him. "There's no one on the surface but savages," Adaolisa says.

"Maybe," he says with something knowing in his eyes. "But I find it difficult to believe someone would come all the way from outer space and swim to the bottom of an ocean just to kill us."

When he puts it like that, I admit, it does sound improbable. But even more improbable is the idea that there are people on the surface with the ability to build submarines and mount the kind of attack we just escaped.

They are lying to you, I remember, and I reflexively seek the handle of my knife.

"Do you know something you're not telling us, Jamal?" Adaolisa asks.

He gives an annoying little shrug. "Maybe."

"Being secretive now will gain you nothing."

"I'll tell you everything soon enough," he says. "I'm just waiting to see if I'm right."

I think he's playing mind games with us. I don't think he actually knows anything. But then again, he did figure out our arrangement with David, so he's not completely full of shit.

Ancestors, David, Benjamin. So many others. The children on the other side of the Habitat.

I try not to think about their crushed bodies floating somewhere at the bottom of the ocean. I pray we weren't the only ones who escaped.

Counselor levels out the submersible once we reach a depth of two hundred feet, and we cut across the midnight-blue waters as fast as the vehicle can take us. Where to, I couldn't say, though Counselor seems to know exactly what he's doing. I find myself recalling all those intermittent absences of his, when he'd disappear from the Habitat for weeks on end without explanation. We all assumed he was visiting the other side of the Habitat. Now I'm beginning to realize he might have been coming up to the surface.

"What is it you thought we'd done, Counselor?" Jamal asks after a prolonged silence.

"What do you mean?" comes Counselor's impatient reply.

"When you entered the mech bay and saw us there, it seemed you thought we'd done something. You were quite angry. Why? And why were you in the mech bay to begin with? Were you sent messages too?"

A long pause, and then Counselor sighs. "It doesn't matter now."

"If you say so," Jamal continues with open insolence. "But what about those horrible things you said to me? You called me a rat. Said you expected bad behavior from me and that I didn't know my place. Isn't that the kind of bias you're not supposed to show, Counselor?"

"I . . . was angry," Counselor admits. "But you're right; I should never have used such words. You have my unreserved apologies."

He actually sounds sincere, but I feel Jamal's grin even without looking at him. "You know, I always thought you and Administrator didn't like me, but I could never be sure. Thanks for clearing up the confusion. The feeling is mutual, by the way."

"Fair enough," Counselor says in a flat tone. "Now be quiet."

Hours pass, and still we swim into the night. I begin to wonder if we'll ever stop—if I even *want* us to stop. Who's to say what lies ahead won't be worse than what we just escaped?

Our lives before now were predictable. We knew who our friends and enemies were. We knew why we existed, what role we were supposed to play. Now I don't know what happens next, and this frightens me.

I'm not used to such feelings. Such maddening uncertainty.

Counselor's oppressive presence took a toll on me, so when my eyes grow heavy, I don't fight the pull, and I let myself drift off into a dreamless sleep.

—

"Damn it!"

I jerk awake at the sound of Counselor's voice. The waters around us have brightened slightly with the approach of daylight. We've slowed to a sluggish drift, and I can see the outline of coral-covered mounds in the near distance. Dry land can't be far away.

"What is it?" Hondo asks, his voice hoarse with discomfort. He must have been sitting there for hours. Why didn't he wake me?

"We have a big problem." Counselor brings up a holo screen that covers most of the front windows. "The shuttle we need to fly safely to the coast is in a hangar on that island up ahead. But there's a squad of commandos waiting for us."

He must have deployed the submersible's drone. Its airborne camera feed shows us an elevated view of a round island in the middle of the ocean. The sun is minutes away from rising. I spot a few aircraft of an unfamiliar make resting on the beach. Several buildings populate the heavily treed island, the kind I'd have expected to see on some rich man's private ocean getaway on the Old World. I count at least six figures walking around in pitch-black bulletproof armor, all of them carrying large rifles.

"More of your friends, Counselor?" I say with open bitterness.

"There's nothing *friendly* about these people, I assure you."

"And yet whoever they are, they clearly anticipated you'd come here. Why is that?"

"If I knew the answer to that question, girl, I'd not be here in the first place."

"Well, we're here," Hondo cuts in. "So let's deal with it. How many commandos, Counselor?"

"Twelve, at least, and they'll shoot us on sight." A shrewd look crosses Counselor's face as he studies Hondo. "But you can take them, can't you?"

"Do we have a choice?"

"I suppose not."

"Then we'll do what needs doing."

I'm prepared to fight if I have to, but I'm not sure Hondo will be up to the task considering he's been withering in Counselor's dead space for hours now. "Can you manage?" I ask him.

"I can manage," he replies in a tone that won't brook argument. "But you'll have to take us closer," he tells Counselor. "We can't exactly swim there."

Counselor deactivates the holo screen and gets us moving. "We'll surface by the pier east of the island. There's more forest cover in the area, and they aren't watching it as closely as they should."

I can't be sure, but I think he can still see the drone's feed through his contact lenses. I also think he'll have a lot of explaining to do as soon as we get to safety. Oh, he'll explain, all right, because something is definitely wrong here.

Adaolisa and Jamal were asleep; they both stir awake and rub their eyes as we slow, approaching the underwater piles of the pier.

"What's going on?" she asks.

"Are we there yet?" he says.

I tell them what we're planning, and Adaolisa is predictably horrified.

"Nandipa! You can't!"

"It's the only way." I take her hands and press them between mine. "You kept me alive in the Habitat. Now it's my turn to keep you alive. This is what I've trained for. I'll be fine."

"You better be," she says, holding back her tears. "That's an order."

I try to project a confidence I don't feel. "Understood."

I glance at Jamal and catch him watching his Proxy with fearful worry, and I think this is the most vulnerable I've ever seen him. But his usual smirk returns as soon as he notices me looking. "Scared, Nandipa? Don't worry. Hondo will be there to save you if you mess up. Isn't that right, Hondo?"

My regard for Hondo goes up a notch when he doesn't reply. Of all the Primes who could have survived the attack, why did we have to be stuck with this one?

"They'll radio for backup, so you'll need to be quick," Counselor warns us. "We should be long gone by the time someone else comes to investigate. Here. Take these."

Both Hondo and I accept little black earpieces taken out of a dashboard compartment. Adaolisa watches me unhappily as I clip mine on.

"We can't stay afloat for too long, or they'll spot us," Counselor says. "We'll be dipping back down as soon as you jump off. Are you ready?"

Adaolisa hugs me tightly. Hondo gives his Prime a quiet glance, then nods at Counselor.

"Go ahead," he says. "We're ready."

Water cascades down the windows as we breach the surface, and I see the sky for the first time. I've experienced dawn beneath the Green's artificial sky, so I know roughly what to expect. The interplay of color—luxurious golds, soft cherries, deeper indigos where the sunlight has yet to reach. The quiet stillness that lends itself to meditation. The breathtaking beauty.

What the Green failed to accurately portray was the sky's true size.

Hondo and I step off the submersible and onto a wooden pier—me armed with my knife, Hondo still with his torque wrench—and the sky immediately imposes its might on my senses so that I almost lose my balance, fighting the powerful urge to drop to my knees and hide my face. My mind keeps telling me that something is wrong. The sky should not be so big. It has cracked open, and in seconds I'll be crushed under an ocean of water.

Breathe, I tell myself. *You're a* Homo sapiens. *Your ancestors were hunter-gatherers who lived under an open sky. The sun's warmth on your face, the sea breeze, the low and distant horizon; this is what is natural. It was the Habitat that was alien. You are finally home, and for fuck's sake get a grip on yourself. Now's not the time to panic.*

The submersible is already sinking back into the water. I notice Hondo swaying next to me, so I grip his arm to steady him. "Are you all right?"

"The sky," he mutters, looking dazed. "It's too much."

He stayed too long next to Counselor. Damn it.

I look around. No enemies in sight, but we need to be off this pier. "Jamal is counting on you," I say. "Ignore everything else. Can you do that?"

It's like I've cast a spell. At the mention of his Prime, Hondo immediately gets a grip on himself, a calm lucidness entering his eyes. "Yes. He needs me. Let's go."

We hurry off the pier, slink into the surrounding woods, and take cover in the profuse undergrowth of fernlike plants. The trees on this island form mazes of twisting branches that interlace way above our heads. Rich scents fill my nose, tempting me to sneeze. I hold it in.

A gravel path nearby leads to a white building just visible between the trees. I'm about to cut through the ferns for the building when I suffer an abrupt overload of the senses, my skin tingling like I'm in a crowded room and no one's bothering to mask their emotional responses.

At first I wonder if perhaps I'm coming down with something, but the longer I pay attention, the more I realize that this sensory racket is coming from two people walking down the gravel path.

I crouch lower, seeking Hondo's gaze. "Do you feel that?" I whisper.

The look on his face is restrained alarm. "Yes."

If Counselor is an emptiness, these two strangers are roaring clouds of static. I've never felt anything like it. I could almost swear they have radios inside their heads, broadcasting the ambient sound of their thoughts with the volume turned all the way up.

Just to make sure I'm not going crazy, I focus on Hondo to see if he's suddenly making as much noise, but no, his presence is mild enough he could sneak up on me if I were distracted.

"What the hell is this?" I wonder out loud.

"It doesn't matter," Hondo says. "Here they come."

The two commandos approaching us have hidden their eyes behind dark sunglasses and covered their chests in ballistic armor. I wouldn't have needed to see them to know their exact positions; the loud static of their thoughts betrays them to us, and we lie low until they're almost on top of us. Then we pounce.

I watch myself rise from the undergrowth behind them. Their thoughts burst into a more furious noise when they notice us, but I'm already striking with my electrically charged tech knife, slicing the soft neck tissue just below the chin. My victim gasps, dropping his weapon, and I help him down to the ground. The second one has already fallen, his skull smashed inward by the dull blow of a torque wrench.

I'm no heroine today, no simpering seductress. I have just killed for the second time in my life, and the blood is still fresh. I can smell it, see it, touch it. I block all my emotional responses, staying in the moment, and crouch down to investigate my victim's rifle. It's lighter than it looks, made of polymer and an alloy of titanium with precision-guided systems. I notice he was also packing a pistol.

"Don't bother with those," Counselor says into my earpiece. *"They'll be keyed to subcutaneous implants on their wrists. You won't be able to use them."*

He must be monitoring us through his drone. I really hope Adaolisa isn't watching.

"That's inconvenient," I say, letting go of the rifle.

"It's better this way." I look up; Hondo's eyes are on the building. Spatters of blood have stained his jumpsuit. I don't think he's noticed. "We'll avoid a firefight," he says, "pick them off before they see us. I sense two more on the other side of that building. Come on."

I don't like the prospect of killing more people in close quarters, but I don't let that weaken me. I can't.

We continue hunting, years of training kicking in, cutting through the strangeness of the surface and its open sky. And the loud static emanating from our enemies, initially disconcerting to us, becomes their own undoing as it guides us to their positions before they know we're there.

It is not sound, precisely. It's the turbulent wake a thinking, feeling mind leaves in the world as it goes about thinking and feeling, the thing Counselor and the other Custodians do not give off, and with these people it's amplified to an almost physical sensation.

A sensation I feel going out with every use of my knife, though not like turning off a switch, here now, gone the next second, but like listening to the outro of a song as it slowly fades into silence.

We make fast work of the commandos, taking advantage of their dispersed patrols of the island. I reaffirm my assessment of this place as some sort of luxurious private paradise, like the home of a tycoon from some Old World drama serial. Ornamental gardens. Open and airy buildings with pristine pools. In another life I might have loved to linger.

Today the static calls to me, so sharp I quickly realize I can tell where the enemy will look before they look there, if they are alert or distracted, if they've heard something approach, and they always do, but too late.

Seriously, what is *this?*

Hondo's presence is quieter, as it has always been, but I can still sense him restraining himself, as though he were fighting to keep a wild beast contained, taking his targets out with just a single swing of his wrench—and one swing is always enough. When our eyes briefly meet as we stalk to our last two targets, I see only focused intent on his bloodied face. I wonder if I look the same. A cold, ruthless killer.

I really, really hope Adaolisa isn't watching.

One of the men ahead is trying to reach the others on his radio. I don't quite catch his words; his accent is unfamiliar. I throw my knife from the undergrowth, and he goes down, clutching at the blood fountaining from his ruptured larynx. His friend has only enough time to emit an alarmed burst of thought before Hondo steps out of the shadow of a tree and swings, shattering his face. And then it's over.

"I don't see any more movement outside," Counselor says into my ear. *"But there might be others in the buildings."*

"I doubt it," I say. "But we'll check just to be sure."

As I expect, Hondo and I find no one inside the lavishly furnished buildings—no one alive, at least. We do find a pile of bodies in one living room with a drooping crystal chandelier, at least a dozen people who were shot, then dragged on top of each other like refuse.

This is not a drill. Not an episode on the holo screen. This is really happening.

"The island's original inhabitants, maybe?" Hondo says as we stare at the corpses. He sweeps his gaze around the rest of the room. "What the hell is this place?"

My body has suppressed so much of my emotional shock I find it only distantly crazy that there were inhabitants anywhere on the surface to begin with. I'm even less shocked that I'm standing in front of a literal pile of corpses.

"We've found bodies in one of the buildings," I inform Counselor. "It looks like the commandos killed them before we got here. We need to leave before anyone else shows up."

"All right, I'm bringing us in."

"We'll meet you at the pier."

Before I leave, I pick up a throw blanket from a nearby couch. On our way out I offer it to Hondo, who gives me an odd stare.

"You have blood on your face," I explain.

"It's not mine," he answers.

"I know."

He seems to grow self-conscious, properly looking down at himself and seeing the bloodstains all over his jumpsuit. He accepts the blanket without making eye contact. "Thanks."

I sense he might be ashamed, though I'm not sure why he'd feel that way. It's not like either of us had a choice.

"You did well," I hear myself say. "We both did." And for some stupid reason I go on to add, "I'm glad you're here."

Beyond the eastern docks, the sun has fully risen, and its reflection is a shimmering line of liquid gold on the surface of the ocean. Both Primes run over as soon as they see us, Adaolisa throwing her arms around me in an embrace, Jamal doing the same to his morose Proxy.

"You were magnificent!" Jamal exclaims. "Ancestors, Hondo. I didn't know you could move like that! And the sky! Have you seen the sky?"

"That was horrifying," Adaolisa says to me. "Are you all right?"

"I'm fine."

She releases me and looks me in the eye. "Nandipa, I know you're not hurt. But . . . are you all right?"

Am I? I could dig deep, look inward, examine myself, but I am two separate beings right now. One knows what I should feel; the other is making sure I don't feel it. And the last thing I want is to burden Adaolisa with guilt for my actions. "Don't worry about me. I'll get over it."

When Counselor catches up, he regards me and Hondo like he's reassessing us. "Well done. It would seem bringing you with me was not a mistake, as I thought. You were more . . . efficient than I anticipated. And perhaps . . . hmm . . . yes, perhaps not everything is lost after all . . ." He trails off, sinking into his own thoughts.

"Counselor, where's the shuttle?" I say, bringing him back to the present. "We need to leave this place."

"Right. Yes. Follow me. It's this way."

The shuttle in the hangar across the island looks to me like an armored truck, large, boxlike, and bulging in the sides as though it might have guns tucked somewhere inside. It could hardly be a truck, however, given the total lack of wheels.

We all jump on board behind Counselor, strapping ourselves into seats a few rows away from the cockpit. This time neither Hondo nor I volunteers to endure Counselor's dead space. We're at his mercy now, whatever he decides to do. There's no point in torturing ourselves just to keep a closer eye on him.

The shuttle whines like a whirling fan, and we gently lift off the ground and float out of the hangar. What I thought were guns turn out to be hidden ion thrusters; they extrude from the sides of the shuttle, tilt downward, and ignite, lifting us even higher into the air.

I reach for Adaolisa's hand just as she reaches for mine, and we hold on to each other as gravity does funny things to our internal organs. Outside the shuttle's windows, the island grows smaller as we bank away from it; then the thrusters realign and we accelerate away from the rising sun.

More hours transpire, the four of us taking in the sudden openness of our world in thoughtful silence. We fly low enough that we can still see individual waves rippling across the face of the ocean, and as it stretches and stretches, boundless as the sky itself, I begin to let go of all the conceptions I made about the surface from my little pocket of air under the ocean. The surface isn't just a surface, a two-dimensional space; it is a world. A universe. I did not know anything could be so big.

The skies become gray and rivulets of water start coursing across our windows, and I realize this is another first for me: rain. The rain strengthens and wanes repeatedly, shrouding everything in a fine silver mist I find oddly peaceful despite it washing all the color from the world.

Islands with visible structures begin to appear below us, then seagoing vessels cutting white slipstreams across the ocean, then other aerial vehicles moving through the wet skies. Pressure builds up inside my chest, but I remain numb even when the coast finally appears ahead of us as myriad lights shining through the rainfall, even as we fly over a busy marina, then over land so densely built up there is hardly a foot of empty space.

I am numb even as we enter a maze of great towering skyscrapers, navigating from one aerial traffic lane to another, turning this corner and then that, bombarded all the while by more lights and holograms than I knew existed in the entirety of the universe.

I remain completely numb even as Counselor rises above a traffic lane and finally settles the shuttle onto a landing pad somewhere high in the maze of glass and concrete, in what is clearly an immensely populous city, the kind of city I thought I'd only ever see in holo videos of the distant past.

The surface of Ile Wura was lost to savagery, they told us. Cybernetic cannibals roved the apocalyptic wastes in packs, mindless and hungry for flesh. The last embers of civilization lay off-world, and only we could rekindle its dying flames.

From here, the city's forest of towers spreads from one edge of the horizon to the other.

They are lying to you. I realize I'm holding Adaolisa's hand again. Alone, I might have wept or screamed in rage, but she's here, so even though the world has changed around me, I take solace in the knowledge that my purpose in it has not.

As for Adaolisa—the faraway look in her eye, the ghost of a smile on her lips—she's already moved past her shock, and I can tell she's approaching our new reality like a fresh war game. She will know what to do next, she will be drawing up plans and counterplans, and I will gladly follow her lead.

In the relative quiet after Counselor turns off the engines, the pitter-patter of rainfall fills our ears, and then Jamal starts laughing like a madman. "I knew it," he says. "I *knew* it. It was all a lie. Fucking incredible."

Counselor remains still in the cockpit for the longest time, his shoulders tensed beneath his suit. When he finally speaks, he does so without turning his head to look at us. "This is a safe house of sorts," he says. "I'm going to leave you here for a while. I paid a great deal of money to make sure this vehicle can't be tracked, but I'll need to throw off our scent just in case. You will be safe here for now."

We wait, but he says nothing else.

"That's it?" Jamal asks. "That's *all* you're going to tell us? Don't you think you're leaving out some pretty significant information? For example, where the hell are we? Or maybe, who the hell were those people who attacked us? Or better yet, why have you been lying to us all our lives?" He's almost shouting at the end, his voice strident in the enclosed cabin.

Counselor still won't look at us. "I know you have questions," he says, subdued. "I know you're confused, but please understand that whatever we told you, we had good reasons. Let me take care of a few things so that you're safe here; then, when I return, I'll tell you everything."

He turns a switch and the door slides open, inviting in a fine drizzle of the first rainfall I've ever felt on my skin. Quietly we step outside and into a cacophony of sound—the whir of passing aerial vehicles, the whisper of rainfall, the static of so many thinking beings it makes me want to slam my hands over my ears.

This isn't a drill. We're in a city.

A real, living, breathing, *noisy* city.

It's far more than I've ever imagined.

Our jumpsuits are soaked in seconds, but none of us care. We quietly walk to the edge of the landing pad to get our first full view of human life on the surface, a city that should not exist.

"It's got to be three hundred years old at least," Jamal remarks.

"It defies everything I thought I knew about . . . well, everything," Adaolisa says. She gives a laugh, though I sense a strong current of despair moving through her. "All our knowledge might be completely useless."

"The cybernetic menace is real," Counselor barks behind us. "And you truly are the last hope against it. That is the truth. Do not be deceived by these shining towers. We kept you hidden for your own protection. If the rulers of this world knew you were still alive, they'd do everything in their power to destroy you. Never doubt that."

The nerve. Warning us against deception when our lives have been one big lie. I should kill him. Torture him for answers.

"You should come inside," he says. "When it's safer, you can gawk at the city as much as you want, and I'll answer whatever questions you have."

As he turns around, I entertain the notion of grabbing him and throwing him off the landing pad. I sense a similar sentiment occurring to Hondo, but neither of us makes the move. I guess we both figure it's not our place to make that decision.

Instead we shadow our Primes as they follow Counselor toward the glass doors across the landing pad.

"At least tell us where we are," Jamal says to his back. "You owe us that much."

Counselor pauses briefly and then sighs before he says, "Welcome to ZimbaTech." The doors slide open, and he walks in. "Now come in before someone sees you."

Part 2:
ZimbaTech

Chapter 5: Hondo

"Don't leave the apartment until I get back. Are we clear?"

That's the last thing Counselor says to us before he heads back out into the rain. From the windows, we watch him lift off the landing pad in his shuttle and fly off into the city, all of us soaked and dripping onto the floor.

"Lying bastard, isn't he?" Jamal mutters. "I wish you'd gone ahead and chucked him off the landing pad like you wanted to."

I guess I didn't mask that impulse very well. Ancestors know it took every ounce of self-control I had to stop myself. "We need him," I say, because it's true. We know nothing about this world, and without him we're sitting targets. Those people from the island could still be hunting us.

I tremble with rage at being so helpless, balling my fists so I don't punch something. My life is a lie. My home, a lie. They said we were civilization's last hope, yet here is civilization all around us, old and brimming and overflowing with noise.

"You knew about this, Jamal?" Adaolisa asks, nodding at the cityscape outside, an endless grid of lights and towers stretching out into the rain.

Jamal's amazement is unmasked as he shakes his head at the view. "Not precisely *this*. But I figured out there was more happening on the surface than we were led to believe."

"And how did you 'figure this out'?"

I expect him to keep his secrets, but he pulls out Counselor's data stick from his chest pocket. "Hondo stole this for me from Counselor's office. I disabled the biometric sensor, so you should be able to look through it without a problem."

Adaolisa blinks at him like he's the most ridiculous thing she's ever seen. "You had your Proxy *steal* from a Custodian?"

"I was sitting right in front of Counselor when he put the stick in an unlocked drawer." Jamal shrugs. "He was practically inviting me to steal it."

Shaking her head, she turns to Nandipa and says, "Remind me never to stow anything important in Jamal's presence."

I try not to think about the amused look on Nandipa's face, whether she's impressed or finds me absurd. And I definitely haven't noticed the way her wet jumpsuit is clinging to her body or that her hair has drooped into long, glistening ringlets.

"Do you want the stick or not?" Jamal says impatiently.

Adaolisa seems to think about it, perhaps the residual fear of crossing a Custodian making her hesitant, but she decides to accept the gift anyway. "What's on it?"

"Look through it yourself," Jamal says. "I need a hot shower. That rain has a bite to it, doesn't it?"

In true Jamal fashion he's already halfway across the room, leaving me alone with the two young women, who watch me openly, like they're waiting for me to make the first move.

It strikes me how alike they seem, right then, both lissome and bright eyed, with faces designed to beguile and gazes that see too much. Under their scrutiny I begin to feel myself wilt, so I excuse myself and scurry after my Prime.

The apartment reminds me of Administrator's office, lots of Old World chic with its mahogany synth-leather; furnishings in dark, earthy tones; and metallic accents in the hanging lamps and ornaments. The staircase to the second floor might actually be real wood. The potted plants might be real plants. And there's a library stocked with real paper books on the first floor.

Jamal selfishly claims the larger of the two bedchambers upstairs, which has its own bathroom amenities and a dormant computer terminal. While he showers, I wander around the room, looking through the drawers, examining the paintings of Old World industrial landscapes, pressing every button I see. I learn how to shut out the city by making the windows opaque and how to invite it back in by making them completely transparent. I turn on the terminal, but it demands biometric authentication, so I turn it off again.

There are clothes in the walk-in closet. Shirts and coats and suits that seem tailored for Counselor's build, meaning they'll be too broad at the shoulders and not quite long enough for me. Better than nothing, I suppose. We'll just have to make do until Counselor comes up with a plan for us.

Jamal emerges from the bathroom in a cloud of steam, enthusing about the excellent water pressure. I hop into the shower myself, and when I come out, I find him already asleep between the sheets of the only bed in the room.

I sigh, slightly annoyed. Jamal can be a fitful sleeper, so I'm not exactly thrilled about having to share a bed with him. But I'm exhausted, so after I towel off, I slip into ill-fitting sleepwear from the closet and join him on the bed.

I dream about home. I did not have friends in the Habitat. I was feared or hated, either because of Jamal or for my own reputation. I have very few fond memories of that place. I shouldn't *care* about my dead siblings. I'm not even sure I do, but their faces visit me in my sleep, and I already know that the sight of my home shattered on the ocean floor will stay with me forever.

Is this me being sentimental? I hate it.

I wake up ravenous a few hours later. It's stopped raining outside, but night has fallen, the lights of passing aerial cars dancing on the wet windows. Jamal is awake, sitting by the terminal, his face illuminated by the purple glare coming off the screens. Like me he has put on a pair of striped nightclothes.

"What are you doing?" I ask groggily. "I thought the terminal was locked."

"I still have Counselor's biometric templates," Jamal tells me. "If there are any secrets he's keeping here, I'm going to find them."

My initial instinct is to ask him to be careful, to not do something that might get us in trouble with the Custodians. But then my brain catches up, and I realize the Custodians don't matter anymore. Counselor may be the last one left for all we know. And good riddance, I'd say.

I get up from the bed and head for the door. "I'm going to get something to eat."

"Bring me something too, would you?"

"You can come and get it yourself."

"I love you too," he calls behind me.

"Go screw yourself."

In the kitchen downstairs, I open the freezer and look over the wide selection of frozen meals in commercially branded little boxes. I pull out a box claiming to have real grilled vegetables inside it, and then I follow the reheating instructions on the colorful packaging.

Figuring out how the oven works isn't difficult, and soon there's a pleasant scent filling the kitchen. My mouth is watering by the time I finally settle down to eat by the counter. I take my first tentative bite, and it's the best thing I've ever tasted.

"Something smells good," Nandipa says as she joins me in the kitchen.

I try not to stare, though I'm not sure I succeed. I've never seen her in anything other than a jumpsuit, but now she's wearing an oversize printed shirt with green patterns, and beneath it her long legs are bare. It's just a shirt, but I'm suddenly aware of my own ill-fitting pajamas.

I eat slowly, watching her as she reheats her own frozen meal, and the silence between us becomes more awkward when she sits down next to me by the kitchen counter. She takes her first forkful of grilled vegetables, and the signals in my brain get mixed up when she gives a sigh of pleasure. I hide my face by frowning down at my food.

"The Custodians have a lot to answer for," she says. "We've been eating kelp this whole time when we could have been having this? The least they could have done is give us good food."

This is the first time she's ever invited conversation with me. I chew my food and swallow, pretending I'm not painfully self-conscious. "Have you wondered what happened to the others who left the Habitat?"

"You mean the previous generations?" She becomes pensive, twirling her fork in a way I find endearing. "I hadn't thought that far, to be honest. There are too many lies to sort through. But it's an interesting question. The off-world story doesn't seem likely anymore."

"Before yesterday," I say, "I wondered if the Custodians were past versions of us. It made sense to me, because who else could they be?"

"Condemned criminals wearing dead-space tech to repel us and make us afraid of them?" Nandipa offers.

I look at her. "Wild, isn't it? How did you know?"

"Adaolisa told me. She's in the library right now, looking through the data stick. Did you really steal it from Counselor's office?"

The laughter in her eyes makes me grin. "Have you never stolen from a Custodian?" I say.

"Not so directly, no."

"I once lifted a snack bar straight out of a warden's pocket."

"That was . . . stupid . . . to say the least."

"Absolutely. But it felt good to pull it off."

Nandipa considers me with an enigmatic smile, and I decide there and then that her face was sculpted to achieve precisely this effect. "You know, Hondo," she says, "you're not what I expected."

This is good, right? "What did you expect?" I ask hopefully.

"A creep," she flatly says.

Ah. My hopes crash and burn, and I look back down onto the kitchen counter. "I apologized for that."

"I guess you did." I remain silent as she gets up from her stool and picks up her food. I think she's about to ditch me, but then she says, "I'm curious what surfacers watch for entertainment. Care to join me?"

It's a miracle I don't stutter or gape like an idiot. "Sure," I say and follow her to the holo screen in the living area.

Sitting beside her on the same couch, I hardly pay attention to the rush of images that inundates my eyes as she sifts through an endless selection of holo streams. But I'm not so distracted by her that I learn nothing.

I learn, for example, that the people of the surface—of this city, at least—speak the Third Dialect, albeit a slightly less formal, slightly bastardized form of it. And when we flip through several soccer streams, I decide that soccer is probably the most popular sport in this part of the world at least. I'm sure Jamal will be delighted. He hardly watched anything else with his hour of entertainment back in the Habitat.

Other sport streams briefly pique our interest. Fluffy drones trying to blow each other up. Bionically enhanced kickboxers having at each other in brutal death matches. I grimace in disgust when a man loses his head to a bionic arm blade.

"This can't be real, can it?" I say.

Nandipa switches to the next stream, and I immediately regret I said something, because there's suddenly a scene of explicit . . . *propositioning* . . . filling the holo screen right in front of us.

While I sit there frozen in deathly mortification, Nandipa is insane enough to be fascinated. "Nothing's sacred to these people, is it?" She tilts her head with morbid interest. "How is she even doing that?"

Dear ancestors, kill me now. "Perhaps we should move on," I suggest, dying a thousand deaths with each passing second.

Nandipa snickers at the look on my face but thankfully changes the stream to something more benign. The images are still stuck in my head, though. Was that pornography? I only knew of it in the abstract sense. And they just have it right there for everyone to see. And Nandipa treats it like it's nothing.

Maybe because she knows more about propositioning than you ever will? . . . No, get your mind out of that gutter immediately.

My embarrassment slowly ebbs as we skim through other streams, many of them trying to sell us one thing or another. Bodymods. Financial credit. Something called Scree. A surprisingly large number of religious streams entreat us to save our souls by registering as new members of this or that faith.

"For a small financial contribution, you can join us and instantly raise your Scree! Make the pledge tonight!"

By force of habit we don't watch the streams for more than an hour. Darkness shrouds us when Nandipa turns off the holo screen, and as the silence elongates, I become more aware of her close proximity.

"I'm going to check on Adaolisa," she suddenly says, getting up.

"Of course."

I get up, too, and we both take our empty food boxes back to the kitchen. She gives me a not-quite smile before she leaves me, and I'm not sure what to make of it.

I take dinner to Jamal because I do actually like him and I don't want him to starve. As I expect, he hasn't left the terminal, and he doesn't notice me placing his food next to him until the aroma reaches his nose.

"Thanks, Hondo. This smells great. You're the best."

I lie back down on the bed, my thoughts scattered, and I try to work through the fuzzy warmth spreading inside me. It takes me a while to understand that this must be what it feels like to look forward to the future; then I start to wonder if it isn't selfish of me to feel this way given all that has happened.

Eventually I give up trying to make sense of my own mind, and I let the strange new ambient sounds of the nighttime city lull me to sleep.

No vehicles touch down on the landing pad throughout the night, and no one knocks on the door to the apartment. There is still no sign of Counselor as morning arrives.

Before Jamal and I head down to the kitchen for breakfast, he shows me the safe he hacked open while I slept, which he discovered hidden behind the painting of an ancient oil rig.

He lays out all the safe's contents on the bed for me to inspect, and I count seven different identity cards with holographic overlays, each bearing Counselor's face and a different name. One of them says it was issued by the ZimbaTech Citizen Affairs Office. The others have seals from other governments.

Now why would a man need multiple identities?

There were other things in the safe, most notably a whole bunch of slender data sticks with steel-plated cases and what I think is the symbol of a currency embossed onto their surfaces. I pick one up, bringing it closer to my face, and a holo of the number *10,000* flashes up at me. There are others on the bed with numbers as high as fifty thousand.

I look at Jamal, and I don't like the giddiness radiating from him. "Is this money?"

"Technically, no. Practically, yes."

"Say something that makes sense."

"Long story short, they are tokens representing electronic wallets with static amounts of digital currency. Think of them as keys to virtual money safes. I've gathered they are the standard medium of exchange for people who want to transact without leaving a digital record. You can cash them in if you want, but if you do, the firmware disables the token and you can't use it anymore. Here, take a look at this one."

Jamal picks up a steel card that was among the tokens and hands it to me. The green characters on the card's little screen proclaim a standing wallet balance of five thousand shillings. I may not be a Prime, but my education was solid enough to grant me a basic understanding of currency, banking, and finance.

"Some kind of bank card, I assume?"

Jamal nods. "Preloaded and anonymous, useless once the balance goes down to zero. I found it inside an unopened envelope complete with the PIN, so it's unlikely Counselor has used it before."

Counselor is going to kill us for this. "How much is all this anyway?" I ask.

"I don't know," Jamal replies, eyeing the card in my hand. "Why don't we go find out?"

So this is why he's so excited. "Counselor said to stay put, Jamal."

"Are you really going to listen to a word that man says after everything? I mean, look at this." Jamal gestures at the multiple identity cards and untraceable money tokens on the bed.

He has a point, but . . . "We don't have a choice."

"I want to see what's out there," Jamal says stubbornly. "And I'm going. With or without you."

Rolling my eyes, I drop the card and the money token and walk out of the room. We both know there'll never be a "without me" so long as I continue to draw breath.

"Don't tell the girls about the money just yet," he says as he rushes after me.

Breakfast is the four of us seated around the dining table, eating reheated eggs, beans, and sausage while we watch the rising sun glimmer on the towers of ZimbaTech. Both young women used silken shirts like sleep bonnets and still have them wrapped around their heads. Nandipa is still wearing her baggy shirt. Adaolisa covered herself with an oversize white bathrobe like she just stepped out of the shower. The puffiness of her eyes tells me she didn't get much sleep.

"This isn't real meat, is it?" she asks, pushing a roll of sausage around her food box with a fork. "Like, the actual flesh of a dead animal?"

Nandipa grimaces at her own box. "Ancestors, I hope not."

The idea hadn't occurred to me either, but now my stomach threatens to rebel. I set aside the sausage and resolve not to eat anything else that might even possibly be real meat. Who knows with surfacers? Better to be safe than sorry.

Jamal stops eating altogether, pushing his food away and wiping his hands like he's lost his appetite. But a grin touches his lips as he stares across the table. "You look . . . disheveled this morning, Adaolisa," he says. "Rough night?"

She continues pushing her food around, not seeming to realize or care that he's poking fun at her. "I didn't sleep at all, if that's what you're asking. But I did improve my basic understanding of history and can speak more confidently about what I know and what I don't."

Jamal slowly loses his smirk. "Oh? Learn anything useful?"

At his change in tone, her lips twitch at one corner with amusement. "Well. In the spirit of sharing information, I can tell you that not everything we know is bullshit. The Tanganyika cluster was indeed settled by pan-African spacefarers. And there *was* a cluster-wide setback a couple hundred years ago, but that's where what we know starts to become fiction."

Jamal and I are both riveted as she goes on to remake our conceptions of history and our places in it.

They call it the Artemis Incident, she tells us, and it began with a weaponized state-of-the-art AI going rogue somewhere in the faraway Artemis star cluster. At first the AI spread in secret; then one day the whole cluster went silent. Almost twenty planets and moons, some of the oldest, most successful colonies in human history: they all stopped responding to communications sent through the cluster's long-range interstellar jump gate. Ships that crossed over to investigate vanished forever. By the time people caught on to what was happening, several other clusters had gone dark. The Artemis AI had stowed away on ships, spreading its corruption through the network of jump gates across settled space.

It never became clear what happened to the affected worlds and their human settlers, but in each and every case, they all stopped trying to communicate.

That was roughly 250 years ago.

"How much damage did the AI do?" Jamal asks.

"It's anyone's guess," Adaolisa replies. "But news of it preceded its arrival to Tanganyika, so the authorities had time to shut down our long-range jump gate before the AI could come through."

Jamal blinks, his lips parted in muted shock. "So you're saying there was no cybernetic apocalypse, as we were told."

"Not precisely. There was an age of societal regression driven by the fear of AI, and since Tanganyika's short-range jump gates remained active, there was also a period of significant internal migration. A lot of restructuring. This world in particular saw the wholesale fall of democracy and the rise of corporate power." Adaolisa pauses, gazing down at the table with a lifted eyebrow. "Or should I say, corporate power in the hands of a cybernetic aristocracy." She smiles wanly. "I was beginning to worry our fabled enemy didn't actually exist. Turns out they do, but only on this world, and they aren't anywhere as bad as what we were told. Hardly any blood was shed when they took over."

"Only on this world?" Jamal repeats like he can't believe his ears. "You're saying there aren't cybernetic warlords terrorizing the rest of the cluster?" When Adaolisa simply shakes her head, Jamal snorts, though I know he doesn't find this funny in the least. "So what about the recent liberation of Dar al Amal and Novo Paraíso? They said it was other Primes that did that. Was it a lie? And what happened to them anyway? Where did our predecessors go if not to help rebuild civilization or whatever tripe we were told? What was the point of all of it?"

Adaolisa gives a tired sigh, her expression going distant. "I can't say. There's so much I still don't know."

The sheer scope of the lies we were told makes me reel, and I'm left even more confused about what the Custodians were doing in the Habitat. Why did they create us? Why did they make us play games against each other, make us kill, make us fear them killing us?

How many of us did they recycle over the Habitat's centuries of continued operation?

An image of Paul and Saul floating helplessly in their tanks flashes across my eyes, and I lose my appetite as well, dropping my fork next to my untouched sausages. We've all stopped eating.

"So our star cluster has been cut off from the rest of humanity for hundreds of years," Nandipa remarks.

"If there's even anyone else left," I mutter out loud.

"Oh, you can be sure there are others out there," Adaolisa says. "There were over two hundred colonies just before the Artemis Incident. We can't be the only ones who self-isolated on time. For all we know, the AI was defeated long ago and the rest of humanity is wondering why our door is still closed."

"Or," says Jamal, "maybe the AI is waiting for us to crack the door open so it can slip in and finish its work."

Adaolisa gives him a thin smile, her eyes taking me in as well. "Are you always both so cynical?"

"Of course!" Jamal proclaims. "Cynicism has kept us alive longer than our expiration dates. One could argue it's our best feature!"

Nandipa snorts, and Adaolisa shakes her head in defeat. "If you say so."

"I do." Abruptly Jamal gets up from his seat. "And by the way. Hondo and I are going out for a walk today. In the city."

I see Nandipa's eyes harden, and I expect Adaolisa to argue, but she considers Jamal as if to gauge his seriousness, then shrugs. "Good luck. You're probably going to need it."

Jamal shifts on his feet, glancing at me, then sits back down. "That's a rather ominous farewell, Adaolisa. Care to explain yourself?"

Guile moves in the depths of her eyes. "There are biometric locks throughout the building. One in the lobby downstairs, another in the elevator, and another at the door. Even if you can bypass them all with your PCU, I doubt you'll be able to do it without being seen."

Jamal watches her for a moment. "You sound like you know a way around that."

"I do. And I'll tell you all about it provided you tell me what you found inside Counselor's safe."

Jamal scratches his chin, a sardonic smile widening on his face. "Now how in the world did you know about that?" At the subtle sense of triumph that radiates from both young women, he blinks, then groans, hiding his face in his palms. "Oh, I'm such an idiot. Well done."

It takes me a moment longer to understand that Jamal has just been duped. Adaolisa only suspected there was a safe, because *of course* there'd be a safe, knowing Counselor. She probably searched for it elsewhere in the apartment and decided it must be in our room. Now she's tricked Jamal into admitting that there really *is* one and that he opened it. I almost laugh.

"Really, Hondo?" he says to me.

"I said nothing!"

"I can feel your lack of support!"

I shrug. "Maybe it'd be better if we stopped keeping secrets from each other. We're not in the Habitat anymore."

"Agreed," Nandipa says, and I think I like the way she's looking at me.

Jamal rolls his eyes. "Fine. Yes, there's a safe. It has money tokens, financial documents, and Counselor's multiple fake identities. You're welcome to look through the contents if you like. Now, do you actually know a safe way for us to leave the apartment, or was this just a clever ploy?"

"As it happens," Adaolisa says graciously, "I do."

It turns out she also received the same illicit programs that appeared on Jamal's PCU, and after we clear up the breakfast table, she shows us how she used one of these programs on the workstation in the library to access information about the building's security systems.

"Far better to add ourselves to the system as authorized residents than to have to hack through every door," she tells us, seated by the workstation.

Multiple windows are open on the three screens, giving me a glimpse of some of the research she's been doing. I also notice progress bars on her docked PCU. *What is she up to?*

"We can do that?" Jamal asks skeptically. "It's that easy?"

"I've already done it for Nandipa and myself," she says, oozing with self-satisfaction. "I could do it for you, too, if you like."

I know Jamal would rather handle this himself so he isn't indebted to her, but he's impatient to leave. "Fine. Hondo, you first."

I let Adaolisa capture my biometric information with her PCU. Jamal goes next, and then we watch as she navigates the building's security system on the workstation and appends us to its list of authorized residents. I'm certain this is a crime, but I'm sure she knows what she's doing.

Afterward Jamal and I both run our jumpsuits through the washer-dryer, and I'm immensely relieved when mine comes out free of bloodstains. Most of Counselor's clothes aren't great fits, but his black trench coats are good enough, so we slip them over our jumpsuits and lace up our Habitat sneaker boots.

On our way out, Nandipa pulls me aside. "Keep your Prime in line," she whispers. "The last thing we need is attention."

Irritation stirs within me, but I keep a lid on it. "Noted," I say in a clipped voice.

Then I open the front door, and Jamal follows me out of the apartment.

—

"What now?" I ask him in the dim hallway outside.

"I want to walk the streets of the city," he says excitedly. "Down. All the way down."

Finding an elevator isn't hard, nor is figuring out its touch-screen interface. Adaolisa's magic must be working, because the security systems let us through without complaint. But as we descend into the bowels of the building and approach the surface, I struggle not to slam my palms over my ears. So many people, so much noise. I could still hear it in the apartment, but it was faint enough I learned to filter it out. It rattles inside my head now, louder and louder. I start to fear my ears will bleed.

The elevator finally stops, and the doors open to a wide multistory lobby interior. A few people are seated on the couches on one side of the room. My eyes immediately find the guard at the reception desk, whose scattered noise tells me he's bored.

"Ancestors, do you feel that?" Jamal says to me as we step out of the elevator. By the amazement radiating out of him, he's not finding the noise as unpleasant as I do.

I force my teeth not to clench. "I felt it back at the island too. The commandos were giving out some sort of . . . noise. Just like these people. It's so loud. I hate it."

"Noise?" Jamal looks at me. "You can hear it?"

"Can't you?"

"No." I follow him as we make our way deeper into the lobby. Jamal's amazement seems to grow as he watches the people by the couches. "But I can almost . . . see it. The colors. Don't you see them?"

I follow his gaze to a mother and her three children, I think. Their static sounds like anticipation, like they're waiting for something, perhaps someone who lives in the building? She and her eldest child are not paying attention to their surroundings, both of them lost behind their glazed eyes. Contact lenses? The static that surrounds them is a cloud I can almost hear, but I see no colors.

I sense the guard becoming aware of us, and I realize we've both stopped to stare at the waiting family. The guard doesn't think we're a threat yet, so I grab Jamal by the arm and nudge him along. "We should keep moving."

A wall of static greets me outside, but it melts away into an overall assault on all my senses. Traffic seethes on the roads. The air is crisp and smells like rubber. Lights flash at us from street signs or the sides of vehicles, on buildings or on aerial drones with holo screens. The sky is a distant ceiling above the noise and activity, hemmed in by the towers that surround us.

For a time Jamal and I wander the streets, our hands in the pockets of our coats. I keep track of each landmark we pass, charting our route back to our building. The people around us are a river of printed fabrics, more color than I've ever seen, their eyes glazed behind contact lenses. It's like they're all trapped in their own little worlds, just cognizant enough to navigate without running into each other.

Strangely, they appear to give us wider berths, parting for us like we might be contagious. Even their static becomes more cautious whenever they notice us. I wonder if it's because we seem to be unusually tall.

I expect to develop a headache the longer we walk, but surprisingly I adapt to the press of consciousness all around me, and soon it doesn't bother me as much.

Next to me Jamal's amazement has evolved into wicked joy, the wolf realizing he's been locked inside a pen full of fattened sheep. "Do you see it, Hondo?" he says to me. "They're wide open. Colors leaking everywhere. I can read them like words on a page. What is this?"

"I think they fear us," I say, concerned by how they keep moving out of our way.

"It's not fear," Jamal says, then laughs. "Don't you see the colors? It's respect. Something is making them conclude we're their social betters." He frowns a little as we come to a stop at a pedestrian crossing, his eyes scanning the crowds of humanity flowing around us. "This is why, isn't it? This is why the Custodians used dead-space tech on us. So we wouldn't see them like this. We were never meant to know what we could do. They were . . . *afraid* of us."

I blink at him, shocked by how much sense he's making. Looking back, there were many moments I almost lashed out in anger against one particularly sadistic weapons master who presided over us when we were sixteen. I knew I was stronger, I knew I was stronger than all the Custodians, but the dead space stood like an impenetrable shield, and I never had the nerve to test it.

I study Jamal and the hungry way he's surveying the people around us. "Do you really see colors?"

"Not . . . precisely," he says, squinting as if to find the right word. "It's like seeing colors that shouldn't exist. They are there, I can see them, but not with my eyes."

"That's not what it's like for me," I say.

"No? What's it like, then?"

"Noise," I tell him, "but like you said, I can hear it, just not with my ears."

Traffic stops, and we join the flow of people crossing the road. Once we reach the other side, Jamal starts singling people out of the crowds and pointing them out to me.

"See that man over there? He's upset. Someone close to him recently betrayed him. That one is anxious about a debt. And so is she. And the man behind her. And those two people as well. Wow! A lot of people are worried about debt! That one is probably sick; I'd go to a doctor if I were him. That one just did something illegal. Ha! You see those four over there?"

I look where he's pointing and see four young people seated at one of the outdoor tables of a restaurant, a blur of dyed Afros and braids and golden designs painted onto bald scalps. I never imagined real-life people could wear so many colors.

"What about them?" I say.

"Two couples, right? But they've all been faithless to each other with a person across the table, and their partners don't know it! Shall I tell them?"

"What? No!"

"Why not? I'd be doing them a favor. Maybe they could even have a foursome."

I nearly smack the back of his head, the idiot. "Don't you dare."

His shoulders shake with quiet laughter. "Oh, Hondo. I think I'm going to *love* this city. Let's buy something."

I fail to stop him before he veers into a store along the street. A sweet aroma tickles my nose as I follow him past a glass door and into a pastel haven of baked goods. A woman in a white apron was slouched and glassy eyed behind the counter; I feel a panicked burst of thought from her as she awakens to our presence.

"Ooh. Surface cookies," Jamal exclaims, leaning down to gaze at the tempting selection.

"Ca-can I help you, boss?" stutters the clearly nervous woman.

Seriously, what is it with these people? I wonder. *What is it about us that's spooking them like this?*

Jamal points at a chocolate-covered muffin. "How much for that one?"

"Five shillings, boss," she squeaks.

He straightens and fishes out the steel-plated money card from a pocket. "I'll take two."

"O-of course." I watch her straighten out the limb of a scanning device on the counter. Her hands are trembling. "Can you please scan your code here?"

Jamal glances at me, then back at the woman. "My . . . code?"

"For your privacy filter," the woman replies, her heart rate climbing even higher. "I can't verify Scree with your filter on, so I need your code . . ." The poor woman's eyes widen with fear. I can almost see the circuitry of her contacts. "Do you not have a code?" she almost whispers.

"Of course I do," Jamal lies. "I simply don't have it with me right now."

The woman blinks. "I'm so sorry, boss. I need to verify Scree before purchase."

From the way she's practically wringing her hands, one would think she expects us to attack her and eat her face.

"This card has five thousand shillings," Jamal says. "The cupcakes are five shillings each. I want only two. Why can't you just take the money and give me what I'm here to buy?"

The woman shrinks deeper into herself. "Boss, no Scree, no purchase. I sell and I lose my job. Please. I'm sorry."

I notice a sign on the wall behind her and almost kick myself for not being more attentive. Turns out we need a minimum of three thousand Scree to be able to buy anything in this store.

"Jamal. Let's go."

He's not happy, but he follows me out of the store. And just as well. The woman's heart might have failed if we'd stayed there a second longer.

"What the hell is Scree?" Jamal asks me outside. I shrug, because I sure as shit don't know.

He tries again at a food vendor we encounter farther down the street. The man is initially excited when we stop by, but like the woman he becomes fearful when Jamal tells him he didn't bring his code, whatever that is.

"Forgive me, boss. I sell with no verification, and I lose my license. Sorry."

Jamal gets turned away from three more food vendors. At the fourth he finally loses his patience.

"Just to be clear," he fumes. "I can't use any of my perfectly valid money in this fucking city unless I have the right amount of something called Scree."

The food vendor is a plump man who dyed his beard to match the swirl of colors on his apron. Similarly colorful holograms dance on the side of his food cart. He gawks at Jamal, his static becoming frantic, and I begin to think he might bolt at any second.

"Pretend I have amnesia and I'm relearning everything for the first time," Jamal says in a less frustrated voice.

The vendor's static mellows, and he breathes out in relief. "Amnesia? Bad implant or something?"

". . . Something like that," Jamal says, playing along, though I practically feel the shiver of disgust that goes down his spine.

"That's rough. You're lucky you're alive, boss."

"Believe me, I know. So back to the Scree."

"My boss, you need Scree for everything," the vendor explains, waving his grill tongs around with his gestures. "You want to buy it? Scree. You want a job? Scree. You want to sell things? Scree. Hospital? Scree. You need it like you need the blood in your veins."

I sense Jamal's thoughts racing. "And how do I earn Scree?" he asks.

The man spreads his arms as if to take in the whole city. "By being good for society, of course! Be good for ZimbaTech! Impress the Oloye! Do well in your job. Don't be lazy. Work hard. Provide the best service. Don't be late. Don't complain. You see me? I was born with nothing, but I work hard, and soon I'll have enough Scree to get a proper job, and maybe one day I'll be uptown, like you! Or maybe I'll be Oloye and have you work for me!" The vendor gives a belly laugh, like he just told a joke.

"That's . . . interesting," Jamal cautiously says. "But what about people with no Scree? How do they survive?"

The vendor whistles. "It's tough. You ask your family if they have some to spare. Maybe your church or your mosque. Else try your luck with the skelem shylocks. They can loan you Scree for money, but if you miss a payment, they put you in a Hive. Not worth the trouble, I say."

"Sounds awful."

"Ah, but that should not trouble you, boss. Your kind never has to worry about Scree."

"My kind," Jamal slowly repeats.

"You know. Uptown folk," the vendor says, like that's supposed to be sufficient explanation.

Jamal feigns a self-deprecating smile, shaking his head. "I was hoping you wouldn't notice. What keeps giving me away?"

The vendor gives a snort. "Everything. No offense, but it's obvious you're bodymodded like crazy. And next time get an alias with fake info. Better than showing nothing, because then everyone knows you can afford a privacy filter." He considers the both of us, and I sense his static stirring again. "But how do you not know all this? Are you pulling my leg or something?" He looks around like a nervous criminal. "Is this a test? Am I being watched?"

I decide we're done here. "Forgive my brother," I say. "I think he's still hungover from last night. Come on. Let's go."

I gently pull Jamal away, aware of the vendor's eyes on us as we leave. I keep my senses focused on him until his static settles down and we're out of his sight.

"I don't appreciate you handling me like I'm a child," Jamal says, shrugging free of me.

"And I don't appreciate you putting yourself in danger with your questions. Are you trying to get noticed?"

"This is bullshit, Hondo." We come to a stop at a wide central intersection and take in the vastness of the city; the traffic, both on the ground and in the skies; the lights and holos; the flow and ebb of a civilization we did not know existed until yesterday. "Something is very wrong with this city," Jamal says.

A worrying glint takes up residence in his eyes, and I recognize it as the same look he gets just before he decides to upend the dynamics of a war game, to throw a wrench in the machine and watch as it falls apart.

Ancestors. The very thought makes me shudder.

"We should head back," I say. He doesn't argue, but that look stays on his face the rest of the way back home.

Chapter 6: Nandipa

I was not built for monotony. There are only so many hours a day I can stare out the windows, wondering if the next aerial vehicle that passes by will be Counselor's. Only so many times I can watch in envy as Hondo leaves the apartment with Jamal to go and explore the city.

Yet over the next half week I find myself having to endure being cooped up while Adaolisa practically melds herself to the terminal in the apartment's library. She shoots me down the few times I gently suggest we go out for a walk, telling me there's still too much she doesn't know, that I should be patient. My only saving grace is the hollow-body guitar that was hanging on the wall in the living room as an ornament. I pass many hours practicing my arrangements of jazz and folk tunes I learned back at the Habitat, but even that stops keeping me from stressing after a while.

I get it. I really do. She can't help her compulsive need to control her environment and know everything there is to know about the people within it—what they think, how they see her, what she can give them, how she can use their wants and needs to her benefit. This is how she operates, how she became the power behind the chair back in the Habitat, and I admire her immensely for it.

But our old home, treacherous though it might have been, was a small universe with far fewer unknowns. Right now she's trying to grasp all the threads of a city and its centuries of history, and I don't need the mind of a Prime to know that this is impossible. I honestly think she might be panicking a little, but I respect her, so I don't push.

On our fifth morning in the apartment, I rouse from sleep just as she enters our room freshly showered and buzzing with calm determination. We were slower to claim space for ourselves, so the room is smaller than the main bedchamber, with only a bed, a closet, and a chest of drawers, and we have to use the bathroom across the hall. The bed's comfortable, though, better than my single bunk in the Habitat, so I'm not complaining.

I yawn as I stretch, watching Adaolisa wrap a white microfiber towel around her wet hair. "You seem . . . back to yourself this morning," I remark.

Her smile is restrained but confident. "I have a plan, I think."

Which is music to my ears because I'm done living in limbo. "Are we finally heading out into the city?"

"Soon," she says, and I wilt a little inside.

"Oh."

"There are more pressing concerns right now, Nandipa," she lightly scolds me. "You should get ready for breakfast. I have a few things I need to discuss with you and the boys."

I sigh, but I wake up and do as I'm told.

After washing my face, I put on an oversize white dress shirt and shorts with strings I have to cinch tightly around my waist just so they don't fall. We cleansed our jumpsuits in the washer and put them away for when we finally venture into the city, but while we're in the apartment, we're forced to make do with whatever garments are in the closets and drawers. I think we look ridiculous.

We're first to arrive in the kitchen this morning, and the freezer comes worryingly close to empty after we each take a box of frozen vegetables for reheating.

Jamal and Hondo, both in striped pajamas that achieve the mildly comical effect of being simultaneously baggy and too short, find us already at the dining table. The two boys would be almost identical if not for their different complexions and hair textures, neither as broad at the shoulders as David and Benjamin nor so thin they are gangling. Hondo gives me the barest hint of a smile when our eyes meet. I feel my lips twitch, and it's one of those moments that pass between us without our Primes noticing.

I'm still . . . deciding . . . what I think of him. For the longest time I've known only his brusque edges, the callous smirks that sit easily on his sharp features, the undercurrent of violence barely restrained behind a cold-blooded gaze. But I've seen glimpses beneath this facade of a surprising vulnerability, a sensitive—

Actually, I think I'll stop myself right here. I'm beginning to sound like those women in the serials who latch on to a man simply because he has a vulnerable side. Whatever softness he might possess, there is enough of Jamal in him to give me pause.

Adaolisa waits until we're all done eating before she shares what's on her mind. "Before you run off to do whatever it is you do out in the city," she says to the boys, "I'd like us all to confront the possibility that Counselor isn't coming back. It makes no sense that he'd bring us here only to leave us alone and unsupervised for as long as he has. Something must have happened to him."

I was beginning to wonder as well, though it seems I have a much lower opinion of Counselor. "Maybe he ditched us," I say. "He wanted to do so back in the mech bay, remember?"

Jamal gives a thoughtful hum, considering my words. "Actually, I agree with Adaolisa. If he wanted to make a run for it, I think he'd have at least taken his money and the documents for his aliases. He didn't, which tells me he was planning on returning."

"Fair point," I concede.

"So what now?" Jamal says. "We're running out of food, and we can't buy anything in this damned city."

"Which brings me to the other thing I wanted to discuss," Adaolisa says, leaning forward and interlacing her fingers on the table. "Right now, we might as well be ghosts. We aren't in any government database. We have no names, no dates of birth, no accounts, no records, nothing. I was able to insinuate us into this building's security system even though it didn't recognize our biometrics, but that won't work everywhere."

"It might not have to," Jamal says. "People here pay hefty sums *not* to appear on the public social network, or the Nzuko, as they call it. So when people look at us and don't see our details, they assume we paid for it. No one has caught on that we don't actually belong here."

She gives a shake of the head. "A stroke of luck. We can't rely on an incorrect assumption to protect us forever. We need legal, proper identities, and I've arranged for us to get them."

And here I was being a petulant child. I cringe inwardly at my own behavior. Adaolisa must think me foolish.

And I'm not the only one impressed. Beaming from ear to ear, Jamal leans back in his chair and folds his arms. "You've been very busy, I see."

Adaolisa returns a weak smile. "Not all of us can run around a city knowing literally nothing about it."

"You disapprove of my excursions?"

"It's not my place to disapprove. We all adapt differently. I prefer to know all I can about a situation before I jump in. You thrive in the chaos of the unknown."

"So you're saying I'm reckless."

"Are you reckless, Jamal?" she throws back.

He doesn't answer the question, though his smile remains. "I assume we'll need to be creative about our identities. We can't exactly go around telling people who we really are. Whoever destroyed the Habitat is still out there, and they might be eager to finish the job."

"Telling the truth would definitely be unwise," Adaolisa agrees. "But any identities we create for ourselves have to be plausible. We can't claim to be from anywhere on the surface; that would be too easy to disprove. Besides, we know far too little about this place to convincingly pretend. So the next best thing is to pose as immigrants from off-world. They are rare but not unheard of, and to be legally documented, all they need is for an officer of the starship they arrived on to vouch for them at the Citizen Affairs Office."

"There's a spaceport in the outskirts of the city," Hondo puts in. "Yesterday we saw a huge ship descend toward it."

"It was probably just a cargo ferry coming down from orbit," Adaolisa says. "The actual interstellar ships are too large to land on planets. And in fact, the starship currently in orbit is a recent arrival from New KwaNdebele. I did some digging and used one of Counselor's aliases to reach out to the first mate; she'll be in ZimbaTech tomorrow and has agreed to edit us into her manifest and vouch for us as her passengers—for a fee. She'll also need to grease a few palms at the Citizen Affairs Office, which means I'm going to need those money tokens from the safe, Jamal."

Jamal stares, a heavy crease forming above the bridge of his nose. "How much?"

"Sixty thousand shillings for the identities, and an extra ten thousand each to start us off with a decent amount of Scree."

"That's almost all the money we have!"

"There's more in Counselor's Nzuko wallets," Adaolisa calmly says. "We won't want for food or other essentials for a while."

Unmasked petulance oozes from Jamal. "Counselor could still come back, you know."

I roll my eyes. "I thought you agreed he probably *wasn't* coming back."

"Well," Jamal says, "that was before I knew your Prime wanted to piss off almost every shilling we have."

I expect we're about to have an argument, but Hondo steps in, coolheaded and reasonable. "Don't you want to see the rest of the city, Jamal?" he asks. "With Scree we could finally walk past some of those checkpoints and see what's on the other side."

When Jamal sighs in defeat, it dawns on me that Hondo may actually be the more levelheaded of the pair, which, knowing Hondo's wild temper, says a lot more to me about Jamal's true nature, and none of it good.

"Checkpoints?" I ask, and Hondo nods.

"Certain zones of the city are sectioned off. We've gathered there's a minimum Scree threshold required to cross over. The other day we saw a man denied entrance to the zone where he works because his Scree had dipped below the minimum. The police had to haul him away kicking and screaming."

A current of envy runs through me at seeing how much they already know about the city. "Scree is a social currency, right?" I say. "The holo streams are filled with ads for how you can earn or spend it. It's really annoying."

"Repulsive, more like," Jamal grumbles. "You can't even visit a barbershop without them asking to verify your Scree."

"They turned obedience and conformity into a currency more valuable than money," remarks Adaolisa. "It's ingenious when you think about it."

"You almost sound impressed," Jamal says in an accusing tone.

I bristle, but Adaolisa remains unflustered. "You can be impressed by something without admiring it, Jamal."

He watches her for a moment, then grunts, the prickliness fading from him. "I'm grateful for the hard work you've done, Adaolisa. You have my blessing to use the tokens. And just so you know, I haven't been running around aimlessly. I've been getting to know the people of this city, how they think, how their colors move and swirl around them without them even knowing it. I never thought anyone could be so oblivious to their own enslavement."

Adaolisa and I exchange confused looks. "Colors?" she asks.

With a smirk, Jamal rises from his chair. His eyes flash at us with hidden significance when he says, "You'll know exactly what I mean the second you step outside. Now, if you'll excuse us, the city awaits."

—

The boys go down to the city, and once again I'm left to haunt the apartment while Adaolisa returns to her terminal in the library.

I try to find something to watch on the holo screen, but surface entertainment is plagued with ZimbaTech commercials and Scree promotions, so I give up in disgust, silently bemoaning the loss of the Habitat's archive of Old World content. A lot of it was dated, filmed before the advent of holographic technology, but at least the actors never burst into regular paroxysms of groveling praise for ZimbaTech or some other corporate government.

Since we've concluded that Counselor is probably not coming back, I decide to disobey his command and go out through the glass doors to watch the city from the landing pad. The safe house is the highest apartment in our building, so I have a great view of the lanes of aerial traffic weaving through the towers. From here I can also see the skyline's crown jewel, a distant spiraling skyscraper of pearlescent glass with a holographic ribbon of the word **ZIMBATECH** revolving around its spire.

The static is also much clearer here. It's been with me since I arrived in this city, coming from the people living below us or caressing my mind from those passing through in aerial cars. I still don't know what it is, and I haven't told Adaolisa because I don't want her to worry, but

I've grown used to it and can almost forget it's there. If I concentrate, though, I can single out particularly agitated sources of static all the way down on the ground. At least three such sources are just out of sight, hidden behind another building. They sound hostile and impatient to me, like the slightest annoyance could set them off. *A Scree checkpoint manned by impatient police officers, maybe?*

"You're going stir crazy," Adaolisa says behind me.

"I'll manage," I reply automatically.

She joins me by the rails on the landing pad, looking out into the city. "I'd have told you to go with the boys if I didn't know you better."

"I can't risk leaving you here alone. I know too little about this place. I don't even know what's on the other side of the door."

She smiles. "Like I said. If I didn't know you better."

Affection wells within me, and I snake an arm around her back. "Then you should also know that I'll wait for as long as you need. You're cautious and diligent, and you're doing important work. Don't worry about me."

Her smile slowly weakens as she looks toward the distant ZimbaTech spire. "I'm more worried about myself, actually."

I search her face. "Why?"

She doesn't mask her anxiety. "I know I can't sit in front of a terminal collecting information forever. I know it's impossible I'll ever control everything around me. But I feel like I'm drowning, Nandipa. Flailing against a tide of all the things I don't know, and that I'm not learning them fast enough. Whenever I step away from the terminal, I begin to fear I'm missing something, some vital detail or piece of information, and if I don't discover it, I'm going to make a mistake and get us both killed."

Concern thickens within me, and I hug her closer to my side. "That's not going to happen, Ada. You won't get us killed. I know because you have good instincts and good judgment. You don't need to know or control everything for you to make wonderful decisions. All you need is to trust yourself a little more, because you're spectacular."

She gives a tired laugh. "Easier said than done."

"Trusting you is easy, believe me," I say. "You should try it."

Her smile is genuine, but again it doesn't last for long. We watch the aerial traffic flow past us for a time, and then she says, "Why us?"

"What do you mean?" I ask.

"Who sent us those messages, Nandipa? Who put those programs on our PCUs? Why did they target me and Jamal, and why does it feel like they saved our lives?"

I have asked myself these questions, too, and the more I think about them, the less our survival feels like luck.

The mech bay would have been one of the last places to collapse, since it was built into the seabed and had no structures of glass. The bay was also one of the few places in the Habitat with an emergency submersible; most other sectors had pressurized escape bunkers. So whoever sent that last message put us in the bay just moments before the attack, with one of the handful of people in the Habitat authorized to use the submersible.

It's hard to believe our escape wasn't engineered.

"So it had to be a Custodian, right?" I think aloud. "Someone with high-level access. For all we know, it was Counselor himself and he's just a really good actor. Or maybe it was Administrator."

Adaolisa exhales loudly, shaking her head. "The one person who might have helped us get some answers is possibly gone forever."

"You think he's dead?" I ask.

"I think someone—or something—got to him. He'd have come back otherwise. But enough of that. I didn't come outside to worry you with questions neither of us can answer. There's a gymnasium a few floors below. It's close enough you won't have to feel like you're leaving me, but at least it's out of the apartment. You should go down and give it a look."

"I . . . don't know," I say. "We're going out tomorrow, aren't we? I can wait until then."

She squeezes my arm, her voice firm. "Go, Nandipa. I may be a control freak, but I won't let that keep you prisoner. Besides, you've never needed to spend every waking hour in my presence. There's no need to start now."

"This isn't the Habitat," I remind her.

"Believe me, I know. But I'm safe here, and I have a lot of work to do, and you're inches away from pulling out your hair."

I gasp, tousling my curls by reflex. "I would never!"

Her eyes glitter with silent laughter. "I know. You love your hair too much, and I don't want that to change by driving you to madness. Now go. That's an order."

With a water bottle in one hand, I take my first step out of the apartment dressed in the gray compression bra and gym shorts I came wearing beneath my jumpsuit. I make it to the elevator and descend to the gymnasium floor without event.

The gymnasium itself is a rectangular room of mirrors and steel, one side with a head-on view of the advertisement holo screen on the building across the street. I'm almost as disappointed as I am relieved when I find no one there.

The treadmills take me a moment to figure out, but soon I'm lost in the percussion of my sneaker boots hitting the moving rubber. After I've warmed up sufficiently, I move on to chest presses, push-ups, pull-ups, and sit-ups, working myself to the satisfying burn of fatigue. Adaolisa's calm presence in the apartment above keeps my anxiety in check, and my restlessness eventually fades away.

I'm cooling down with stretches by the mats near the mirrors when I sense a cloud of static approaching the gymnasium. A young woman in a gray bodysuit and golden box braids tied up in a bun joins me seconds later, and she does a double take when she spots me, her static ramping up with curiosity.

She tries to be casual about it, but I sense her eyes on me as she steps onto an exercise bike, and they follow me as I move to fill my bottle at a water fountain. She finally gets off her bike to accost me on my way toward the exit.

"Sorry, sis," she says, "but you're new here, right?"

Never say more than you have to, is what Adaolisa would tell me. *And always lie with the truth if you can.* "Yes, I'm new."

The woman looks me over with a mixture of envy and admiration that makes me uneasy. "You've gotta tell me what skin mod you're using."

Um. What? "Excuse me?"

"Your bodymod," she says, still looking me over. "I like it. It's so subtle. I'm using Adore by Cerise. What about you?"

". . . I don't use mods?"

She snorts in derision, folding her arms. "Okay. Keep your secrets. But I bet you're some Oloye's sidepiece, huh. He pay for your privacy filter too?"

I think she's implying I'm some sort of prostitute or kept woman, but I decide it's not worth challenging whatever assumptions she's made about me. ". . . Maybe," I say.

"No judgment here, sis. We all do what we gotta do to survive. And whatever *you're* doing looks like it's working." Her curiosity satisfied, she turns away from me and returns to her workout.

I feel a laugh bubbling inside my chest as I leave the gymnasium. My first conversation with a surfacer, and I get accused of being someone's "sidepiece." I think I'd be horrified if it weren't all so absurdly different from what I dreaded as I lay in my bed in the Habitat.

Later that night we reheat the last four meals in the freezer and eat them silently in the dining area.

I know hunger exists. I have felt it myself as I trained under instructors who forced me to subsist for weeks on just enough rations to keep me alive. I know hunger is a motive that has driven my species ever since we took our first steps on the Old World and that wars have been fought because people were hungry and had no viable means of feeding themselves or their children. I understand scarcity.

But it's only now that I'm properly glimpsing what it might feel like to *actually* live with scarcity and hunger, and not because my trainer took my food away but because I literally have no more access to food.

It feels almost surreal as we clean up afterward, burdened by the knowledge that there'll be nothing for us to eat come morning tomorrow. We can no longer expect our needs to be met simply because we exist. No food will magically reappear in the freezer. No masked Custodian will be there to dish us a healthy serving of kelp-based eggs and ham. We are truly alone and on our own.

I can't decide how I feel about this.

It's become a habit for Hondo and me to spend an hour every evening after dinner occupying ourselves with cooking holo streams or hate-watching overly dramatic celebrities as they go about their vapid lives, where the only thing that seems to ever matter is what they're wearing and who they're sleeping with.

These "lifestyle" holo streams are invariably asinine and ridiculous, but I derive a perverse sort of pleasure from mocking and criticizing the people on-screen.

"Ancestors, can you believe her?" I say halfway through an episode following a rather attractive but scatterbrained socialite. "If she were any more stupid, her head would be buoyant."

Hondo coughs, covering his mouth to hide a smile, and I feel myself flushing with minor embarrassment.

I guess I do get too engrossed in these kinds of shows. I know he watches them only because I want to.

Sometimes Adaolisa and Jamal join us. Tonight they slink away to their respective terminals, leaving us to our own devices. We don't talk about our Primes or how we spent the day—a Proxy never shares anything that might compromise their Prime's activities. We don't talk much at all, but our silences feel combustible, me being aware of Hondo being aware of me.

I'm not new to sexual desire. Benjamin and I had our fun when the fancy took us. And before Benjamin there was Haroun. But either boy felt to me like a shallow pool I could take a dip in and then wade out unscathed. We all knew the boundaries and expected nothing more from each other beyond the barest bones of what might be generously called friendship.

The intensity I sense from Hondo feels like quicksand. A dangerous thing that might ensnare me if I let it. He has a physical pull that has surprised me, a fascinating thrill that keeps drawing me into the depths of his dark eyes. But I can't help the feeling that if I let things ever go that far, we'd destroy each other.

I excuse myself at the end of the hour, not lingering too long in the silence after I turn off the holo screen. If Adaolisa has sensed anything, she says nothing about it when she eventually joins me in our room. I almost ask for her input but ultimately decide against it; I don't want her thinking I'm considering the idea. Because I'm not.

Sunrise the next morning finds us all dressed in our jumpsuits and ready for Adaolisa's contact to arrive. There is no breakfast beyond mugs of coffee, but I'm so excited to finally leave this building that food is the last thing on my mind.

At the appointed hour a boxy old vehicle with a rusted sky-blue coat rises out of a traffic lane to descend onto the landing pad outside.

"She's here," Adaolisa says with a nervous hitch in her voice. "Let's go."

"This better work, or we'll starve to death," mutters Jamal as we file out the glass doors.

The individual who proceeds to emerge from the vehicle almost literally takes my breath away. She is long and thin, like a mantis, and as colorful as a butterfly. I cannot tell if she's wearing eyepieces or if those shining red lenses were grafted onto her face. A fluffy pink Afro covers one side of her scalp, while coils of chrome thread out of the other.

As we approach each other, my eyes are drawn to the many holographic patches sewn onto her red, grease-stained jumpsuit and the dark leather jacket she's wearing over it. Many of them are written in the Second Dialect, which I've gathered isn't spoken much on this world. Her noise is different as well, fuzzier, though the sensation of static is much stronger in my ears. I wouldn't be surprised if there were actual electrical components inside her head.

She stares at us for a beat, her noise inquisitive. "So who's the one I spoke to?"

Adaolisa is so surprised by the woman she takes a whole second to respond. "Are you Zandi?"

"That I am."

"Then we're the ones you're expecting. These are my siblings, as we discussed."

The stranger considers us again, the strength of her noise kicking up a notch. "Where did you say you were from?"

The boys and I remain silent and let Adaolisa do the talking. "You said your services came with no questions asked."

"They do. It's just that you don't look like the sort of people who typically need my services."

"We have our own reasons."

The woman grins, showing us two rows of chrome teeth. "Hey, this isn't an interrogation. It's your money, and I appreciate the business. Speaking of which."

Adaolisa nods at Jamal, who reluctantly extracts five steel-plated data sticks from his pocket and presents them to the woman on his palm. "One hundred thousand shillings in cold tokens," he says, but when she reaches forward to grab them, he retracts his hand. "Ahp. No touching. You can look, make sure they're valid, but I'll keep them until you've met your end of the bargain."

The woman gives a high-pitched laugh. "Yeah. No deal." And just like that she's walking away, getting back into her vehicle, and firing up the engines.

Jamal and Adaolisa make no move to stop her even as she takes off the landing pad and flies off, joining an aerial traffic lane.

"Well, isn't this just great?" I moan as I watch the vehicle retreat. "Looks like we'll be starving to death in this damned apartment. You could have handled that better, Jamal."

His smugness remains infuriatingly strong. "Don't you worry, Nandipa. She'll be back."

"How the hell do you know?"

"Ask your Prime."

I look at Adaolisa. Her surprise still hasn't left her, and above that she is intrigued. I can sense the puzzles coming together in her mind. "What is he talking about?" I ask her.

She gives the barest hint of a smile. "I . . . can't explain it. But he's right. She judged us naive and foolish by our appearance. If Jamal had given her the money, she'd have taken it and disappeared."

"It's the colors," Jamal says. "And you haven't even scratched the surface. Oh, look. Here she comes again."

He's actually right. Zandi's rusty sky-blue vehicle touches down on the landing pad for the second time, finding us standing exactly where she left us, as if we knew she'd be back. Which, apparently, some of us did.

Without stepping out, she opens the doors and nods at us to come in. "You're lucky I need parts for my ship," she grumbles as we join her inside the vehicle.

Hondo agrees to let me sit up front while he and the Primes take the back seat. Then we lift off and bank into a fast-moving lane of traffic, the towers rushing by outside our windows.

The interior smells like grease, the leatherette covering the seats is cracked, and an electric beat rumbles out of the speakers. The vehicle races through a tunnel of green holographic squares produced on the front window to delineate the bounds of the traffic lane.

A minute into our flight, Zandi turns down the music and looks at the others through the rearview mirror. "My contact is at the Citizen Affairs branch in the Jondolos. I hope you're not too fancy to rub shoulders with the riffraff."

Jamal, seated in the middle seat, leans forward and says, "Zandi, right? We don't mind where you take us so long as we get what was agreed upon."

"You'll go far with that attitude," Zandi says with an amused cadence. "Tell me something. Do any of you speak Second?"

I can feel the frown on Adaolisa's face even without looking at her. "Why is that relevant?" she says.

"If you do, it'll make it easier to sell you as passengers from New Kwa. But it's okay if you don't. Your money will speak for you."

"We can speak for ourselves if required," Adaolisa replies in the Second Dialect.

I sense Zandi's static growing cautious. "Who *are* you people?"

"Trust me," Adaolisa says. "The less you know about us, the better."

"For your own sake," Jamal adds with an ominous bite to his words.

Zandi watches them through the rearview mirror. "I have a feeling you're not joking."

"That feeling," Jamal says, "would be correct."

The city appears to have been built on an estuary, with large island districts separated by rivers and straits. We fly across the busy waters of the bay to the island south of the city, bordered on the north side by the bay and the ocean and separated from the mainland by a tidal inlet.

The buildings on this island aren't as tall as the towers across the bay but are nonetheless wide and massive, dour monoliths of concrete stained olive with age and disrepair.

We come to a building so large it literally swallows us as we fly into the massive square cavity built into the upper third of its structure. The sky vanishes behind a concrete ceiling with bright lights; then Zandi pilots the vehicle to a parking bay and settles us down among hundreds of other dormant vehicles.

The inside of the cavity is several stories high. Across the parking area, a holo of the words **ZimbaTech Citizen Affairs** hangs on a wall above a row of glass doors leading into the building. Zandi motions for us to follow her as she disembarks, then leads the way through the parking area toward the glass doors beneath the sign.

A wave of static hits me as we approach the entrance. I'm suddenly in an ocean of noise, drowning in the sheer number of people thinking and feeling all around me. There must be thousands of people in this mammoth building alone. I can't even hear myself think.

"Don't fight it," I hear Jamal say. "Don't try to take it all in. Let it wash over you. Soon you'll learn to pick and choose where to focus your attention."

I belatedly realize he's talking to Adaolisa, but his advice works for me all the same. The noise becomes tolerable the second I stop trying to make sense of it and let it exist without my input.

The smell, though, is another issue. An almost overpowering urine stench follows us from the parking area all the way to the entrance, where body odor joins the mix, emanating from the long line of glassy-eyed, miserable-looking people waiting outside the entrance. The line leads inside, disappearing beyond a glass door. I don't know what they are waiting for, but Zandi ignores the line, taking us in through an adjacent door.

The central hall inside is even worse. More people with absent stares, more body odor, more noise, not just static but the hubbub of hundreds speaking at the same time, a baby wailing somewhere unseen. I count multiple lines of people waiting to be served at one counter or another, other lines going up the stairs, others disappearing behind corners, perhaps into offices. I have never seen so many people in my life.

Zandi takes us deeper into the hall to a seating area tucked into one corner. We attract quite a few eyes along the way, leaving a wake of curious static, and the people already seated there come out of their blank stares to gawk at us. We find a bench of four empty seats; the faded plastic on the seats doesn't look like it's been wiped in a good stretch of time, but we go ahead and settle down when Zandi tells us to get comfortable.

"Speak to no one," she tells us in the Second Dialect. "My contact has to make everything look aboveboard, so he'll call us in for an interview. When he does, let me do the talking. Understood?"

"How long is this going to take?" Adaolisa asks, grimacing as she inspects the grime on the concrete floors, walls, and ceiling.

Zandi gives a laugh, spreading her hands. "This is the Citizen Affairs Office, princess. It's designed to crush your soul with waiting. But don't you worry your pretty little face. You won't have to stand in any lines today. Now wait here. I'll be back."

We watch her disappear into the sea of humanity, and I'm suddenly grateful Jamal held on to the money. I have a feeling we wouldn't be seeing her again if he hadn't.

"Do you smell that?" he says, still using the Second Dialect. "Give it a good whiff. That, my friends, is the stink of poverty, and ZimbaTech reeks of it."

A man with gaunt cheeks seated two rows ahead keeps looking over his shoulder to sneak glances at us. His static is aggressive, and I can practically sense him building up the courage to address us.

"Mind your business, sir," Hondo barks, sending the man's static into a fearful spike.

The aggression remains, but he stops looking at us, and I sense his desire to start something dissolve.

"Was that necessary?" Adaolisa whispers reproachfully.

Hondo gives a shrug. "I've found that it's best to be forward. Otherwise people will keep bothering us."

"He's right," Jamal says. "If you haven't noticed, we don't exactly fit in around here."

I have noticed. The people in this place aren't like us. I can see the haggardness on their faces, the gauntness, the pockmarked skin, the imperfect teeth, the premature wrinkles. They weren't raised in sheltered Habitats, their every need catered to. Their genetic traits weren't chosen in a lab somewhere under the ocean before they were even born. Their faces and bodies weren't sculpted according to mathematical equations of physical beauty. Even Jamal and Hondo, who are expies, are the result of centuries' worth of genetic science. We stand out, and I don't think I like it.

"What are they all waiting for?" I say.

"Social security, probably," Jamal replies. "It's a neatly designed little cycle of slavery and decrepitude, you see. Most people in this city have Scree so low they can only work jobs that pay a pittance, which in turn means low Scree-earning potential. And because their wages are a pittance, they have to come here to trade what little Scree they've earned for financial support, which in turn keeps them working those low-paying jobs, and so on and so forth."

"*Most* people in the city?" I say, finding this hard to believe.

"Oh yes. You've only seen the pretty parts. I reckon a good two-thirds of ZimbaTech's population lives in the Jondolos." Jamal's disgust is so strong it's like a heat source. "Just look at them. Lost in the false world of the Nzuko. That's what they see behind their lenses; did you know that? A fake world that lets them pretend they aren't walking around in filth."

"I think you're being too harsh," Adaolisa says, echoing exactly what I'm thinking. "None of them chose this. And it wasn't always like this, you know. In the beginning, this city was part of an egalitarian democracy. I read their original constitution, and . . . I was inspired," she breathes. "They were so hopeful. They wanted to build a haven of free thought and scientific advancement without the corporate greed that devastated the Old World. I can't wrap my head around why things ended up this way."

Jamal makes a contemptuous sound. "Unless that egalitarian constitution explicitly acknowledged human greed in its first paragraph, then this was inevitable. If I were to write a constitution, I'd start it like this: *People are greedy. Here are the strict and robust measures we're putting in place to stop our own greed from destroying us.*"

"There you go again, being cynical." Adaolisa sighs.

"It's realistic. Greed is the human instinct of survival without the brakes on, and few people have the self-control not to keep reaching for more when there's more for the taking. More success. More wealth. More market share. More trophies, medals, awards. We can't help ourselves."

"Do you include yourself in this generalization?" I butt in even though I should know better than to insert myself into an argument between Primes.

"I include us all," Jamal says with a look I'd like to punch off his face. "Not even you are immune, Nandipa. I should know. It was you and your Prime's greed for the chair I exploited to keep myself alive. You didn't need it. You could have survived a year without it and won it back again. But you just couldn't let the prize go, and Paul was recycled instead of me."

I seriously think about hitting him. Hondo would come to his defense, but I'd get there first, maybe crack his skull or pull out his tongue.

Before I decide, Adaolisa places a hand on my thigh, enveloping me in a sense of calm even though I can feel cold anger moving through her. "I suppose you're right," she tells Jamal. "I get nervous when I'm not in control, and maybe that *is* a form of greed. I don't mind owning that. But you will never shame me for doing everything I could to keep Nandipa safe."

He lets a moment elapse before he feigns contrition, dipping his head. "I apologize. I should not have said that. I think this city is screwing with my head. I take back every word."

I don't believe him, but Adaolisa's composure soothes my temper, and I relax my balled hands. Jamal enjoys bringing out the worst in people. That's what he was made for, after all, and I should know better than to give him what he wants.

Hondo's expression has remained blank this whole time, and he's masked himself so well I can't tell what he's thinking. How he tolerates being in Jamal's presence for any period of time is a mystery to me.

We wait in silence for the next two hours, the glassy-eyed crowds shambling all around us without pause, their static absentminded.

I wanted to get out of the apartment, but I find myself wishing I could go back, if only to leave this miserable place. My empty belly is the sole reason I find the patience to sit still.

None of us masks our relief when Zandi finally shows her face, beckoning us over. We follow her up a concrete staircase, skirting the line of people waiting along the steps, and on an upper floor she takes us through a claustrophobic corridor with ancient fluorescent lamps, where the line continues along one wall, snaking into an office farther along the corridor.

Zandi takes us to another office two doors down, a tiny room with an even-tinier window and a workstation too wide for such a small space. The bald and rather short man seated on the other side of the workstation has the ZimbaTech logo printed on the chest pocket of his white shirt. The pristine color of that shirt and his general aura of health and tidiness tell me he doesn't live in this part of the city. As we enter his office, his static intensifies so dramatically I almost look behind me to see what has excited him so much.

"Boss," Zandi says to him. "I was told to bring these four in so you could see them. You should already have the paperwork."

The man takes a moment longer to overcome his surprise. "Yes, yes, come in," he says. "And shut the door behind you."

Over the next few minutes, we let him take photographs of us and collect all the necessary biometric information needed to give us identities. He works with the proficiency of someone who's done this kind of work for eons. When he's finished, he tells us to sit down, but there are only two chairs available, so Hondo and I let the Primes take the seats while we stand behind them.

"So they're really from New KwaNdebele?" the man says, playing with the graying bristles on his chin while looking at our information on the screens of his workstation.

"Noble exiles," Zandi says from where she's leaning against the door. "Forced to run after their houses made an unsuccessful play for the throne. You know how the story goes. They might be all that's left of their families."

That last part strikes dangerously close to the truth, but I show nothing, and neither do the others.

"Fascinating," the man says, and I'm not sure if he actually believes this or if he's in on Zandi's act. He does something on the terminal before he asks, "Do they understand Third?"

"Like I said: nobles. Fancy education and everything."

"Is that so?" After tapping more keys on his workstation, the man grins widely at us, revealing a number of golden teeth. "I hope you don't mind. I've put your last names down as Ndebele. It's protocol for off-worlders, you see. Makes it easier to keep track of who's from where, that sort of thing."

We all look back at Zandi, who nods.

"It's fine," Adaolisa says, also speaking in Third. "We're here for a fresh start anyway. Best to leave past attachments behind."

In fact, we've never had last names, so we don't have any attachments in that regard, but there's no need for them to know that.

"I can already see you'll be valuable additions to our society," the man says with a smarmy grin. "Anyhow, you're in the system now. But before you leave, allow me to . . . clarify . . . a few things so there aren't any misunderstandings. I'm sorry to say that whatever privileges you enjoyed on New KwaNdebele by virtue of your noble birth will not be honored here. ZimbaTech is a meritocratic society. Here the value of an individual is measured by their productivity and hard work. Questions? Concerns? Objections?"

We all shake our heads.

"Good. That said, we are not heartless. As a gesture of welcome, we will start you off with gold-tier social credit, or Scree, as we like to call it. That means you can work and live in any gold-tier zone so long as you maintain the appropriate level of Scree. If you don't, you might have to be bumped down to a lower tier, but don't worry; you'll always be placed wherever you can bring the most value to ZimbaTech. And if you have what it takes, you can work your way up to the platinum tier and maybe even the diamond tier. The sky is the limit! Questions?"

I sense Jamal boiling with an acidic remark; Hondo places a hand on Jamal's shoulder before the remark can spew out. Jamal behaves himself.

"All right then," the man says. "Welcome to Ile Wura, and thank you for choosing ZimbaTech. I hope you'll find our city productive enough to stay here indefinitely."

Chapter 7: Hondo

The first thing Adaolisa and Jamal do with our new gold-tier status is split Counselor's funds between themselves. They spend most of an evening at the dinner table after a meal of take-out couscous with vegetable stew, seated across from each other with their PCUs like lawyers negotiating a divorce settlement. Most of Counselor's money was tied up in accounts whose paperwork was in the safe; it's spread out on the table now, and both Primes seem equal to the task of figuring out ways of extracting the money without rousing legal scrutiny.

Nandipa and I leave them to it and negotiate our own settlement on the holo screen in the living room, first deciding on which of the available Nzuko remote grocery services to use, then deciding on what items to order, all of which, supposedly, will be promptly delivered to our landing pad via drone.

"That'll rot your teeth," Nandipa says, removing the box of chocolates I just added to our virtual cart.

I gesture to add it back. "I don't care. I can get new teeth. I want to taste real chocolate."

She sighs, moving us along. "You just like the color of the box."

"The drawings on it are very nice," I admit with a grin. "Wait. What are those?" I squint to get a better look at the items she just added to the list, but she quickly scrolls away. "Nandipa?"

There's bite in her voice even as she smiles. "I'm beginning to like you, Hondo. Don't change that by asking me to explain feminine hygiene to you."

I burn with sudden embarrassment, studiously not looking in her direction. "Oh. Er. Sorry. Take as much as you need." I wince at that last part, closing my eyes. Trust me to be so tactless.

By the way she laughs, she's enjoying my mortification. Thankfully we don't dwell on the subject and move on to restock on frozen foods.

"What now?" I say when she lifts out yet another item I've just put into our cart.

"It has meat."

"Eek." I shudder with revulsion and don't reach back for the box of frozen pies. How anyone can stomach the idea of consuming dead flesh is beyond me. "Wait. No, don't buy that."

Nandipa refuses to remove the packets of frozen peas she's added to our cart. "Why not?"

"They're raw," I point out. "They'll need to be cooked. Or something."

She blinks at me. "So?"

"So . . . none of us have ever cooked anything before?"

She shrugs, turning her attention back to the holo screen. "Doesn't mean we can't learn." When I keep staring at her, she shoots me a defensive frown. "What? It'll give us more options. Besides, it's a useful skill."

"I think that's a great idea, Nandipa," Jamal calls from the dinner table. "I've always wanted to learn how to cook."

I feel blood draining from my face. Has he been listening this whole time? "We didn't ask for your opinion," I tell him.

"You have it anyway."

I sigh, leaning deeper into my couch. "Suit yourselves, I guess."

"Oh no." Nandipa gives me an arched eyebrow. "I'm not cooking for you without your help. We'll learn together, or you don't eat anything I make."

"Great. Chores," I complain, but I'm secretly very pleased.

She said *together*. As in, me and her. The tiny smile I see on her face tells me she knows how I feel. I'm only a little ashamed about it.

We continue browsing the virtual store, but my ears prick when I catch Jamal and Adaolisa discussing the possibility of getting separate apartments. I hold my breath, listening. Nandipa and I don't get to decide what happens next. Our Primes do, and we have to follow because they know better.

Ultimately they decide to stay put as a means of saving money. The rush of relief that pulses through me must leak out to Nandipa, given the odd way she glances at me. But then I realize: we were both listening, and some of that relief wasn't coming from me.

We finish our virtual grocery shopping and make no mention of it.

Over the coming days we all spend less and less time in the apartment and more time out in the city, though while Adaolisa can only tolerate crowded spaces in low doses, much to Nandipa's mild but obvious disappointment, Jamal takes to exploring ZimbaTech like he's conducting reconnaissance on an enemy.

Which, I slowly realize, much to *my* disappointment, might be exactly what he's doing.

First, he has us shop for local garments so we can blend in, and I experience the novel joy of shucking off my jumpsuit for something I chose to wear myself. I find I'm most comfortable in the sensibly smart styles worn by the city's working upper-middle tiers—simple button-downs, chinos, denims, leather boots. At first I expect Jamal and me to share the same tastes, but I'm surprised when he adopts a rather flashy sense of style: high-waisted trousers and fancy dress shirts and three-piece suits with silken scarves and shiny oxfords.

He's a snappy dresser, so very much unlike me, which makes me wonder if I'm finally seeing him the way he's always seen himself or if I'm looking at the man he intends to become.

One morning before we take the maglev to visit yet another part of the city, he pulls me along into a bodymod parlor, and I watch in silent shock as he gets his ears pierced and purchases a selection of platinum earrings. He smiles into a mirror with deep satisfaction at the way his little crosses dangle from his earlobes, and when I catch him studying the tattoo artist and the butterfly splashed across her back in neon colors like a street sign, I decide to drag him out of there before he gets any more ideas.

"That's cybernetic tech, Jamal," I hiss at him in the Second Dialect, which we've gotten into the habit of speaking when we don't want to be overheard. "You can't!"

Maybe the Custodians lied to us about our supposed enemies—the hordes of cybernetically enhanced savages who were holding back civilization—but the hatred of cybernetic tech is so ingrained into me I can't abide the idea of Jamal putting it into his body.

He doesn't fight to go back into the parlor, but he huffs, pulling his arm away. "It's a bodymod, Hondo. It modifies patches of skin at the genetic level. There aren't any implants involved."

"It was flashing," I point out.

"Bioluminescence." Jamal sees the look on my face and snickers. "I wasn't actually going to get one, you know. I was just looking."

Now it's my turn to scoff. Jamal is never "just looking." Even as we pretend to be tourists, visiting every island of the city, riding every maglev route, walking every promenade, I know he's not just looking; he's absorbing, analyzing, plotting. What exactly he's plotting, I cannot say, but I know I'll find out soon enough. I always do.

We tour the squalid streets of the Jondolos, remnants of the pre-Artemisian settler period when the colony of Ile Wura was still new and everything was built for purpose rather than beauty. Exposed and frankly unsettling bionic prostheses—eschewed elsewhere in the city—are a common sight around here, worn proudly by members of local skelems. A few such individuals tail us when they notice us walking through their territories, watching our every move, but otherwise leave us alone.

I've never seen so many children. They run unsupervised in the shadows of the district's utilitarian tower blocks, filthy and stinking of neglect. So many of them wear bionic prostheses, too, that Jamal decides to find out why.

On our way to an open-air market, we cross paths with a rather skinny boy of around thirteen, whose entire left arm is a grotesque mechanical appendage with all its internal machinery visible. His static pipes up only a little when he spots us, but something Jamal sees makes him decide to call him over for a chat.

"I'm new in town. Just wondering why so many folks around here have arms and legs like yours." Jamal points at the prosthetic. "Do they indicate allegiance to a skelem?"

The kid eyes us skeptically, his contact lenses glazing over. We haven't paid for privacy filters, so our names and Scree ranks should be fully visible to him. We obviously don't belong here, but he must decide we won't get him in trouble. "Some of them do," he answers, though his eyes still watch us with suspicion. "But I'm in no skelem. I was in an accident where I work. At the meat vats down on Factory Side. You can ask my boss. He's a Goldblood. They run the factory."

Kid almost sounds like he thinks we'll call him a liar. And if I had to guess, the Goldbloods are one of the skelems who run this island. Seems they have no qualms about putting children in dangerous situations for profit, and the way the kid's wearing that arm, they probably convinced him it's a badge of honor.

"You have a job?" Jamal asks, not hiding his surprise. "But you are a child!"

The kid frowns like he wants to scream: *Who the fuck are you calling a child?* "Course I got a job," he says. "Not gonna feed myself sitting on my ass, am I?"

"Thank you for your time. Carry on."

I feel the kid's eyes on our backs as we continue on our way. I also feel Jamal's thoughts weaving together into plots, conclusions, action plans. How I wish he were someone who "just looked" at things and left them as they are.

It's also in the Jondolos that we attend our first religious service, in a crowded temple of a faith that syncretizes Christian and Islamic traditions of Old Earth. The sermon runs so long we end up leaving before it's over, but the temple's musicians leave me with a newfound liking for contemporary neo–soul punk and post-Artemisian Afro jazz.

We visit as much of the upper districts as we can, too, and I learn to appreciate all the different tastes in apparel that exist in the city.

The industrial, almost space-worthy coveralls of the manufacturing bronze- and silver-tier districts, supposedly influenced by a wave of off-world immigration from Tripoli V some two decades ago.

The chromatic vogue of the high-tier theaters, jazz clubs, and waterfronts, combining high fashion with eye-catching bodymods like brightly colored hair, skin with a golden radiance, or bioluminescent tattoos.

The cultured and elegant Africana surrounding the city's platinum-tier university, where the kente, shukas, kanzus, and ankara fabrics of Old Africa are worn and upheld as symbols of refinement and erudition.

The corporate grandeur of the business districts: suits, gowns, silk scarves, high-heeled shoes, and the smell of money.

It's as we walk down the seafront promenade of one such district that Jamal and I first encounter a member of the city's cybernetic aristocracy, the diamond-tier ruling class, or the Oloye, as they are called.

He's a young man in an expensive silken suit, tall as we are, and not much older, walking with an attractive woman clinging to either arm like a decoration. His face is chiseled like stone, almost unnaturally, and a curious shimmer plays on his dark skin.

It was raining the morning we first saw the city from the landing pad outside Counselor's apartment, our jumpsuits drenched as we stared out into an endless grid of towers and lights. *"If the rulers of this world knew you were still alive,"* Counselor said to us, *"they'd do everything in their power to destroy you."*

That warning echoes in my mind as our paths cross with the Oloye and his two companions. When we pass each other, his silver eyes skim over us; perhaps he checks our names and Scree ranks to see if we're anyone he should note. We must not be, because he doesn't stop walking, and neither do we, and soon he's behind us.

I'd have known what he was even with my eyes closed. Many of the wealthier folks in this city have implants installed into their heads, mostly ocular so they can better interact with the Nzuko. I can usually tell when someone's wearing such an implant, because their static comes stronger than usual, almost like an actual radio signal.

But this Oloye's static is a musical trill. Electric. His thoughts are so intertwined with whatever tech is embedded within his mind he's probably just as much of a machine as he is human.

Jamal says nothing, but his disgust is a heat wave, his heart beating with a strength that echoes in my own chest. That man is everything we were raised to destroy. He's the enemy. An abomination, a plague on human progress. We were lied to, yes, but that gets hard to believe when Oloye can walk on such splendid waterfronts in the same city where a boy lost his arm working in a meat factory.

Personally, I don't really care. I'm not built to care about anyone or anything other than Jamal and his well-being. But I know it'll eat at him, the contrast between this pristine promenade and the depressing tower blocks of poverty lining the Jondolos. It'll make him restless, give him ideas.

Dear ancestors, please don't let him get any ideas.

When we return home later that afternoon, I suggest to Nandipa that we attempt to make our first homemade pizza, deciding I need to distract myself from trying to figure out what's inside Jamal's head.

Adaolisa took her shopping, so instead of Counselor's shirts, these days Nandipa walks around the apartment in tank tops and denim shorts, her curls pulled back and tied by a ribbon. It really shouldn't be anything remarkable, but I often catch myself staring like an imbecile. She's also started using this subtle fragrance that hits me like a narcotic.

I'm very carefully and deliberately not a creep about it.

The pizza will probably be a disaster—everything we've tried to make thus far has turned out inedible—but I relish the easy laughs between us, watching Nandipa's elegant fingers working through the dough, the way she tries to wipe off a dusting of flour from her cheek only to make it worse, the heat of her skin whenever we come too close to each other as we work in the small kitchen.

Unfortunately we leave the pizza in the oven for too long. When I pull it out and it looks just as heinous as I expected, we grimace, and then our eyes meet and we both start laughing.

"I think we're getting better," I reason.

Nandipa peers down at the culinary ruin, skeptical. "I suppose it does look like food if you squint."

"It'll be better next time," I say, taking the pizza and discarding it into the recycler. I remove the mittens I was wearing and place them on the counter. "I guess it's reheated frozen meals again? To be honest, I'm getting tired of that."

Nandipa regards me like she's having a thought. "We could go out to eat," she suggests. "The four of us. We never do anything together. Isn't that a shame?"

I glance up the stairs. Jamal will probably be working on the terminal in our room, and Adaolisa is ensconced in the library. The Habitat is long gone, but the way those two carry on sometimes, it might as well have followed us here. They don't trust each other. They are too different, I think. But maybe Nandipa and I can show them that we don't have to be the same people we've always been.

"Let's leave in half an hour," I say to her.

She smirks like she knows I'm not going to give Jamal a choice in the matter. "Wear something nice," she says. "Might as well make a night of it."

"Oh. Okay." I turn away from her and rush up the stairs so she doesn't see me wondering what she'd consider nice on me.

—

With a snide comment about my poor dress sense, Jamal lets me borrow one of his sport coats, a fedora, and a pair of dress shoes. He wears something similar but somehow ends up looking better than me. Maybe it's because being fancy comes natural to him. I feel like I'm putting on airs.

The feeling strengthens when we meet up with Adaolisa and Nandipa downstairs, both in cleverly made metallic cocktail dresses and shoes with heels that might gouge dents on the floor. Adaolisa has paired her outfit with an ankara turban, while Nandipa has flared out her hair and worn large silver hoops on her ears.

Ancestors, they both look amazing.

There's a moment when we all stare at each other like it's only just hitting us that we're no longer children of the Habitat. We're free to do as we please. We could dress like this every day, and who would stop us?

By the appreciative smile Nandipa spares me, I must not look too shabby myself. I hold that thought and let it percolate through me, washing away my self-conscious awkwardness. I resolve to enjoy the night regardless of the foolish little knot of inconvenient feelings tangled together inside my chest.

We take an aerial cab to an uptown lounge with a live jazz band, paying a hefty sum just to walk in through the doors. Nandipa's face practically glows as we enter, and when I catch her nodding along to the music, that knot in my chest gets even more tangled and smarts like a physical pain. I brush it aside and stop staring.

We get a table and order from a waiter; I ask for a spiced cauliflower roast. I've had alcohol exactly once before—when we were allowed shots of brandy at our eighteenth birthdays—but I follow Nandipa's lead and also order a gimlet cocktail like I know what I'm doing.

Her eyes sparkle with laughter, though not unkindly. I realize she's probably been here before with Adaolisa.

The two Primes order spritzers for themselves but remain reserved. Adaolisa has barely spoken a word since we left the apartment. I don't think she's unhappy to be here; I get the sense that her thoughts are elsewhere. I guess she and Jamal have that in common right now.

"How's your search for Counselor going?" Jamal asks during a lull in the music.

Adaolisa was twisting the stem of her cocktail glass in an idle motion. She gives Jamal a wan smile. "Now what makes you think I'm looking for him?"

"Seems like something you'd want to do. Am I wrong?"

"Don't *you* want to find out what happened to him?"

"Not enough to do it myself," Jamal says with a halfway grin, then shrugs. "He's the past. I'm more interested in the future."

"His disappearance could have a direct bearing on our future," Adaolisa counters. "Finding out who took him may lead us to whoever destroyed the Habitat."

"We already know who destroyed the Habitat," Jamal claims, and when we all stare at him, he rolls his eyes. "Who else could it be? You all heard what Counselor told us that day: the rulers of this world, meaning the Oloye and their city-states, have a bone to pick with us. How could they not? The Custodians built us to destroy them. We'd be dead if they found out who we are. And the city-states are realistically the only force who could muster the firepower to attack the Habitat."

"It could be the Free People," Nandipa suggests offhandedly. "Don't they have multiple fleets of ships and submarines?"

I privately wonder if she's been reading up on her own. Everything I know about Ile Wura's politics is what Jamal has told me.

"The Free People also trade ammunition and grain as currency," Jamal replies. "They're practically scavengers, not to mention they're far too busy fighting the city-states for coastal land. Destroying the Habitat would gain them nothing."

Adaolisa shakes her head, not quite satisfied with Jamal's theory. "I can believe the Oloye having a vested interest in our destruction. I've looked at the dead-space designs, and it's clear the Custodians achieved some esoteric understanding of the mind and were possibly using us to refine that understanding. I think eventually they were going to weaponize us against the surface—us or the next generation or the one after that. But I digress. What I'm saying is, I can believe the Oloye wanting us dead. *If* they knew we existed. But I'm not convinced that they do."

Jamal regards her with a deepening frown. "What makes you say that?"

"From what I've seen, the cities like to boast about their military exploits. They rarely clash with each other—mostly, they keep the Free People off the coasts—but no military operation remains a secret. And yet so far there's been no mention anywhere on the planet of an underwater base being destroyed. Whoever did it is keeping very quiet."

"Maybe one of the cities acted on their own," Jamal posits.

"Then why keep it quiet? If they knew about us, why not boast about our destruction?"

A thoughtful pause stretches languidly over the table. Then Jamal says, "If you want answers to those questions, Adaolisa, you'll probably need more . . . access."

Nandipa and I exchange a silent glance. By the slight narrowing of her eyes, seems she knows exactly where Jamal is taking this discussion, and she hates it just as much as I do.

"The Nzuko is a tightly woven network," Adaolisa says in a rather weak dismissal. Clearly she's already considered the idea of expanding her "access."

"It's possible, though." Jamal gives a cryptic smile. "You'll just have to be creative about it."

Fuck. And I was supposed to be enjoying myself tonight. Now I'll have to worry about what plots Jamal has hatched.

"The food's here," I say, pointing at the approaching waiter. And for the rest of the night, I actively steer the conversation away from any dangerous discussions.

Chapter 8: Nandipa

ZimbaTech. SalisuCorp. Molefe Star Industrial. Heynes Group. Nkala Interstellar. Kenrock City. Transworld. These are the seven city-states that rule Ile Wura.

While I don't wade as deep into their politics as Adaolisa—I doubt I could if I tried—some light browsing on a tablet computer in the mornings gives me a basic understanding of why the hell all the governments of this world sound like they should be corporations, not political entities.

Turns out they *were* corporations once upon a time, specialized in one thing or another. They paid taxes to their respective governments. Obeyed rules and regulations. Yes, they took every opportunity to maximize profits and influence legislation by getting cozy with politicians, but it seems they otherwise respected the democratic institutions they operated under.

But when the Tanganyika jump gate was closed to ward off the Artemis AI, thereby isolating the cluster from the rest of humanity and cutting off the flow of trade and information, these corporations saw an opportunity in the chaos, and the much-weakened governments of Ile Wura could hardly do a thing to stop them.

They began by merging or buying each other out, then buying out everything else, from little corner stores to churches to universities, until they owned entire cities. Then they bought out the land surrounding those cities and the land surrounding that land, until much of the world's real estate belonged to one conglomerate or another. By now the old governments had become largely nominal, but they were allowed to cling to the illusion of control for a good long while.

Eventually, though, the corporations got tired of pretending, and thus the corporate city-states were born. Those who opposed them were driven out to sea, where they live to this day in nomadic flotillas, occasionally skirmishing for valuable coastal land if they're not too busy fighting among themselves.

It amazes me to think that ZimbaTech was once a manufacturer of technology and nothing more. It's a government unto itself now, owning every square inch of land in the city, all the surrounding farmland, and much of the coast and unsettled wilderness beyond that. Every citizen is both an employee and a customer. Earning money and, to a greater extent, *spending* money—or being productive, as they call it—is rewarded with greater social credit. Those who aren't productive are forgotten, left to rot.

I still don't know how the Oloye came into the picture, but at some point the corporate masters of the city-states became an aristocracy with access to powerful cybernetic technologies, and of course, they hoarded that tech for themselves.

My first encounter with the musical static peculiar to the Oloye comes on the day Adaolisa decides to start coming out of her shell.

It's been three afternoons since our dinner out with the boys, and I'm alone with her in the apartment, strumming my guitar in the living room, when she comes in and tells me she wants to go out.

"An exclusive jazz club is hosting a famous off-world musician tonight," she tells me, sounding excited. "All the way from Novo

Paraíso. Platinum Scree and above only, but I've scored us some invitations. Am I not the best?"

I want to be excited. An off-world jazz musician performing live? Ancestors, yes. But all our trips out of the apartment, with the exception of our impromptu outing with the boys, have thus far been carefully planned beforehand to minimize Adaolisa's exposure to crowds and strangers. We'll visit these three stores, go to this hair salon, go here for lunch, then come back home; no detours.

I've gotten used to this and have accepted her introversion as my reality. She's always been an introvert. I've never held it against her.

This sudden change in behavior has my mind going back to her conversation with Jamal the other night, the one about "access." Something is definitely up.

I consider her, my guitar lying silent in my arms. "Ada, are you doing this because you want to have a fun night out, or . . . is there another reason?"

She gives me an innocent look, but I know her too well for that to work on me, so she sighs and drops down onto a couch, blinking at the windows facing the city. "Nandipa, someone attacked the Habitat. They *destroyed* it, and they almost killed us, and we still don't know who they are. What's more, the only person who could have told us what's going on is missing. You of all people know how much I can't stand being out of balance, and right now, our lives are *severely* out of balance. I need to recover some measure of control."

Her distress bleeds into me, and I suffer a wave of concern. "All right. So what does the jazz club have to do with it?"

"There are . . . individuals . . . whose attention I'd like to draw. I've determined we can do this quite effectively by leaning deeper into our false identities. If we present ourselves as noble castaway socialites, we'll carry a certain mystique the right people may find appealing."

Access, I hear, and she's decided to go out and get it. I'm not sure how I feel about this. Worried mostly. "I follow your lead," I say in as level a tone as I can manage.

"It'll be harmless, I promise," she reassures me. "And did I mention the off-world jazz? You wouldn't want to miss that, would you?"

I let out a long breath. "How am I supposed to say no to that?"

"You're not," Adaolisa says with a fond twinkle in her eye. "Now come. Let's start putting all those nice clothes we've been buying to good use."

And thus it is that the two of us make our first public appearance along the fashionable platinum waterfronts, where the entertainments are lively and exclusive enough to draw even those from the highest tier of the city.

We wear voguish party dresses straddling a very thin line between corporate class and come-hither, Adaolisa with accents of Africana in her beaded jewelry and ankara turban and myself with a more metallic look, from my silver necklaces to the large hoops on my ears.

To everyone watching, and oh, do they watch, Adaolisa is perfectly in her element. They don't feel her battling the nerves tingling across her skin as eyes rake over us. They don't feel her suffering the urge to draw her faux-fur coat closer around herself. They don't notice the careful steps she takes in her stilettos. They see a foreign princess and her sister, as glamorous as the most bodymodded socialites, graceful as they are mysterious, because that's what we sell them.

That first night, the music turns out to be as good as I expected, but I fail to enjoy myself, what with Adaolisa being a nervous wreck next to me. We don't attempt to talk to anyone else, thankfully, but an Oloye whose age I can't pin down buys us drinks and comes over to our table to introduce himself.

A subtle metal gloss lies hidden just beneath the surface of his skin, visible only when seen from certain angles. Supposedly that weave of circuitry can harden an Oloye's skin to be tough as rock if necessary.

Ultraware is what they call it. Not just the skin weave but all that advanced and mysterious cybernetic tech used exclusively by the Oloye.

The parts of it embedded in their minds stream their conscious experiences to high-security server farms hidden in bunkers outside the city. Should an Oloye's body suffer irreparable damage, apparently their digital backups can simply be printed onto new bodies, and then for all intents and purposes, it'll be like they never died. And at age 150, every Oloye is fully digitized and uploaded to a closed-off virtual paradise, where they supposedly live in blissful perpetuity.

The reality of an Oloye is one of wealth and ease from birth to afterlife, and it shows on every inch of them.

Despite all this, I can still hear their static. It's smoother, less agitated, maybe because they're less conditioned to a life of hardship. But I can read them all the same, and so can Adaolisa.

This Oloye must not be one of the people she's looking for, though. I let her do the talking, and she's polite enough with him, but I detect no further interest.

Tonight is a test run, I realize. *The people she wants might not be here at all. We'll probably have to make more public appearances like this before she can get whatever it is she's looking for.*

I turn out to be right. After that first evening, invitations to clubs in the platinum entertainment quarter start pouring in. The socialites who frequent the area start noticing us and coming over for a chat, asking questions about New KwaNdebele I don't bother attempting to answer.

I leave it to Adaolisa and consequently gain a reputation as the cold and standoffish sister, the one you don't talk to because she thinks she's above it all, still angry she's no longer a princess or whatever the hell they have on that backward planet they came from, don't even buy her a drink because she'll roll her eyes, heard she even doused a guy in his own drink after he told her she looked nice, talk to her sister instead, she has a friendly smile and a calming voice.

And all of this is perfectly fine with me. I complement Adaolisa; I make her look better. That's my job. But as much as I enjoy the live jazz, I quickly grow to hate all the small talk and the dressing up and the pretending.

By contrast, Adaolisa grows more confident with every outing. The glamour becomes less of a pretense, the charm more natural.

Back in the Habitat, she was never one to call attention to herself. I was the shield that stood between her and the world. If she needed someone persuaded, I was the one who did it. If someone needed to be distracted, I did the distracting.

It's interesting to watch her gradually adjust to the power of her physical presence. Maybe it's because she can see it now, how she affects people, how they react to her appearance.

Two weeks after our first trip to the waterfronts, she confidently approaches a young Oloye sitting alone at a table in an exclusive lounge, eyes hidden beneath a fedora even in the dim interior. "Hi. Sorry to bother you, but our usual table is occupied," she says. "Are you amenable to company?"

It's unusual to see a member of the ruling class sitting alone at any table. Even more unusual to meet one who's shy, yet this one looks around to make sure we're asking to join him, not someone else. His golden eyes eventually climb back up to Adaolisa. "I've heard about you," he says. "You're the off-worlders from New Kwa, right?"

"The name's Adaolisa, and this is my sister, Nandipa. We can find another table if you'd rather be alone."

"No, no," he says quickly and gestures at the other seats at his table. "Please. Join me."

They say it's impossible to successfully lie to an Oloye. Their ultraware eyes supposedly see beyond the visible spectrum, and they can detect changes in heart rate and temperature. True for most people, perhaps, but Adaolisa and I are both capable of masking our emotions and producing the expected physiological responses, so lying to an Oloye is rather trivial.

As we join Marcel at his table, I know right away that we'll be lying an awful lot to this particular Oloye, because he's exactly who Adaolisa has been trying to fish, and now she has him.

—

"So you've been going out a lot these days. I feel like I hardly see you."

Sometimes, if we're both at home in the afternoon, I invite Hondo to join me down in the gymnasium. We run side by side on the treadmills or work up a sweat on the weight machines. We usually avoid conversation while we train, but after our stretches, we sit down on the mats by the wall mirrors and just . . . talk.

I've been surprised to learn just how much I like talking to Hondo. Especially here in the gymnasium, while our Primes are far enough that I can let my thoughts run to places they wouldn't otherwise go.

Like how distractingly attractive Hondo has suddenly become. Not just when he's exercising in his white tank tops that cling to his defined chest in all the right ways, but also when he's walking around in his prim button-downs and knit shirts and woolen sweaters. Frankly, the guy is adorable, even more so for the fact that he doesn't know it. He's unsure of himself and too easy to embarrass. His smiles come easier these days too. It's actually getting really hard to reconcile him with the dangerous expie I knew in the Habitat.

I guess I've been realizing just how much personhood and individuality that place robbed from us. I always thought Adaolisa liked being inconspicuous, but apparently that was just a survival instinct born of necessity. She actually enjoys dressing up. And Hondo, who I thought was a cold-blooded creep, is reserved and sensitive and would spend most of his free time sketching on his tablet if Jamal didn't drag him along into his mischief.

I took a peek at his sketchpad after he left it lying on the dinner table the other day, and my heart almost stopped. Proxy Haroun's face stared back at me from the tablet, drawn in such detail I'd have believed it a photograph had I not known better.

Hondo had gotten everything right, down to Haroun's particular half smile, one eye more crinkled in the corner than the other, like he had an inside joke he was about to tell you.

I know for a fact Haroun disliked Hondo intensely and that the feeling was reciprocated. And knowing Haroun, I don't think he'd have spared Hondo a second thought.

Hondo spent hours on that one drawing.

It's . . . noble, I guess. Not at all what I expected.

I wish I'd known him before now. I wish I could let myself get to know him.

We're facing each other where we're seated on the floor, towels draped around our necks; me cross-legged, him with his knees bent, arms loosely hugging them.

"You go out with Jamal all the time," I say in reply to his comment. "You've never heard me complain."

"Yeah, but we're always back by evening," he says with a hint of accusation.

He has the ability to mask himself from me, but sometimes he's too easy to read. "I didn't know there was a curfew," I tease.

"There isn't a curfew. It's just . . ." He looks down at the space between his legs. "I miss learning how to cook with you."

I'm not a simpering child. I shouldn't feel so glad to hear him say that, and yet here we are. "Jamal's in the kitchen right now," I say, continuing to tease. I love seeing him get flustered. "Why don't you go help him?"

He huffs, dismissive. "It's not the same. I miss learning how to cook with *you*."

I give a long internal sigh. *What a pickle you've gotten into, Nandipa.* I'd have an easier time if this were only about sex. But I know it's not. He doesn't just think I'm nice to look at, like he told me in that tunnel back in the Habitat. He thinks other things, too, feels other things, *wants* other things, things I shouldn't want to give him.

I'm a Proxy, and I can't allow anything to distract me from my duty to Adaolisa. Especially not right now.

Maybe I should just be blunt. "Hondo . . . I don't think this is a good idea."

He keeps his eyes on the floor. "What's not a good idea?"

"Huh," I say. "I guess I must have misread the situation if you don't even know what I'm talking about. Never mind." I remove my towel from my neck and lift myself off the floor.

"Wait!" He gets up, too, scratching the back of his head like he's confused. He takes a moment to gather his thoughts, then says, "Nandipa, are we friends?"

The question takes me aback, if only because I've never considered anyone other than Adaolisa a true friend. Yet the answer seems so obvious. "I think so, yes."

"Okay." He lets himself smile just a little. "But if we were other people, in another life . . ."

A weird warmth fills my chest at that rebellious idea. "You mean . . . without the responsibilities we have now."

"Yes." He comes closer, suddenly more confident. "If we were strangers in another life. Would you—"

"Yes," I say, not letting him finish. "Yes, I think I would." I'd never say this anywhere else, never even think it, but here, in this little box of glass, treadmills, and weight machines, I can let my thoughts wander to forbidden places. "Or at least, I'd seriously consider it."

That smile. I could never have guessed that his sharp features, so suited to sneers and cruel smirks, could produce a smile like this, like he could stop the near-constant rain outside if he aimed his smile at the sky.

"Who knows," he says after a moment. "Maybe . . . maybe that life will find us some day."

I hold his gaze. I've seen him kill, seen what he looks like with blood on his face, but there's still an innocence in his eyes. A naivety. How else can he believe there's any chance we could ever know such a life outside our dreams and fantasies?

"Maybe," I say, though I wouldn't bet on it. I don't say that last part out loud.

We head back to the apartment, morose silence pressing down on us more heavily than all the weights we lifted today.

—

Jamal proudly serves us red-lentil stew with freshly made chapati later that evening. To my mild annoyance, he went from not knowing how to operate a stove to being a decent cook practically overnight, surpassing my and Hondo's bumbling attempts and generally making us feel like idiots who can't follow a recipe. His food actually tastes good. Looks good too.

As the four of us settle down at the dinner table to eat, I begrudgingly tell him this.

He beams, dishing himself a helping of stew. "Why, thank you, Nandipa. I suppose the food is the one thing about this city I don't absolutely abhor."

"And the clothes," I say, gesturing with my spoon at his outfit.

He's wearing checkered gray trousers, suspenders, and a white dress shirt with the sleeves rolled up, a little platinum ankh dangling from one ear. A predilection for fanciness is definitely one of the things he has in common with Adaolisa. He looks down at himself rather self-consciously and shrugs. "Yes, I suppose it's nice to have options now."

"And the music."

He gives me a funny look, eyes narrowing a little. "You're enjoying yourself, I take it."

"Oh, the city's not so bad. It's not perfect. But I could get used to it."

"Ah, but could she?" Jamal's gaze lands on Adaolisa across the table, a challenge in his expression. "How are you finding the city, Adaolisa? Is it as pleasant for you as it is for your Proxy?"

Adaolisa is already in pajamas, her hair wrapped in a silk bonnet in preparation for an early night. She lets herself finish chewing before she answers. "I'm getting along fine. Thanks for asking."

"But you feel it too, don't you?" Jamal presses. "The . . . itch . . . to fix things."

I watch my Prime, waiting for her to tell him off. The fact that she doesn't all but confirms his assertion.

He leans back in his chair, looking triumphant, like he's proved some kind of point. "It's what we were made for, isn't it? To fix, to save, to liberate, and this city needs us more than it needs anything. This whole world even. I'm talking about a clean slate. The Custodians were dirty liars, but they were right about the evils of cybernetics. The Oloye have built a stagnant society. There's no room for new ideas. Everyone gets stuffed into boxes they can't get out of, and those at the bottom trample on each other for scraps. I don't know about you, but it feels wrong to just sit here doing nothing. We were trained to do better."

Hondo and I listen carefully, our emotions fully masked. In the Habitat, at the beginning of every war simulation, Primes would often meet one on one to suss each other out and determine where they'd be working together and where they'd be opposed. If they could be allies or if they needed to start moving against each other. I suddenly feel like I'm sitting in on such a meeting.

"I assume by *clean slate* you mean *tear everything down*," Adaolisa says without expression.

"Naturally," Jamal replies. "When an edifice is rotten and crawling with worms and termites, you don't try to patch it; you tear it down to the foundations and rebuild anew."

Adaolisa's lips stretch into a grim smile. "And then what happens? Suppose you succeed. Congratulations, Jamal, you've destroyed the government and its Oloye masters. What now? How will you ensure what comes next won't be worse? Who will govern, and how?"

Jamal loses a touch of his confidence but remains stubborn. "The people can decide that afterward," he says.

This time Adaolisa laughs. "The rebel who thrives on tearing down the status quo but seldom pauses to think about what comes next. How terribly cliché. Don't you ever wonder why so many revolutions fail, Jamal? Why so many rebel leaders wind up worse than the tyrants they overthrew?"

"I'm sure you're going to tell me."

"It's almost always because they forget that the end of a revolution is only the beginning," Adaolisa says, "not a happily ever after or fade to black. Once the euphoria of victory subsides, someone has to pick up the pieces and rebuild. But rebels never plan that far ahead, so they get stumped when they're faced with a problem they can't burn down."

Jamal lifts a glass of water and takes several gulps without breaking eye contact with Adaolisa. He thunks the glass back on the table and says, "Let me guess. You'd rather 'change the system from the inside.'" He makes air quotes with his fingers.

"You mock, but yes," she says. "Change is usually lasting and peaceful when it comes through the mechanisms of the existing system. When the entrenched powers are party to the change, rather than actively opposed to it. Revolution needs not be chaotic, Jamal. It can be organized, executed in stages, the old seamlessly giving way to the new. Violence must be a last resort. The correct and effective application of words—winning people's hearts and minds—this can be enough.

Admittedly, it may not be as fast or satisfying as watching a city burn, but it works."

Jamal watches Adaolisa with a fixed smile. It's not a nice look. I want to smack it off his face.

"Have you been to the Jondolos since we got our IDs?" he asks.

"No, I have not," Adaolisa admits.

"Maybe you *should* visit. Walk the streets there. Smell them. Maybe then you'll understand why pretty words and winning hearts and minds isn't going to save those people." Jamal picks his fork back up from his plate and goes on to add, almost like an afterthought, "But I suppose you have your way of doing things, and I have mine. We shall have to see which strategy works best."

I freeze with a spoonful of stew halfway toward my mouth. Only for a moment, though. I quickly recover and continue to eat, but my chest tightens as I wait for Adaolisa's reaction.

She smiles, cold and without joy. Almost regretful. "I guess we shall," she says.

And my heart sinks. Hondo catches my eye, and the masked despair I see on his face might as well be a reflection of my own.

They didn't say it out loud. They didn't have to, but we both know it: Our Primes have just declared war on each other. Which means Hondo is now effectively my enemy, as surely as I am his.

Chapter 9: Hondo

It's a crisp and cloudy morning when I stroll down a street three blocks from our apartment building, my hands in the pockets of my charcoal-gray overcoat to ward off the chill. I've hidden my eyes behind silver wraparound sunglasses that augment my vision with parts of the Nzuko, tagging everyone in sight with their names and Scree ranks and applying cosmetic filters over their bodies. Such filters are the much cheaper alternative to bodymods, but generally, the more expensive the filter, the better it looks.

I've timed my walk down this particular street to coincide with the morning routine of one particular man. I know he'll be stopping at a bakery along this same street in just a few moments. I also know that his name is Isaac Yakubu and that he's a records clerk at the city's main police station.

I know these things because Jamal has been privately tailing his movements around the city, scheming in secret while I foolishly thought we were sightseeing. He only revealed what he was doing when he decided he needed my help with the next part of his plan, so here I am.

The man is about to reach the door to the bakery. I keep walking, blending into the early-morning crowds rushing to work. With his synth-leather briefcase, his smart printed dress shirt, and skin so flawless it's probably a bodymod, he looks like any other middle-class pen pusher in the city. I brush past him just as he opens the door, and his static barely registers the contact.

I don't look back as I continue down the street, crossing to the other side of the road a moment later. Across the street I keep walking until I come to the outdoor seating area of the café I thought Jamal liked for its Old World charm. Now I know it was really just a good place for him to watch his target. Even right now I find him seated at his favorite table, which has a clear view of the door to the bakery.

As I join him at the table, my back toward the bakery, he raises a mug of coffee in salute, his earrings twinkling with the motion. "Smooth as silk, Hondo. Well done."

I try not to sound sulky in my response. "What now?"

"Now we wait for him to come out. Then"—Jamal lifts his personal mobile and wiggles it, jangling the platinum bracelet on that hand—"I'll give him a call."

A waitress bounces over to deliver the coffee he ordered for me in my absence. Her cosmetic filter is on the cheaper side, so it doesn't quite fit her face, giving her skin an obviously unnatural gloss. I might have found it funny if I didn't understand that this is probably the best she can afford.

I resist the temptation to immediately take off my sunglasses, waiting until she's left before slipping them off and dropping them on the table. The flood of augmented information ceases, and my eyes thank me for it. It breaks my mind to think these glasses are the least intrusive form of the Nzuko and that most people allow deeper levels of digital augmentation into their eyes.

"I honestly don't know how you manage with those," Jamal remarks absently, still watching the bakery across the street.

"I hate them," I admit.

But wearing the glasses, as I've come to learn, is a good way to remain inconspicuous, because when we walk around without Nzuko-enabled eyewear, people are alerted to the fact that their expensive cosmetic filters are wasted on us. And that can draw attention.

Jamal enjoys this; he *wants* people to know he can see them as they are, unfiltered and unedited, that he's not participating in the lies they tell themselves, but some people find this upsetting, so I compromise with the sunglasses whenever I need to blend in. Jamal tried them on once and never again.

"Our friend just walked out," he informs me. He fires up his PCU, which was lying dormant on the table. "Shall we?"

I don't bother turning around to look. I take a sip of my coffee as I try to come up with something, anything, that could sway him. "It's not too late to stop this," I say. "Whatever you've planned, you can stop it right now. You don't have to make that call."

His eyes find mine, and he leans forward, his intensity so potent I can feel it in my own veins. "Do you agree that there's something fundamentally wrong with this city?"

"Of course I do," I say.

"But you think we should ignore it. Get used to it. Lay low. Do nothing because hey, everything is fucked, but at least we'll be safe. Is that it, Hondo?"

He says my name like he wants me to remember what it means. *War. Change. A fire that will not be cowed.*

I look down at my coffee. Whatever he named me, the parameters of my existence are narrow and focused: his life and health above all else. But even I get angry when I think about those scrawny kids running about the Jondolos with missing limbs and no one to look out for them, preyed on by violent skelems or forced to join them just to put food in their mouths. It's not right, and knowing Jamal, he was never going to look and leave things as is. That's not how the Custodians made him.

Still. "My concern is your safety, Jamal. This isn't the Habitat anymore, and this isn't a war game. The consequences of your actions won't exist on a scoreboard; they'll be out in the real world, and if you miscalculate, it could backfire so badly I won't be able to protect you."

His features soften, though the intensity continues to burn strongly in his eyes. "Have a little more faith in me, my brother. I'll be careful. I promise."

I don't like it, but I give him my blessing with a reluctant nod.

Lips twisting up in one corner, he places the call, using the PCU to disguise his voice and connect himself to my earpiece so I can listen in.

"Hello?"

"Tell me something, Mr. Yakubu," Jamal says in smooth Third Dialect, his modulated voice low and textured, like he's been smoking a pack of cigarettes every day for the past thirty years. "How does a lowly police clerk afford to live like an Oloye's plaything?"

A few seconds of complete silence elapse before Yakubu responds. *"Who is this?"*

"Secretly docking Scree from low-tier folk brought in for questioning, knowing they'll think it's a fine and won't dare to complain, selling your ill-gotten gains to skelem shylocks for anonymous tokens, which you collect at prayer service every week. You've been a very bad man, Mr. Yakubu. Do you know the penalty for social credit fraud? You should, since you work for the police."

"Who the hell is this?"

"The question you should be asking right now is, How are you going to convince me to keep your little secret?"

"I don't know what you're talking about."

"Your son Philip goes to that nice uptown school, doesn't he? One call from me to your supervisor, and Philip and the rest of your family will be sleeping in the darkest corner of the Jondolos tonight.

Such a sweet, sheltered boy. How long do you think he'll last in skelem territory?"

I don't need to see or sense Yakubu to know he's rattled. His voice is practically trembling. *"What do you want?"*

"Look in your pockets," Jamal says.

"What?"

"Check your pockets, Mr. Yakubu."

The sound of rustling comes through my earpiece. *"A . . . drive? What is this? Who put it there?"*

"Again with the wrong question. You should be asking me what I want you to do with that drive. And the answer is, you're going to plug it into your workstation today. First thing when you arrive. That's all you need to do. Plug it into your workstation and keep it there for five minutes. Do this, and you won't hear from me again. Defy me, and Philip will pay the price."

"Are you insane? I could lose my job for this!"

"You won't if you're careful."

"Go fuck yourself."

"Do we have an agreement?"

Heavy breathing comes through the earpiece for a long second. *". . . Damn it. Fine."*

"Five minutes, Mr. Yakubu. No less."

Jamal disconnects the call and brings his coffee mug to his lips, looking satisfied with himself. I'm used to him doing . . . questionable things—it's how he kept us alive in the Habitat when almost everyone wanted to see us recycled—but the way he broke that man's will makes me uncomfortable, to say the least.

"Did you really have to be so ruthless?"

Jamal sips his coffee, unconcerned. "I had one chance to convince him my threat was credible. I couldn't afford to tip him off that I don't actually have any evidence of his crimes."

"Then how did you know what he was doing?" I ask, perplexed.

He sets down his mug. "The second I laid my eyes on him, I knew he was guilty of *something*. It took careful observation and a little research to figure out exactly what."

"So he doesn't actually have to listen to you."

"I could still give his supervisor a call, but I wouldn't be able to prove anything."

"What if he figures this out?"

"He won't," Jamal says with a confident grin. "That's why I chose him."

I shake my head, but I don't argue, because I know he's probably right. I've seen how easily he can identify someone's worst fears just by looking at the way they smile or brush a strand of hair from their face. He's always been observant, but being in the city has honed his ability to read people to surgical sharpness.

It's gotten very clear to us that our . . . auxiliary . . . senses are likely the main reason we were sequestered at the bottom of the ocean, far from the eyes of the world. As Adaolisa put it, we are weapons the Custodians were building against the surface, and while I hate to think of us in such terms, our existence being a threat would go a long way toward explaining why someone was so determined to destroy us.

After coffee, Jamal and I head to the barbershop for our weekly haircuts. My first time inside the shop's brickwork interior was an almost transcendent experience. There was always a hairdresser at the Habitat, but visiting them meant enduring dead space while trying not to squirm as cold fingers slithered over my scalp. I expected a similarly unpleasant ordeal; instead I walked out with the best damned haircut of my life.

The owner is a grizzled but spry old man named Ode who likes to practice what little Second Dialect he knows whenever he sees us. He has metal ring splints to support his arthritic fingers and occasionally has to pause to flex them, but his hands remain dexterous as he works on Jamal while his grandson works on me in an adjacent chair, their cordless clippers giving off twin buzzes as they touch up our fade cuts.

Jamal lays on the charm, asking seemingly innocent questions. Folks here don't like to speak ill of ZimbaTech or the decisions made by the Board of Directors, but Jamal coaxes out of the barber an admission of his disappointment at the recent hike in Scree requirements across every tier.

"A barber with arthritis?" Ode gripes, shaking his head. "Not good for business. And I was inches away from a free treatment at the clinic down the road. Inches, I tell you."

Jamal puts on a worried frown, watching the barber through the mirror. "I'm sorry to hear that."

"Don't you worry about it. These things happen. I'm not dead yet, besides." Ode lifts an eyebrow as he shaves a neat hairline onto Jamal's upper forehead. "Though you wouldn't know it from the way my daughter acts these days. She keeps insisting I go to the Jondolos to get myself metaled like a skelem hoodlum. Can you believe that? These old hands chopped off and replaced with machines. They'd never let me back uptown."

"I think it's good advice, Papa," his sullen grandson puts in from behind me. "Better than letting yourself suffer."

"And what do you know of suffering, hmm? I love my hands. And those metal things are just ugly and unnatural. A chore to maintain as well, probably. No. I kept your mother away from that nonsense, and I'm sure as hell not getting it myself."

"But Papa—"

"I've been through worse, my boy, and I'll get through this," Ode cuts in. "I just gotta work harder. That's all."

His grandson pauses the side part he's shaving onto my scalp so he can glare at the old man. "You said that two years ago, and you're not getting younger. Feels like every time you get close, they raise the price."

"Silly boy. You think they'd raise the price just for me?" Ode kisses his teeth in annoyance. "I'm not that important. Like I said, these things happen. My grandfather had nothing when he came here from Tripoli V. But he worked hard every single day to give his family a chance, and now his grandson owns a shop in a gold district. I've lived in this city my whole life, and I can tell you this: if you want something, you work hard for it. Anything is possible so long as you set your mind to it and put in the effort." He eyes Jamal through the mirror. "You understand, don't you, young Jamal?"

I sense the scathing response Jamal keeps to himself. Outwardly he remains charming and affable. "I defer to your wisdom, Papa," he says.

The barber turns to his grandson with a lifted brow. "See? Now why can't you be more like him?"

Jamal's quiet outrage remains strong even after we leave the barbershop and begin a slow walk back to the apartment. "The human capacity for self-deception is astounding, isn't it?" he says. "That poor old man lives in a society advanced enough to extend his life indefinitely yet instead chooses to make his arthritis treatments unattainable; and he thinks the solution is to work harder."

"It's all he's ever known," I say in the barber's defense. "It's what he's been told his whole life. The same way we were told if we impressed the Custodians enough we'd help civilization, or whatever."

Jamal lets out a sigh, shaking his head. "A fair point, I guess."

Right then a beeping sound comes out of a pocket on his black felt overcoat. He reaches into the pocket and takes out his PCU; I glimpse myriad lines of text on the screen, but I see nothing I can make immediate sense of.

A smile breaks on his face as he scrolls through the text. "Looks like our friend just came through for us. Let me send him a message of thanks."

Speaking into his mobile, he says, "Good work, Mr. Yakubu. You've met your end of the bargain, so your secret is safe with me. I'd get rid of that drive if I were you. Crush it or throw it into the bay—doesn't matter. Just don't get caught with it. And for fuck's sake, stop stealing from people who already have so little. Life is hard enough in this city without you adding to their misery."

Jamal breaks off the communication and puts his PCU back into his pocket, thrumming with the kind of self-satisfaction that always fills me with dread.

"I take it you now have your paws in the police database," I say.

"That might come in handy, I suppose. But it's really their access to the Nzuko I care about."

I almost miss a step. That word again. *Access.* Plots. Schemes. Danger. "Jamal, what are you planning?"

"It's like you said." The determination in Jamal's eyes wouldn't take a Prime to see. "We were fed lies all our lives, and we believed them because we didn't know better. The people on this surface are no different. I just want to see what happens when they learn the truth."

There's no one home when we arrive. As usual, Jamal retreats to the terminal in our room to plot or scheme or whatever else he does there. Left alone, I turn on a news feed on the holo screen, then take my stylus and sketch tablet and sit on a comfortable chair by the windows, facing the lanes of aerial traffic outside. I rest my feet on a low stool and resume the drawing I began yesterday.

There's something about the Free People on the news. Apparently two of the biggest flotillas have decided to stop fighting and reached some kind of agreement to cooperate. Highly bodymodded analysts and government spokespeople with artificially perfect faces drone on and on about what this means for the cities and their ongoing conflict with the Free People.

I tune their voices out, my stylus moving on the tablet in sure but idle strokes. If Nandipa were around, we might have gone down to the gymnasium. I love it there. Even with our Primes engaged in a cold war, nothing's changed between us. When we're alone, I feel I'm not just imagining the lingering looks, the meaningful smiles. *"Yes,"* she said when I asked her if she would, in another life.

Save my first meeting with Jamal, I can't recall anything that's ever made me so happy.

My mind strays into my drawing, my hand deepening the shades of black in the pair of eyes staring up at me with the sharpness and confidence of a shrewd queen.

"I didn't know you felt so strongly about Clarice," Adaolisa says behind me.

I knew she was there even before she opened the door and entered the apartment. Now her perfume fills my nostrils as she grabs the sides of my chair's backrest, looking over my shoulder at my sketch tablet. I've already blanked my mind of all emotion, shrouding my thoughts the way Jamal taught me so I don't inadvertently give anything away. To the untrained ear, Adaolisa and Nandipa might sound alike. But Adaolisa's voice has a weight to it, a gravity that can pull you in if you're not careful, making you sit up straighter and listen, making you *want* to listen, and it's a subtle thing all too easy to miss.

I keep my attention on my portrait of Prime Clarice, exerting deliberate control over every movement of my body. "Clarice despised my Prime and thought me a dog," I say. "She never even spoke to me. Not once in nineteen years."

"And yet here she is," Adaolisa points out, "rendered in loving detail by you."

I make a noncommittal sound. "I'm working on portraits of all our siblings."

"Is that so? May I ask why?"

In the Habitat, a wise Proxy always knew better than to get trapped in conversation with someone else's Prime. I have already erred by letting this conversation go on for so long. "We all have our own ways of grieving, I suppose. Where's Nandipa?" I ask to change the subject.

Adaolisa lets go of my chair and moves to stand closer to the windows so that I can see her from the back. She folds her arms as she stares out at the traffic, a statuesque silhouette against the busy skyline. "Running an errand for me in the city," she says.

I can't help myself; I stare at her. With her patterned head wrap, a sheath dress of cream-colored silk, and dark boots with a low heel, she would be eye catching in any high-tier neighborhood. As with Jamal, I can't say if this new style of dress is more expressive of who she is or if it's simply another weapon she realized she could add to her arsenal.

While Jamal and I went gallivanting through the Jondolos, she and Nandipa leaned into their supposed noble heritage and made friends in the highest places of the city. I don't know what they're planning, but it would be foolish to assume it isn't as far reaching as whatever Jamal is about to do.

"She let you come back here alone?" I ask. I'd have at least made sure Jamal was in the apartment before I let myself go off on my own.

"She trusts that I'm safe here." Adaolisa turns around with a raised eyebrow, arms still folded. "Am I not?"

"Of course you are," I rush to say, giving myself a mental kick. "That was not a threat. In fact, I'd not let Nandipa's Prime come to harm if I could help it."

"Yes, the two of you have become good friends, haven't you?" She watches me for a reaction. I make sure I don't give her one. She tries again. "The Rat and his Dog. I don't imagine you ever liked that moniker."

"I didn't care for it, no."

"It was because our siblings saw you as something wild to be kept on a leash. And while you certainly possess the necessary cold-blooded streak to complement your Prime's ruthless ambition, I now see that we completely misunderstood the dynamics of your relationship." Adaolisa's gaze bores into me. I begin to feel like she's a cat and I'm the food she's playing with. "You complement him, yes, but it is *you* who holds the leash, not the other way round."

All right. This has gone on for too long. "Prime Adaolisa, I sense you have something to say to me. Perhaps you should say it so we can end this conversation."

She gives me a little smile that lets me know I've gained a measure of her respect. "You are the only person in the world whose opinion Jamal actually cares about; do you know that?"

"Naturally," I say. "I'm his Proxy."

"Yes, but you're the only person he'd ever listen to."

"He respects your opinions," I argue.

"To an extent. But I cannot change his mind if he has set it upon a course of action. Only you can do that."

"I follow his lead. I don't tell him what to do."

"And I'm not saying that you should," Adaolisa counters. "What I'm saying is, you have a restraining effect on him. You temper his wilder impulses, and I'm now convinced this is what kept you both alive in the Habitat when most other expies would have been recycled after the first war game."

I'm getting annoyed now, but I keep it masked. "What's your point?"

"I know Jamal is planning something—"

"With due respect, Prime Adaolisa, so are you."

"Yes, I'm not denying that," she says firmly. "But take my advice or leave it: Jamal will go only as far as you let him. It might fall on you to remind him of the difference between changing something and destroying it. That's all I'm trying to say."

I don't like this, how she's getting into my head. I shouldn't let her. "Consider me warned, Prime Adaolisa."

Her point made, she leaves me alone with my sketch tablet once again, and I return to the drawing, pretending not to think about what she said.

Chapter 10: Nandipa

Getting the audition is easy. The bar is in a bronze-tier neighborhood close to the largest technical college in the city; it sees a lot of traffic, but they don't get to be picky about entertainment options. When I stumble in like a tipsy wannabe starlet and ask for a performing gig, the mustached bar manager takes one look at my silver stilettos and the glittering tassels of my dress and shows me to the stage.

"If you sing half as good as you look, you're hired."

My privacy filter has told him nothing about who I am, but given my appearance, my slight intoxication, and the fact that I'm asking for a job in some run-down bronze-tier bar, I know he's made a few assumptions about me. *Probably some rich man's ditzy plaything who got cast aside and is now feeling desperate.*

It's early enough the lunch crowds won't be arriving for a few more hours, and the students don't show up until after dark, so my audience is no more than a pair of janitor drones, an absentminded man taking stock of the inventory behind the bar, and the manager himself. I still suffer a nervous tingle as I wobble onto the stage with my archtop guitar.

I've never performed for anyone before—Adaolisa doesn't count; she's incapable of being critical of my music. I've never even wanted to perform. Music has always been a personal experience for me, a pastime like watching drama episodes, something that belongs to me and me alone.

But I don't show my nerves, putting a lid on my drunkenness and beginning my rendition of a pre-Artemisian Afro-soul number with the confidence of a seasoned performer. My hands never stumble on the fretboard; the lyrics ooze from my lips like syrup.

And slowly the tenor of the static changes in the room. The man behind the bar stops what he's doing. The manager sits down near the stage, his cleaning cloth draped over one shoulder, eyes shining as he looks up at me.

I barely understand this gift the Custodians built into me. Are these pheromones? Do I have an extra lobe in my cerebral cortex? Whatever it is, I feel it working. I find myself performing for their static, drawing it around me, reeling them in like fish on a hook.

The manager doesn't stop me when I improvise my way into another song. The man behind the bar folds his arms, watching me with eyes that carry a blue cybernetic luminescence. He's light complexioned, with short fuzzy hair and a trimmed beard bodymodded to the color of ivory. My expensive Nzuko-enabled eye contacts tell me his name is Aart Mwila and that in addition to working here, he moonlights as a freight handler at ZimbaTech's spaceport. Scree status: bronze.

I play just one more song before I stop. As I come down from the stage, the manager gets up, clapping his hands. He's trying to play it cool, but his static is all over the place.

"Tell me something: Ever played in a band?" he asks.

"No. But I'd love to," I say, and this isn't exactly a lie.

"Come by at around six, and we'll talk some more."

I shouldn't be excited, but I don't have to fake a smile. "Really? Oh, thank you!" I surprise the manager by throwing my arms around him. "Thank you so much."

Cybernetic irises watch us from across the room.

"You're welcome," the manager says with a somewhat uncomfortable laugh. "Just don't audition for anyone else, all right?"

I smile back and promise not to. As I leave the bar, my guitar case slung over my back, I frown to myself, analyzing the spark of excitement I suddenly feel.

Is this something I actually want to do?

The world blurs around me as I make my way toward the nearest maglev station. I draw my coat closer to ward off the crisp air, but it sobers my walk, though I'm still careful with any stairs I have to navigate.

This part of town isn't as dicey as the Jondolos, but poverty leaves its mark in the age of the concrete buildings and the muck gathering along the sides of the roads. In my desire to get to the station faster, I decide to take a shortcut, turning into a narrow alleyway that even in the morning is draped in shadows from the adjacent buildings.

The alley is empty. The windows on the buildings have bars of steel bolted over them on the outside and give the impression that they've never been opened. This is no place for a lone young woman, but the station is not far away, so I should be fine.

My stilettos click on the ground as I walk. I hear another sound behind me, so I look over my shoulder, but there's nothing. Maybe I imagined it, but I pick up the pace anyway.

Suddenly I hear footsteps. I look again, and this time there's a white-haired man running toward me. I let out a scream and try to flee, but I'm not quite sober, and my ridiculous stilettos were not meant for running, so he catches me. My guitar case falls away, and I'm pushed violently against the wall. My eyes widen with terror when the point of a knife comes to rest against the skin of my throat.

"Scream again and I'll cut you," he whispers.

Aart Mwila smells like sweat and beer. His white shirt and denims strain against his physical strength, excitement shining in the electric blues of his cybernetic eyes. He wants me to put up a fight, to struggle and resist. He's done this before and knows he'll win. I'm nothing but a foolish drunken girl.

I don't let him realize his mistake. Faster than he can think, my hand chops the side of his neck, striking a carotid sinus and temporarily cutting off the flow of oxygen to his brain. His static dulls as he crumples in a dead faint, hitting the ground hard enough he'll have a terrible headache when he regains consciousness. I plan to be long gone by then.

With one ear paying attention to the surrounding static, I pull out the blood-microsampling device and the syringe that were in my coat pocket. I use the first to collect a sample of his blood. When that's done, I use the syringe to inject a microchip tracker into his bloodstream; it's supposed to be so stealthy he won't know about it unless he goes for a full-body scan.

A cold rage takes me as I stand over his unconscious form. It shouldn't have been so easy. All I did was exist in his space, minding my own business, and for that he decided I was yet another thing to victimize.

I should kill him.

But that's not what I was sent here to do, so I pick up my guitar and walk away before I do something stupid.

A few minutes later, I claim a lone seat inside a maglev heading back home. As we depart the station, I pull out my mobile and make a voice call to Adaolisa, using the encryption system she set up. "It's done," I tell her.

"I saw the tracker going active," her voice says into my ear. *"Excellent work. Did you have any trouble?"*

"Leaving that slimy bastard alive took everything I had."

"He'll get what he deserves. Where are you now?"

"On the maglev back home."

"Marcel wants to meet up for cocktails. He'll be sending a car over soon. I think now's the time to make our move."

We've gone so far already. I have a blood sample in the pocket of my coat. Adaolisa never acts unless she has contingencies in place; I know she knows what she's doing. But I have a niggling worry in the back of my throat, and I think speaking to her on the mobile, with distance between us, makes it easier for me to voice my doubts. "Are you sure about this?" I ask.

I hear the sound of boots on concrete. I think she's out on the landing pad. *"Can we ever be sure of anything these days?"*

"We don't have to do this, you know."

"Yes, we could sit back and watch Jamal burn the world down around us."

"So this is about stopping Jamal?"

"You know me better than that, my love. I don't like to react. Better to set my own agenda." Adaolisa sighs, and I can picture her standing outside the apartment, one hand on the rails of the landing pad, eyes looking out over the city. *"This world is a powder keg waiting to go off. It would be so easy for Jamal to light the fire and make things worse. I'm not specifically trying to stop him. I think we both seek the same end. But I want to make sure there's something still standing when all is said and done. You trust me, don't you?"*

"Of course I do," I say automatically, and guilt throbs through me at the realization that this isn't completely true. Yes, I trust her judgment, but I'm not sure I trust her not to put herself in danger.

"I need you with me, Nandipa, and I value your advice. If you feel strongly that I shouldn't do this, say the word and I'll back off."

Well . . . damn. Could it be so simple? I say *don't do it* and that's the end of it? "I trust you, Ada," I hear myself say. "Don't let me get in the way. It's not my place to tell you what to do."

"I disagree with so much in that statement, but I appreciate your support. Let's talk more when you get back, okay?"

As we end the call, part of me wants to punch myself in the face for wasting an opportunity to nip her schemes in the bud. But she's the smartest person I know. What if telling her to stop is the wrong decision? Who am I to challenge her wisdom?

I stare outside my window as the maglev races across one of the city's main tidal waterways toward a gold-tier district where the towers are taller, newer, and more slender. A tingle of anxiety curls around my core. I recognize it as the feeling I always get at the beginning of a new war game.

—

It's midmorning when I step into the apartment. As I emerge from the foyer, Hondo gets up from where he was seated across the open living room, setting his stylus and sketch tablet on the coffee table. "You're back," he says, and his eyebrows climb up his forehead as he takes in my outfit. "Wow."

A smile teases the corners of my lips. "Don't ask. Just admire." I set my guitar down and remove my coat, draping it onto the kitchen counter. I feel parched, so I open the fridge to pull out a bottle of water.

As I pour myself a glass and quench my thirst, Hondo pads closer to the kitchen on socked feet, his hands in the pockets of his bottle-green chinos. He looks like he wants to ask a question but isn't sure how to go about it.

Despite myself my skin tingles with anticipation.

"Hey, can I have a quick word with you?" he says in a voice low enough I know he doesn't want the Primes to overhear him.

I place my half-empty glass on the counter between us, curious where this is going. "Something on your mind?"

"Yes. So, uh, your Prime spoke to me earlier today."

Uh-oh. What have you done, Adaolisa? I keep my cool. "Oh? What did she say?"

"She asked me to restrain Jamal. Stop him from going too far, whatever that means."

"Sounds like good advice. I'd take it if I were you."

Hondo folds his arms over his striped knit shirt, his forehead creasing in a little frown. I think I've offended him, but I'm not going to do or say anything to undermine my Prime.

"Well, I have some advice for you too," he says brusquely.

"Is that so?"

I expect he's about to give me a piece of his mind. Instead he closes his eyes briefly, getting his temper under control. "Actually, it's more of a request. I know you don't like Jamal—"

"He's a jerk," I say, to which Hondo dips his head, his lips twitching.

"Yes, I suppose he is, and I think he knows that, but he's not a bad person. He'd never go out of his way to hurt someone—not unless he felt he was fighting for his life."

"All right," I say in a deliberate tone, making it clear I'm still waiting for him to get to his point.

"I think Prime Adaolisa can be ruthless," he says. I bridle at this, but I let him continue. "My worry is she'll decide to go after Jamal if he gets in her way."

"Then don't let him get in her way. Problem solved."

"I don't know what your Prime is planning, Nandipa. And even if I did, it's not my place to stop Jamal from following his convictions. Would you stop Adaolisa from following hers?"

I almost let myself become a hypocrite. It's what a good Proxy would do. I should say whatever will convince Hondo to get Jamal to back off. "I guess not," I admit. "So what are you saying?"

We both know our Primes are out of earshot, but Hondo looks around the apartment just to make sure. When he's satisfied, he lowers his voice even more. "I want us to make a pact. Let's not let our Primes destroy each other. I'll make sure Jamal never does anything to harm your Prime, and you do the same for me."

I'm not new to this kind of deal. In the Habitat, secret alliances between Proxies happened all the time—*keep your Prime off mine's back, and I'll return the favor*. The Primes never needed to know. But I'd really like to stop living like we're still stuck in that fucking place. "From the way you're talking, one would think we're in a war game," I say.

His eyes shimmer with the specter of regret. "I think we both know we might as well be," he says, and I fail to disagree with him. "Look, as far as I know, you're the biggest physical threat to Jamal. You're the last person I want coming after him. And I'm sure, given the option, you'd rather not have to worry about me lurking behind every corner."

Okay. He has a point. If there's someone alive who can get to Adaolisa before I can stop them, it would be Hondo. The very thought almost makes me shiver. "That would not be ideal, no."

"Exactly. So for the sake of our Primes, let's not let things get to the point where you and I have to watch out for each other."

A part of me wants him to admit why he doesn't want to face off against me. I *want* him to say it. But that's a dangerous thing to want, so I let it go. "All right, Hondo." I extend my hand. "We have a deal."

A little smile moves his lips as he reaches out to shake the offered hand, and the contact drives an unexpected tingle of electricity into my arm and straight down my spine. He has a nice hand, doesn't he. Real solid, warm, and his eyes are magnets, drawing me in, cold and dark but with a fire in their depths—

We jerk away from each other when we hear the sound of Adaolisa's boots on the floor. She appears in the living room seconds later with a black handbag hanging on one arm. Hondo is suddenly halfway across the room.

"There you are. Our ride is about to land outside." She stops by a mirror to check the subtle shades of her makeup, adjusting her ankara head wrap. "Are you ready?"

To be frank, I'm tired of playing at being a socialite. I don't mind dressing up on occasion; I know how well I pull it off, and yes, sometimes I do enjoy bringing silence to a room just by walking in. I've always had a flair for the dramatic. But I've found I much prefer the simplicity of leggings, leather jackets, and boots with low heels, if only for the increased mobility. How the hell am I supposed to be a good Proxy if I can't run for shit?

"Shouldn't I get changed first?" I ask hopefully.

"What? No. You look delightful, my love." A sleek gunmetal aerial car makes no noise as it descends gracefully onto the landing pad. "I believe that's our ride. Hondo, tell Jamal we're going out for a bit. Stay out of trouble, all right?"

I narrowly avoid a sigh as I pick up my coat from the counter and slip back into it. Hondo gives me a sympathetic smile on our way out. I stick my tongue out at him for thinking I need his pity. I'm perfectly capable of pitying myself.

The car lifts off with a low whir and whisks us away into the cloudy sky above ZimbaTech. The spacious interior has a smell of newness about it—in fact, I wouldn't be surprised if Adaolisa and I were the very first passengers to ever ride inside.

I open the various compartments within reach of my seat, inspecting the wines and spirits inside and the glasses with which to drink them. This is definitely no aerial cab.

"I think Marcel is trying to impress you," I remark.

Adaolisa keeps looking out her window. "He's infatuated, but I'd rather have his trust and respect."

"Well, I'd say you're already halfway there."

We've been meeting with Marcel regularly since that first night Adaolisa approached him. At first I thought she intended to seduce him, but then she shot down that idea almost right away.

"I'm a lesbian, Marcel," she said that night. "And I'm definitely no prostitute. I'm not here to try and get into your pants. I'm sure you have enough people for that and could have your pick of them."

Marcel seemed shocked and mesmerized at the same time. "Oh! Then . . . why would you . . ."

"Be interested in you?" Adaolisa shrugged, amusement and confidence sparkling in her eyes. "You looked like you could use a friend. And frankly, so could I."

I didn't think it would work, but a grin slowly spread across Marcel's face, like he'd been offered his heart's desire. It frightens me a little that Adaolisa can just look at a person and see them so clearly. I wonder what she sees when she looks at me.

The clouds part outside my window, and I glimpse the hologram spinning in a slow ribbon around the ZimbaTech Spire, now so close I'd be able to see through its pearlescent windows if they weren't so reflective. Our car descends toward a much smaller, though no less glittering, conical tower in the neighborhood, aiming for the landing pad jutting out on one side just below the building's rounded top. But what looked small from above grows and grows as we draw closer, until it dominates the view outside.

"Before I forget." I pull the microsampling device out of my coat pocket and hand it over to Adaolisa.

She accepts it with a grateful smile, slipping it into her handbag. "I know you have reservations," she says. "And I know you've chosen to have faith in me despite those reservations. I promise I'll do my best not to betray this trust."

I don't think she could ever disappoint me, but her reassurance loosens some of the knots of anxiety that had tightened inside my stomach.

We touch down on the landing pad, and I draw my coat tighter around myself as I step out of the car. We're supposed to be near the top of this building, but there are still many stories towering over us.

Our host is there to welcome us with a nervous grin on his rugged face. He wears a burgundy suit over his lank frame, a black wide-brimmed fedora on his head, multiple chains of platinum, and a patterned silk scarf hanging loosely around his neck.

I'm still wearing my contacts, but no augmented information appears about him in the Nzuko. No cosmetic filters cover him either. Not that he'd need one. Oloye, after all, are the pinnacle of bodymodification and can sculpt their bodies however they wish.

His perfect grin widens as we meet. "Ladies. I'm glad you could make it."

"Marcel." Adaolisa greets him with a chaste hug. "It's good to see you."

"Likewise." He gives me a shy glance as they separate. "Nandipa."

I wink at him, knowing it'll make him blush. "Hey, Marcel."

His grin becomes timid. "So. I reserved a table. Join me?"

"Lead the way," says Adaolisa.

Our table is on a mezzanine floor with a good view of the live band serenading our ears with ambient jazz. I don't have to pretend to be more interested in the musicians than I am in the conversation.

I don't tune out completely either. I listen to Adaolisa play Marcel like he's an instrument and she a maestro. I used to think strategy was her biggest strength, that *I* was the people person, but watching her gently worm her way into the diamond district has been an eye-opening experience. I'm now convinced she could have charmed the mask off a Custodian if she ever set her mind to it.

Take Marcel Muzinga, twenty-four years old, a bastard child whose father was a gardener from the Jondolos. He grew up a recluse, mocked by his peers for his low parentage, but his mother's family was and still is powerful, so now he's the associate director of ZimbaTech's Internal Security Agency, or Int-Sec.

Sounds impressive on the surface, until you find out it's a sinecure in a largely redundant agency, one of those cushy but empty jobs doled out to less important Oloye to give them something they can say they do. Even so, Marcel has a hunger to prove himself, a hunger Adaolisa spotted the second she laid her eyes on him and knew he was her way in.

She presented herself as a breath of fresh air, someone who understood him and didn't care what people whispered. With calculated words she made him pliant, made him crave her approval, her friendship.

Personally I find him rather dull. He has everything anyone in this city could ever want, but he lives in his own little world of self-pity, desperate for glory yet lacking the spine to reach for it. Too impressionable, which I suppose is why Adaolisa chose him. Sometimes I feel guilty about our charade and wonder what she really thinks of him, if she's using him and it's all just an act or if part of her actually likes him. I haven't asked.

She doesn't get to business right away. We enjoy cocktails and jazz and light conversation for an hour before she finally reaches into her handbag for the used microsampler along with a small mobile.

"I have a gift for you, Marcel," she says as she places both items on the table. "Consider this a job application."

Marcel's deeply expressive eyes reflect the golden glaze coming from the light fixtures all over the restaurant. "You want a job?" he asks. "But why would you want to work? I could support you financially, and your whole family would never have to work."

I think about what Jamal would make of such an offer and almost laugh. "Sounds like a deal," I say with just enough humor that I might be joking. "Work is boring anyway."

Playing along, Adaolisa rolls her eyes. "You're too kind, Marcel, but unlike my sister, I don't like being idle. I guess I'm a lot more like you in that regard. I like to earn my keep. I also like to learn, and as the youngest associate director of Int-Sec in generations, I believe there's a lot you could teach me."

The flattery goes straight to his head. I don't even need Adaolisa's advanced empathy to see it happening. His whole face lights up. "And I'd be willing to teach," he says. "But . . . what would you even do? I don't really have much to delegate."

That's because whatever duties Int-Sec was created to perform are now completely covered by the police service and, if that fails, the Criminal Investigation Department.

"We could be your personal assistants," Adaolisa replies. "You'll need us once Int-Sec gives you more responsibility."

A touch of sadness weakens Marcel's smile. "That's never going to happen, Adaolisa."

"Are you sure?" she says, moving in for the kill. "Not even if you personally tracked down and brought in the Pest himself?"

"The Pest?" Marcel lists his head in confusion. "As in, the terrorist kidnapper guy? Isn't he hiding out at sea with the Free People?"

The Pest, real name Joseph Banda, has a list of crimes that could fill a ledger, from rape all the way to murder. He was so good at covering his tracks no one looked too closely at him until he decided to add kidnapping Oloye children for ransom to his list of misdeeds and, worse, making antigovernment posts on the Nzuko.

He became one of the city's most wanted criminals after that, but he remained elusive, using underground bodymods to change his appearance and fool biometric scanners. He might have lived the rest of his days under his false identity had Adaolisa not set her eyes on him for her own purposes.

"He's hiding in this city, Marcel," she says. "Lives and works under the alias Aart Mwila. He changed his face, his hair, his eyes, even his hands, but I have a DNA sample that can prove his identity. This mobile is also tracking his location as we speak. Here, take a look."

Marcel leans forward, and Adaolisa shows him the program on the mobile stalking Joseph Banda as he goes about the city.

"He doesn't know it, but there's a tracker in his bloodstream," she says.

Marcel's brow knits into lines as he gazes at the mobile. "Is that really him?"

"The blood sample can prove it. The tracker will lead you to his location. If you and Int-Sec were the heroes who brought him in . . ." She leaves that hanging, inviting him to reach up and bite.

"The Board would be impressed," he muses. "They might even give me Sidibe's job."

Sidibe is his boss, the current head of Int-Sec. Complaining about him is one of Marcel's favorite pastimes.

Now he sits back in his chair, the static of his thoughts revving up with excitement, though outwardly he remains calm. "How did you do this?"

"The tracker and the blood?" Adaolisa asks with measured casualness. "I hired someone."

"But *how* did you find him?"

"My sister was raised to rule, my dear Marcel," I say, giving Adaolisa a look between mockery and endearment. "She has a talent for seeing patterns where most of us would miss them. And she's been oh so desperate to impress you."

Adaolisa affects an annoyed huff. "I was only trying to help. I just wanted to show Marcel how useful I can be."

"No, no. It's fine," Marcel says, coming to her rescue. "I'm not complaining. This is great, Adaolisa. More than great. Thank you."

She smiles at him coyly, and I sigh like I'm bored, which isn't completely a pretense.

"So do we have a deal?" she presses gently. "Can we work for you as your assistants?"

"If I bring in the Pest, you'll have whatever you want." Marcel picks up the microsampler and stares at the drop of blood contained inside the plastic chamber. "The Pest himself. They'll make me director for sure." The light of ambition strengthens within his eyes as he looks at Adaolisa. "I'll need to verify the sample. Then I'll take a small team and ambush the son of a bitch. Preferably today. As soon as possible. Now, in fact. You don't mind, do you?"

"You're a busy man, Marcel," Adaolisa says. "We understand."

He grins as he gets up, pocketing the mobile and the blood sample in the inside of his jacket. "Feel free to order whatever you like. My car will take you back home when you're ready. I'll let you know when the job is done."

He bids us farewell and leaves us at the table, rushing off to claim his destiny. There could be surveillance in such a place, so we don't break character, but Adaolisa radiates with satisfaction the whole time.

I mask my growing worry so tightly she doesn't notice it.

Chapter 11: Hondo

I'd grown accustomed to not being permanently worried about Jamal like I used to be back in the Habitat, but things change once he acquires administrative access to the city's all-knowing network.

Dreading all the trouble he could cause with such power, I become hesitant to let him out of my sight. I frown every time I see him with his PCU. I lurk behind him whenever he's seated at the terminal in our room. Even as the weeks go by without the world ending, I fail to relax, knowing there's an axe hanging over the city and it might come down at any time.

One early evening, he gets fed up with my hovering and orders me to leave the apartment.

"Where am I supposed to go?" I snap back at him.

He grabs my mobile and marks a location across the city. "There. Get a drink or two. Go dancing. Go wild. I don't care. Just give me some space, or I swear I'll jump off this building."

The girls are out—they're always out these days—so the apartment is empty. But I know Jamal has control over the building and can restrict access to the landing pad, so I'm not too worried about leaving him alone. And maybe some time apart will do us both good.

Reluctantly, I obey. I dress up and take an aerial cab to the location, some drinking establishment in a bronze-tier district. Upbeat jazz greets my ears as I step inside. Almost everyone in sight looks to be around my age; my augmented reality spectacles tell me most of the patrons here are students at a nearby technical institute. The place is so crowded there are no free tables, so I keep my coat on at first, wondering why the hell Jamal would send me here.

That's when I see her, up on the stage.

A band is playing behind her, but their faces remain a blur. My attention fixes on Nandipa, on her melodic voice, on her lips as she sings me into a near trance. A flower adorns the cloud of ringlets around her head, its petals a lustrous gold like her blouse. Large hoops dangle from her ears, black like her eyeshadow. She's a vision I immediately commit to memory, one I'll try to sketch in the future, though I already know I'll never get it right.

I gravitate toward the bar when I spot a free seat just far enough from the stage for me to watch in relative shadow. She's confident while she sings, then shy when applause breaks. Some songs she joins the band's syncopated rhythms with her guitar. Others she takes center stage, the instruments mellowing to let her liquid voice sail over them. I could almost believe she's been performing all her life.

I thought she followed Adaolisa whenever they left the apartment. Has she been coming here instead? And since when?

After a particularly lively song the band announces they'll be taking a break. I know I've been spotted when Nandipa makes her way toward the bar. She exchanges smiles and greetings with people along the way, some of them by name, and she remains outwardly pleasant when she stops next to me and addresses the bartender.

"The fruitiest cocktail you have for my friend here."

The bartender gives me a glance, then chuckles. "Sure thing, boss."

"So," Nandipa says to me, switching out of the Third Dialect and into the Second. She's still smiling, but I sense something venomous under the surface. "Are you spying on me?"

I could strangle Jamal right now. "If I said I'm not, would you believe me?"

"So you just happened upon this place while you were taking a stroll," she deadpans.

"Not exactly," I admit. "Jamal wanted me out of his hair for a while, so he sent me here. I didn't know what I'd find."

She watches me through her shadowed eyes, making me tingle all over. I keep it off my face. I also sense her anger mellowing, though the look in her eye turns sardonic. "So it's your Prime who's been spying on me. Not that I'm surprised."

I'm saved from responding when the drink arrives. The bartender pushes it toward me with a grin. "On the house."

It's indeed a fruity-looking drink with cherries and strawberries. "Should I be worried about this?" I ask Nandipa.

She picks up the drink and sips from the straw, her eyes never leaving mine. "Only if you can't handle having a good time."

I have to clear my throat and look away. "I thought you worked at Int-Sec."

"I do," she says, placing the glass back on the counter. "I come here sometimes after work."

"Does Adaolisa know?"

"Would you keep a secret from Jamal?"

"Fair point." *Ancestors, I'm messing this up.* "You're amazing," I blurt out. "I mean, you sound good. You're very talented."

Quiet laughter brings wrinkles to her eyes, and I just know she finds me ridiculous. "Why don't you stay until I'm finished here?" she says. "We'll head home together."

"All right," I say, completely cool and not unreasonably excited at all.

She leans closer. "And Hondo?"

"Yes?"

"Don't come here again. It's nothing against you. I just can't have you keeping tabs on me for Jamal." She pulls away, her smile widening. "Enjoy the drink."

Back at home, I don't give Jamal a hard time about sending me to Nandipa's bar. Mostly because I don't regret going there, but also because I don't want to have to ask him why he thought sending me there was a good way to distract me.

I'm not ready to have that conversation.

I do ask him, though, if he's spying on the girls.

He swivels on his chair by the terminal to give me a smirk. "Adaolisa made sure I couldn't. It was the first thing she did when she set foot into Int-Sec. Right after getting admin access to the Nzuko."

Access. I think about that for a second. "Then how . . ."

"How did I know what Nandipa was up to?"

"Yes."

"I saw it on her face. The joy, the cocktails, the jazz. I knew she was performing somewhere." Jamal shrugs, turning back to his work. "After that, it wasn't too difficult to trawl the Nzuko for mentions of a new sensational singer and connect them to a place."

"I see."

"How was she?" Jamal asks casually.

"Good, I guess." I don't say more.

The next evening he pads down the stairs to find me alone in the living room, working on my sketchpad.

"Get dressed," he says, a mysterious air about him. "There's something I want you to see."

It's cold and rainy outside, so we dress accordingly. Tonight Jamal decides he's a platinum uptowner, wearing dark pinstripes complete with a suit vest, a silk scarf, ankle-high dress boots, and an iron-gray overcoat. I slip into my usual. Denims, a white button-down, a woolen sweater, a black trench coat, and cap-toe synthetic-leather boots.

Instead of a bright-green aerial cab, a plain white cargo vehicle is waiting for us on the landing pad, rivulets of rainwater pouring down its tinted windows. I unfurl an umbrella as we exit the apartment, holding it over our heads.

"Whose car is this?" I ask. I sense no static inside.

"It's mine," Jamal replies. "Or at least, it's mine to do with as I please. I bought it with a fake alias. Feel free to jump behind the wheel if you want."

While Jamal hops into the passenger seat, a weird feeling I get from him tells me to check the cargo compartment. I open the sliding door and find myself staring at six cases of black polymer.

"Hondo . . . ," Jamal says cautiously, looking at me over his shoulder from the passenger seat. "Please don't overreact."

I open the first case, and my guts turn to ice. I go ahead and open the other cases. Guns. Ammunition. Ballistic vests and helmets. Even a compact utility drone with armored plating. And for some reason the sixth case is full of packaged crop seeds.

Jamal preempts my brewing outburst before I can even find the words to express myself.

"Whether we make use of those weapons will be entirely up to you," he says. "Let me show you something. Then you decide."

I want to drag him back into the house and keep him away from danger, but he's my Prime, and I should let him follow his convictions. At the very least I should let him make his case.

I collect myself with a breath. Then I jump into the driver's seat and take manual control of the vehicle, trying not to enjoy the feel of driving something real for a change, not a simulation in the Habitat. The energy-dense fluoride-ion batteries are almost at full charge; the ion thrusters respond eagerly when I fire them up, and the controls are smooth as I guide the vehicle off the landing pad and into a traffic lane.

I fight back a grin, not wanting Jamal to think I approve. "How did you afford this car, Jamal?" I ask. "Forget the car—what about the weapons? *When* did you even buy them?"

"I got the money from dead rich people," he says matter-of-factly. "You wouldn't believe just how much liquid cash is sitting untouched in secret Nzuko wallets people took to their graves." He pulls out his PCU from his coat and extends the keyboard, setting it on his lap. "Here, take us to this address."

A map marker appears on the vehicle's dashboard, pointing to a place across the bay, in the Jondolos. Not a place I want to visit, especially after dark, and definitely not with a car full of weapons and ammo. I switch lanes anyway, turning southward.

"You stole from dead people?"

"It's hardly stealing if they're dead," he says. "Most of the time it's some rich exec who opens a wallet with an alias to hide money from their spouse for whatever reason. Usually an affair. Then they die unexpectedly, having told no one about the alias, and the money is as good as lost. Not to me. I skimmed a little here and a little there, used the profits to buy anonymous tokens from the minting exchange, used drones to deliver the tokens to a broker, used the broker to buy the weapons and the vehicles. And here we are."

I glance sideways and catch him frowning into the well of light coming out of his PCU.

"Don't worry," he says distractedly. "The broker can't be tied back to us. I made sure to choose someone discreet. And whatever we do won't be tied back to him either."

"Did you say vehicles?" I ask.

He takes a second to reply. "I guess I did."

"Jamal, should I expect trouble tonight?"

"It'll depend."

"On what?"

He looks over and our eyes meet. "On what you decide after you see what I want to show you."

The nighttime rains have just begun to taper off when we arrive at the marked location across the bay, a residential neighborhood full of crumbling brutalist concrete structures several stories high.

A concentrated burst of static coming from one particular building complex draws my attention.

"What is this place?" I ask as we descend toward the mostly empty parking lot near the complex.

"Set us down here," Jamal says. "We'll walk the rest of the way. Don't forget to put on your shades."

Following his own instruction, Jamal slips on a pair of wraparound augmented reality shades. After I set the car down, I do the same.

The Nzuko is much more tolerable these days. Jamal unlocked a host of useful features our accounts previously denied us, including privacy filters and the ability to reduce the amount of augmented visual noise fed to our eyes.

I notice that the filters he's given us now are fake aliases complete with facial disguises. Whoever sees us will think we work for Citizen Affairs. I don't bother asking.

It's still drizzling, so we huddle beneath my umbrella as we make our way to the complex on foot. Behind us the car lifts off on its own, following Jamal's instructions to find a secure parking tower and stay there until we summon it. The people of this world are still suspicious of artificial intelligences even centuries after the Artemis Incident, but the autopilots on vehicles are robust enough I know the car can quickly make itself available should we need a hasty getaway.

Three young women are guarding the building's main entrance, beneath a porch sheltered from the rains. They were laughing among themselves, but they stop when they spot us, standing up straighter. One of them has a rifle on a sling. The other two are packing handguns in holsters. Their static ticks up with nervousness, but they make no moves to reach for their weapons.

By the disconcerting bionic prostheses taking up most of their necks and chins, visible articulated metal tubes in place of arteries and airways, I know these women are enforcers for the Silvernecks, one of the three major skelems that run the Jondolos. Suddenly I wish I'd been wise enough to bring one of Jamal's new guns.

"Relax," he whispers to me. "Just follow my lead."

"Here comes the boss," says one of the young women in an irreverent voice, making her friends laugh. "You here for an inspection, boss, or you here to be my friend?"

They giggle again, meaning to intimidate us, but I know our sudden appearance has unsettled them.

"Why not both?" Jamal says with a wolfish grin. "And since I'm your friend, let's not use words like *inspection*. I'll take a quick walk around, just for the record; then I'll get out of your hair. Sounds good?"

"Of course, of course," says the young woman, her static mellowing with relief. "Want someone to give you a tour?"

"No need. I'll be quick. I have places to be."

"Then go on in, boss. Door's not locked."

Just like that, the three women let us in. A low-security operation, it seems, whatever this place is. I saw only a single camera watching the entrance and no barricades of any kind. Inspections from Citizen Affairs must be regular and common for them not to ask further questions.

Jamal and I proceed to enter some kind of decrepit hospital. Or the neglected remains of what may have once been a hospital. Some of the windows broke and were never replaced. Fluorescent lamps cast a sickly yellow light over everything. The brown floors could be white, but they haven't seen a mop in decades. I wince at the sour chemical odor that immediately assaults my nostrils. *What the hell is this place?*

There's a Silverneck enforcer seated behind the grimy reception desk with his booted feet up on the counter. He watches us with indifference and doesn't stop us when we pass him. We come upon more Silvernecks bustling about the gloomy corridors, some in scrubs. They all ignore us like they see people from Citizen Affairs all the time. Even I almost believe Jamal belongs here and has been here before, the way he walks like he knows where he's going.

"Hold any questions you have," he says as we approach a pair of steel doors. "For now, I just want you to look."

He shows me into a large ward with at least twenty beds, all of them occupied. My skin crawls with revulsion at the squalor of the room, the mildew staining the cement walls. The sour chemical smell is also stronger here, mingling with the stench of piss and shit. Even worse is the state of the patients languishing on the beds, frail and emaciated, all hooked up to tubes and catheters and electrodes attached to their shaved heads like the tentacles of an octothon.

I'm a Proxy. I was built to be tough, to kill without flinching. I once tore a sibling to pieces with my bare hands. My stomach should be tough as iron. And it is. Even as my soul recoils in horror, I remain calm, lucid.

"Come," Jamal says, inviting me deeper into the ward.

I follow him quietly, forcing myself to look at the patients. What puts me on edge is how active their static is, like they're fully awake, not sleeping or unconscious, as they appear.

I see a boy not older than fifteen. I see a woman with gray in her eyebrows. I disconnect myself from the worried voice at the back of my head, becoming cold, logical, searching for the pattern that unites these people. But I find none save the fact that they are here.

I stop near a bed carrying a young woman. Her eyes are fluttering beneath her closed eyelids. An enteral feeding tube punctures her abdomen, but she must not be getting enough nutrition, since I can see the outline of her ribs against her skin. I trace the electrodes connected to her shaved scalp; they merge into a thick black cable that connects to a boxlike machine behind her bed.

I look around. Every bed has its own machine, with lights that blink on and off in the quiet gloom.

"Jamal. What is this?"

"No questions, remember? Just look."

He gestures at me to follow, so I do. And throughout a tour of the building's many wards, I hold my tongue. I stop counting the patients once I get to five hundred. They are packed wherever there's room to fit them, on some floors even in the corridors. In one ward we come upon a group of Silvernecks in scrubs trying their best to revive a patient who's flatlined.

"Carry on," Jamal tells them when they notice us.

After a minute of failed CPR, the Silvernecks give up. "He's gone," one of them says, removing her gloves. "Clean this up and bring in a replacement."

I've seen enough, but Jamal shows me more rooms, more wards, all of them stinking and filthy and full of beds with patients hooked up to machines. I hear a scream coming from several floors below, and I want to believe I imagined it, but I can't ignore the accompanying burst of panicked static that scrapes against my mind before going dull.

Someone has been knocked out, and they were scared.

The replacement? I try not to think about what's probably going to happen to that person.

At the closed doors to yet another ward, I put my hand out to stop Jamal from going in. "Enough," I say, a little louder than I intended. "I've seen enough, okay?"

His eyes pierce into mine, quiet and frosty with anger he's been holding in all along, and then he pushes through the doors anyway.

Ancestors. "Jamal!" I hiss after him.

The ward holds more occupied beds, more machines with flickering lights, more grime-coated floors and walls with crumbling chips of paint. Jamal stops at the foot of a bed and peers down at the husk wasting away on the dirty sheets, a man who should be in his prime.

"Does he look like an angel to you?" he asks me without taking his gaze off the patient.

I stare, beginning to doubt he's still sane. "What?"

"That's what he might as well be. A faithful servant helping the afterlife dream. An angel."

He begins a slow walk down the row of beds. I follow.

"To be effectively immortal," he says, "Oloye stream their conscious selves in real time to remote backup servers. But the tech that does this—the ultraware, as they call it—has limits. Live long enough, and it begins to strain under too many decades of high-resolution memory. So what happens is, the Oloye go full digital. They retreat into their own private heaven, where they'll live until the day technology solves the memory problem, allowing them to return to the physical world."

He stops at another bed, tilting his head as he gazes at the anorexic figure sleeping there. "They call it the Abode. A computer network capable of hosting thousands of digitized minds. Probably one of the most advanced systems ever built, and yet, there is still some unidentified and, dare I say, ephemeral aspect of human consciousness that can't as yet be simulated on hardware. Actual human brains must be recruited to provide this element. A wetware-based processing unit, if you will." Jamal sweeps his gaze around the dismal ward before locking eyes with me. "A Hive."

Revulsion tightens its coils around me, my fingers curling into each other, forming fists. Why is Jamal showing me this?

"Officially, Hives are illegal," he goes on. "In practice, ZimbaTech pays a lot of money for the service. There are two other Hives in the Jondolos, each run by a different skelem. They put you inside one if you owe them a debt you can't pay, or if you're so desperate you're willing to indenture yourself for payment. Most people leave as shells of who they were when they came in. Half of them die within five years of their stay. Few live past ten years. And it's not just ZimbaTech. *Every* corporate state has its own Hives, its own Abode. An entire ecosystem feeding off the minds of people like this," Jamal says, gesturing at the hapless figure on the bed.

I hear a bubbling sound from somewhere nearby, a tube doing its work, perhaps. An unholy stench hits my nostrils, and I almost gag. *I need to get out of here.* "I think I've seen enough," I say.

Jamal regards me with muted frustration, but he's merciful enough to end the tour.

Relief courses through me when we return to the reception and leave the building through the main entrance. I almost break into a run.

"Everything in order, boss?" says the young woman who let us in.

"No complaints," Jamal tells her cheerily. "Carry on."

The rains have strengthened again, so I cover us with my umbrella.

"Are you disgusted?" Jamal asks me as soon as we put the women out of earshot.

"You know I am," I growl at him.

"Then what are you going to do about it?"

This is the crux of the matter, isn't it? This is why he brought me here. But what the hell does he expect from me? "I don't know what you want me to say."

He's already summoned our car. It whines as it lands where it left us, eddies of watery mist swirling beneath the ion thrusters. I take him to the passenger side, but instead of hopping in, he glares at me beneath the umbrella.

"Let's cut the bullshit, all right? I'm tired of feeling like I'm dragging you around against your will. I'm not your master. You don't have to listen to me. You could turn your back on me and walk away, and there's nothing I could do to stop it."

I open my mouth with a fierce protest, but he shushes me.

"No. I'm not having this. I know you want to stay out of some sense of loyalty the Custodians engineered into you—"

"Oh, fuck you."

"—but if you don't believe in what I'm doing, then what's the point? Why stick around? You've seen what this world stands for. The cybernetic corruption we were told about is *real.* You know I have to do something. But if you're going to help me, I'll need to believe that this is *our* cause, not mine alone."

The rains batter the fabric of the umbrella, making me feel even more cornered. I don't understand why Jamal is being like this. "Your cause is my cause, Jamal," I say, hoping it's what he wants to hear.

His eyes are wet. I don't know if it's because of the rain or if those are tears. "So you'll care only if I care, is that it?"

"What do you want me to say? That I *want* to help those people? I don't. I can't, because what if you decide to do nothing? Am I supposed to hold that against you?"

"Yes!" he shouts. "Exactly. Hold it against me. Have a conscience, for fuck's sake. Think for yourself."

"I don't work like that," I snap back. "I already have a cause. I don't have room for another one. I can give you advice, but ultimately—"

"Great!" Jamal says, cutting me off. "Then what's your advice? You saw those people in there. What do you advise me to do about it?"

"I advise you to be careful, whatever you decide," I say. "You want to go home? We go home. You want to go in and put a stop to what we just saw, I'll lead the charge. You don't lose my respect either way."

The wetness spills out of one eye. He shakes his head with an ironic laugh. "I don't know why I expected anything different. Ancestors forbid you ever become your own person with your own opinions."

"I can't change what I am, Jamal."

"Would you, given the chance?"

"I wouldn't take that chance," I answer bluntly.

"And that's the thing, isn't it? I can never be sure your loyalty is genuine, not something hard coded into you, and that somewhere deep inside you don't resent me for it. Would you even like me if you didn't have to, Hondo?"

I stare at him, shocked that he would even ask me such a thing. Is this why he wants me to share his cause? So he can be certain I'm with him because I want to be?

But why would he ever feel—

I freeze, a cold realization hitting me like a slap in the face. I'm such a fool.

I put a firm hand on his shoulder. "Jamal, you are and will always be the most important person in my life. That will never change. Yes, you annoy me sometimes, but I don't resent you, and I don't regret the bond between us. Do you understand?"

Jamal keeps watching me, looking through me like he's trying to spot any sign of deception, but I spoke honestly. "What if that's what they programmed you to feel?"

"Then it's a part of who I am," I reply. "And I like who I am. Don't you?"

He sniffs, wiping the corner of his eye. "I guess you're okay."

"I'm the best and you know it. Now what's the plan?"

He collects himself. "There's an ultraware data center where all three Hives connect to the Abode. It's here in the Jondolos. It'll be guarded, but we have everything we need to get inside."

Sounds dangerous, but I'm committed now. "Then what?" I ask.

Malice flashes across Jamal's face, his old self returning. He finally opens the door to the aerial car. "Then the fun begins."

While our car flies along the traffic lanes of the Jondolos in aimless circles, Jamal fills me in on his plan, showing me maps of the data center and the layers of security we'll have to penetrate to get to the servers within.

Turns out the facility is hidden beneath a disused electrical substation north of the island, in what is probably the city's oldest district. Most of the buildings in the area are old industrial properties that were condemned and left to rot many years ago.

Midnight is approaching when I finally land the car behind a vacant warehouse within sight of the substation. We get out of the car, and then we get ready for battle.

Despite myself, I suffer a thrill as I take stock of our gear.

The guns? Lightweight alloy and polymer, as sturdy as the best weapons we had in the Habitat and designed to fire various types of caseless ammunition. The tactical helmets? Both are equipped with non-intrusive true-to-vision displays and onboard software that can interface with the targeting modules on our guns. Our high-tech ballistic vests are interlocking slats of ultralight cermet that expand and adjust into chest plates with near-perfect fits. I wear mine over my sweater, Jamal over his suit vest. We both wear the same armored tactical gloves.

Jamal's main weapon will be the utility drone and his PCU, but he also carries a compact machine pistol on a shoulder belt just in case, along with two extra magazines of homing rounds. I choose a shotgun, but I also holster a heavy pistol in the sheath of my shoulder belt and carry twice as much ammunition as I intend to use.

Faces concealed beneath the opaque visors of our helmets, we stalk toward the substation. Jamal's drone, powered by two small ion thrusters, follows us quietly from above. Spherical, with a steel-blue coating, the drone has a coilgun mounted on its underside, visible by the telltale loops of metal surrounding the barrel. It'll probably have a low firing rate, but it's good to know there's an extra gun if we need it.

A fork of lightning cuts through the night, briefly etching the falling raindrops against the black sky. From this side of the bay the distant towers of the upper districts are columns of light crowned by the ZimbaTech spire. We stop when we get close enough to read the yellow reflective signage on the substation's fencing warning us to KEEP OUT.

For a supposedly disused place, the fencing is in rather good condition, unlike the mangled circuit breakers and rusted-out transformers enclosed within. While Jamal turns his attention to his PCU, my helmet follows the motion of my eye and zooms in on the small, flat-roofed concrete building inside the fence. It looks like it was built a century ago, but the double doors are reinforced steel.

"Are you ready?" Jamal says, his voice delivered to me through my helmet's comms.

I nod.

"Jamming firewall is now active," he says. "Beginning assault in three . . . two . . . one . . ."

A flash blooms in front of us as the drone melts a hole into the fence with a plasma round. My eyes would have been dazzled, but the helmet filters out the worst of it, keeping my sight clear. As soon as the glare dies down, I race for the newly opened entrance, Jamal a shadow behind me.

Alarms will be going off inside the facility. The security system is air gapped from the Nzuko, so there's nothing Jamal can do about it from this end. They'll know we are here and see us coming, and they'll be prepared, but what they won't do is use the Nzuko to call for outside help. That line of communication is currently being jammed by whatever clever program Jamal has deployed.

A pair of sentry guns rises from the roof of the building ahead of us. I expected them, so my gun is already loaded with EMP slugs. I fire two slugs before the guns can shoot at us; they are both equipped with electronic countermeasures that jam targeting systems, so I don't use any aim assist.

I don't need to. My aim is solid, and the two slugs detonate when they hit, releasing electromagnetic pulses that fry the electronics on the guns, rendering them useless.

"Sentry guns disabled," I say.

"Good work."

With the guns off-line, the drone can now safely approach the building. It zips over us, then descends, stopping to hover as it extends a limb and begins to cut through the metal doors with an intense laser beam.

I sense a single source of static on the other side, fearful and armed, ready to fire as soon as the doors open. Jamal said to avoid killing if I can, so while we wait, I draw my pistol from its holster and sling my shotgun across my back. If they work the way they're supposed to, the electroshock rounds I've loaded into the pistol should be nonlethal.

Off to the side, Jamal shakes his head at his PCU. "I still can't access the security system," he tells me. "I need to get closer to a terminal."

"There's one hostile inside. Stay out of the way until I deal with him."

"Got it."

The drone takes less than two minutes to do its job, making precise and targeted cuts to the doors without much input from Jamal. I don't barge in immediately; I know from the static on the other side that there's a gun aimed in my direction. I wait, listening.

We now know that the Custodians wore some kind of tech to hide their minds from our senses. What we felt as dead space was simply their tech doing its work. We grew into adults not knowing the full extent of what we were capable of. We thought it was normal that we could feel and mask ourselves from each other. We didn't know that we were weapons engineered by a secretive group of geneticists.

I know this now, and my senses have sharpened since that first day on the island.

The static on the other side falters; I can practically feel the gun trembling in the hand holding it. I move, kicking the doors open, then fire an electroshock round even before sighting the target.

The man inside doesn't get to fire his weapon. The round strikes his chest with enough force to bruise and knock him down, delivering an incapacitating shock. He spasms a few times on the floor before going still.

I know there's no one else in the immediate vicinity, but I go inside to check anyway. Red warning lights flash on the walls, and there's an alarm beeping out of the surveillance terminal near where the guard fell. Old electrical equipment takes up the rest of the square room.

"Target is down," I say. "You can come in."

Jamal doesn't waste time. I stand guard by the doorway while he gets to work at the terminal, gloved hands flying on the keyboard. After a minute, I begin to think that perhaps the security system is too robust for the mystery programs on his PCU to crack, but I'm proved wrong when the lights suddenly stop flashing and the alarm goes silent.

"I've gained access to the system," he informs me. "Locking out all other users. Canceling lockdown protocols. Taking control of sentry guns."

I move closer to the terminal, watching him tighten his grip on the facility with each keystroke. It all looks so easy, but I don't fault the people who designed the system. They couldn't have known that someone like Jamal existed and would one day cut through their security like a laser through a rusted pipe.

Suddenly the camera feeds on the screens change from views of the building's exterior to the brightly lit hallways of the facility beneath us. I count about twenty confused people on the screens, most of them dressed like regular office workers. A few others are in light tactical gear like the guard I just shot and have positioned themselves to defend a corridor facing the closed doors of an elevator.

The pocket handguns they're nervously pointing at the elevator tell me these guys aren't there to protect the facility from external threats but to police the employees. The true defenses are the high-powered sentry guns hidden in the ceilings in nearly every room and passage leading to the server floor.

Those same guns now unfold from their recesses in the ceilings and release short bursts. No one is hit, but everyone on the screen runs for cover. After the screams stop, Jamal patches himself through to the facility's public-address system.

"Sorry to drop by unannounced," he says. "But if you cooperate, everyone and everything will be just fine. First things first. You, the gentlemen in the elevator corridor. Lay down your weapons."

The men hesitate, so Jamal commands the sentry gun in the corridor to shoot out another burst of fire. The bullets hit the floor, making the men flinch away.

"Drop your weapons, gentlemen. I won't ask again."

This time they obey, lowering their pistols and lifting their empty palms.

"Excellent. Now, as you can see, I'm in control of your automated guns. In about sixty seconds, those guns will start firing on anyone who isn't inside the break room. This is not a drill. The timer starts now."

Jamal punctuates his message with another round of automated gunfire, and I'm surprised by how well his plan works. Almost everyone leaves whatever they were doing and flees for the break room, shoving each other through the door. *Almost* everyone; there's a technician on the server floor, where there are no guns. There's also a biometric security interlock barring the entrance to the floor, so he's probably decided he'll be safe if he stays put.

Meanwhile the rest of his colleagues make it into the break room on time, and Jamal rewards them by engaging the locks on the door.

"Thank you for your cooperation. Now please remain where you are. Don't try anything stupid, and in a few minutes, it'll be like I was never here." He disconnects from the announcement system, then does something that brings about the hum of working motors. "The elevator is on its way. We should have a clear path forward."

Seconds later the elevator emerges from the floor in the corner of the room, its gleaming silver walls exposing the lie this substation exists to conceal. While the drone stays behind to keep an eye on things on the surface, Jamal and I step into the elevator and descend into the facility.

My skin tingles as we step out into the elevator corridor. All five surrendered pistols are still on the floor. All sources of static but one are gathered in a single section of the facility. The sentry gun hanging from the corridor's ceiling could have already eviscerated us, but it remains inactive. Everything is as it should be, yet my heart won't stop racing.

I follow Jamal, our boots making echoes in the hallways. All that remains between us and the server floor is a security interlock. But just as we turn a corner, my instincts scream at me, and I reach forward to pull Jamal back.

"Jamal!"

A projectile ricochets off his helmet, striking me in the chest. He yelps, taking cover.

"I'm fine! I'm fine!" he shouts.

I've already exchanged my pistol for the shotgun. I take a brief peek around the corner, and a spray of bullets immediately peppers me, a few striking my helmet and making the display flicker. I retreat.

"What the hell is that?" Jamal squeals.

I ignore him, bracing myself, and this time when I duck out of cover, I fire four EMP slugs before I draw back. They detonate one after another, followed by silence.

After a few seconds, I risk a peek around the corner again. When I'm sure the danger has passed, I come out of hiding and head down the corridor, my gun still aimed. Jamal follows.

The three-wheeled mech that was firing at us from a barrel protruding from its round head is now releasing smoke and sparks from its internal machinery. There were mechs just like it in the Habitat, although this one is somewhat taller, coming up to our chests when we stop in front of it.

Jamal releases a curse. "Where the hell did this come from? There was nothing about a mech in the security blueprints."

I'm not surprised. I know from instruction and experience that security mechs are typically built to be autonomous, with no wireless modules so they can't be compromised. Programming or reprogramming requires direct access to their physical ports. I've also come to learn that this is why people on the surface don't like mechs so much, what with the universal fear of autonomous machines. This is the first security mech I've seen since I left the Habitat.

"We should move on," I say.

Jamal gets a grip on himself. "Yes. We've already wasted valuable time. This way."

He's already given us full access rights to the building, so the interlocking door system down the hall lets us through, and finally we enter the cooled interior of the server room. Rows of black cabinets with glass doors stretch down a floor as wide as a ship hangar. Lights inside the cabinets suffuse the area with an ambient blue light. The hum of powerful air conditioners almost sounds like ion drives at low thrust.

I home in on the fearful source of static hiding among the cabinets. The poor guy is not making a sound. He can hear the echo of my footsteps—I'm not even trying to conceal my approach. I really shouldn't know he's there, but to my senses his fear is a beacon that leads me right to where he's crouched against a server rack, trembling.

When he sees me, his feverish eyes shine at me with terror. "Please!"

I raise my pistol. "This is going to hurt," I say and shoot him in the chest.

The electroshock round instantly stuns and knocks him out. Wetness spreads from his groin as he pisses himself. He'll have a bruise or maybe a cracked rib when he wakes up, but at least he'll be alive.

"Was that necessary?" Jamal says behind me.

"Get to work," I tell him.

He shakes his head, but he gets to the business of why we are here.

The technician I just shot was using a wheeled cart with a dedicated console for accessing server hardware. While Jamal commandeers the cart and connects it to a nearby server rack, I do a quick patrol of the area to make sure there aren't any more surprises.

That mech should teach me. I could seriously punch myself in the face. As capable as Jamal may seem at times, I should know that he can and will get himself killed unless I keep my eyes open. What if his helmet had failed? What if the mech had been more powerful? Where would I even be right now?

I return to him when I'm satisfied we're alone, finding him working on the console on the cart. He's connected a data stick to one of the ports, using whatever he loaded onto it to complete his infiltration of the network. The lines of code on the console's screen are gibberish to me, but he told me he'd be installing rootkits and opening a number of back doors.

"So this is the Abode?" I ask, peering into one of the cabinets. From afar the machines inside look like typical servers, but now I glimpse squares of glass stacked horizontally in some kind of illuminated gel. Must be ultraware. "Are there dead minds in these machines?"

"No," Jamal says absently. "This is just the control center of the Hives. A confluence, if you will. The true Abode is running on a server farm hidden outside the city."

Probably guarded like the gates of hell, I think. "How long is this going to take?"

"Not long. I should be done in a minute." Abruptly Jamal's mobile pings in his pocket. He pulls it out and glances at the screen, then chuckles as he pockets the mobile again, getting back to work. "Adaolisa. Nice of you to join us."

I don't know how, but my helmet displays an augmented hologram of her standing with her arms crossed, peering at Jamal with disapproval. Brass rings cascade down her neck like she's a royal from New KwaNdebele. The heels of her shoes could gouge out a man's eye. These days I often wonder how it wasn't obvious to everyone in the Habitat who was the true power behind the chair. Or maybe it's obvious to me now that she wears her power out in the open.

"What the hell do you think you're doing?" she demands.

"Nothing much," Jamal says as he continues working on the console. "We're just taking a walk. Was there something you needed?"

"Jamal, if you destroy the Abode—"

"Destroy it?" Jamal interrupts. "Now why would I do that? They'd just build another one. It's the idea itself that needs to be challenged."

"Reckless and divisive acts like this will only entrench political positions. You'll be causing more problems than you solve."

Jamal pauses, giving her a long stare. "You know, Adaolisa, you're making me wonder whose side you're on. The people or the Oloye? You can't serve both."

"Stop this. Or I won't protect you from the consequences."

I've been silent all along, but she gives me a searing gaze, like this whole thing is my fault, then disconnects, pixelating out of my helmet's display.

"I thought you said she couldn't spy on us," I complain to Jamal.

"She can't. She must have noticed I was jamming comms in the Nzuko and figured out where I was." Finally he pulls out his data stick and shuts down the console. "We're done here. Let's get the hell out before the place is crawling with cops."

"You think she called the cops on us?" I ask.

His helmet shimmers as he gazes at me. "She *is* the cops, Hondo. Now come on."

Chapter 12: Nandipa

When an abandoned and normally uninteresting electrical substation in the sketchiest neighborhood of the Jondolos suddenly becomes host to the firepower of a military base, a lot of people are going to notice.

It's barely morning, but crowds have gathered from everywhere to investigate; by the press of static all around me, I could almost believe half the island's population is here.

A large police helo makes a low pass in the cloudy skies above us, red and blue lights strobing on either side of its fuselage. More lights flash at us ahead, coming from the parked police vehicles and holographic **Do Not Cross** lines that have been placed to keep the crowds at least a block away from the substation.

When we get to the perimeter line, following Marcel, Adaolisa and I are allowed through without question on account of our statuses as his secretaries. In her white satin dress, zebra-striped head wrap, and platinum jewelry, Adaolisa cuts a refined contrast to my close-fitting black denims, boots, and leather jacket. Fitting styles for both our personalities but also chosen for effect; when we stand next to Marcel, she makes him look elegant, wiser, and mature, and I make him look strong willed and assertive, not a man to be trifled with.

An illusion, perhaps, but one Adaolisa is more than happy to live with.

Another perimeter has been set closer to the substation's fence, this one manned by helmeted soldiers all holding rifles in ready positions. Little silver pins shaped like spinning wheels are attached to the collars of their midnight-blue armored uniforms, marking them as soldiers of the Kolovrat. As we draw nearer, one of the soldiers raises a gloved palm in indication that we should stop.

"Director Muzinga, only you have clearance to enter the facility. Your assistants must wait here."

Behind the soldier, Criminal Investigation Department agents in their green jackets are crawling all over the crime scene. Seeing them, Marcel becomes instantly indignant. "This was a cyberattack on ZimbaTech soil. Internal Security has as much jurisdiction here as the CID."

"Our orders came directly from the Board, sir," the soldier says, not budging. "If you have a complaint, take it up with them."

Damn it. I know Adaolisa desperately wants to get inside, but short of fighting our way in, there's no way we'll be getting past these soldiers. All I have is a small personal defense weapon clipped to my hip. And these guys aren't exactly average grunts.

Mostly descended from Slavic military contractors who were operating in the cluster when the Artemis lockdown went into effect, the Kolovrat are elite mercenaries known for their incorruptibility and political disinterest; exactly the kind of reputation that makes them desirable to the boards of corporate city-states as bodyguards or personal militaries. They are loyal and answer only to the people who pay them.

The ambient static coming off them is fainter than usual, and still as a windless night. I'm pretty sure they received some kind of rigorous psychological training. If ZimbaTech's Board has sent them here, they must be really spooked.

"But I need my assistants!" Marcel argues.

"It's all right, Director," Adaolisa says. "We'll wait for you here."

Marcel frowns, clearly unhappy. "This is bullshit."

Don't push your luck, you fool, I think. *You should be grateful they're even letting you in.*

His fortunes have certainly changed over the last several weeks. After he took credit for capturing the Pest, the city's Board gave him the highest office at Int-Sec HQ. It also didn't hurt when Adaolisa dropped a string of more newsworthy arrests into his lap, helping him raise the agency's profile and importance. Unsurprisingly, it has all gone to his head.

He concedes, in the end, entering the substation's perimeter on his own. Adaolisa and I are ordered to step back from the barricade; we obey, though we remain in sight of the door to the square building inside the fence.

Next to me, I can feel Adaolisa thrumming with anxiety. "If I could only get inside," she mutters quietly. "If I could access the servers, I might be able to find out what Jamal did."

We might have tried simply asking him what he did, but the boys didn't return to the apartment last night, and all attempts to reach them have failed. A cold suspicion inside my gut tells me they might not ever return. I don't know why I should feel betrayed by this.

"Are you sure you can't reach the servers from the Nzuko?" I ask.

Adaolisa shakes her head minutely. "The Abode is ultraware. It runs on a separate network with different protocols, and connections to the Nzuko can only be initiated from the inside. That's why Jamal needed physical access to the servers. If I can get inside, too, I might be able to close whatever doors he opened for himself."

We watch Marcel exchange tepid greetings with the CID officer in charge of the crime scene.

"I don't think that's going to happen," I remark.

"You're right, I'm afraid." Adaolisa sighs. "All we can do now is damage control."

The distinctly melodic static of another Oloye draws my attention to the side. When I look, I see an imposing woman being let through the police line along with an entourage of suited platinum-tier attendants trailing behind her. I surreptitiously nudge Adaolisa with my elbow and point.

That's none other than Director Abuk Dieng, head of the CID. It's her people already working inside the substation, but she's only just arriving. I guess being effectively immortal means you don't have to rush for anything.

She's really quite the sight, all angles like she was carved from diamond: high cheekbones, a box cut for her Afro, wide shoulder pads on her ash-gray suit, eye shadow that emphasizes the wicked tilt of her brows. She's already unusually tall, but the heels of her black stilettos put her a head over her entourage. When she spots us, the metal weave beneath her dark complexion shimmers as she grins like a shark sighting prey.

Uh-oh. Looks like she's coming over.

"Ah. The young off-world royals I've heard so much about. Whatever are you doing here?"

I often wonder if we weren't perhaps a little too good at selling our new identities. Our reputations have certainly spread farther than I'd like.

"Director Dieng," Adaolisa says, polite, fearless. "An honor to meet you. We're waiting for Director Muzinga. He's inside, taking a look at the crime scene."

Dieng purses her red lips, and one of her eyebrows climbs even higher as she gives the silent Kolovrat soldiers a sidelong glance. "He was allowed through, was he? Getting too big for his shoes, that boy." Her gaze returns to us. "I suppose I have you to thank for that. To think all that spirit was hiding under the surface, and all he needed was a pair of pretty young things to bat their eyelashes at him." She takes a few steps closer to us, her shark grin returning. "A word of advice. Make the best of your time clinging to his coattails. Mortal beauty is fleeting, but diamond eyes are forever, and often too easy to distract."

I offer no reaction. Adaolisa gives none either. "We'll keep that in mind, Director," she calmly says.

Dieng smiles again, though her static ticks up slightly with annoyance.

I wait until she's gone beyond the perimeter with her entourage before speaking again. "Maybe we should have let her think she intimidates us."

"We would have only emboldened her," Adaolisa says coolly. "Don't worry. She can be dealt with if she becomes a nuisance."

Marcel is gone for about thirty minutes. He comes back tugging nervously at the lapels of his wine-colored suit.

"There's not much to go on," he tells us. "There were two eyewitnesses; both saw a lone gunman before he shot them with stun rounds. They didn't see his face. Everyone else heard his voice when he ordered them to lock themselves in the break room after taking control of the turrets. There was also a security mech, but its hardware got fried. It's like the attackers were ghosts."

They were certainly clinical, I think. *How long had they been planning this?*

"The only thing we know for certain is that the electroshock rounds and EMP shells the attackers used were of SalisuCorp origin," Marcel says. "So was the pulsed laser beam that cut through the doors and the plasma shot that tore a hole in the fence. Could be that SalisuCorp is declaring war on us."

"Let's not jump to conclusions," Adaolisa advises. "This could be exactly what the attackers want us to think."

"Of course," he says. "So what now? The Board wants to meet with me and the other directors, and they expect us to be on top of things. What am I supposed to say?"

"Why don't we get back to HQ?" Adaolisa suggests. "We can talk more on the way."

"Yes. Excellent idea." Marcel grimaces as he glances at his decrepit surroundings. "This place smells bad anyway."

The three of us make our way back to our aerial transport, an armored Int-Sec cruiser we left on the other side of the police line. The doors slide up for us; a young Int-Sec agent and Marcel's designated driver was dozing at the wheel, but he jolts awake as we file into the passenger cabin.

"Take us back to HQ, Agent Sambo," Marcel tells him. "We're done here."

"Of course, sir."

I settle down on the rear-facing seat across from Adaolisa while Marcel takes the seat next to hers. The cruiser has barely lifted off the ground when Marcel starts grumbling.

"I still can't believe they kept you outside while letting Dieng's idiots roll all over the crime scene. *We're* the ones who noticed something and raised the alarm. No. I won't abide by it. Absolutely not. But don't worry. When we find the people who did this and bring them in ourselves, everyone will see just how much better we are . . ."

I hate it when Marcel whines like this, so I zone out, looking out the window. We rise into a traffic lane taking us through the island's commercial district. When the massive Citizen Affairs building where we bought our identities races by, I'm suddenly reminded of Zandi, the curious woman who helped us.

She's probably halfway back to New KwaNdebele by now. I've heard trips through short-range jump gates take only hours, but the gates are so far out from the inner solar system it takes months just to reach them.

Sitting in this vehicle, listening to Marcel prattle on while trying to ignore the growing worry inside the pit of my stomach, I begin to wonder if the four of us didn't make a mistake by deciding to live on this planet. Forget about Counselor and whoever attacked the Habitat. Forget about the Oloye and their cybernetic tyranny. Maybe we should have bought passage on Zandi's ship and left it all behind.

". . . we need to prove that this case should be ours," Marcel says. "So what are you thinking? You two girls are like my talismans. So full of ideas. Hit me with them."

I don't even get the chance to ignore him. I'm jerked violently in my seat like we just hit something, and then the cruiser tilts to the side, throwing me against the door. My stomach drops as we pitch downward, the ion drives coughing and sputtering dangerously.

"We're under attack!" Sambo shouts. "What the hell? There's a gunship firing at us!"

I was far away, but now I'm suddenly in the present, the details of our predicament coming together with too much clarity. The static all around me has gone up several notches, people in the vicinity reacting to what they are seeing, but I immediately latch on to a particular source in a vehicle keeping pace with us.

The hostility in the static is unmistakable, a naked desire to destroy everyone in this cruiser. I even sense fingers on a trigger right before bullets pepper the roof of our armored vehicle.

"Get us out of here!" I shout.

"I'm trying," Sambo shouts back. "The drives aren't responding. Shit, there's another gunship ahead. What the hell is going on?"

Marcel screams something. Adaolisa is quiet, but her fear is a physical thing to me, flooding my bloodstream with stimulants, forcing me to act. I claw my way between the two rear-facing seats and into the cockpit.

"Move over," I tell the driver.

He frowns, but something in my tone gets him to obey. I take the controls while he shifts over to the passenger seat.

We've lost so much altitude we're close enough to the crowded streets to see confused faces looking up at us. The black-and-silver gunship helos attacking us keep firing, showing no regard for collateral damage and causing panic on the ground.

Just as I careen around a corner, a missile explodes against the rear of the cruiser with a bang, jolting us like rag dolls. I struggle to keep us from crashing into the side of a building.

"What the fuck!" Marcel shouts. "What the hell!"

"We won't make it!" mutters Sambo.

Like hell we won't. I go full throttle, pushing the damaged drives as hard as they'll let me. We won't last much longer out in the open, so I search for shelter, anything to get us some cover. As soon as I spot the dark opening to an underground parking lot, I dive for it and duck inside just in time for a missile to strike the upper lip of the entrance.

We last only a few seconds before we crash-land onto the concrete driveway, skidding with a loud racket and coming to a stop when the front end of the cruiser strikes a pillar.

"Everyone out, now."

As we crawl out of the cruiser, I draw my personal defense weapon, extending the stock from its collapsed configuration. It's an Int-Sec-issued diamond-tier firearm with the punch and accuracy of a rifle in a frame as light and compact as a small submachine gun—good enough for deterring petty criminals, but I didn't think I'd need something heavier in the presence of an Oloye.

Seriously, who the hell is trying to kill an Oloye?

"What the hell was that?" Marcel screeches. "Did they not know I was on board?"

"They seemed very deliberate," Adaolisa says tensely. "And if they're serious about eliminating us, they'll be here soon."

She's right. I can already feel a net closing in on us. Whoever these people are, they want us dead.

Sambo has a pistol, but his static is so ramped up his grip on the weapon is tenuous. I wouldn't be surprised if he's never fired it before. After all, his navy-blue uniform was little more than a glorified costume before Adaolisa walked into Int-Sec HQ.

I'm on my own then.

The lighting is poor down here. Rows of parked vehicles stretch away from us and vanish into the shadows. A man saw us crashing and is wandering over to investigate. I look past him, fixing on the foot of a staircase leading up. Three hostiles are running down from the surface level.

"Everyone, hide," I hiss, pointing behind a parked red four-seater. While they obey, I take cover behind a pillar and wait.

"Hello?" says the man who saw us. "Do you need help?"

Run away, you idiot, I think.

The hostiles arrive and immediately open fire on the crashed cruiser. Finally getting that he shouldn't be here, the man cries fearfully and runs, and he's lucky the hostiles are too preoccupied to notice.

Rifle fire pummels the armored cruiser so loudly I think I'll go deaf if this continues for much longer. What the hell do they think they're accomplishing?

Doesn't matter. I let their static guide my aim as I come out of cover.

All three women shooting at the cruiser have silver bionic prostheses covering their necks and lower chins. By the hateful snarls on their faces, I'd almost believe I'd done something to personally offend them.

My weapon is set to burst fire; I pull the trigger three times, firing consecutive bursts of four tungsten armor-piercing rounds.

The rifles immediately go silent, three bodies dropping to the ground. I'm not in the headspace to care about it, not right now. These three women were only the first arrivals of a squad closing in on us.

"We have to get out of here," I say.

Marcel and Sambo poke their heads from behind the red car, eyebrows drawing apart when they see the bodies.

"Those are Silvernecks!" Sambo exclaims. "Why would they attack us?"

"Are they dead?" Marcel asks.

I look toward the stairwell. There'll be more people here soon, I can feel it, but there's a gap in the encroaching net we might be able to use to escape. "Everyone, to the stairs."

"Wait."

I frown while Adaolisa takes out her PCU from her handbag. Her eyes narrow with focus as she scans the parked vehicles around us; then she points at an old gray van some several rows away. "That one."

She sets off for it at a fast walk without explaining herself.

I grit my teeth and follow at her heels. "Ada, my dear, what the hell are you doing? We need to get out of here."

"Yes, Adaolisa, we need to leave," Marcel says nervously, him and Sambo coming up behind me.

"Let's be smart about this, okay?" She's doing something on her device—what, I could only guess. When we reach the van, she stops and keeps tapping on the screen of her PCU.

Hostiles are about to reach the stairwell upstairs. More will be pouring in through the parking lot entrance. That gap I sensed has closed.

I hold my gun, waiting. I came with a full magazine, but I don't think I'll be able to shoot our way out of this. "Ada . . ."

"Hang on," she says. "Almost there."

"By the ancestors, what *are* you doing?"

Abruptly a clicking sound echoes across the floor, coming from every direction. "There. Get in, and keep your heads down."

I don't stop to think; I simply open the door and usher everyone inside, then roll the door closed behind me.

The dark, windowless interior has no seats and smells like grease. Old tools and toolboxes litter the floor. We all crouch down so our heads can't be seen should someone walk past the front of the vehicle.

It's only in such close quarters that I catch a whiff of piss and realize Marcel has wet himself.

"Now what?" Sambo whispers. "We hide in here until they go away?"

"No. We leave in this vehicle," Adaolisa tells us.

She's afraid but also calm, so she believes her plan will work. But surely this can't be the plan, can it? "Those gunships are still out there," I reply. "They'll shoot down anything they see coming out."

"Not if everything goes out at the same time," she says.

A scream of rage comes from someone outside; looks like the hostiles have discovered their dead comrades. If it wasn't personal before, it will be now.

"Everyone, don't panic," Adaolisa whispers, and then our van turns itself on.

For a split second I worry she's drawn attention to us, but the static from the people outside dulls with confusion, only to ramp up with alarm. I risk taking a peek through the windshield and see that it's not just our vehicle acting strangely; the whole parking lot has come alive. Our van is just one of many vehicles lifting off the ground and easing its way out of its bay.

As the vehicles begin to zip for the entrance in fast but orderly lines, we hear shouts and gunfire, our hunters shooting blindly into the automated convoy. Marcel covers his mouth when a bullet makes a hole not far from his head, but soon sunlight floods through the windshield as we exit the parking lot, and then we're out.

By now the two gunships lurking above the street have already given up on firing on the vehicles. It would be a waste of ammunition anyway. The vehicles scatter in almost every direction as they leave, and we're no more conspicuous than the others as we lift into an aerial traffic lane bound for the upper districts.

Only once we're flying across the bay do we release a collective sigh of relief. At least, Adaolisa, Sambo, and I do. Marcel is hyperventilating, perhaps suffering a belated panic attack.

Adaolisa touches his back with a comforting hand. "Slow, deep breaths, Marcel, come on. There. We're safe now. You're all right."

"I . . . I'm fine," he manages to say between breaths.

I'm only just coming down from an adrenaline high myself, so I sympathize.

What the hell just happened?

Sambo suddenly curses like he isn't in the presence of an Oloye. His eyes have glazed over behind his contacts. "Turn on your news feeds, everyone. The Silvernecks have declared war on the government. That's why they attacked us!"

Adaolisa must have already figured this out considering her complete lack of surprise. The barely masked annoyance stabbing out of her like sharpened knives immediately answers my unasked question: *Yes, Jamal had everything to do with this.* I use my mobile to find out what's going on.

The government must be failing to suppress the story, because it's all over the Nzuko. Files—video, audio, documents—proving a conspiracy by the government to stoke animosity between the skelems. I skim one of the most circulated articles on the subject and find myself oscillating between a greater disgust for this city and anger at Jamal for almost getting us killed.

"Last year the Silverneck boss lost her daughter to a shoot-out with a Goldblood," I report. "Or so everyone thought. Turns out the real killer was a freelancer hired by the CID to frame the Goldbloods, and that this wasn't the first such plot hatched by the government to pit the skelems against each other. They've been doing it for decades."

Sambo's eyes remain vacant behind his contacts. "This . . . can't be true, can it?"

"The skelems are convinced," I reply. "What matters now is how the government responds. If they play this wrong, there'll be a lot more blood before it's over."

Marcel gasps, his breaths becoming shallow again. Perhaps I should have chosen my words more carefully.

"You need to collect yourself, Director," Adaolisa says in a gentle voice, rubbing his back in soothing circles. "Your meeting with the Board is even more important now. The city is under attack." To no avail. Shaking her head, she reaches for her PCU and begins to tap on the screen. "He cannot miss that meeting, Nandipa. We'll take him home and get him cleaned up."

The van begins to descend, banking into a traffic lane heading in the direction of our apartment.

"Understood," I say, then glance at Sambo, who's still preoccupied with the augmented news streams of the Nzuko. "What about him?"

"Agent Sambo," Adaolisa says, drawing his attention.

He blinks as he comes back to reality. "Yes, madam?"

"The director needs to prepare for an important meeting, so we'll be taking him to our apartment. After we drop off, take the van and report back to HQ. To anyone who asks, we survived by stealing an unlocked vehicle, and you drove us out of danger. Do not reveal the specifics of how we escaped, understood? You are now a member of the director's inner circle; you cannot compromise his secrets."

Any questions Sambo had about what happened in the parking lot dissolve away in a bright burst of static. He licks his lips, eyes shining with eagerness to prove himself. "Don't you worry, madam. The director's secrets are safe with me."

"He'll be very grateful."

"I'll earn his trust, madam, and yours too."

Well. That's one potential problem sorted out, I guess.

A minute later, we touch down on the landing pad outside our apartment and guide a disoriented Marcel out of the van. Sambo departs for HQ with another promise to be discreet, and then we head inside, finding the apartment quiet and empty.

I trail behind Adaolisa as she takes Marcel upstairs to the boys' bedroom. I lean against a wall and watch her herd him into the shower, telling him to get cleaned and she'll lay out fresh clothes for him on the bed.

She comes back out, closing the door behind her, and for a moment she stands there like she's trying to summon her last reserves of patience and tranquility. Besides the grease stains she collected from the van, she looks to have already gotten over the attack. But I can sense the slight tremor in her hands.

"Are you all right?" I ask, concerned.

She breathes in, breathes out. "I will be once we put out the fire Jamal has started."

Composure restored, she makes for the walk-in closet to find Marcel something to wear. The clothes there should fit him, since he and the boys share similar tall and slender builds. I feel a little weird about it, though.

Inside the closet, Adaolisa considers a white three-piece suit I've never seen Jamal wear. "We were lucky, all things considered," she mutters. "I doubt Marcel was the only government official who was attacked today. I think this will do." Satisfied, she takes the suit to the bed. "Now for some underwear."

Yep. This isn't weird at all. "I'll go check the news," I say, inching toward the door.

Adaolisa is already rummaging through the drawers in the closet. "You go on ahead. I'll need to get cleaned up and changed myself."

Downstairs, I fish out my mobile from my jacket and try to ping Hondo. He doesn't answer. I annoy myself by suffering a twinge of worry. His Prime almost got us killed today. If anything I should be furious.

I swipe the comm interface away from the screen to check on the news feeds again, expecting to hear more about the skelem attacks. But something else is causing commotion in the Nzuko.

With a frown, I move to sit down on a couch, linking my mobile to my contacts and opening an augmented reality stream so I can see what the fuss is about.

And when I do see, my blood turns to liquid frost in my veins.

A grid of twenty faces hovers in front of me, and above them are these words:

Do you think it's fair that these people get to live forever? Here are their sins. Look, read, judge for yourselves, and then decide their fates.

My heart racing, I select the face of a man with a square jaw and silver stubble. He looks fatherly, or at least, he has the type of face I could easily imagine my father having, if I had a father.

I almost immediately reconsider that thought when I find myself watching a recording he apparently made as he was raping an unconscious girl. I swipe the video out of my sight only to be confronted with another one. And another. Then another. I come out to the directory and see that there are at least a hundred such recordings, each with a different victim.

Horrified and disgusted, I swipe his face away. The videos disappear, but his portrait returns, along with these words:

Adam Zimba. Unrepentant defiler of children. Do you think he should live forever while the rest of us die? You decide. Voting ends in thirteen minutes.

There's an interactive beneath the words, a simple choice between *Yes, he should live* and *No, he should not live*. Over four hundred thousand people have already voted, and I can see that number ticking up by the second.

I stare at the *No* option for a long minute, wondering what will happen if the public condemns him.

Ultimately I decide against it and return to the grid of faces. Numbing myself, I browse through the sins of the people those faces belong to. A mother who knew her son was a serial murderer but paid CID officers to cover up his crimes. An executive who knew a food product was tainted but chose to sell it anyway, resulting in the deaths of hundreds.

Abusers. Rapists. Murderers. Their sins laid bare for people to see and judge.

And I *do* want to judge. Ancestors, I want nothing more than to see those people denied eternity; no one deserves it less. But this is Jamal's plot. I can't let myself have anything to do with it.

I turn off the stream and get up, deciding to send Hondo a message. Instead of giving voice to it, I type my words out on the screen.

N: We got shot at in the Jondolos because of the war you started. We could have died.

I'm about to pocket my mobile when it pings with a response.

H: I'm sorry. We didn't plan for you to be attacked. Are you all right?

Relief, then anger. I begin to type out a furious response; thankfully, I come to my senses and start again.

N: Fine. Where are you? And what are you doing with the Abode?

H: Can't talk right now. Can we meet later? I'll send you time and location.

I think about it. Something tells me he means for us to meet alone, without our Primes. Is that wise?

N: I'll let you know.

H: Okay.

Adaolisa's silver heels drum on the stairs as she comes down. She's changed into a strapless black gown, long gloves of black lace, simple silver chokers, and an ankara turban with black and silver patterns—a blend of corporate and Africana that makes her look simultaneously cutthroat and refined. I'm guessing she intends to meet the Board with Marcel.

"Have you seen what's happening?" I ask her. "There's a vote in the Nzuko to decide who gets to stay in the Abode."

"I'm aware." Adaolisa sighs. "Can't say I'm surprised. You can always trust Jamal to choose the most dramatic course of action." She walks to gaze at herself in the dining room's full-length mirror. "How do I look?"

Like a ruthless platinum executive with the cultured temperament of an academic. "Great," I say. "You always do." I stare at her for a beat. "And you don't seem bothered at all by what's happening."

She turns to the side, still looking at herself in the mirror. "Perhaps it's for the best. If the Board sees exactly what's at stake for them, they'll be less likely to underestimate the threat."

And therefore more receptive to your suggestions, I work out. *But why help them in the first place? Why not let Jamal burn them all to the ground? What is it you see that I don't?*

Before I can ask, we hear Marcel coming down the stairs in Jamal's dress shoes. The white suit seems to fit him well enough, though both vest and jacket are unbuttoned, the patterned silk scarf is draped carelessly around his neck, and the look on his face is utter misery. Halfway down, he bends his knees and sits down on the steps, peering at us with rheumy eyes.

"Whose clothes are these?" he asks, voice hoarse like he's been crying.

"Our brother's," Adaolisa tells him. "He's out of town right now, but he won't mind us helping a friend."

"I see." Marcel lowers his eyes, blinking hard. "Adaolisa, I can't do this. I can't meet the Board. Not in my condition. Did you see? People are being deleted from the Abode."

I check my mobile, and he's right. All twenty faces from the grid are now grayed out and overlaid with red diagonal crosses. The voting tallies have also been released; over 98 percent of the million or so who voted condemned Adam Zimba as unworthy of the Abode. Every other Oloye went down with similar margins.

And now there's a second grid of faces with active timers, another twenty people for the public to judge. I have no illusions about what will be decided. The people of ZimbaTech have tasted blood, and they will want more.

"We don't know if this is real," I say. "Maybe it's fake. A hoax to scare people."

"It's real," Marcel says with a choked cry. "One of the women on the list was my great-aunt. She didn't like me very much, but I could reach her if I wanted to. I can't reach her anymore. She's gone." Marcel pulls the scarf off his neck with a visibly trembling hand. "Oh God. What if they delete everyone else? Did you see the votes? Everyone hates us, Adaolisa."

"We can still stop this from happening," she pleads with him. "And you don't have to be in the Boardroom in person. We can join the meeting from your office. But you have to advise them, or they might not make the right decisions."

"I can't," Marcel says, shaking his head. "But maybe you can."

She considers him. "What do you mean?"

"Speak to them on my behalf," he says. "Tell them I'm sick, or that I'm recovering after the attack. I'll even give you my Mark." He closes his eyes briefly, and I sense something transpiring within his static. "There. It'll let everyone know you speak with my authority."

Using my mobile, I let the Nzuko into my contacts. Adaolisa has her privacy filter on, but since we are friends on the network, I can see past the filter to the diamond icon now attached to her name. Focusing on the icon brings up a virtual certificate confirming that she is indeed acting on Marcel's behalf and with his authority.

She looks at him doubtfully. "Marcel . . . are you sure?"

"Yes," he says. "I just want to go home and lie down on my bed."

"You may not be safe there," I say. "If the skelems are targeting high-ranking officials, they may attack your home."

Marcel's eyes become even more watery. "Shit. You're right. Dear God, you're right."

"You can stay here for now, Marcel," Adaolisa offers. "No one knows we live here, and I can restrict access rights to the landing pad. You'll be safe."

He blinks tears from his eyes. "You don't mind?"

"Not at all. And if you need to rest, the bed upstairs is available."

"Thank you."

Guilt moves me at his heartfelt sincerity. I may not like the rest of his kind, but I don't think he deserves to be afraid for his life.

Adaolisa glances at the clock on the wall. "We have to leave soon if we'll make it to the meeting."

"I've summoned my car," Marcel tells us, standing up. "You can use it since I'm no longer going home." He starts walking back up the stairs. "I think I need to lie down. Let me know how the meeting goes."

Adaolisa decides her introduction to the Board will take place from the comfort and safety of Marcel's office at Int-Sec HQ. In the car on our way there, I watch her until she notices.

"What?"

"You knew, didn't you?" I say. "That he'd ask you to take over."

She exhales, looking out the window. "This was always the plan, my love. I just didn't know it would happen so soon. You disapprove?"

"It's not that. I'd just hoped . . ." *How to say this? What am I even trying to say?* "I'd hoped we'd left such games back in the Habitat."

"I know," she says quietly. "But this is the peaceful alternative." She turns her head to face me, her eyes boring into mine. "You have a question. Ask it."

I almost demur, but I think better of it. "Why help them, Ada? The Oloye are tyrants. And some of them are really evil. Have you seen the stuff Jamal put up?"

She smiles, not unkindly, but there's no humor in her gaze. "My love, even if the Oloye fell today, there'd be a new tyrant ruling ZimbaTech within the year. Do you know why?"

"Why?" I oblige her.

"Because tyranny isn't just an individual or a group of individuals. It's a culture. It's endemic. A system whose roots of complacency, corruption, and hopelessness extend across every level of society. The faces of the tyrants themselves are almost always arbitrary; remove one, and another will rise to take their place."

"So . . . keep the Oloye as tyrants?"

"Of course not. But the culture must change. People must first be convinced that freedom is not only worth having but worth fighting for, because ultimately, a freedom won by the people is a freedom they won't easily give up, and that's how you defeat tyranny. But what Jamal is doing? It's terrorism, Nandipa, and terrorism only crystallizes resistance to change."

The Int-Sec HQ building appears ahead of us, and we descend toward its highest landing pad. Shaped like a glass bullet, the building sits on a narrow platinum-tier island in a major tidal waterway. The south-facing promenades of the island, lined with the city's premier jazz clubs, look toward the ZimbaTech spire and the rest of the diamond quarter.

Since we're Int-Sec employees, everyone else who works here sees right through our privacy filters. The Int-Sec police officers guarding the entrance from the landing pad greet Adaolisa like she's an Oloye. Int-Sec agents and pen pushers part for us as we walk through the halls. No one stops us when we enter Marcel's large office, and no one comes to ask questions when I close the doors behind us.

The office looks southward and boasts a commanding view of the ZimbaTech skyline. Adaolisa seems perfectly at home as she settles down at the desk, though she gives the chromatic lights and industrial accents a passing glance—I guess a few things will be changing around here soon.

The appointed hour is near, so she fires up the holographic cameras in the room and requests a connection to the Board. On the surface she appears cool and collected, but she doesn't mask the mild current of anxiety running through her.

"Are you ready?" I ask her.

She smiles to reassure me. "I'm always ready, my love."

I lean against the wall, out of view of the cameras, but Adaolisa connects us both to the call so that I can watch from out of sight. My lenses cloud over for a disorienting spell, completely overriding my vision; then they clear up, and I find myself standing inside the city's Boardroom, a chamber so high above the ground there's a layer of clouds outside the pearly windows.

The ten members of the Board sit like judges on the same side of an elevated table, chiseled silhouettes in expensive suits and gowns. Their faces are shadowed so that their features are indistinct, and from where they sit, they look down on the smaller table where Adaolisa has appeared along with five other people.

I recognize the dreadlocked woman to her left as a high-ranking officer of the CID, but the others are strangers, and as they are holograms, I have no direct insight into their minds. They look nervous, though, blinking rapidly or staring fixedly or tapping their fingers against the table.

The Board tortures them with an extended silence until finally a central figure speaks. "I'm confused," says the figure, her voice low and lordly. "The Board requested a meeting with the people responsible for the defense of this city—people we selected ourselves because we knew and trusted them. So why do we now find ourselves in the company of strangers? What is the meaning of this?"

Adaolisa exchanges looks with the others. The dreadlocked woman clears her throat and speaks first. "Madam Chair, I'm sorry to report that Director Abuk Dieng and her party were attacked in the Jondolos about an hour ago. They didn't make it. The director is currently being decanted into a new body as we speak, but she won't be directly available for at least the next two weeks."

I look up to the Board to see how they react. Their faces remain in shadow, their postures serenely self-possessed. How I wish I were in that room so I could sense their static.

"The police commissioner?" says the central figure on the high table, who apparently is the city's executive chair herself.

A woman in a police uniform seated to Adaolisa's right answers without looking up from the floor. "Commissioner Domingos was attacked and killed as he left his home earlier this morning. The Board will have to choose a replacement for him soon."

If I remember correctly, the commissioner was not Oloye, so in his case, dead means dead.

The two men representing the Intelligence Service and Defense Force respectively give similar reports: the leaders of their organizations were ambushed and assassinated by skelem enforcers earlier this morning. Both were Oloye and will be in new bodies soon, but their aides were unfortunately lost.

This time the Board members whisper to each other.

Hidden from view, I shake my head, begrudgingly impressed. One skelem was able to strike at the heads of all the city's military and law enforcement agencies in the space of an hour. No wonder the government went to great lengths to keep the skelems divided.

There's one other man seated with Adaolisa, short, with stocky limbs and a receding hairline—a rather unusual look in the upper districts, where bodymods are almost a culture. Given how he says nothing, I get the feeling he's possibly the only person on that table who was actually meant to be here.

"I assume you have similar news," the chair says to Adaolisa.

"Not exactly, Madam Chair." The chamber's attention pivots toward her. She wears it like a second skin, remaining as poised as the Oloye on the high table. "We were attacked, but thanks to the quick thinking of an Int-Sec officer, Director Muzinga made it to safety with no injuries. He has decided to keep his current whereabouts a secret while he continues to assess the situation. I am here on his behalf."

"That's a relief," says a Board member. "At least there's a competent person still in charge. He will be given every resource available."

"I'm certain he'll appreciate your support, honorable member."

The chair finally turns to the last man. "Give us some answers, Mr. Petrus. How is this possible? Your technology is supposed to be infallible."

My ears prick. I notice Adaolisa sitting up straighter, taking a closer look at this Petrus. *Your technology?* Does she mean ultraware?

Petrus clears his throat, visibly nervous, but there's no tremor in his voice. "Madam Chair, we're still trying to work out the specifics, but we cannot take responsibility for the poor security around your data centers. The attackers should not have been able to gain physical access to your systems. The failure was not on our side."

The chair lets silence stretch and loop around the chamber. "True enough, I suppose," she finally says. "We'll interrogate our security systems to find out where they failed. In the meantime . . ."

She turns her scrutiny to the others, infusing anger into her words. "What's happening today is unacceptable, people. The skelems are brazenly attacking us on the street, and now they've desecrated the Abode. Forty of our ancestors—*my* ancestors—have been taken from their resting places, murdered with the push of a button. Centuries of wisdom lost to us forever. Every other Board on the planet has defederated their Abodes from ours, and who can blame them? We've lost control. *You* have lost control. But I don't want to hear excuses. I want to know how you're going to make this right."

She's come to the wrong conclusion, I realize. *She's decided the Abode hack must be the work of the skelems as well, not an element of a broader attack on the city by an unknown enemy.*

And she's not the only one who thinks this, it seems. Over the next ten minutes I listen to a string of violent proposals to invade the Jondolos and crush the skelems until they submit, and the Board keeps nodding like they approve; the more violent the idea, the more they seem to like it. Adaolisa says nothing to correct their erroneous assumptions, and I'm surprised by how little she contributes to the overall discussion. I thought the whole point of being here was to influence what the Board decided.

It's only as the meeting ends that I realize why she stayed so silent. While the other representatives disappear from my lenses, and while most of the Board members get up and leave the chamber, the chair remains seated, and so does Adaolisa.

"Adaolisa Ndebele, is it?" the chair says once they're alone. "Your message said you wanted to speak in private. I'm a busy woman, so be quick."

"Madam Chair, whoever attacked the Abode could have compromised any number of systems, and there might not be enough time to figure out exactly what they did—"

"We have the best technicians on site as we speak," the chair interrupts. "Petrus and his people will gain back control before the end of the day."

"Perhaps," Adaolisa says patiently. "But how many minds will be deleted from the Abode in the meantime? And what happens if the technicians fail?"

"I don't see what other alternatives we have."

"Director Muzinga strongly recommends that you shut down the Abode immediately. The attackers mean to erode the public's confidence in your strength and authority. The longer they are seen to be in control of the Abode, the more damage they'll do to your reputation."

The chair watches Adaolisa. "And how long does the director suggest we shut it down for?"

"Until a fresh install of the entire system can be arranged, using original copies of the hosted personalities."

A low chuckle comes down from the high table. The Oloye leans forward, and even with her face in shadow, I can see the glimmer of teeth as she smiles. "My girl, it has long been established that two copies of the same conscious mind are separate entities altogether. What you're asking us to do is wipe thousands of conscious beings from existence and replace them with copies of themselves. I'm going to forgive such foolishness on account of the director's youth and your newness to our world."

I know Adaolisa is not afraid, but she strikes the right balance with her outward reaction, not so nervous she can be easily dismissed, but not so bold she seems disrespectful. "The director knows this is an unpleasant choice to make," she says. "But think of the alternative, Madam Chair. If you fail to recover control of the system, those minds will perish anyway, and they'll do so in a way that serves the aims of the attackers. You cannot allow them such a victory."

"Even if I agreed with you, I alone cannot authorize a reset of the Abode. I'd need the consent of the rest of the Board, and I can tell you now, they'd never agree to it."

"Then your best option is a complete shutdown of the system, Madam Chair. Put it on ice until the attackers have been caught and we know the full extent of what they did."

"Your director's message has been heard, Ms. Ndebele. You are dismissed."

And just like that, the meeting ends, and we both disconnect from the Boardroom, returning to Marcel's office. Adaolisa sits back into her chair, releasing a long breath.

"Do you think she'll do it?" I ask, still standing against the wall with my arms folded.

"A reset? Never. She wouldn't want to establish such a precedent. Otherwise she'd have to live with the fear that someone in her future might do the same thing to her, wipe her from existence without her ever knowing. No. Shutting down the system is her only good option; she'll see that soon enough. And if all goes according to plan, she'll never turn it back on again."

"So you agree with Jamal about the Abode," I observe.

"It's a cybernetic parasite feeding on the minds of the desperate; of course I agree it has to go," Adaolisa says. "But it didn't need to be so violent. People are dead, Nandipa. And a lot more are going to die."

"Then why didn't you convince the Board not to respond to the skelems with violence? Shouldn't they try to appease them?"

"They should, but Jamal's actions have accelerated my timeline. I want the skelems weakened. Ultimately their partnership with the government is why this city has no prodemocracy activists, labor unions, or any other advocacy groups—they've been very good at suppressing dissent at the grassroots level. But with a change in leadership and strengthened antipathy toward the government, they can become vehicles for positive change."

Adaolisa rolls her chair back and gets up, bringing the tips of her fingers together like she's about to break some unpleasant news. "Of course, for any of this to work, Nandipa," she says as she walks closer to me, "I can't have Jamal interfering. I know his reasons for hacking the Abode go beyond what we've seen today, and I realize I can't stop those plans, not without doing something drastic." She stops and looks me in the eye. "He needs to leave. Find somewhere else to run amok. Either that, or I'll have to make neutralizing him a priority. Do you understand?"

I narrowly avoid a gulp. "Don't you think that would be going a little too far?"

"My love, are you speaking as my Proxy or as Hondo's friend?"

I open my mouth. Words fail me, so I close it. Anger takes me, so I scowl. "It's not like that!"

"Find Hondo," she simply says, like she knows all about what's in my head, like she's always known. "Tell him to get his Prime out of ZimbaTech and never return. Can you do that for me?"

She's wrong. How could she even suggest that I'd—no. I'll show her. "Of course," I say coldly. "And if they don't leave, I'll take care of them myself."

I arrange to meet Hondo in the outdoor seating area of a café close to our apartment building. I get there first and order an herbal tea for myself.

The afternoon streets are quieter than usual today, and the few people I see walking around seem glued to the augmented news feeds being streamed into their contacts or ocular implants. Even the waiter's attention is elsewhere; he trips on a chair as he brings my tea, and it's a miracle he recovers his balance just in time to avoid dousing me with the stuff.

He apologizes profusely, but I wave his concern away. It's not like I blame him. The Abode polls are still ongoing, a new batch of twenty people presented for judgment every half hour or so. Supposedly over two hundred digitized Oloye have already been deleted from the Abode. I'm pretty sure the whole world is riveted.

Hondo appears minutes later, eyes hidden behind darkened sunglasses. His checkered sky-blue button-down is tucked neatly into khaki chinos, the sleeves rolled up to the elbows. Light-brown dress shoes and a black leather backpack complete the ruse of a harmless filing clerk or an urbane university student.

He even manages to look nervous as he removes his backpack and sits down on the chair across my table.

The gall. He should thank his ancestors I don't attack him on sight.

He removes his glasses and stares at my nose, like he can't even look me in the eye. "You're angry with me," he observes.

"Of course I am," I snap. "Your Prime's fucked-up schemes almost got Adaolisa killed. People are dying because of the war he started, and *you* helped him."

He puts his hands on the table, posture hunched like he doesn't know what to say to defend himself. "I didn't mean for you to get hurt."

I want to stay angry. Prove that Adaolisa was wrong, that I'd never put anything or anyone above her needs or ambitions. And if this were Jamal, I'd have no problem telling him to piss off. But Hondo . . .

He didn't plan for any of this. "I know," my lips say, almost of their own accord. I wince inwardly at my weakness. "Well? You wanted us to meet. Here I am."

Hondo finally looks into my eyes, and something electric passes between us. "I . . . wanted to say goodbye," he says. "Jamal has decided to leave the city."

I draw everything into myself, masking my emotions so well not even I can tell what I was about to feel. This is why I came here, isn't it? Makes things easier.

"Where are you going?" I ask, a casual question.

"I can't tell you that," he says automatically. Then he shakes himself out of it, his shoulders relaxing. "Mostly because I don't know."

"Are you coming back?"

"I doubt it."

There. A problem solving itself. I should be celebrating. "Goodbye, then. I guess."

We sit there, the sounds of the shiftless streets filling the silence between us, and I begin to fear that the mask I've constructed is slipping.

Abruptly, Hondo sits forward and speaks in a near whisper. "Nandipa," he says, and the way he says my name does things to me he has no right to do. "These last few months have been the best of my life. I'll . . . I'll miss you. A lot. I wish . . ."

Momentarily a searing wave of emotion engulfs me, and I'm filled with so much hatred for him, this naive and gentle boy, this foolish, honest boy who would make me doubt myself and question my devotion to my Prime. The hate consumes me, and I try to hold it in my heart, crystallize it into something I can grab onto so I can be glad to be rid of him. But it suddenly melts, and I realize what I'm feeling isn't hate at all but a deep vein of sorrow that's been torn open right through me.

I reach forward and take his hand, and now my mask has chipped away, but right now I don't care. "I know," I say. I don't need to hear the rest, because I know. Ancestors, I, too, wish we were different people with different lives, whose duties to the people we love didn't have to drive a wedge between us. "I know," I say again. "And I'll miss you too."

He smiles, and I burn that image of us sitting there into my mind. In an alternate universe, we're just two ordinary people out for a coffee.

"I have to go," he says, and I release his hand.

He picks up his backpack, getting up from his chair. "Take care of yourself," he says.

"You too," I reply, and then he's gone.

I try to enjoy the rest of my tea, but it's suddenly turned bitter in my mouth. So I pay the bill, tip the waiter, and go home.

Part 3:
Ile Wura

CHAPTER 13: HONDO

We started a fire in ZimbaTech, and now we're running from it.

I don't find out where we're going or how we're getting there until Jamal brings me to a marina north of the bay, where he shows me the used omni-vehicle he bought through his broker.

I know what it is by the telltale bulges of concealed ion thrusters on the sides of its narrow hull, a lustrous ivory in the waning daylight. This thing isn't just a submarine; it can fly, hover, float, and dive, an almost omnipotent machine, hence the name.

The word **SEAJACK** is printed on the sides of the raised top deck. Jamal leads the way across the gangway to the starboard entrance, lugging two brand-new rucksacks filled with essentials we bought using anonymous cash. I follow behind, pushing cases of the gear we used last night in a trolley cart, unable to keep the indignant scowl off my face.

I thought we'd be going back home after our attack on the Abode, but all of a sudden Jamal got paranoid and decided we needed to leave everything behind and escape the city. I'd gotten used to the comforts of the apartment. And it was nice getting to pretend we were normal people who didn't have to worry about getting recycled or shot at. At the very least he could have let me pack a few things.

I look around as the hatch closes behind me. Omnis are supposed to be recreational vehicles built for luxury, but the spartan, almost industrial amenities and the overabundance of computing equipment in the *Seajack*'s interior tell me it's a custom retrofit.

The glazed cockpit is visible up front, submerged in water, and in the aft sections I see a kitchenette, a small bathroom, and two narrow bunk beds way in the back. The rest of the habitation area hosts racks upon racks of processors, monitors, and other computing equipment installed on either side of the cabin, with a main multi-display terminal mounted in front of a single swivel chair.

This would have taken time to organize. Weeks at least. Jamal must have been planning our escape since the day he gained access to the Nzuko.

I put a lid on my ire and stow the cases away in a storage compartment toward the rear of the ship. Nearby Jamal drops our bags onto the lower bunk bed and begins to undo the buttons of his coat. Beneath it he's still wearing the pin-striped suit vest from last night.

"Where are we going?" I ask.

"Far from this place," he answers.

"I thought you wanted to change things in this city." I don't mean it as an accusation, but it comes out like one.

"I do, and I will." He tosses his coat onto the bunk and rolls up the sleeves of his shirt. There's enough room for him to walk past me on his way up front without us touching. "But I don't think my dear sister will tolerate our continued presence after what we just did."

I watch him settle down at the terminal and fire up the computers. The processors begin to beep and blink with lights, and I hear the liquid cooling systems humming as they come online.

"We should probably start moving," he says. "Take us out of the bay, then dive. We'll head southeast for a while, until I'm sure we're off Adaolisa's radar. She can't know where we are."

"I think you're being paranoid," I grumble, but I make my way to the cockpit. As I reach the pilot's seat, Jamal calls my name. I look over my shoulder. "What?"

Seated on his swivel chair, he fails to look me in the eye. "I'm sorry about Nandipa," he says. "I know you two were . . . close."

Conflicting emotions pull me in too many directions. "There's nothing to be sorry about," I say, then settle down by the controls.

—

With its robust life-support systems, the *Seajack* could keep us submerged for as long as there's power in its fluoride-ion batteries. Seawater is drawn in and made potable through reverse osmosis or electrolyzed into oxygen. The onboard computer makes any needed adjustments to maintain optimum air composition.

I take us southeast of the city's coast in a slow subaquatic trek, keeping us at a depth of one hundred feet. Jamal deploys the omni's antenna drone so that it tails us from the surface, connecting us to the world through a wireless optical telemetry system.

I've come to love the open skies and the crisp winds of the surface, but being back in the ocean improves my mood a little, to my surprise. I'd forgotten how peaceful it can be down here, how humbling to have the unknowable expanse of the deep pressing toward me, kept away by mere inches of reinforced glass and metal. It's like coming back home.

I remain too prickly for Jamal to bother attempting conversation with me, so we spend our first night away from ZimbaTech in brooding silence. Jamal offers me the lower bunk by way of silent apology. I also find a brand-new sketch tablet next to my pillow, and in the morning, I wake up to the smell of cooking breakfast. The plant-based fry-up looks amazing, but I still feel waspish, so I give him a tepid thanks and take my plate to the cockpit. I'm a little annoyed when he follows me to sit down in the copilot's seat.

"I'm sorry that the person I am is incompatible with the things you want," he gripes, finally losing his patience.

"What I want," I say, "is to not have this conversation."

He glares at me. "Then stop being miserable."

"I'm *not* miserable."

"He said miserably."

"I'll get over it."

Jamal frowns at his own plate, pushing his eggs around with a plastic fork. "You could go back if you wanted. You don't have to stay with me. I've told you this before."

"Now you're just pissing me off."

"You know what? Go fuck yourself," he tells me, then storms off.

Left alone in the cockpit, I feel a weight of guilt settling over me. *It's never pretty,* I remember Counselor telling me. *Ancestors.* Nothing even happened between Nandipa and me—correction: we held hands, once—but it's already putting a rift between me and my Prime.

I can still feel the warmth of her hand in mine. I hold that thought for a moment, and then I let it go, promising myself never to reach for it again.

I clean up as my way of apologizing. Jamal has never held a grudge against me, so the air between us gradually mellows. As I finish wiping down the kitchenette, he looks over at me from his seat by the terminal.

"Are we good?" he asks.

"We're good," I tell him, and I try to pretend we are.

We stay submerged for another two days. During that time, I get acquainted with some of the systems Jamal installed, including the surveillance station with live satnav data tracking pretty much every vehicle on the planet.

I use the station to monitor the movements of the Free People flotilla some several hundred miles south of us. The Free People rove about the seas of this world in their floating mobile cities, away from the reach and control of the corporate states. Jamal tells me we'll need to visit the flotilla to recharge and restock, but for now it's better to stay out of their way.

If I'm not on the surveillance station, I'm sitting in the cockpit with my feet up on the dashboard, drawing on my tablet or browsing the news. Jamal forbids any direct interaction with the Nzuko since Adaolisa will probably be watching for us, but there are other networks from which to get news about what's happening in ZimbaTech.

The Abode has been temporarily shut down, apparently, which means Jamal's automated judgment polls are no longer running. Last time I checked, over three hundred minds had been deleted. After what I saw at the Hive, I still don't know why Jamal didn't go ahead and wipe the whole thing out.

All three skelems have now declared the Jondolos autonomous. Government forces are preparing to invade, and someone on the Board publicly threatened to obliterate the whole island with a Rod of God. I know what these are; release a tungsten rod the size of a streetlamp from a satellite in orbit, and it will gather enough kinetic energy as it falls to hit like a nuclear bomb, except without any radioactive fallout. Their speed and slender profiles make them incredibly difficult to intercept.

"Aren't you concerned by this?" I ask Jamal from the cockpit.

It's our third day in the omni, and Jamal is at his workstation, as usual.

"Nothing like that will happen unless Adaolisa lets it happen," he answers.

I turn in my seat so I can look at him. "You seem very sure of that."

"Because I *am* sure. If the city isn't already under her control, it will be soon. She can't help herself. It's a pathology, you see. She hates anything she can't directly influence, and if she can't bend it to her will, she destroys it." Jamal glances at me. "In fact, I reckon your friendship with Nandipa is the only reason she didn't take us out at the earliest opportunity."

I simmer with residual bitterness at the mention of that name, but I've told myself that I should forgive him, so I don't make a fuss. "Adaolisa isn't that cold blooded," I argue.

"No, she wouldn't have us killed," Jamal agrees, turning back to his monitors. "She'd have us arrested and imprisoned. Or something like that."

"So what was the point?" I ask. "Why pit the skelems against the government or set up those polls if we were only going to run away?"

"To keep Adaolisa too busy to notice or care about what I'm really doing," Jamal tells me, confirming what I've been thinking all along: he had ulterior motives for attacking that data center. Motives he kept from me.

Perhaps sensing the tenor of my thoughts, Jamal sighs loudly. "It's not that I didn't trust you, Hondo. I just didn't want to risk you unwittingly giving something away to Nandipa."

I turn away from him and face the front of the cockpit. "Good to know you don't think I can keep a secret."

"It's not like that," he protests. "All right, fine. Come take a look. I'll show you everything."

I want to be petulant, but I'm curious to know what he's up to, so I get up and go take a look.

"They built this thing like a tower of dominoes," Jamal explains with a sparkle in his eye. "Pull one, and the whole thing falls down."

And he's right. Turns out each of the seven corporate city-states has its own version of the Abode as well as its own supranetwork—that is, an omniscient network like ZimbaTech's Nzuko. The supranets are closed off from each other to prevent corporate espionage, but the Abodes are essentially a federated network with free communication among themselves, an interlinked heaven for Oloye from every city.

"When I compromised the Abode in ZimbaTech," Jamal says, "I infected the whole federated network, which allowed me to access each city's supranetwork from the inside. I still have two more to go, but the rest are now under my thumb."

The scale of his actions almost makes me dizzy. On his screens are live feeds from the cities whose networks he's hacked. ZimbaTech. SalisuCorp. Molefe Star Industrial. Kenrock City. Transworld. He still hasn't cracked into Nkala Interstellar and Heynes Group City as of yet, but I spot running scripts and progress bars that tell me it won't be long before he controls those networks too.

"What are you planning on doing with all this access?" I ask him.

"The cybernetic menace is worldwide," he says, not bothering to hide his zeal. "It won't be enough to change ZimbaTech alone. The other cities would be warned and take steps to protect themselves. They must be brought down swiftly and all at once. It's the only way to win."

"The only way for who, Jamal?" I ask.

His confidence falters only for a moment. "For the people of this world, Hondo. Who else?"

Chapter 14: Nandipa

I am a weapon, designed by my creators to kill with coldhearted efficiency, but tonight I'm a star, and all eyes watch me as I sing my deceptions up on the stage.

In my glittering jewelry and tasseled silver dress, I lie to my audience with my voice, singing of love and sunshine and bright days to come even as Rods of God threaten to rain down onto the city.

The bar's patronage has grown since I started performing here every other night. Most of them are students from the nearby technical institute, but a good deal have come from other parts of the bronze-tier district to enjoy the bar's lively new entertainments and, more illicitly, the political discussions that have started to follow.

I move my body in tandem with the jazz from the band behind me. I make eye contact with members of my audience as I sing, coaxing them with my smile to believe that my song is for them and them alone. I've gotten used to this, the addictive rush that goes through me when I see the impact of my performance on the faces watching me.

I have grown used to the way their static bends around me, letting me know I have their full attention. But tonight a different flavor of static draws my gaze to a figure at the back of the busy bar, both quiet and inquisitive, and sharp like the tapering point of a honed knife.

My voice doesn't waver, nor does my performance, but I become less interested in my audience, my senses shifting to focus on this new presence. The lights shining on me prevent me from seeing clearly to the back, so I fail to make out any facial features, but I know it's not Hondo. I'd have sensed his virtually silent static the second he walked through the door.

I finish the performance as usual, to rapturous cheers. The student activists going next, dressed in green leather jackets and black bandannas as headbands, are ready to take the stage, and as their leader steps up to the microphone, she gestures at me and whistles.

"Another round of applause for the sensational Ms. Lindiwe!"

The crowd obliges. I have done my part. This is why I continue to perform here, to start a trend that Adaolisa intends to spread to other lower-class social spaces in the city: lure people in with entertainment, then confront them with political discourse that is only now possible because of the city's chaos. This bar has already become an epicenter for a burgeoning student-and-labor-activist movement.

I start making my way to the visitor I sensed, but their static is receding. I'd run, but far too many people want to address me, congratulate me, shake my hand, have me smile and acknowledge them.

"Tonight, comrades," says the activist on the stage, her voice booming through the speakers with righteous confidence, "I want to talk about the power of Us. The power of the many. It is the power of not what I say but what We say. A single drop of water can be flung away with the flick of a finger. But put enough of them together, and you'll have a mighty river that can sweep away cities."

The sound of fists and mugs banging on the tables in an angry rhythm rises around the bar, encouraging her to continue.

"A single voice can be silenced. But a multitude can be heard even from across the highest mountain peak."

"Speak!"

"The power of Us, my comrades, is a power none holds alone but one known by the multitudes."

"Amen, sister!"

"A power this world once knew but was cast aside by greed . . ."

I finally escape the crowds, following the static outside the bar's entrance. I'm not wearing a coat, so the night's chilly air makes me shiver. I look down the narrow street. Lights and holos cast dancing shadows onto the wet asphalt, but there's no sign of the person I sensed inside the bar.

The hairs on the back of my neck have stiffened. What worries me is the feeling that this stranger was here not to watch my performance but to watch me specifically. And that perhaps they knew I'd notice them.

I've kept my two identities separate. Adaolisa has made sure no one would tie the alias I use when I come here to my Int-Sec identity. Is it possible that I've been compromised?

I should have moved quicker.

The boom of a distant explosion reaches my ears, a now-common reminder of the continued fighting on the island across the bay. Hugging myself, I go back inside the bar.

I decide not to burden Adaolisa with news about the stranger. Besides, she returns to the apartment much later than I do, hours past midnight, the hint of wine in her breath. I know where she's been and with whom, but I guess that's something else we've yet to explicitly confront. I think I'll wait until she's ready to talk about it.

Despite her late night, we're both ready to leave for Int-Sec HQ at the crack of dawn. On the jazz stage I'm a shimmering starlet meant to draw the eye, but everywhere else I'm a standoffish Int-Sec operative clad in black leather jackets and black tight-fitting denims, armed with a personal defense weapon, the brawn to Adaolisa's corporate elegance.

Neither of us spends much time in the apartment these days. Marcel has turned it into his personal pleasure-house, where he hosts a revolving door of young women he invites to entertain him. I don't know if this is his way of dealing with what's happening to his city, but he's showing no sign of stopping.

The official story is that he's still in hiding and acting remotely through his assistants. Two weeks after the attack, and people have already stopped asking to speak directly with him and have accepted Adaolisa as the de facto head of Int-Sec. Even the Board now accepts her word without question.

While Adaolisa heads to her office, I veer down the hall to the building's refurbished ops room, already bustling with activity. Over a dozen agents sit engrossed in front of their screens and workstations, monitoring satellite data and camera feeds from everywhere in the city. They know I'm here to be their link to the director's office, so they don't pay me much attention as I lean against the wall and watch them work.

With the other agencies rendered temporarily leaderless, Int-Sec was granted unprecedented access and became the main source of intel for the city's military operations in the Jondolos.

Not that this has helped. For decades the skelems were allowed to run their criminal enterprises unmolested by the government in exchange for suppressing dissidence; they are well armed and well equipped, and they seemed to have anticipated that the government would one day turn against them.

By contrast, the Defense Force is only used to engagements with Free People wanderers outside the city; they were woefully unprepared for urban warfare.

I don't interfere with the work happening on the floor. The priority right now is locating the leaders of the three skelems, but they were smart enough to create blind spots across the Jondolos where the

Nzuko cannot see. Finding people in that maze who don't want to be found is a tall order.

"You're here," says a voice off to the side. "Again. You know, I'm starting to think maybe you come here to watch me. Do you like to watch me, Ms. Nandipa?" The woman who spoke gives me a lopsided grin, folding her bionic arms as if to call attention to them.

"Your thoughts misguide you, Ms. Angelique," I calmly reply. "I am the director's eyes in the ops room. Nothing else."

"Of course. My apologies. Carry on."

Chrome plating hides the inner workings of those arms, but I don't doubt she could punch through a wall if she wanted. Jet-black ballistic armor covers the rest of her body. She's a bit of a giant, probably a bodymod, muscular and taller than me by a few inches even with her bald scalp, and by the restraint I sense in her static, I'd guess she was trained by the Kolovrat.

I know her only as Angelique, and she's been a nuisance from the day I met her.

Even from her decanting tank, Director Abuk Dieng of the CID somehow maneuvered the Board into letting a CID "consultant" slither into our ops room. I have no idea what the director hopes to achieve, but I'm already sick of Angelique's prying and meddling presence.

"Secretary, I think I've found something."

I approach the agent who has hailed me, a man old enough to have children my age, yet the platinum Scree rank that came with my job means I am his senior officer.

"This footage was taken from a comm tower last night," he tells me, and on one of his screens I watch a hulking brute of a man walking up the steps to the entrance of a run-down building. The tower must have been far away by the grainy texture of the footage, but even from a distance the metallic luster of the man's left hand is visible. If I'm not mistaken, that is the leader of the Mercuries, one of the three skelems now fighting for the Jondolos.

"Do we know when he left the building?" I ask.

"He hasn't, not since he entered it last night," the agent tells me. "By rights he should still be in there. I'd send a drone to investigate, but they shoot them down pretty quickly."

"They'll run out of ammunition soon enough," Angelique says with a grunt, shamelessly eavesdropping on our conversation. "Send the intel over to the DF and the CID immediately."

"Disregard that," I say. Ignoring Angelique, I reach for Adaolisa through my earpiece. When she responds, I privately relay the situation to her.

"It's most likely a trap," she says. *"The skelems know every inch of the Jondolos. He would have known about the tower. If we have a visual of him entering a building, it's because he wanted us to see it."*

"So what should we do?"

"Pass the intel along but append a warning with my suspicions."

"A warning they won't heed, I'm sure."

"There's nothing for it. I'm sure your friend is already aware of the information."

I glance in Angelique's direction. She smirks at me like she knows what we're talking about. "Unfortunately, yes."

"Then send the intel along."

I relay the instructions to the agent, and Angelique snorts derisively at the suggestion that the footage might be a trap.

"As if that pile of human refuse could ever ensnare us. We will crush them." She looks at me sideways. "And where's your sister anyway? She's the director's pet, isn't she? Shouldn't she be here, directing?"

My stay with Jamal must have deepened my reserves of patience, because I don't even twitch a muscle. "The director has assigned her many duties. She comes to the ops room only when she must."

The large woman gives off another grunt.

I get a reprieve from her infuriating presence when she leaves in the early afternoon, as she usually does. I head over to Adaolisa's office and catch her seated at her desk just as she reaches the tail end of a voice call.

". . . and when do you think you can send me a prototype?" she says.

I shut the door softly behind me.

"Three days. Maybe more. These designs are highly unusual—"

"Can I trust in your discretion? I don't want this on any records."

"Of course, madam. I'll let you know when the prototype is ready."

"I'll be looking forward to it," Adaolisa replies, then ends the conversation.

Since she took over Int-Sec, this office has been less jazz-club chic and more sit-and-you'll-make-it-dirty chic, a bit like the occupant herself, I guess. Immaculate behind her glass table in her ivory gown and turban, as if a single touch would mar her delicate beauty.

I lower myself onto the large cream-white couch on one side of her office, watching her. "What's this about a prototype?" I ask.

She takes a moment to consider how much to tell me. Evidently, she decides to be candid. "I'm having our resident engineer look into the dead-space designs on Counselor's data stick. I want to see if they can be incorporated into helmets for our raid teams."

I gape, dumbstruck, the blood draining from my face. "Ada, why the *fuck* would you do that?"

"A contingency, Nandipa," she says, blinking at me with tired eyes. "Nothing more. Hondo might be worthy of your trust, but Jamal is capable of anything. You can't blame me for preparing for all eventualities."

She knows better. She does. I don't doubt that. But the idea of weaponizing dead space, of all things, makes me want to take a shower and scrub myself clean. "What if these engineers figure out what it is or what it was used for?"

"I doubt they will," Adaolisa says confidently. "And I chose someone discreet. But I'll be keeping a close eye on them all the same."

I study her for a while. I feel like her exhaustion has infected me, because I'm suddenly very tired. "I hope you know what you're doing."

"I hope so too." She gets up from her chair and moves to look out the windows. "Also, I just spoke to the young man I hope will take over the Goldbloods once this war is over. He's the last holdout, in fact. I've already confirmed successors for the Silvernecks and the Mercuries. If he's on board, the war could be over by this time tomorrow."

My breath almost hitches at the casual way she says that last part. Sometimes I forget she knows exactly where the current leaders of the skelems are hiding and could betray their locations to the government at any time.

While they were wise enough to build a shadow network to communicate among themselves, separate from the Nzuko and thus inaccessible to the government, they weren't so diligent as to ensure no devices could connect to both networks. All Adaolisa needed to do was trawl the Nzuko for such a device and remotely compromise it; then she was in. It took her less time than it takes to ride in a car from here to our apartment.

"All three potential leaders are young and hold a genuine desire to make this city a better place," Adaolisa tells me. "Can you imagine? A free media. Student activists. Trade unions. All guaranteed protection by a militia that has already proved its might. Democratic change would be inevitable even without my further involvement."

I sense her mood shifting, and abruptly she turns around to look me in the eye. "You think I'm a bad person, don't you," she says. "For doing this. For letting people die when I could have stopped it. The victims of the war now number in the thousands. Jamal might have started this conflict, but I had the power to end it before things got so bad. And I didn't. What does that say about me?"

I lean back, unable to mask my surprise. I've felt uncomfortable with her plans from the beginning, but not because I thought they were immoral. I've never thought that. She's always done what she felt was right. "If you'd given up the skelem leaders, you'd have only strengthened the Oloye's hold over the city," I say.

"Then I guess the question is, How many lives are worth sacrificing to destroy the Oloye? When is enough enough? A hundred? A thousand?"

That's not a question I can answer.

She recovers her composure with a slow exhale, then says, "In other news, someone has been looking into me. I set up trip wires all over the Nzuko to alert me if this ever happened, but the trails all lead to fake aliases. I have no idea who it is."

Whatever tiredness was trickling into me flushes out of my bloodstream all at once. I'm instantly alert. "You don't think it's Jamal?"

She shakes her head. "This person doesn't know me, but they're curious. I think perhaps they suspect."

"Suspect what?" I ask.

"That we might not be who we say we are," Adaolisa says. "In fact, the way they've been able to hide from me has echoes of what happened to Counselor. Despite my access, I still can't find out what happened after he left the apartment. He might as well have vanished into another dimension. But now . . . this could be how we find him."

This is serious, but Adaolisa seems more fascinated than concerned. Why isn't she more worried? "What do you mean, this is how we find him?" I ask, my heart beating faster.

A distant aerial car briefly reflects a beam of sunlight through the windows, illuminating one half of Adaolisa's face. She was upset not too long ago, but her eyes have hardened with strange purpose. "I think we're dealing with the same people who took Counselor," she says. "I'm going to let them reveal themselves to us. Then I'm going to hunt them down."

I stifle a groan. This day just won't let up. "Ada, you said the people who took Counselor could be the same people who destroyed the Habitat. If they know about us—"

"They don't know; they suspect."

"That's not great either."

"There's not much we can do regardless. Not until they show themselves."

I close my eyes, take a deep breath, let it out. "They might already have."

Still standing by the windows, Adaolisa eyes me curiously. "Explain."

"Someone came to watch me perform at the bar last night. Their static wasn't hostile, but it was odd enough for me to notice. I didn't mention it because I didn't want to worry you with something that might turn out to be nothing."

She's not as annoyed as I expected her to be, but she sighs and shakes her head. "You have good instincts, Nandipa. If you noticed, it probably wasn't nothing."

"I'll let you know if it happens again."

"Make sure you do." She walks closer to her table and gestures, pulling up a holo screen. The image of a man appears on the screen, along with an array of documents and news articles. "Do you remember Petrus? First name Fillemon."

I frown at the image, recognizing the pudgy face and the receding hairline. "He was at your first meeting with the Board, wasn't he?"

"Yes. I've been looking into him, and I have to say, for someone important enough to speak at a crisis meeting with the Board of Directors, there's a surprising lack of information about him."

She gestures and brings up multiple documents with the same spherical corporate logo on the headers. "I did find out that he's the leader of an independent group of scientists who call themselves the Stewards. Turns out these Stewards are, as a matter of fact, the makers of ultraware, though you wouldn't know it for how few mentions of them exist. It's likely the city-states actively censor any media reports about them."

"Makes sense," I reason. "They're protective of the technology they put inside their heads. Wait." My eyes widen as I make the connection she's trying to draw. "You think these Stewards are the ones looking into us. The ones who took Counselor and destroyed the Habitat."

Her flat stare confirms my guess. "They operate independently without scrutiny from the city-states. They have the money, the resources, and the motive. Look at us; look at where we are: clearly we're threats to their creations." Adaolisa points at the holo screen. "I have searched and searched, and if there's someone who could destroy an underwater base without anyone else ever finding out, it's them. This is the only group that fits."

I look at the screen, and suddenly Fillemon Petrus's face, so unremarkable a moment ago, takes on a new gravity, attaching itself to my memories of the Habitat in ruins, my life forever changed. I don't know what to feel.

On the one hand, this is the face of the man who killed so many of our siblings, all of whom were just trying to survive, like us.

On the other hand, the Habitat was never a home. We were scientific experiments. Living creations our minders controlled with dead space. Without the attack on the Habitat, Adaolisa and I would still be none the wiser. We'd still be somewhere under the ocean, plotting against our siblings to impress the Custodians.

In a way, I owe this man my freedom. The very idea disgusts me. I already know I'll be seeing that face in my nightmares.

"What are we going to do?" I say. "If these people come after us—"

"Let them." There's a honed edge in Adaolisa's voice as she cuts me off. "I have eyes and ears everywhere in this city. They won't know it, but I'll be waiting for them." A beeping sound on her terminal interrupts us. When she reads the caller ID, her lips twitch into a cynical sneer. "Director Abuk Dieng has returned from the dead, it seems. This should be interesting."

Sensing that she'd rather be alone, I get up from the couch. "I'll give you your privacy."

As I reach the door, she addresses me. "Nandipa . . ."

I look over my shoulder, but her gaze drops to the table.

"I won't be coming home with you later. I have . . . an engagement."

All right. I don't think I can ignore this anymore. "Adaolisa, are you sure about this?" I finally ask. "Michelle Zimba is the executive chair. What if—"

"I'm fascinated by her," Adaolisa cuts me off. "She's intriguing. And it's harmless fun. *And* an opportunity. Don't worry about me, my love. I know what I'm doing."

I can't help but sigh. "Just be careful."

"I have to take this call."

"Of course," I say and dutifully leave her office.

Chapter 15: Hondo

I watch the footage on my tablet for the twentieth time, maybe. A man walks toward an aerial car in the early hours of the morning. The camera watches from a building across the street, but I can still see the nasty scar on the right side of his stubbled face, filled in with a metallic material. He gets into the car. It lifts off, briefly ascending out of view, and then seconds later it drops from the sky like a rock, hitting the ground with enough force to flatten everything inside.

The next vid was taken on the same day, just minutes later, apparently, from the inside of an elevator. A heavily armored woman walks in with two others, and as soon as the doors close, the elevator plummets, taking them down with it. The fall lasts at least twelve seconds before the footage cuts out. There are no survivors.

Seated on a folding chair on the *Seajack*'s topside deck, I watch the vids again, memorizing the facial structures of the victims, the curvatures of their mouths, the emotion in their eyes, details I'll use when I get around to sketching them.

In one fell swoop, these incidents took out two of the most powerful and vicious gang leaders of Kenrock City, and all signs point to the Kenrock corporate government as responsible. But I know better.

I know that these are yet more souls I have helped send to their graves; therefore it is only fitting that I sketch them. I tell myself I don't really regret that they are dead, that they had to die. They were cruel, they forced people into Hives, they killed, and they suppressed; Jamal had to remove them. It was necessary.

It was the right thing to do.

Once I've committed the faces to memory, I browse through my news feeds. With ZimbaTech and now Kenrock suffering criminal gang uprisings, other cities have begun to notice. Molefe Star has already seized control of their Hives from the gangs they had running them. Nkala Interstellar has set up checkpoints and no-fly zones to insulate its upper districts from any potential bad actors. From a little submarine in the ocean, Jamal has engineered the perception of a worldwide criminal gang uprising, and my list of people to sketch is growing faster than my hand can sketch them.

I swipe the news feeds away when he climbs up a nearby ladder, coming out of the water from his swim. I reach for the towel on the chair next to mine and toss it to him. He flashes me a smile as he catches it.

"The water is great today," he tells me as he wipes himself down. "Are you sure you don't want to go in?"

It's our second time coming up to the surface this week. I don't mind the water, but I'd much rather use my time up here soaking up as much sun as possible. "Maybe next time," I say. "If there'll even be a next time. Our batteries will need a recharge soon."

Jamal drapes the towel over one shoulder. "How far to reach the nearest flotilla?"

"If we take it slow, we'll be there by morning tomorrow." He looks out into the distant line of the blue horizon, and I sense uncertainty passing through him. "Something you're worried about?" I say.

He shrugs it off, sitting down next to me. "Maybe Adaolisa's need for control rubbed off on me," he replies with a scornful laugh. "The flotillas are an unknown, and I'm close to the next phase of my plan. I guess I just don't want any disruptions."

I feel my sketching hand twisting the grip of an imaginary stylus. So many faces already. More to come. It's necessary.

"Take us to the flotilla," Jamal decides. "We can't avoid it forever."

—

I keep the *Seajack*'s top deck above the waterline as we make our slow approach, broadcasting the omni's identifying information as is supposedly the custom when dealing with the Free People to indicate friendly intent.

A Free People vessel hails us as soon as we come within two hundred miles of the flotilla. *"Omni-vehicle* Seajack, *you are entering sovereign Free People waters. Turn back or submit to boarding for a full inspection."*

The water around us has lightened to an aquamarine blue with the coming of sunrise. Both Jamal and I spent the night in the cockpit, though Jamal drifted off to sleep in the copilot's seat a while ago.

I glance at one of the screens on the dashboard, which has a live data feed from the satnav station. The ship hailing us is the FV *Khama*, apparently, a large frigate equipped with substantial antisubmarine weaponry. We'll be finished if they decide they don't like us.

Better not piss them off, then.

"Free People vessel, this is the *Seajack*," I say. "We request permission to dock with the flotilla, recharge our batteries, and trade for supplies. We will submit to boarding for inspection."

Jamal stirs awake and listens quietly as the voice on the radio responds. We are directed to cut off our speed, maintain position, and prepare ourselves to receive a boarding party. I accept and end the communication.

"We don't have anything to hide, do we?" I ask Jamal.

He gives a sleepy laugh. "We have everything to hide, my brother. Just nothing that isn't already in plain sight."

"I'm reassured," I say flatly, then look down at my naked chest. "At least we should put on shirts. For modesty's sake."

With no one to impress, we've both gone lax in our clothing habits, getting by on shorts and flip-flops alone. I pull a simple white shirt over my head while Jamal slips into a floral button-down, and then we head topside to receive our guests.

Jamal whistles as the FV *Khama* approaches us, his spike in anxiety rippling through me and causing my eyes to dilate. It's not so much the size of the thing that impresses us; though it towers over the *Seajack*'s single exposed deck, it isn't especially large for a ship. But its sleek, geometric structure of sharp edges, few windows, and heavy armor plating makes it look practically indestructible, a moving bunker that could withstand anything thrown at it.

Three radar domes crown the *Khama*'s daunting silhouette. I'm sure we've already been scanned and they know the omni has no weapons. A large five-pointed black star is painted on the hull amidships. As the *Khama* comes up along the *Seajack*'s starboard side, the frigate keeps its distance, and I begin to wonder how the boarding party intends to make it all the way across.

Then we see a platform ascend from the *Khama*'s main deck, carrying aloft several figures on the power of ion thrusters attached to the bottom of the platform. I pick up seven sources of static on board, not imminently hostile but alert, coiled like springs. *Armed, and highly trained.*

"Seven commandos," I warn Jamal as we watch the platform. "They'll fire at the slightest excuse."

Jamal licks his lips. "Then let us not give them an excuse."

The platform descends close enough to allow the Free commandos access to our top deck, and the seven rifle-toting men and women who join us pique my interest as much as they put me on my guard.

Loose patterned cloths drape over their ballistic armor, while interesting designs painted in white cover their arms and faces.

The leader of the group is a large man whose scarlet cloth leaves most of his chest bare. Long braids fall to cover the left half of his face, and the iris looking out from the other half holds a synthetic white glimmer, giving the impression that he can see through walls.

I struggle not to put myself in front of Jamal when the man steps forward with his massive rifle, which has a jagged knife implement attached to it. The deepening interest I detect in his static as his white iris looks us over has me wishing I had a gun in my hands. The abrupt spike of worry I sense from Jamal doesn't help matters either.

"Lieutenant Jotham Lukwiya of the Black Star Navy at your service," the man says in a friendly baritone, though he glances around the deck as if he expects to find someone hiding. "Anyone else on board, fellows?"

I don't know what Jamal has seen, but he's tensed up inside like he regrets ever coming here. "It's just the two of us, boss," he politely replies, putting up a ruse of calm.

"Any weapons or contraband?"

"We have six firearms and three cases of ammunition, all stowed in a storage compartment. No contraband."

The man nods at his people, and three of them head inside the *Seajack* to commence their search of the interior. The other three stay behind, holding their guns like they want a reason to shoot us. I feel like their focus is squarely on me.

What the hell is going on?

If I thought I could move fast enough without getting Jamal killed, I'd have already attacked.

"So what brings you all the way out here?" says Lukwiya, throwing the question casually, though the coils of his static have wound even tighter. I think his eye contact might be a recording device, and I see an earpiece in his right ear. I have a feeling someone on the ship is watching and communicating with him. The same might be true for the others.

Despite the invisible but growing air of danger, Jamal steps forward to hand the lieutenant a tablet showing the aliases he created for us. We are currently pretending to be data-recovery experts from SalisuCorp.

"I'm Joshua, and this is my brother, Caleb," Jamal says. "We're wanderers trying our hand at life outside the cities. We're considering joining a flotilla."

Lukwiya smiles without humor as he scans the information on the tablet, no doubt to be verified by whoever's listening in. "I hope for your sakes you're not wanted men, Joshua and Caleb. The flotillas are not havens for criminals running from corporate justice. If you are such individuals, you have come to the wrong place."

"We have nothing to hide, Lieutenant," Jamal says. "Our identities are verifiable."

Lukwiya stares blankly for a moment, his static patient. I think a communication comes into his earpiece, and then he nods. "It would seem you are right." He hands the tablet back to Jamal. "Once we complete our search, you can proceed to the flotilla."

I don't believe him. Something's wrong here.

"I'll take a look inside, if you don't mind," Lukwiya says. "You can wait out here."

"Of course."

We don't move. The three remaining Free commandos watch us with near-unblinking stares, like they know we could pose a threat to them even unarmed. They'd light us up faster than I could take the first one.

Jamal leans closer to me and whispers in the Second Dialect, "I think we're in trouble."

"Are they pirates?" I ask.

"No. But I don't think they plan to let us go."

"Something interesting, gentlemen?" says the one with white dotted stripes painted down her cheeks. She's younger than the others, and despite the smile on her face, her static tells me she desperately wants to point her rifle and pull the trigger.

"Nothing at all, boss," Jamal says. "We'll keep quiet."

"It would be best."

Lukwiya is gone for only minutes, but time crawls, and the sensation of being trapped grows so strong I begin to convince myself to act. Maybe I'll be fast enough. I can't just stand here and let them take Jamal. I have to do something.

"Don't do it," Jamal whispers.

Reluctantly, I rein myself back in.

"I see you came prepared," Lukwiya says as he comes back out onto the deck. "Grain seeds and ammo are desired mediums of trade among the Free People."

Jamal remains polite. "Is everything in order, Lieutenant? We would love to be on our way."

"In a bit. Why don't you tell me about the setup you've got going down there? Seems like a lot of tech to be hauling around."

"We decrypt data for a living," Jamal lies. "We help people who've lost their encryption keys. We don't always succeed, but the computing power required is substantial."

"I see." I know the lieutenant doesn't believe us. My muscles want to tense, I'm flooded with stimulants screaming at me to act, but I don't move.

Lukwiya glances at me, then looks back at Jamal. "You said you're brothers, yes? You know, it's uncanny. You look so alike, yet I'd hardly believe you share the same two parents. Are you half brothers?"

"We're fraternal twins, Lieutenant," Jamal answers, infusing a touch of impatience into his voice. "Is there a problem here?"

"As a matter of fact, yes, there is." Abruptly there are six rifles aimed at us, the lieutenant's people acting on some silent cue.

Jamal and I both lift our palms. It was Jamal keeping me from losing it all along, but now I project a sense of calm in his direction. *I won't let you get hurt. Just do what they tell you.*

For his part, Lukwiya remains at ease, a deceptively affable smile curling his lips. "See, I think you're lying to me, Joshua, if that's even your name."

"Our identities are verifiable," Jamal says, his voice steady.

"I'll give you that, but see, we've been told to be on the lookout for any strange siblings traveling together in pairs. They'd be intelligent, good looking, and well spoken. I don't know about you, comrades," the lieutenant says, addressing his people without taking his eyes off us, "but I say they fit the bill."

"They fit, sir," says the young woman who spoke earlier.

"We were also warned to watch out for the silent one." Lukwiya's white iris lands on me. "That would be you. Caleb, is it? Try anything and your brother dies first."

Ancestors. We're done for. All I can do now is obey and hope it'll be enough to save Jamal. "Understood."

"Good boy. Now put your hands behind your head and turn around. Slowly. Both of you."

I glance at Jamal. I know he's afraid, but he's kept it off his face. "Just do what they say."

He nods, and we both turn around, our hands behind our heads.

"Patience?" Lukwiya says.

"Right away, sir."

The young woman named Patience comes to cuff me first, binding my hands in metal shackles. She does the same thing to Jamal. A spike in her static tells me I'm about to be attacked, but I remain still only because I don't sense the same hostility directed toward Jamal. The next thing I know, there's a hand reaching up to smear a red paste above my upper lip.

The pungent fumes of the paste hit me like a punch to the jaw. My head spins; I stagger, then sink to one knee. I struggle against the sudden urge to laugh.

"What have you done?" I hear Jamal say. "What have you given him?"

"Just a little something to help your brother relax," Patience says. "We're not taking any chances."

I try to fight it—I was built to be resistant to such things—but the psychoactive fumes are powerful. With my hands bound I drop awkwardly to the deck, and it feels like I never stop falling.

"Don't worry," comes Lukwiya's baritone. "Cooperate, and you will both be fine."

The last things I see before I black out are Jamal's flip-flops, Lukwiya's sandals, a pair of boots, and behind them all, the blue sky.

—

I return to awareness in a seated position, a painful crick in my neck. I groan, lifting my forehead off a hard and cold surface. As I blink my eyes open, my heart kicks into gear immediately, my thoughts racing, reaching, then flooding with relief when I feel Jamal's quiet presence nearby.

"Jamal?" I croak.

"I'm here. I'm fine. Ancestors, Hondo, are you all right? I damn near pissed myself."

I try to move but find my hands cuffed and my ankles fettered to a steel table. Unharmed and seated calmly next to me, Jamal is similarly bound to the table, though it seems they allowed him the kindness of looser restraints. My head is still spinning as I look around. We're in a windowless cell with a single lamp on the ceiling, so dim we're practically sitting in the dark.

"How long?" I say.

"A few hours."

"Where are we?"

"Inside the frigate."

I flex my shoulders, trying in vain to work the cramp out of my neck. I can still taste that foul red paste at the back of my throat. "Do you think your sister did this?"

A breath pours out of Jamal like he's asked himself the same question. "Maybe, but this isn't like her. And she didn't know we'd be coming out here."

"Then how?" I ask.

Jamal slowly shakes his head. "I honestly don't know."

There are at least twenty people on board the frigate. I sense one of them approaching, restive like they're itching for a fight. I don't need to guess who it might be.

They must know I'm awake. But of course they'd have a camera watching us.

"I think Patience is coming," I warn Jamal and brace myself for whatever's about to happen.

"They haven't killed us yet," Jamal says despite his spiking nerves. "We might be able to talk our way out of this."

It's only when the Free commando is almost to the door that I realize there are two other sources of static moving with her, masked so well I might not have noticed were I not paying attention.

Goose bumps rise all over my skin. "Someone else is with her," I whisper.

"Who?"

Before I can answer, the door swings open. Light floods in, dazzling my eyes, and then the silhouettes of a pair of tall and broad-shouldered figures fill the doorway. Behind them I sense Patience waiting quietly.

Jamal hisses out a curse.

"As I live and breathe," says one of the silhouettes.

He steps into the cell, and my heart almost stops as I find myself staring into David's smug eyes. Which means that figure behind him could be none other than Benjamin.

"Didn't think you'd be seeing me again, did you, Jamal," David says, and my heart sinks at knowing we're completely at his mercy.

Chapter 16: Nandipa

I have a good view of the hotel down the street from where I'm sitting, by the second-floor windows of a music lounge. The building looks like a protea flower, giant glass petals arranged into a cone with a neon-rose bloom. The salmon light coming off it reflects on the nearby waterway in a dancing shimmer.

I lift my champagne cocktail to my lips and take a sip, my gaze fixed on the hotel. The glass is close to empty, but the alcohol has done nothing to ease my restlessness. I should be more patient. Less of a hypocrite.

Ancestors. I'd be one to judge Adaolisa after what didn't but possibly might have happened with Hondo. And it's not like I didn't sneak away with Benjamin or Haroun for the occasional quickie in some secluded closet of the Habitat. I should remember that I'm not the only one with hormones and physical needs. I should allow Adaolisa the same courtesies she's allowed me.

But there are people looking into us. People like Fillemon Petrus and the Stewards, who might want nothing more than to see us dead. People who might have taken Counselor.

Adaolisa keeps reassuring me she's the safest woman in the city, that she knows what she's doing, but that doesn't mean I can't memorize the layouts of every hotel she decides to visit and lurk nearby just in case.

Keeping her safe is literally why I exist.

But maybe I should give her a little more credit.

Draining my glass, I decide to stop being a stalking, smothering, overprotective creep and go home. The song currently oozing out of the speakers is an experimental blend of synth melodies and Zimba jazz. Laughter and chatter drone over the music, the strands of static mixing together so well I can barely tell them apart.

It's funny, that, how the static of a group of people doing the same thing in the same place at the same time can sort of meld into a singular whole, like the combined voice of a choir, and they don't even know it's happening.

The waiters here are pretty men wearing little more than silk loincloths around their waists. Skin bodymods make their muscles reflect the light like polished gold. As I leave, one of them catches my eye and gives me a suggestive wink. I smile back, but I can't muster the energy to be more interested.

I need to make myself walk away. I need to let Adaolisa be her own person.

Outside, I stuff my hands in the pockets of my leather jacket and decide to make my way to the maglev station on foot. A cease-fire has been active for a week now, so the streets see more traffic even at night. The air is getting slightly warmer, too, though seasonal changes on this planet are mild, and torrid summers are a thing only to be seen in Old Earth drama serials.

I do my best not to look back at the hotel as I walk. My instincts need me to stick around, to lurk even closer, right outside the door even, but Adaolisa wants to be more independent. She's not pulling away from me, exactly. I don't think she is. But she seems to have decided she should be able to go places without me. And I shouldn't begrudge her that.

But. Couldn't she have chosen someone less . . . problematic? Michelle Zimba is young enough, I suppose, recently come to her position after her grandfather retired into the Abode, but such a powerful woman could bring us a world of trouble if their relationship were to turn sour. Not to mention she's married, even if the rumors claim she married out of convenience and that her affairs are an open secret.

Maybe Adaolisa is planning something, using the chair the same way she used Marcel, but I hate that thought even more than the idea of a simple and harmless affair.

I don't stop when a familiar brush of static tickles my senses just out of reach. I keep walking, and there it is again, keeping pace with me at the very limits of my auxiliary perception. As if whoever it is knows I can sense them.

I don't need to debate with myself what to do next. I break into a run. I turn a corner and vanish into the neon glow of the waterfront streets. Even in this part of town, there is no shortage of narrow alleys nestled between uptown bars and nightclubs.

Along a backstreet, I am the wind as I leap up to catch the rails of a first-floor alleyway balcony. I climb over the rails and quickly lie prone against the floor, my heart a beating drum inside my chest. Flashing lights and holo screens near the mouth of the street deepen the shadows around me. This is why I always like to wear black whenever I'm not impersonating a jazz starlet.

Seconds later I watch unseen as a lank figure comes sprinting down the street, a pistol in one hand. His steps waver just after he passes the balcony; then he slows and stops, looking around.

I hear him hiss out a curse. He's breathing hard like he overexerted himself. I watch him turn around and start heading back, but he's already made a mistake by letting me see him.

Just as he passes my hiding spot, I pounce, landing behind him. His static explodes with alarm, and he begins to turn around and lift his gun, but I'm already twisting his wrist to disarm him.

He's faster than I thought. Stronger too. Knows what he's doing. His other hand rises to chop at me, and I barely move in time to block it with the side of my forearm. The impact almost makes me cry out in pain—it feels like I got hit with a metal pole.

As we battle for his gun, our arms trying to outmaneuver each other, I glimpse a greenish fluorescence in the depths of his hollow eyes and a flash of metal on his face. I move too slow, and he punches me in the gut so hard I almost double over, pinpricks of light dancing at the corners of my vision. And here he is lifting his gun to finish me off.

I slide forward and redirect his aim just as he fires. Three near-silent pops make holes in the wall nearby. Someone farther down the street screams and runs away. This is a platinum-tier neighborhood; cops will be here in minutes.

Fueled by stimulants, I knee my opponent in the abdomen and seize upon his shock to finally wrest the gun from him. Before he manages to wheeze out his next breath, I have the weapon pointed right between his eyes. I take a few steps back to move out of his range.

He lifts his palms, licking his lips, eyeing me with malice. He might be twice my age, maybe a little younger than that. A goatee hangs off his chin. One cheek was shaved off and replaced with metal plating. I don't recognize him at all.

"Who the fuck are you, and what do you want from me?" I demand.

In answer he spits onto the ground separating us, his static fearless and hostile. I keep the gun aimed, my mind racing in two different directions. I should kill him, eliminate a threat, but I also need to know why he's been following me around. I'm fairly certain this is the same person I sensed at the jazz club the other day.

A moment passes. He must sense my hesitation, because he turns tail and runs. My senses coalesce around my trigger finger as I watch him pull away from me, but he ducks behind a corner before I've made my decision.

I put him out of my mind and run in the other direction, heading for the hotel.

The distant call of a siren follows me as I run. The glittering denizens of the nighttime waterfront part for me on the cement walkways, muttering insults and complaints as I barrel through them with a gun in my hand.

I don't give a shit. I'd kill them all without remorse if it meant getting to Adaolisa even a second quicker. I should have never let her out of my sight. What was I thinking?

A visible Kolovrat presence would betray the chair's activities, so I find only a single security guard on duty at the main entrance. I pull out my mobile and activate my Int-Sec filter so that I don't have to explain myself; the guard shoots me a displeased look but lets me through without stopping me.

I use the east staircase, racing up to the seventh floor, which I know will be entirely vacant save for one room. I fully expect the whole floor to be heavily guarded, and I'm not disappointed. As soon as I fling the door open on the seventh-floor landing, I find myself staring at a well-armed Kolovrat soldier, blond and pale skinned, multiple magazines slotted into the pockets of his navy ballistic chest piece.

Except he's sprawled on the ground, unconscious. I see the legs of another fallen soldier farther down the hall, the rest of his body hidden behind a corner. The next breath I take almost makes me sneeze.

To most humans fentanyl has no distinct smell, but I was made to be able to identify and be resistant to a wide range of harmful substances, including fentanyl-based incapacitating agents. I start to feel dizzy, but my thoughts remain my own, my will unbreakable. I will reach Adaolisa even if I have to tear through the walls to get to her.

My legs carry me forward. There are multiple sources of static on this floor, most of them dulled to unconsciousness, but I home in on the one I came for and almost cry out with relief when I confirm whose it is.

Adaolisa. She's alive. But something is wrong.

I turn onto a hallway lined with doors. At the far end I see a man in black armor and a breathing mask. The figure was crouched down, but now he snaps closed a small polymer briefcase and rises to face me, surprise in his static, the briefcase dangling from one hand. I immediately know he's an enemy, so I raise my gun and fire as I run forward.

Bullets hit his mask as he turns around and runs. He ducks behind a corner and is gone. Much as I want to, I don't run after him; something is wrong inside room 713. I race for the door and try to open it, but it's locked.

"Adaolisa!"

Silence, but I'm close enough to her to know she's scared and fighting for her life. I yell as I kick on the door. My limbs are not bionic machines, but the Custodians treated biology as their steel, nature as their nuts and bolts. Strength surges within my unnaturally fortified bones, and at my next kick the lock gives way and the door opens.

I don't have time to process what I'm doing before I've done it. I run inside the room, and all I see is Adaolisa on the large bed as she struggles against the hands that have closed around her throat.

I give only one warning. "Stop!"

And when the attacker refuses to comply, I shoot. Two bullets straight into the head. Adaolisa frees herself, and the attacker falls on the bed next to her, limp and wide eyed.

"Ada, are you all right?"

She sits up, rubbing at her sore neck. "Fine," she says, her voice hoarse.

I move closer, the gun still aimed, my heart battering against its restraints. Michelle Zimba, the executive chair of ZimbaTech herself, now stares unblinkingly at the ceiling, her naked body lifeless, blood soaking out of the bullet wounds and into the sheets. Judging by Adaolisa's equally unclothed state, something else was happening here, until it wasn't anymore.

Despite everything, I remain in control, calm, composed. "Ada, you're going to have to explain to me why I just shot the city's chair in the head to save your life."

She's still rubbing at her neck, tears spilling out of her eyes. "I don't know," she says in a broken whisper.

"You have to do better, my love."

"I don't know! One moment we were . . . and then she changed all of a sudden. I don't know what came over her. It's like she . . . like she lost her mind!" Adaolisa looks to her side and gasps, then looks away, covering her mouth with a shaking hand, the sound of her ragged breaths filling the room. She's panicking.

I almost prod myself to check I'm not in some twisted nightmare. Ancestors. What are we going to do now? I need to salvage this. I need to think like a Prime. Or like a smart Proxy.

I look at the gun in my hands, the pistol I took from my attacker, with ten more rounds left in the magazine. My mind goes to places I never thought it could go, places so revolting my guts almost tie themselves into knots.

"Ada, I need you to be brave right now," I say. "Can you do that for me?"

She nods but covers her mouth to keep in a sob.

"Someone drugged all the guards outside," I say. "They probably tampered with the security cameras, but I'll need you to check and scrub any footage of me on this floor as soon as I leave, do you understand? I'll also need you to make sure there's a record of you sending me a message for help, maybe ten minutes ago. Can you do that?"

Her eyes widen as she catches on to what I intend to do. She glances at my gun, taking a shuddering breath. "Okay," she says, then: "Will it hurt?"

"Yes. Quite a bit."

Adaolisa, the brave and intelligent other half of my soul, she looks me in the eye and doesn't flinch. "Do it."

Every muscle in my body screams at me to stop, but I don't have a choice. I raise my gun, and then I shoot her.

—

Every law enforcement agency is there within minutes, helos and drones circling the hotel like carrion birds around a corpse, strobe lights flashing in the night from a fleet of ambulances and cop cars.

I get muzzled with an oxygen mask next to an ambulance outside the hotel while the recently resurrected Director Abuk Dieng relentlessly interrogates me. The whole time she watches me like a bug she'd like to squish beneath her expensive booties, her pencil-thin eyebrows tilted as if glued in place that way. Angelique's hulking form lurks just within earshot, bionic arms folded, eyes glowing at me with cynical amusement. Neither woman likes me, but I provide them no reason to doubt my account of what happened.

"Tell me again," Dieng demands, "how did you know to come here?"

The oxygen therapy isn't necessary, but it does help ease my light-headedness. Also, I'd draw suspicion to myself if I didn't need it. My voice comes out muffled. "I was having a drink at the lounge down the road when I got my sister's message."

"And what did the message say?"

"It said *Help*."

"And why didn't you immediately call Int-Sec for backup? Or the police? Why did you come here alone?"

A sigh pours out of my mouth, misting the inside of my mask. I think I breathed enough of that gas to kill an ordinary human being. I don't know if those guards will survive. "I didn't know what the situation was. I just acted."

"Then what happened?"

"I ran here. I knew she'd be on the seventh floor, so I took the stairs. But when I got there, I found the guards unconscious, and there was something in the air making me dizzy. I left before I breathed in too much. Then I called it in."

Dieng's lips twist with displeasure, but I don't sense that she doubts me. "We'll verify all you have told us, Ms. Nandipa. And if you have lied to us . . ." A shark smile with brand-new teeth flashes at me. "We will know."

As I watch her walk away, I suffer a brief spell of nausea and sheer terror. Ancestors, I really hope Adaolisa removed any digital trace of me entering that floor; otherwise we'll both be screwed.

Three hours later a nurse at a small uptown hospital shows me to the doors of a pristine ward, and for the second time tonight I find Adaolisa in bed inside a strange room. Except this time she's wearing a hospital gown, and there's gauze covering her left shoulder.

My heart breaks at the sight of her lying there looking fragile, her back elevated so she's almost sitting up. She should be resting, but I find her working on a sleek mobile computer, her fingers flying across the keyboard. The tremors haven't left her hands.

News feeds on the Nzuko are already running wild with speculation. Some are blaming the skelems for the chair's assassination, even though all three groups agreed to a cease-fire. Others are spreading rumors of an interfamilial plot to unseat the Zimba family from power.

I can't refute either theory. All I know is, the chair was crazed and tried to kill Adaolisa, and the man I saw in the hotel was involved somehow.

"How are you feeling?" I ask as I walk in, and I immediately feel foolish for such a trite question.

"Now is not the time for guilt, my love," she says breezily.

I sit down on the chair next to her bed, emotions roiling in the pit of my stomach. "I think you need to rest, Ada. Vengeance can come later."

"I'm all right," she says, a note of frustration creeping into her voice. "And none of this is your fault. I should be the one apologizing for being so stupid—" Her voice breaks with emotion.

I sense her embarrassment and annoyance with herself for failing to anticipate what happened. I sense her love and gratitude for my timely arrival. Mostly, though, I sense her blistering fury.

I put a hand on her thigh, my palm settling on the white duvet covering her legs. "You have nothing to be ashamed of," I tell her. "You couldn't have predicted this."

She takes a deep breath to banish the tremors. While the other emotions subside, the fury rises to the surface and hardens the lines of her face. "It doesn't matter. I'm alive, and so are you. And the enemy has revealed themselves. Now we can find them."

Before I can open my mouth to advise against acting too brashly, my mobile pings inside my pocket. "Check your mobile," Adaolisa tells me. "The bastard doesn't know I have control of every camera connected to the Nzuko. You should be able to track him wherever he goes. I want him collected and prepared for interrogation by noon tomorrow. And keep this private. I don't want anyone else getting to him before we do, understood?"

My hand is still on her thigh. I squeeze just a little to draw her eyes to mine. "Ada, I don't think I should leave you here, and I really think you should let yourself rest."

Liquid anger shimmers in her gaze for a moment. She takes another deep breath to fend off the tears, but I hear them in her voice. "I made a mistake, but I'm not powerless. I have an army of drones watching me as we speak. I'll rest once I know that whoever made Michelle . . ." Speaking the name makes Adaolisa's breath hitch, and despite her efforts a tear escapes the corner of one eye and leaves a wet streak down her cheek. "Please, Nandipa. I need this."

I well with protectiveness and anger on her behalf. The last time I saw her this torn up was when we'd just witnessed our old home breaking apart on the seafloor. I need to fix this.

I nod. "It will be done."

Chapter 17: Hondo

David and fucking Benjamin. Alive.

For a moment we stare at each other inside the tiny cell, and despite the air of danger, an emotion I can't identify twists inside my gut, something bright and not precisely unwelcome, mixed with enough grief to nearly knock the breath out of me.

Someone else from home is *alive.*

Someone else survived that ruin on the ocean bed, the end of everything I'd ever known and loved and hated.

The force of my emotion takes me by surprise. Until now I had no idea just how much I wanted this to be true, how much I needed to know that someone else had made it. All those faces I sketched on my tablet—my eyes prickle at the knowledge that two of them no longer need to be mourned.

David's slanted smile sobers me very quickly, though, the old loathing rising to overshadow whatever sentimental nonsense was beginning to cloud my judgment. Benjamin reacts to my quiet hostility by narrowing his eyes at me. Patience has leaned against the doorpost, arms folded, watching us with open suspicion.

When David takes a step forward, I attempt to get up from my chair, ready to fight. My shackles jangle as they resist me.

"Easy there, Hondo," he says, blithe like he knows I can't escape. "You'll hurt yourself needlessly." He pulls a chair across the table and settles down, eyes sweeping back and forth between me and Jamal. His grin widens as he lays a hand flat on the table. "Jamal."

"David." Jamal has retreated behind a cool exterior and masked himself so thickly I hardly know what he's thinking.

"The surface has been kind to you both. You look well."

"Do we?" Jamal quips. "Because my definition of *well* does not include being kidnapped and tied up."

"Still a smart-mouthed little shit, aren't you," David says with an easy laugh. "Are you thirsty?" Before either of us can answer, he looks over his shoulder. "Could we get them something to drink, Comrade Patience? Water will be fine."

Patience straightens from where she was leaning and gives us an uncharitable look before she nods. "Yes, Comrade David."

As she leaves, "Comrade" David flashes his teeth again, no doubt enjoying having us at his mercy.

"No need to be scared, Jamal. If I intended you harm, I wouldn't have bothered coming here to speak with you."

"Maybe you wanted to gloat," Jamal says. "Let's not pretend you don't hate me with every fiber of your being. You must be having the time of your life, seeing me like this."

David's lips curl downward with displeasure. "*Hate* is such a strong word. I disliked you, sure, but I didn't actively wish you harm. I still don't."

"Your people drugged Hondo and shackled us," Jamal hisses. "That feels pretty harmful to me."

"They *detained* you to give me a chance to speak to you," David says. "I had a feeling there might be others out there, so I warned them to be on the lookout." For some reason David hesitates. "You won't believe this, but you're exactly who I hoped would come along. You have no idea how happy I am to see you, Jamal. I thought you were dead."

I can't have heard that correctly. I trade a bewildered look with Jamal. He doesn't seem to believe his ears either. The only thing that still makes sense in this room is Benjamin's scowl as he stares down at me.

"Why the fuck would you ever be happy to see me?" Jamal asks, and David lifts an eyebrow at the language, but the smug grin has mostly gone from his face.

"Maybe because I owe you my life." When the confused creases deepen on Jamal's forehead, David expels a long breath. "During the attack on the Habitat," he explains, "Benjamin and I made it to the bunker beneath the kelp-processing plant. I'm guessing you never saw the inside of a bunker, did you?"

Jamal shakes his head. "We escaped with Counselor on a submersible."

"What?" Shock and the glint of something violent flashes across David's eyes. "Counselor is alive?"

"I don't know." Jamal gives a shrug. "He disappeared the same day we surfaced."

David continues to eye Jamal in a way that irks me, but the look slides off his face, and he seems to relax. "You'll have to tell me more," he says. "Anyway, the bunker we ended up in was rather large. Three floors buried deep in the seabed. There were about two dozen of us there, including Administrator and a team of wardens. The plan was for us to hole up for a week or two, then find someplace else to rebuild. We were fully on board at first, myself included." David's tone is easy and matter of fact, but that violence shimmers back to life in his gaze. "At least until we got your message."

"My message?" Jamal asks, not bothering to mask his confusion.

"Your message, Jamal," David says with an intense stare. "You exposed the Custodians for who they really were and the lies they'd told us. You opened our eyes."

"The dead man's switch," I breathe in amazement, recalling the digital blackmail contingency Jamal created in the hours before we left for the mech bay.

It was supposed to save us from Counselor's retribution in case he found out we'd stolen his data stick. I think Jamal was supposed to disable the switch every day. It must have gone off after we left.

"He speaks!" David says to me, his grin making a comeback. "How have you been, Hondo?"

I will myself not to frown. In all the years I've known him, David has never addressed me directly, and certainly never by name. I was always *the Rat's Dog* or *expie filth*. I don't think I'm ready to pretend those years never happened. "I've been well," I force my lips to say. "You?"

"Never better." David's grin slowly fades into wistfulness as he sits back into his chair, interlacing his fingers behind his head. "Ancestors, this is so surreal. I still can't believe someone else survived. I'd begun to lose hope."

Patience returns right then with a plastic jug filled with water, which she nearly slams onto the table in front of me. She places a cup next to it, and all the while her heated eyes never look away from my face. I'm not sure what I've done to piss her off, but she's obviously taken an instant dislike to me.

I avert my gaze until she walks back to lean against the doorpost.

With our hands bound we can hardly reach for the jug, so David does us the favor of filling the cup and pushing it closer.

"Drink," Jamal says before I can offer him the first sip.

I shouldn't put my welfare over his, but I don't want to argue with him in front of these people, so I awkwardly lift the cup to my lips and drain it of every drop. The water has a subtle but pleasant citrus tang. I find that I'm still thirsty. David pours me a second without question. Then a third.

When Jamal finally has his turn, he drinks only half his cup before he sets it down on the table. "So what happened after you got the message?" he asks.

David harrumphs. "What do you think? We turned against the bastards, of course. Killed them all eventually, but . . . well. They had guns and we did not. Most of us didn't make it. Haroun . . ." A haunted look crosses David's features. "He wouldn't leave Moussa's body. Wouldn't follow us to the escape pods. Benjamin and I had to leave him there. We took the last pod, expecting to meet the others on the surface, but there was no one else when we got there. To this day I don't know what happened to the other pods. Benjamin and I drifted on the water for two days before the Free People found and rescued us."

Tightness wraps around my gut, an ember of hope flickering in my core. I sense an echo of the same feeling from Jamal. "So there could be other survivors?" he asks in a near whisper, as if he fears giving voice to the hope.

"I don't know," David says with a weary sigh. "I've been searching. Haven't had any luck until now. All I know is, if it wasn't for your message, we'd still be stuck down there, or worse. Like I said, I owe you my life."

I half expect Jamal to say something snippy, but I'm surprised by the wave of sorrow that envelops him. "Sounds like the message did more harm than good, though," he says. "You might have gotten away, but it seems everyone else died or disappeared."

"As opposed to what alternative?" David puts both elbows on the table so he can lean forward, teeth almost bared. "Trust me when I say this, Jamal. When we decided to fight those evil bastards, none of us thought we'd survive. We knew we'd probably die, but we weren't living another second as their prized experiments. You freed us from a delusion, and we were all grateful for it."

I have to consciously avoid scratching my head. David, deigning to thank my Prime for saving his life? Reality is beginning to feel like the dream of a mad god.

"I'm sorry about Moussa," Jamal offers. "I know you two were friends."

"We all lost so much that day," David says, then gives a sad smile. "But we gained a lot too. I mean, look at you. Sailing the seas in your own submarine. Who'd have ever thought?"

"Speaking of which." Jamal tugs at his restraints to bring attention to them. "Are you going to let us go now?"

"On one condition," David says. "Take a walk with me. I have a proposal to make. After that, what you do is up to you."

Jamal thinks about it. "Sounds fair."

David's eyes crinkle in the corners, and I really don't like the guarded smile Jamal returns. He of all people should know better than to trust anything David says.

"Please untie them, Comrade Patience. They'll behave." David eyes me. "You'll behave, won't you, Hondo?"

I stir with irritation, but I nod.

Patience reluctantly unties us, and then David beckons us to follow him out of the cell. Rubbing his wrists, Jamal complies. I come up behind him, stretching my back, but at the door, I stop to face off with Benjamin. He's even bulkier in his composite armor and draped wax cloth, but I don't shy from his glare. I'm not afraid of him. I've also never liked him. I still don't, and I can tell that the feeling is intensely mutual.

"Hondo," he says.

"Benjamin," I say.

Nearby Patience snorts like she finds us ridiculous.

We've said what we need to say to each other, so we leave it at that and follow our Primes.

Chapter 18: Nandipa

He goes by the name Njabulo Mnisi and lives in a silver-tier neighborhood dotted with pleasant little treed parks where the sickly sweet smell of rotted fruits wafts on the cold breeze.

A skinny, twitchy man with a scraggly beard, when he's not lurking in gassed hallways outside hotel rooms with mysterious briefcases, Mnisi pretends to be one of the myriad coders who work for ZimbaTech's massive digital infrastructure. He seems to be aware of the placement of street cameras, the way his face is rarely fully exposed in any of the surveillance feeds I watch of him.

His cold eyes are constantly moving, assessing his surroundings. One might mistake his overall demeanor for a nervous temperament, but I recognize in his eyes the alertness of a trained soldier.

One afternoon he returns to his apartment and finds me waiting for him. I don't give him a chance to react. While he lies unconscious on his floor, I use his biometrics and a code-breaking application on my mobile to open the safe in his bedroom.

The mysterious briefcase is inside. I unlock the latches and lift the lid open. It's a computer of some kind, though it can't be an ordinary computer if it can incite the executive chair of a city to commit mindless murder. There are other things in the safe. A heavy pistol, some ammunition, documents, money tokens.

I take everything, then clean up any sign of my presence in the apartment. All cameras that saw me will have their feeds edited. The digital filter masking my appearance means no one wearing contacts or lenses will remember what I look like.

Minutes later I fly my black coupe through a light drizzle and into the upper floor of a parking tower still under construction. A silver luxury two-seater is the only other vehicle there. As I exit my car, I unholster my gun and grasp it firmly with a gloved hand. Adaolisa comes out of the other car, dressed in a white pantsuit and a matching turban.

She has to be in pain from her gunshot wound, but she's put on a brave face, and I know almost nothing will make it come off. Wordlessly, she comes over to my car and stands nearby as I open the trunk.

My quarry has regained consciousness and is now struggling against the ropes binding his hands and feet, but he stills at the sight of a gun barrel pointed at his face. I reach forward with my free hand to pull out the cloth gag I shoved into his mouth.

He doesn't scream. His static is high strung but steady. This isn't his first dance with peril.

"So here's how it's going to work," I tell him. "We ask you a question, and you answer it truthfully. Lie, and we'll know. Trust me, you don't want us to know you're lying."

"You might as well kill me," he calmly says. "You'll get nothing out of me."

His Third carries an eastern accent. He might have originally come from Transworld or Nkala Interstellar.

Adaolisa steps closer, her expression empty, but a smoldering heat sparks in her gaze at her first look of the man. I catch her wincing a little as she pulls out a syringe from the pocket of her white jacket.

"Mnisi, right?" she says. "If that is even your name. Do you know what this is?" She holds the syringe for Mnisi to see. The liquid inside is milky and only slightly transparent. By the minute widening of his eyes and the higher pitch of his static, he recognizes it. "One dose of this, and every nerve in your body will become as a lit flame. A second will feel like an eternity. Without binds you'd tear your skin off just to make it stop."

She leans closer to Mnisi, caustic venom dripping from her words even as she lowers her voice. "Now, I don't actually need to use this to get the truth from you. I suspect you already know who I am and what I'm capable of. You know I can read you like words in a book. But I *want* to. I want to make you suffer. I want to hear you scream, do you understand?"

Mnisi's heart is beating so hard it's adding a regular thrum to his static, but his limbs remain perfectly still, the light of intelligence clear in his eyes. "Yes," he says.

"Who do you work for?" she demands.

"I literally can't tell you that," he says.

I glance at Adaolisa, confused, but she's watching Mnisi with dawning understanding. "It's an implant," she tells me. "He's been compelled not to speak of certain things."

"Not just a pretty face, then," Mnisi replies, lips curling in smugness and spite. "You're wasting your time. Kill me or let me go."

"What's in the briefcase?" Adaolisa asks. "How did you make the chair turn violent?"

"Can't say."

"How many of you are there?"

"Don't know."

"That's a lie." Adaolisa nods at me. "Shoot him in the knee."

I point my gun.

"Wait!" Mnisi cries. "Fine. There are many of us. I don't know exactly how many, but we're everywhere. Some of us know more than others. I'm really just a grunt. I follow orders. That's it. I don't know much."

"How did you know about us?"

"We didn't, not at first," Mnisi says. "We only suspected. You came out of nowhere, and all of a sudden you're chumming around with some very powerful people." He grunts. "You weren't subtle."

Adaolisa takes a moment to digest that. "Who ordered you to attack me?"

Mnisi licks his lips, eyes darting to my gun. "I don't know. I received a message with instructions, and I followed them."

"Why would your people want to kill us?"

Mnisi's chest rises and falls with rapid breaths.

"Don't think about lying, because I will know," Adaolisa warns, to which he snarls like something has snapped inside of him.

"Because you shouldn't exist!" he growls. "You are chaos and regression, and your creators would shackle us to mortal flesh when we could aspire to be so much more!"

His forehead has dampened with sweat. For someone who was determined to tell us nothing just a short while ago, he's suddenly very emotive.

"He knows what happened to Counselor," Adaolisa tells me, sounding amazed. "What did you do with him?" she asks Mnisi, bringing the syringe closer. "He was one of our creators. He disappeared a while ago. Did you take him?"

Mnisi eyes the syringe. "Someone might have taken him, yes."

"Where?" I demand.

"I don't know."

My heart rate picks up. "Is he alive?" I ask.

"Last time I checked—" Mnisi screams abruptly, his eyes rolling up into his skull. His back arches unnaturally, and he starts to quake like he's having a seizure. I begin to wonder if I missed Adaolisa sticking him with the syringe.

"Nandipa," she says nervously. The syringe is still in her hand.

I sense his static sputtering and jerking; never a good sign. He gives one last shudder before he goes still, and his eyes, so aware just seconds ago, never blink again.

"What the fuck just happened?" I ask.

"He said too much, I think," Adaolisa mutters. She takes a few pacing steps away from my car, a hand on her chin, calculations racing behind her eyes. "The Stewards. It's them. The makers of ultraware. That's how they made Michelle . . . and they took Counselor, who could still be alive and somewhere in this city."

I stare helplessly at her. I haven't slept since the attack on the hotel, and I don't have the brainpower to make sense of anything she's said. "So what now?"

"Do you have the briefcase?"

I nod toward the passenger seat and watch as she goes to fetch the briefcase and the other items I collected from Mnisi's safe. She has a determined look on her face as she closes the door. "If we retrace his steps through the Nzuko, we might be able to find who else is part of his group, and where they might have taken Counselor."

"I can do that," I offer, then eye Mnisi's corpse. "As soon as I take care of this first."

"Good. In the meantime . . ." Adaolisa lifts the closed briefcase so she can take a better look at it. "I'll try to find out exactly what this thing is." She glances one last time at Mnisi, then walks away. "I'll see you back at HQ."

"All right."

My heart aches as I watch her return to her vehicle. Mnisi's dead eyes don't blink as I shut the trunk.

Chapter 19: Hondo

I lift a hand to protect my eyes from the sun's glare as we come out onto the frigate's weather deck. I expected the flotilla would be a large collection of ships, and I'm not disappointed. There are more ships in my immediate line of sight than I've ever seen in one place. Warships, cruisers, yachts, aircraft carriers—most with a black star marking their hulls.

But they sail at the periphery of a much more impressive structure: a constellation of hexagonal neighborhoods floating mostly in a ring and connected to each other through detachable walkways. Neat but visibly aged prefabricated buildings rise up to four stories high on these floating neighborhoods, many of which were built with platforms for ships to dock and refuel.

As we follow David down a long gangway off the ship, a knot loosens in my stomach at the sight of the *Seajack* docked to a nearby charging port, its white hull seeming to glow in the sunlight. Despite my lingering anger over being kidnapped, I feel myself thawing just a little, though I've already decided we'll be leaving and getting as far away from here as possible at the first opportunity.

David takes us on a slow walk down a treed pathway in one of the larger neighborhoods, a leisure park, I think. I see an old couple sitting on a bench, enjoying the sunlight while watching over two little girls chasing each other on a well-tended lawn. A woman greets David with a smile as she jogs past us, a light sheen of perspiration covering her face. I could almost believe we were on an island, or somewhere along the coast.

More people we pass incline their heads at David. One man even stops to shake his hand. I don't think he's universally known; not everyone seems to recognize him. But those who do greet him with a clear measure of respect.

Jamal observes this with a slight tilt of an eyebrow, but for a while he lets David speak without interruption.

The Black Star flotilla is home to one of the larger and more powerful tribes of the Free People, or so David tells us. There are at least five other major tribes that sail the oceans of the planet, some more democratic than the others, but the one thing they have in common is an unshakable hatred for the corporate cities.

Most of the tech they use, including the blocky prefabs and the helium-3 nuclear reactors that power everything, is pre-Artemisian. And so are their societies, David tells us. They are the last remnants of the settlers who arrived from the stars in pursuit of a better life, the last holdouts driven off dry land by rising corporate powers who were determined to destroy anything they couldn't dominate.

Patience, Benjamin, and I stay two steps behind the Primes the whole time. When they come to a stop by the rails of a seaside walkway, we stop, too, though I'm sure the others are listening as attentively as I am.

I'm surprised Patience is still with us. I wonder if the lieutenant sent her to watch me or if David has acquired himself a second Proxy.

"They've changed very little over the past century," David says to Jamal, his face turned toward the fantastic view of the ocean and the flotilla's many glittering ships. "In a lot of ways, this is something to celebrate and admire about them. But they've also grown stagnant, I'd say, and proud, too caught up in the tiny details to see the bigger picture. Disagreements over the silliest things, like the meaning of a flag or the true name of a dead war hero. They fail to see how much power they could command if they only stood together. Things are beginning to change, though."

Jamal leans against the rails and watches David with a lopsided near smile. "You know, I heard there was commotion going on among the Free People. I don't know why I didn't realize there was more to it. So what, are you their leader now?"

Patience makes a scoffing noise, and I note the way Benjamin's expression flattens like he's holding in a frown. *So she doesn't like David either.* I don't know why, but this pleases me greatly.

"Oh, I'm far too young for that," David says. "Besides, they elect their leaders here. But I'm good at getting people to sit down and work around their differences toward a common goal. I helped end a decades-long turf war, so now I get sent to mediate between the tribes. They see me as a genuinely neutral party. It's the best place to start building alliances that transcend traditional tribal lines."

"I'm impressed," Jamal says, a little too honest for my liking. "Although I can't say I'm surprised."

David flashes a sheepish grin. "We can't help ourselves, can we? The compulsive need to change things for the better was built into us."

"You mean the compulsive need to control."

"To change something, you need a measure of control over it. And you're one to talk. I've seen what's inside your ship. I know for a fact you're the one causing all that trouble in the cities."

There's nothing sour in David's tone, but Jamal turns his face away. "You don't know what it's like in the cities. The Habitat might have been a prison, but I'd take that over what many people have to endure up here."

"Then I'm glad the Free People found us," David says. "And good timing, by the way. It's a much-needed boost in morale for everyone to see that the cities are not untouchable. What you did in ZimbaTech . . ." Something hungry skitters across David's eyes as he regards Jamal, instantly raising my hackles. "I'm beginning to realize just how much we all underestimated you, my friend." He laughs, throaty and slightly resentful. "I guess that's how you were able to play both me and Adaolisa."

"I was only trying to stay alive," Jamal says.

"I know. And I . . . apologize for how I reacted." David looks down at his sandals like he can't meet Jamal's eyes. "Honestly, I don't even remember how I let myself become her puppet. She had a way of getting inside your head, you know?"

"You mean, she *has* a way of getting inside your head."

David's head whips up, a stricken look on his face. "What?"

"Adaolisa is in ZimbaTech," Jamal clarifies, showing only the barest hint of glee at David's reaction. "She and Nandipa were with us when Counselor took us up to the surface."

"Nandipa is alive?" Benjamin utters, his eyes uncharacteristically wide. It shocks me a little because I've never heard him speak of his own accord in David's presence.

"She is," Jamal says to Benjamin, and this time he lets his smirk show. "In fact, we lived together in the same apartment for months. Got to know each other quite well."

"So that was her work then, in ZimbaTech, with the hacks?" David says, still looking like he's seen the ghosts of his ancestors.

"Oh no, that was me," Jamal says flippantly. "In fact, that's why I had to leave."

"Ah." Abruptly David's shock transforms into a contemptuous curl of the lip. "She has plans of her own, I take it, and you were interfering." He snickers. "I'm guessing she's already in control of the city."

"That would be a safe guess."

"You know what her next move will be, right?"

"Take control of the other cities?"

"We can't let her do that," David says with venom that has clearly simmered for a while. "Adaolisa is like a black hole. She gravitates toward the center of power. She *is* the center of power; she wants to suck everything in. If she takes control, no one will be able to stop her."

Jamal remains thoughtfully expressionless, perhaps not wanting to reveal too much of his own opinion on the matter. "You said you had a proposal."

"Yes," David says. "I want us to work together."

"Doing what?"

"Hitting the cities where it hurts. That's what you want, isn't it? To tear down the rot so there's a chance people will wake up and build something better?"

Jamal's lips part like he's surprised. "Yes."

"I can help you. The Free People are used to life at sea, but they had cities and towns on dry land before the corporations drove them out. They've always wanted their land back—it's easier to build and grow things on dry land—but it's a tough ask. The corporate cities don't want their enslaved populations infected with democratic ideas, so they keep the Free People as far away as possible."

"So you want to invade," Jamal asks.

"I want to force the cities to the negotiating table. That means crippling them until they don't have a choice. Here's the thing, Jamal. You have your computers and your hacks, and I have motivated people and lots of guns. Together, we'd be unstoppable."

My heart sinks when Jamal appears to consider the idea. "Perhaps."

They proceed to spend the rest of the day together, comparing notes on what they've seen and done since the attack on the Habitat, Patience, Benjamin, and me tailing them like shadows.

Miserable shadows, at least where Benjamin and I are concerned.

David helps Jamal barter our grain seeds and ammo for more food and supplies than they're worth. And with one smile and a wink, he gets the docking officials to recharge our *Seajack* for free. The ease with which Jamal settles into a lighthearted rapport with him makes me unreasonably ill tempered.

I don't trust David. Even the Free People don't trust him; otherwise why would Patience stick to him like a fly on fresh shit? I see it in the way she watches us all, listening, making notes and observations with the awareness of a trained Proxy. No doubt every word said between the Primes will be relayed back to Lieutenant Lukwiya.

We return to the park later that afternoon, licking cones of locally made plant-based ice cream so good I almost forget that I don't like this place. The Primes tacitly dismiss us and wander off to go sit on a bench out of earshot. For some reason Patience stays with me and Benjamin, and the three of us sit on our own bench, watching the Primes laugh at each other's jokes like old friends.

"They're getting too chummy with each other," Benjamin grouses.

"I know," I say, and we both scowl at each other, annoyed there's something we agree on.

Patience catches on and snickers, hiding her smile behind her ice cream.

Benjamin chomps down on his cone like it's a thankless chore, then says, without looking at me, "So you lived with Nandipa for months?"

I lick my ice cream, savoring this feeling. "I did."

I don't need to look at Benjamin to know he's frowning. I can almost feel the creases on his forehead. "She thought you were a creep, you know."

"Once, maybe," I say deliberately. "But things changed."

A dangerous edge enters Benjamin's voice. "Did they, now?"

"I'm not looking for a fight, Benjamin."

I sense he has something else to say, but he swallows it down and sighs. "Neither am I."

When I turn my head to the side, I catch Patience staring at me with something much less hostile, more curious than the withering looks she's been giving me all day. "What?" she says defensively, like I'm the one guilty of staring.

"Nothing," I say, and it's my turn to hide my smile.

I almost kneel and loudly praise the ancestors when Jamal finally decides it's time to head back to our ship. David walks us to the docks, Benjamin and Patience trailing behind.

"I'll see you tomorrow, then?" he says, standing far too close to Jamal for my comfort.

"I'm not running away, if that's what you're worried about," Jamal says.

"Mmm." David folds his arms with a stupid grin on his face. "Then maybe you can walk away, and I'll stand here and watch."

To my dismay, Jamal's cheeks darken with a deep blush. "Careful, David," he says with a playful cadence. "Hondo is about two seconds away from caving your face in with his fists. Come, Hondo. Before you and Benjamin have to kill each other. Enjoy the show, David."

David winks. "I will."

Back inside the *Seajack*, I immediately take the helm and prepare the vessel for departure.

"What are you doing?" Jamal says, coming to stand behind me.

A drone fills the cabin as the newly charged batteries come online. "Getting us the fuck out of here."

"What? Don't be a fool, Hondo. They'll blow us to bits."

I don't stop. In a minute we'll be leaving the docks, and I'll dive as deep as the omni can go. "They won't. David said we could go if we wanted to, and I'm not letting you spend another second in this place."

"Hondo, I'm not leaving."

I glare at him over my shoulder. "Are you crazy? You're not actually considering his proposal, are you?"

Jamal regards me like he's caught between two difficult choices. "David has a point," he says at length. "There's only so much I can do from a terminal, but with his help, we can bring real change to the world."

Knowing I won't win this argument, I slump in my seat, feeling drained. "Unbelievable."

"I'm sorry, but this is what I want," Jamal quietly says, though the words are laden with meaning. He's not just talking about David's help.

"You can't be serious," I say. "It's *David*, Jamal. You used to call him a hypocrite, a *puppet*. You said he wasn't worth the dust beneath my shoes! Not to mention how he tried to get us recycled. We hate him, remember?"

"Yes, but that was then, and this is now."

"That's how time generally works. It's linear. It moves forward. But David is still David. He's still an asshole."

"And he's still stupidly attractive," Jamal says in a drawl. "Except now I don't have to feel guilty for wanting to get railed by his—"

"Don't," I say, "finish that sentence." I rub my temples with my fingers, grimacing at the imagery. "For fuck's sake, Jamal. I can't even look at you right now."

"Oh, grow up." Jamal's voice retreats from me as he heads aft of the cabin. "I never said anything about your little infatuation with Nandipa, did I?"

"So you're infatuated with him, are you?"

"Of course not," he calls. "Now turn off the engines and stop behaving like a child."

Ugh. *David.* Everything about him irks me. Him and Benjamin both. Their smugness. The way they think they should be in charge of everything. The way David got angry at us for daring to survive and beat him at his own game. I don't think of myself as vindictive, but I won't ever let that go. I'll never like him, no matter what Jamal says.

But he's the boss here, so I turn off the engines and find refuge in the lines of my sketchpad.

Chapter 20: Nandipa

Retracing Mnisi's steps through the Nzuko to find out where Counselor might be hiding is like trying to find a rock in an asteroid belt. The number of people to watch grows exponentially with every new contact he interacts with, because then I have to trace those contacts, too, and whoever they interact with, and so on.

I have few parameters to refine my search, so I let my instincts guide me through the widening web of contacts, following anyone who even slightly raises my suspicion. After three days spent in a locked office at Int-Sec HQ, hidden away from the eyes of a prying Angelique, I narrow down the possibilities to five different locations.

The first is a church in the Jondolos. From a jollof restaurant a block away, I deploy a stealthy spider drone to infiltrate and scout the building, watching the drone's feed on a tablet. The drone discovers a cache of guns and ammo hidden in a secret room behind a bookshelf but nothing else. Radio frequency scanning reveals no other hidden chambers. I rule the church out and return to HQ.

The next day I lose Angelique's tail and drop my spider drone as I walk past a launderette in a bronze-tier district. The drone skitters inside and crawls unseen along a wall, sending me its camera feed.

There are more guns hidden in the back room, which doesn't surprise me. I'm beginning to think that whoever these people are, they have stashes of weapons and ammunition hidden all over the city. There's no sign of Counselor, so I leave, marking the launderette as a point of future interest.

The third location is a large section of interstellar ship rusting away in the eastern outskirts of the city, deeper inland and close to the spaceport. Ostensibly it was converted into a hostel for freight handlers and other employees of the spaceport but was abandoned some years ago when more permanent accommodations were built. A delivery drone spotted one of Mnisi's contacts in the vicinity, so I'm almost certain there's something more to the ship than meets the eye.

I park my aerial car within sight of the ship's stationary hulk. Out the windows on the passenger side, ZimbaTech's skyline is a haze shrouded in the morning's fog. On the driver's side the farmlands that stretch away from the city's boundaries are visible as a line of green on the horizon.

I open my door just wide enough to let out the spider drone, then send it crawling toward the ship. The structure is only a small section of a much larger vessel, but it still boasts the height and width of a five-story apartment block. The spider drone scurries up the rusted hull on the side facing me and crawls in through a broken window. I've barely made out what's in the room when there's a shout, and then the camera feed goes dark.

Shit. No use being stealthy about it now. I put on my helmet and get out of the car, pulling my gun out as I make a beeline for the ship. Five different minds brush against my senses when I get close enough, and I almost stumble to a stop.

Four of those static sources are ramped up and alert, but something about that fifth mind is so familiar I immediately *know* whose it is.

Heart sprinting inside my chest, I crouch behind an abandoned car and activate my earpiece. Adaolisa will have weaponized drones lurking nearby, ready to come to my aid at a moment's notice. When I address her, she answers almost immediately. "I think this is the place," I say. "I'm going in."

A slight pause. *"Are you sure that's wise?"* comes her voice into my ear.

"I might have tipped them off already, so it's better I go in now."

"I'll send in the drones."

I wait until I spot two spherical drones descending from the sky, then spring forward, running for the ramp going up to the ship's boarded-up entrance.

Gunfire pours out of the darkness as soon as I kick down the boards, a bullet striking my helmet. I duck out of the way and let the drones go in and take the barrage on their armored plating. They return fire with mounted Gatling guns, and both shooters go down.

I move into the ship, my senses alive. There's someone one deck above me, armed and waiting. Probably the same person who shot my spider. There's someone else one deck below. Also armed. And there, three decks beneath me, at the very bottom, I suspect: a weak but scattered buzz. For most of my life that buzz was hidden behind a layer of dead space, but there were moments during our ascent from the Habitat when I felt something.

It's uncovered now. Faint, weak, but there.

This structure was part of a commercial ship; its bulkheads were not designed to resist high-caliber tungsten rounds. Closing my eyes and letting the static guide me, I aim my gun up and fire twice. I aim down and fire again. Twin echoes of heavy objects dropping to the floor reach my ears. I don't see who it is I've just killed, but I feel their minds go dull.

"Search the rest of the ship," I whisper to Adaolisa. "There's someone three decks down. I'm going to investigate."

"Understood."

The drones zip away in different directions. I find a staircase and descend, my gun still ready in case there are surprises.

The lights here flicker on and off. The ship groans with every step I take, a concert of rusted joints that feels like it might come down around me if I sneeze. I don't believe there are other enemies nearby, but my steps are measured as I approach a closed door. There are armed drones at my back. I have a gun. I know the person on the other side of this door is unarmed, so why are my hands shaking?

I open the door.

Counselor, once proud and imposing, loved to peer down at us from above the rims of his spectacles. His disapproval could mean death. I remember how afraid I was when he walked into the mech bay in a fury.

Now he sits on a dirty floor with his head bowed between his knees, gaunt and huddled up in the corner like he's shying away from the bar of sunlight coming in through the single window. His feet are bare and unwashed; his shirt, once white, is tattered and filthy; and his trousers are threadbare. These might be the same clothes he was wearing the day he left us in his apartment.

I don't see any binds on him, and the door was unlocked, so I'm not certain what has kept him in here. I take a cautious step closer.

"Counselor?" I hear myself say, as if I spoke from outside myself. I can hardly believe this is the same man who was once such a towering figure of my childhood.

He lifts his head, showing the thick and unkempt beard covering his face. His weathered and wrinkled skin has aged him by decades. I find myself dithering between rushing to his aid and keeping my distance. I ultimately decide to stay put.

"Counselor, can you hear me?"

Bloodshot eyes blink at me, at first with empty confusion, then with deepening horror. "Nandipa?"

"He's alive and lucid," I inform Adaolisa. "Counselor, can you stand up? I can get you out of here."

He shrinks away from me, shaking his head forcefully. "No. No! What are you doing here? They'll find you!"

"Who'll find us, Counselor?"

Abruptly his face goes blank, his eyes crinkling once more with confusion. "How long has it been? They've been trying to get inside my head, but I've fought them. They don't know about you. You have to leave!"

Perhaps I declared him lucid too soon. "Adaolisa, what are your instructions?" Now that I've found him, I'm suddenly at a loss.

One of the drones wheezes into the room and hovers next to me. There's a flash of laser light as the drone begins a holographic recording. My contact lenses flicker, and Adaolisa materializes nearby as an augmented reality hologram. She takes in Counselor's hunched form expressionlessly. Without lenses or an earpiece, he isn't able to perceive her presence or see the slight pursing of her lips as she looks him over. I see her lifting a tablet and tapping rapidly on the screen. "I think this is a conversation we all need to be here for."

"What are you doing?" I ask her.

"What?" Counselor babbles. "No, no, no, you must go! What are you still doing here? Is this a dream?"

"I'm calling a family meeting," Adaolisa tells me. She appears to wait for something, then says, "Put on your lenses, Jamal. There's something you need to see." Another pause. "I hardly have time to play tricks on you. I can always send you a recording later, but I think you'd rather see this in person." More silence.

I'm starting to get nervous about lingering here. "Are you watching the outside?" I ask Adaolisa.

"Yes. You'll know long before any danger arrives."

Jamal's hologram suddenly pops into being inside the room, wearing his usual cynical grin. By his floral shirt, shorts, and flip-flops, I could believe we interrupted him from sipping cocktails in some distant and sunny island paradise. I feel a sharp pang in my gut at the knowledge that Hondo can't be far away from him.

"Ladies. It's been a while," he says. "Now what was so important you needed . . ." Jamal trails off when he finally sees Counselor's huddled form. Lips parting in disbelief, he moves to get a closer look, crouching to bring himself almost face to face with the other man. He breathes out a curse as he straightens back up, eyes wide as he looks at Adaolisa. "What the hell happened to him? And how did you find him?" Jamal looks around the room; then his eyes flick to me. "Where is this, Nandipa?"

"What's important right now is that we're here," Adaolisa interjects before I can answer. "He can finally answer our questions. I thought you'd want to hear them yourself."

"I do," Jamal says, and something cryptic enters his voice. "In fact, I think there's someone else who should be here too. Hang on."

He vanishes, and I hold my breath, expecting to see him rematerialize with Hondo standing next to him. I almost choke on that breath when instead of Hondo, the ghost of someone I thought long dead pixelates into view. *That face.*

I'll never forget the hate I saw on that face the day we forced him to betray his friend. I suffer a residual flicker of guilt at seeing him standing there next to Jamal, alive, but also an unexpected joy that not everything from that old life was destroyed.

Adaolisa touches the tanzanite stones of her necklace, her shock plain even through the hologram. "David," she whispers.

Unlike Jamal, David is wearing sleek ballistic armor adorned with a drape of patterned yellow-and-green cloth. He stands proudly with his hands behind his back, his smile neither venomous nor friendly. "Adaolisa. Nandipa. It's been a while." When Adaolisa and I fail to speak, he lifts an eyebrow. "Benjamin and I are fine. Thanks for asking."

Jamal snickers, clearly enjoying our shock.

Benjamin is alive. Ancestors. My eyes begin to burn with the promise of tears.

"I . . . forgive me." Adaolisa attempts to shake herself out of it. "I'm just . . . surprised. It's good to see you."

"Likewise, I suppose," David allows. He seems to dismiss the matter altogether, turning his attention to Counselor's still-cowering form. "So the bastard is alive, is he? Go on then, Nandipa. I'm impatient to hear what he has to say."

Since I'm the only one actually present in the room, the three Primes look to me expectantly, and I have to force myself to get over my shock at David's sudden aliveness. *Right. Interrogate Counselor.*

He's muttering things I can't quite catch and shaking his head. He recoils into himself when I come closer. "No! Go away! Please! Don't let them see you here!"

I crouch so that I'm level with him. "Counselor, if you want me to leave, there are questions you need to answer. I need to know who you are, who *we* are, and why you created us."

He lifts his eyes and blinks at me consideringly, and I see the remains of his sanity rising to the surface. He breathes out, his shoulders relaxing, and his next words are spoken with lucid calm. "Yes. I recall I promised you answers once."

"You did," I say. "And now's as good a time as any." I nod at the drone. "The others are listening."

Counselor's eyes widen slightly as he glances at the hovering drone, and then he coughs out an unexpected chuckle. "I knew you'd survive. Of course you did. I should have never doubted you."

"Counselor, we don't have much time. Who are you, and what was the Habitat? Who are the people who took you?"

He lowers his gaze and breathes out again, one hand rubbing the back of his neck. "In the beginning, I suppose we were idealists. A group of scientists who fancied ourselves the custodians of Old Africa's genetic legacy. We were determined to build a new Africa on the foundations of a healthy and prosperous population, so we delved into our genetic history for traits we thought were desirable and attempted to build new genomes around those traits."

"They were eugenicists," Jamal puts in with a note of disgust, but Counselor doesn't hear him and continues.

"At first the changes we made were minimal. We selected for good health and longer life, weeded out genetic disorders. Gradually, though, our work took on a life of its own. Why not make them smarter? Stronger? Why not splice this in, add a new lobe here, a new pathway there? And later, why not test our changes on real subjects and then refine?"

"Bastards," David mutters.

"My great-grandfather was the one who started the Program," Counselor says, oblivious to his invisible audience. "By then, we'd already strayed far from our original goal. We now existed solely to build and refine the perfect humans. Even as the world changed around us, we cared only for the work, which we funded by commercializing some of our successes, like bodymods and life-extension therapies."

My stomach roils. I feel dizzy. How many of us were created and recycled to achieve such successes? I want to throw up, but I keep listening.

"We weren't the only ones trying to shape the world's future, though." Counselor rubs the back of his neck again, eyes looking haunted and far away. "There'd been a schism in the beginning, a splinter faction who changed their minds about pursuing genetic perfection and decided it would be better to merge the human body with machines instead." Counselor sneers. "They called themselves Stewards because we called ourselves Custodians. If we were for it, they were against it. They wanted a more democratic and inclusive method of human improvement, they argued, not the creation of unequal castes. Hypocrites."

Counselor snorts like he's said something funny, but his haggard sorrow returns. "We coexisted in peace at first, though our progress was rapid where theirs was slow. We were making groundbreaking discoveries about the human mind while they were still trying to figure out how to keep their implants from killing their hosts. They knew it was only a matter of time before our creations surpassed theirs.

"So they tried to destroy us," Counselor says, "and they almost succeeded. In the aftermath, we vanished from the surface and retreated to the Habitat. We started recruiting staff from prisons. We sowed rumors that we were hiding somewhere in the North Pole, and for many years, we continued our work in peace."

"Until they found you," Jamal says.

"Until they found us," Counselor echoes as if in agreement.

Silence falls over the room like a heavy drape. Even after all the evidence I've seen testifying to the lies we were told, to hear the truth spoken so plainly still takes my breath away. The games we were forced to play in the Habitat were never about survival, not really, because we weren't actually ever supposed to leave that place.

"What happened to those of us who survived your games?" I ask. I don't think I want to know, but I *need* to know. When he doesn't answer, I prod him. "Counselor, you owe us the truth."

"No one ever left the Habitat," he confesses in a broken voice. "We'd gas them all on the night before they were supposed to leave and recycle them. Then we'd begin the experiment again, hoping the new batch would be better than the last."

I detach myself from my emotions the same way I do when I have to kill.

It was all for nothing.

All the plots and betrayals, the games, the hope for a future on the surface.

We were pigs in a pen, bred for slaughter.

David has been watching Counselor with an unforgiving glower. "Put a bullet between his eyes. He can't walk free after all the things he did to us."

"You might actually be doing him a favor," Jamal intones. "I think he deserves *much* worse than a quick death. Leave him to rot."

"That's not your decision," I say, looking to Adaolisa and awaiting her instructions. She chews her lower lip in thought.

"Are you talking to them now?" Counselor says, looking at the drone.

"Yes."

"What are they saying?"

"Deciding what to do with you."

I don't miss the grimace that briefly touches Counselor's face, the lines of regret that add half a century to his age. "Then let me make it simple for you," he says. "You need to kill me."

"Even he agrees," David points out.

I ignore that comment, watching Counselor. "Why are you in here?" I ask him. "You're not bound. Why can't you simply walk out of here?"

He shakes his head slowly. "I can't leave. They put something inside me." I note the way he rubs the back of his neck again. "It hurts if I disobey. Please. I've tried so hard to keep you a secret. I don't know how much longer I can last."

"They already know about us," I reveal to him.

"Oh." He hangs his head, his shoulders sagging. "Then I've failed." Abruptly he looks back up, his eyes misting over with a mad light. "Please, kill me before they find out more. There are other secrets. Other things I shouldn't say. You have to kill me now."

I look at Adaolisa, still waiting for her to tell me what to do. Conflicting emotions show on her face. I don't need to be near her to know what she's feeling. She hates Counselor. But he's the closest thing to a parent any of us have ever had.

"Give him what he wants," she says at last. "But let him do it himself."

I did not expect to be relieved, but a knot that had tied itself up in my stomach loosens. I guess I don't want Counselor's blood on my hands.

I offer him my pistol. "You'll have to do it yourself."

He eyes it for a second, then slowly reaches for it with a shaking hand. I back away, my heart growing heavy inside my chest.

He lied to me all my life. He killed so many others like me in service to his ambitions. I should feel nothing for him. I shouldn't want to take back the gun and drag him out of here.

He raises the barrel to his lips. A tear escapes from one eye and disappears into his beard. "We lit a fire in your hearts," he says. "And in our fear, we tried to extinguish it. You deserved better. I'm sorry."

The barrel enters his mouth. The longest second of my life passes. I don't look away when he pulls the trigger.

I'm in my car five minutes later, flying back toward Int-Sec HQ. Adaolisa ended the conversation with the boys immediately after Counselor's death and wiped every Nzuko-linked camera in the vicinity while I made my escape.

I drum my fingers on the silver steering wheel, pondering what it means that Jamal and David are somehow in the same place. Together. It can't be a coincidence. "Do you think Jamal knew David was alive all along?"

"I don't know," Adaolisa says into my earpiece. *"Either way, they're working together now. It'll be a complication, but it might also be an opportunity."*

"What are you thinking?"

"They'll do something extreme, no doubt. Create chaos and scare people, as Jamal is wont to do. And when they do, we'll be there to offer the world a more agreeable alternative."

It's what she did with ZimbaTech, I realize. Jamal started a war between the city and the skelems and then left—he has always been good at destroying things. But it was up to Adaolisa to turn that war into an opportunity.

There'll be a prodemocracy march later today in the Jondolos, the second one just this week, watched over and protected by members of all three skelems. Many low-tier jazz clubs are now hot spots of political discourse that would have been criminal just a few months ago, and the authorities don't dare to crack down on them lest they inspire another rebellion.

Things are beginning to change. Slowly, perhaps. But I think this is better than setting the world on fire and hoping for the best, as is Jamal's modus operandi.

"What are we going to do about the Stewards?" I ask. "Fillemon Petrus and his people are still out there. We now know for sure they're the people who attacked the Habitat, and now they know about us. We have to do something."

"I agree, and they might have inadvertently given us the key to their own destruction."

I frown. "What do you mean?"

"I've figured out what the briefcase does."

"Let me guess. It's a mind-control device?"

"In a sense, although I'm realizing just how little control the Stewards must have over their technology if this is what they have to resort to. The device broadcasts a signal that interacts maliciously with ultraware. Any Oloye within range will lose control of themselves and fly into a violent frenzy. I think Mnisi used a weak signal because he didn't want anyone else affected, which was why he needed to be right outside the door. Such an imprecise way of going about things, no? Desperate, even."

"If killing you was the goal, a gunshot would have been easier," I agree.

"Given what we now know, I think they fear us. In fact, I think they aren't certain of the full range of our abilities. Perhaps they decided it would be safer not to come after us directly. Maybe they knew we'd see them coming."

My thoughts flash back to my scuffle with the stranger the night Adaolisa was attacked. He'd followed me from a distance, like he knew I'd sense him the second he came too close. And even that wasn't enough to keep me from noticing.

Maybe they do fear us, and maybe they're right to.

"There's still the matter of the attack on the hotel," I remind Adaolisa. "Dieng and Angelique won't rest until they find the truth. They know something's up."

Adaolisa's voice goes quiet for some time. *"We might already have a solution to that problem."*

Something in her tone makes my ears prick, dread rearing up inside me like a disturbed serpent. "Do I want to know?" I ask.

"I'll explain later. I'll see you when you get back."

The call ends just as Int-Sec's glass arrowhead building comes into view on the island up ahead. Seeing it, I suddenly feel tired. A chapter of my life has closed, I watched the last Custodian blow his brains to bits, and yet I still feel enslaved to the games they created us to play.

For a brief moment I allow myself to think about Hondo, somewhere in a sunny place. And not for the first time I wish to the ancestors we'd gone up to the stars with Zandi and left this fucking world behind.

Chapter 21: Hondo

I listen to the mission briefing from the back of a crowded ready room inside an aircraft carrier. The mission is a foolhardy scheme, but David and Lieutenant Lukwiya deliver their briefing to the gathered commandos like they've mapped out every detail.

It'll be a joint operation between the Black Star and Harambee flotillas, so commandos from both navies are here, listening intently. Whenever David speaks, my brow furrows unintentionally. I think I'm going to get premature wrinkles, the way I can't stop scowling these days.

I fold my arms and lean against the wall behind me, my frown deepening as my eyes settle on Jamal. He's seated a little closer to the front and to the side of the room, paying attention to the briefing, conspicuous in his lack of armor and relaxed state of dress. Lukwiya introduced him as a reliable tech consultant with insider knowledge of mainland defense systems and has let him clarify a few details about the harebrained assault they cooked up together.

I don't want him to be here. It's not that I don't want him to have friends or, dare I say, love, if those are things he desires. So long as I know he's safe, I will be satisfied. But I can't get over the fact that the person he's chosen to take these things from is David, who once tried to get us both recycled not very long ago.

I can't forget that. Forgetting would be against my biological imperatives, and I'll never relax so long as he continues to wield any influence over Jamal.

"I still think we're taking a big risk on an unproven quantity," says the commanding officer of the Harambee contingent once David and Lukwiya open the floor to questions. She watches Jamal beneath eyelids smeared with yellow paint. "How can we be sure your *consultant* can deliver what he's promised?"

"As I said earlier," Lukwiya answers her, "we've already performed multiple test runs, all successful."

"With *one* drop ship. Today there'll be five. How can you be sure we won't get blown out of the sky before we come within a hundred miles of the coast?"

Lukwiya manages to sneer without moving his lips. It's something he does with his synthetic white iris and maybe the inflection of his baritone voice. "You and the Harambees are welcome to back out, comrade. The Black Stars will be content to take all the glory when we return triumphant."

The Harambee officer glares back, then makes a scoffing sound as she gets up. "It'll be your head they put on a spike if this goes belly up, Lukwiya. Come on, then. Let's get this over with."

The five drop ships that will transport the commandos to an inland Molefe Star arms depot are parked on the carrier's massive flight deck. I stick close to Jamal as we watch the commandos file onto the ships from a distance, all of them heavily armed and ready for battle.

David and Benjamin will be joining the assault with Patience and Lukwiya. The four of them wore their heaviest composite armor today, all draped in colorful fabrics as usual, and are carrying heavy rifles.

We see them off on the flight deck, but Lukwiya pauses to give me an assessing glance. "You know, Hondo, if you can shoot a gun half as well as Comrade Benjamin, we'd greatly appreciate your help. It'll be a good fight."

"No thanks," I easily say and detect in Lukwiya's static that I have caused offense with my terse reply.

David laughs. "He'll die before he parts from his brother, Lieutenant. I told you; we come in pairs. You don't get one without the other."

Lukwiya's face contorts with faint unease as he regards me. "Sounds like an unhealthy codependence."

"It's the only reason any of us are still alive," David tells him, then grins at Jamal. "Wish me luck?"

"Good luck," Jamal says, pretending not to know what's being asked of him.

"Please?"

He chuckles and steps closer to David, bringing their lips together. Benjamin and I both look away, gritting our teeth.

I'd honestly feel happy for Jamal if the man he'd chosen to be with were someone other than David. My dislike for the guy has only intensified since we got here, and I just don't see how I can ever work my way toward accepting him. It just won't happen.

"See you later, boys," he says, flashing teeth I'd really like to pull out with my bare hands.

I say nothing to Jamal as we watch them board their drop ship and lift off the carrier with the other four aircraft. They're barely into the air when Jamal tugs at my shirt. "Come. Let's get back to the *Seajack*. I've got work to do."

They tried to convince him to move his operations onto the carrier, but I was relieved Jamal retained enough sense to decline.

So long as there's nothing tying us to the flotilla, we can always leave, and there's no reason to hand over that kind of power to people who might stop being charitable the second we're no longer useful to them.

A platform takes us from the carrier to the *Seajack*'s exposed top deck. Inside the submarine, I head over to the cockpit with my sketch tablet while Jamal settles down by his station.

I don't think anyone else knows just how much power he holds in his hands when he sits on that chair. David and Lukwiya are aware he can hack into certain networks and maybe manipulate the flow of certain channels of information, but I don't think they fully appreciate just how much control he can exert.

They'll figure it out, though, sooner or later. Then we'll see just how friendly David really is.

Comm chatter fills the cabin, Jamal responding to it in a calm voice as he helps direct the operation. He'll be jamming and manipulating the Molefe Star supranet systems to stop them from detecting the drop ships, calling for backup, or coordinating an organized response.

The cities have gotten very good at keeping the Free People off dry land, often blowing Free ships and aircraft to smithereens for coming even within a hundred miles of the coast. But today the drop ships make it all the way to an inland arms depot without being detected.

I can't bring myself to care, even if part of me recognizes that not caring is precisely what drove Jamal to David in the first place. From the beginning Jamal has wanted someone who believes in his cause, and I've only ever been someone who believes in keeping him alive. I'm not enough for him anymore.

Still, I can't help it. My instincts don't trust this place, and I can't make myself pretend otherwise. I'd much rather Jamal fought for his cause on his own, with my help. We were doing just fine all along. We don't need David or his people.

I hear Jamal give a warning about automated sentry guns. The assault must be underway; the comm chatter is more excited now, peppered with gunfire.

I stare down at my sketch, curling my fingers around the imaginary warmth of a slender hand resting in mine. I usually sketch the dead, but my current subject is so full of life it makes my chest ache. I can almost hear the liquid sound of a saxophone, painted lips accompanying it with a voice like a soothing massage. There's a rose in her hair, stars on her glittering dress.

In a moment of weakness, before I even know what I'm doing, I connect to the Nzuko and send the sketch in an empty message. My heart races as I wait, the seconds stretching. I'm beginning to regret what I've done when a reply finally comes through. Three simple words.

N: Is that you?

My chest simulates the sensation of free fall, like I've dived off the *Seajack*'s top deck and I'm about to plunge into the sea. Several times I start typing out a long message only to delete and start again. Eventually I send one word.

H: Yes.

N: Are you supposed to be talking to me?

Jamal gives a warning about not straying from the flight path. He doesn't yet know I've done something rebellious.

H: Probably not. I just wanted to check on you. I heard about Counselor. Are you all right?

N: I am. Look, I have to go.

Like plunging into the sea and finding that the water is frigid.

H: All right. Take care.

Just as I'm about to swipe the comm interface away, one last message comes through.

N: Thanks for the drawing. It's . . . beautiful.

—

The raid on the arms depot is a stunning victory. Five drop ships went out; five return, along with a fleet of heavily armed helos, shuttles, and gunships, all loaded with tons of high-tech weapons and ammunition.

A victory celebration is held in the flotilla's main park that night, which has been festooned with many little lights on strings. The elected premiers of both the Black Star and Harambee tribes are in attendance, and both give exultant speeches.

The public is kept in the dark about the specifics of the operation and Jamal's involvement, so we attend as regular tourists, far removed from the fanfare at the heart of the celebration. By contrast, David stands next to the premiers and the commanding officers of both tribes and is even given the opportunity to make a speech, where he announces that a portion of the loot will be sent to the other tribes as gifts and invitations to greater cooperation.

There are rousing cheers from the gathered crowds, and the admiring look I catch in Jamal's eye makes me want to climb over the seaside rails and drown beneath the waves. After the speeches, David joins us on a tour of the many food stalls that have been set up around the flotilla, each offering its own unique type of free food and strong alcohol.

I allow myself to get somewhat drunk, knowing I'll probably be heading back to the *Seajack* on my own. For once, Benjamin is absent, and I haven't seen Patience since she left for the raid. I eventually decide I've had enough of being a third wheel and let Jamal know I want to go home.

"I'll see you in the morning," he tells me, squeezing my shoulder. He doesn't even look back as he walks off with David, already laughing at whatever inane thing the other Prime has said.

I slowly walk back to the docks, a half-empty bottle of whiskey dangling from one hand. I'm self-aware enough to realize that my issue with David goes beyond my distrust of him. I think the bigger problem is that I don't trust Jamal either.

What if he decides he doesn't need me anymore? What if David gives him everything he wants and I end up being superfluous? Deadweight.

It's selfish of me, but I don't think I ever want him to stop needing me. Because then, what would be the point of my existence?

Patience is waiting by the docks near the *Seajack*. I've only ever seen her in armor, but tonight she's in a low-cut black top and a pair of baggy pants. Her hair falls in two long braids that reach down to her chest. There's something oddly delicate about the way she's standing there, looking out into the ships of the flotilla. It's an interesting change from the usual rough edges and the heated glares.

She notices me as I approach and gives my boat shoes, shorts, and simple shirt a contemptuous once-over. "I've been looking for you," she says.

I almost sigh. I'm not in the mood for a fight, but I humor her. "Why?"

"I don't like you," she tells me.

I snort. "I noticed."

A moment passes, her eyes never leaving mine. "I never like the guys I want to fuck."

"Oh." My addled brain fails to come up with something to add to that.

"Yeah, I don't understand it either," she says, and when I simply stare back, her lips curve with faint amusement. "Did you swallow your tongue?"

"Er . . . no. I, uh. It's just . . . you're very forward," I manage to blabber.

She laughs lowly at my expense, and I let her take the bottle of whiskey from me and watch her as she unscrews the cap and takes a swig. She grimaces as she swallows, then shudders. "So? Do you want to do this or not?"

I don't trust myself to speak, so I nod at the *Seajack* in invitation and lead the way in.

Her kisses are rough. She bites a lot. In the dark and cramped confines of my bunk, I let her take what she wants from me and give as much as she lets me. I end up on my back, pinned down by her weight, losing myself as we piston into each other in a desperate rhythm. A strangled grunt comes out of me as I empty myself into her, and then I feel drained.

Afterward she rolls off me, and we both take a moment to catch our breaths. Then she says, "That was your first time, wasn't it." And it's not even a question.

I gulp, slightly mortified. "Was I that bad?"

She laughs, not unkindly. "No, not bad. But . . . you have a lot to learn, I think. Lucky for you, I'm willing to teach."

I smile. This was . . . good. Even if for a moment there I imagined something else. I sigh as the momentary high begins to subside. "I'm your willing student."

We lie side by side for a while, staring at the bunk bed above us. If she were someone else, I'd have wanted to hold her against me and bury my nose into her hair, but I don't think Patience would like that.

"You hate it here, don't you," she says abruptly, another not-question. "I see it on your face. Are the Free People not good enough for your exacting standards?"

There's some bitterness in there, so I tread carefully. "You wouldn't understand."

It's not the answer she wants, but she doesn't get angry. "Perhaps not."

"I worry about my brother," I admit. "He's all I have. I just don't want to see him get hurt."

Patience turns her head to look at me. "And you think this place will hurt him?"

"I think certain people in this place will hurt him, yes."

I feel her penetrating gaze on the side of my face, and then she says, "I see." She gets up to a seated position and starts to pull her clothes back on. "Well, I can't help you with that. David has done a lot of good for our people. He's a bit of a show-off, but he has good ideas. This raid is the biggest victory we've had in decades. The other tribes are finally ready to join us and fight back for our land. We could have a permanent home again within my lifetime."

The passion in her voice doesn't move me. I almost say, *That's not Jamal's problem*. "A worthy cause, I suppose," I say instead.

Somehow my true intent must come through, because she kisses her teeth in annoyance. "At least I have a cause. You choose to live only to serve someone else's whims."

"It's not really a choice, Patience."

Now fully dressed, she scoffs, looking at me over her shoulder. "David told us a little about where you came from, you know. How Primes and Proxies were made for each other and all that bullshit, but I've watched you and Benjamin, and I know you're not slaves. You both have agency. You both want things of your own. You're just too cowardly to do something about it."

Irritation stirs within me. "Cowardly?" I demand.

"Yes. You're too scared to imagine being your own people. You'd much rather let your Primes decide who you are for you."

The gall. Who does she think she is? "You don't know me," I tell her.

She smiles at me in the dim cabin, eyes hard and fearless. "You know what? Maybe you're right." She gets off the bed, and I watch her walk away. "Thanks for the good time, Hondo," she says to me before she leaves. "Maybe we'll do this again soon."

Chapter 22: Nandipa

The evening is still young, but the biannual Founders' Gala is well underway, champagne and conversation flowing inside the richly decorated hall while I lurk at the edges, silent and observant.

The place is so baroque I feel like I've stepped into an Old Earth European ballroom. The people dining beneath the sizable crystal chandeliers are no less expensive, from their tailoring to their cosmetic body-mods to the cybernetic implants giving their eyes lurid and unnatural colorings.

This is my first time attending such a gala, though I've already figured out it's less a celebration of the founders of ZimbaTech and more an opportunity for the who's who of the city to gossip and pat each other on the back for building such a great and meritocratic society.

I don't imagine there's usually so much anxiety on display, though. As I skirt along the walls of the room, serving in my role as a member of the gala's security, I catch snippets of heated conversations here and there, all about the Free People and their recent attacks on the cities.

Used to be that the cities could detect enemy forces long before they reached dry land. These days Free commandos seem to pop up wherever they please, attacking arms depots and out-of-city manufacturing plants, razing farmland, destroying maglev lines—moving like ghosts across the mainland.

"Maybe it's a new stealth technology," I hear someone say.

Or maybe someone infiltrated your networks so completely they can simply tell your instruments to ignore what's right in front of them, I think to myself and keep moving.

"Maybe they're behind the attack on the Abode," I hear someone else say a while later. He lowers his voice and adds, "In fact, what if they're behind everything else? The skelem rebellion? Michelle's assassination? The gang riots in Kenrock? Hell, we aren't the only ones under attack. And now we've got snot-nosed kids screaming about democracy on the streets. I'm telling you. This is their work."

Close, but not close enough, I think sardonically.

"My grandfather will be furious when the Abode comes back online," someone replies. "I'm seriously not looking forward to that conversation."

"You might not need to worry. I heard those stupid judgment polls start running the minute they switch the system back on. The Abode might not be salvageable."

"I should count my blessings, I suppose."

I continue moving, watching, listening.

"Rotten Free People," someone else grumbles. "We should just drop rods on the lot of them and be done with it."

"They have nuclear missiles, my dear. We would be obliterated too."

"Bah. We can intercept their nukes."

"I'm not so sure. I've heard they have new stealth technology."

"So what are we supposed to do? Let them destroy us?"

"Well. Perhaps we should try listening to what they want for a change."

I've checked and double-checked. This room is probably the most secure place on the planet right now. There's a heavy Kolovrat presence and enough police in the building to crew a military spaceship. If protecting Adaolisa is my prime concern, then I should be satisfied with the state of things.

But I feel my throat constricting as I glimpse her towering white turban among the dining guests. She's seated next to a member of the Board, splendid in a white-and-silver evening gown with cuts and vents in all the right places so that she looks not only like she belongs in this moneyed hall but like she could command it too.

I have a heart to rebel, to grab her and run away, but this is what she wants, and I exist to make sure she gets it, so I stay.

I check my mobile, and my chest flutters when I notice Hondo has sent me another sketch, the third one this week. I've told him to stop, and I suppose I could cut him off if I wanted to, but . . .

But. I can't stop looking at the woman in his drawings. It's like being shown the person I could have been, or the person I want to be, yet so far from who I actually am.

Is this how he sees me?

A wave of sorrow takes me by surprise, and I suddenly want to get out of here. Adaolisa must sense something, because she glances in my direction, and I feel her eyes following me as I leave the main hall, heading for the bathrooms.

At the sinks I open a faucet and let it run, wetting my fingers before wiping my eyes. A good thing I wore no makeup tonight.

I don't know what's gotten into me, why a simple sketch should make me feel so much loss. It's like I'm nostalgic for a life that never happened. Isn't that foolish?

I am not that singer on the stage. I am a Proxy. I am a killing machine. I am—

The door opens, and someone else steps into the bathroom. I sigh as I turn off the faucet. I'm really not in the mood for this. "What do you want, Angelique?"

She folds her bionic arms. Like me, she's wearing a ballistic vest and a clearly visible personal defense weapon. "What are you planning?" she demands.

I roll my eyes. "If I get my way, to spend the rest of the night without seeing your face. Now if you'll excuse me."

She moves to block my way out. Normally she'd taunt me or flirt aggressively, but tonight her stare is cold. "I saw you here two days ago. In this hotel. You were wearing a filter, but I *know* it was you. You came in with a bag and left without it. What was in it? Where is it now?"

Fuck. I scream that curse inside my head so loud I wouldn't be surprised if the whole city heard me. The stupid woman has gotten better at following me. "I don't know what you're talking about," I say, forcing calm into my veins.

"Try again."

"I don't have time for this." I make to walk past her, knowing she'll try to stop me.

Her hands are machines. They are stronger and faster than ordinary hands, but her mind is not. While she reaches to grab me by the arm and push me back, she doesn't see me unsheathing a knife from my belt with my other hand and fails to react in time to stop me from driving the knife deep into the side of her neck.

I twist, enduring her crushing grip, wide eyes watching me with shock and accusation. She knew I was no good from the second she laid eyes on me, and perhaps given time, she would have found her proof.

I respect that. I wish she'd been worse at her job; then maybe I wouldn't have to do this.

I hold her up as her machine grip weakens, the life leaving her limbs. There's already so much blood, though most of it has soaked down into her clothes. Still, if someone walks in here now, I won't be able to talk my way out of this.

I quickly drag her to the farthest stall from the door and deposit her onto the toilet in a seated position. After locking the stall from the inside, I heave myself up and over the door to land on the other side.

I pay attention to the surrounding static as I gather paper towels from the dispenser. By the time two women enter the bathroom in a swirl of laughter and expensive perfumes, I've already cleaned up the blood from the floor and washed my hands. With my Int-Sec filter active, the women don't even look at me. I silently wait for them to pass before I walk out the door.

Cameras watching this hallway will have to be scrubbed, but that was always going to happen anyway. I reach for my mobile and call Adaolisa.

"Yes?" She sounds a little annoyed. We weren't supposed to call each other.

"I had to remove Angelique," I tell her in a low voice. "She saw me come here the other day. Is Dieng in the room?"

"It would seem so, yes."

"We have to do this now."

A pause. *"Of course."*

I want to tell her we shouldn't do this. *Let's not. Let's run away to another world. Let's be ordinary people.* "Be careful," I say.

"I will. Have a good night."

I stare at my mobile, tempted to take another look at Hondo's sketch. The moment of weakness passes, and I bring up an application connecting me to the briefcase.

Two days ago, an alias rented a hotel room three floors above the gala hall. Among her things was a specific briefcase capable of broadcasting a specific signal, preprogrammed to deliver the signal at the highest strength when activated.

I walk back into the main hall just in time to witness a Board member stabbing his wife in the eye with a dessert fork. Gasps ensue as she steps back in shock, covering her bleeding eye with a hand. Then her perfectly chiseled face twists with inhuman rage, and she leaps upon her husband, bringing him down to the floor as her teeth sink into his neck.

From there it seems everyone starts screaming.

All at once, people in glittering gowns and expensive suits erupt into a violent melee, attacking one another with cutlery, chairs, and plates along with teeth and bare fists.

I knew what was coming, but even I'm shocked by the display. As I search for Adaolisa, I spot Director Dieng clobbering one of her aides with a champagne bottle. The aide collapses, and another one screams.

"Director, are you well?"

Mindless, Dieng snarls and makes a swipe at her other aide, but before she can get closer, someone else smashes a chair into her back.

"What's going on?" someone shouts.

"The Oloye have gone mad!"

Those not affected by the sudden insanity flee for the exits. Adaolisa has hidden with a few others behind a group of Kolovrat mercenaries, who all seem at a genuine loss, holding their guns like they don't know who to shoot.

Uniformed police officers are the first to run into the fray and unwittingly find themselves having to fend off ravenous Oloye.

"Subdue them!" I hear Adaolisa shout. "Stop them from hurting themselves and each other!"

While the unaffected guests trample each other to be first out through the doors, the Kolovrat finally burst into action, moving to subdue their employers. I join in with the other Int-Sec agents present; even with my strength, it's a struggle to pull Oloye off each other while keeping them from attacking me.

The Kolovrat mercenaries are efficient from the beginning, but the police officers take a little longer to realize that being gentle is counterproductive. Hundreds of Oloye were in attendance at the gala; by the time we have them all bound in zip ties—those still alive and lucid at any rate—we're all sweating and panting.

Off to the side, Adaolisa is already delegating tasks to a senior Int-Sec agent. "Get a list of everyone who was here and make sure they know to keep their mouths shut," I hear her say. "We'll go after anyone who spreads false rumors. This applies to the staff as well."

The agent is clearly shaken, but she nods. "Yes, madam."

"Commissioner Ingabire?" Adaolisa says.

The recently promoted police commissioner is standing nearby, along with Dieng's surviving aides, but they all look aghast, transfixed by the scene of Oloye writhing on the floor as they struggle against their binds.

"Commissioner Ingabire?" she says again.

His wide eyes swivel to her, dazed.

"Commissioner, we need your people to set up a wide cordon around this hotel. Immediately. Until we know more, what happened here must be contained."

He blinks, then seems to come back to himself. "Er. Yes. Of course. A cordon. I'll . . . get right on that."

A shift has occurred in the room, though I think at present I'm the only one aware of it. The leaders of this city have been incapacitated in so shocking a manner that everyone is desperate for a bit of normalcy, and someone has stepped up to give them exactly that.

Adaolisa has never been more powerful than she is now, with the police commissioner taking her orders, aides from the CID and the Defense Force looking up to her, and the commanding officer of the Kolovrat unit coming over and saying, "What do we do now, madam?"

She takes a moment to look around the room. The Oloye are still snarling like feral animals. The doors have been closed, guarded by men and women who all look like they've seen the world end. My expression can't be far from theirs, though for a different reason. There are dead bodies on the floor, and Angelique's corpse is going cold in a bathroom not far away.

This is who I am, not the woman in the sketch.

Adaolisa shakes her head, looking appropriately somber. "This must be an ultraware hack of some kind. No one else appears to be affected, but it could be infectious to other Oloye, so we need to keep them isolated."

She meets my gaze briefly before coming to a decision. "Clear up a hospital, and put them all there. Make sure they're comfortable but contained. We *will* get to the bottom of this. Order *will* be restored."

Chapter 23: Hondo

It's while we're having breakfast in the FV *Khama*'s mess hall—me, Benjamin, and the two Primes—that David reveals the next target he wants to attack: a base on an island some several hundred miles northwest of Heynes Group City.

And it's not just any base, he tells us. It's not even city property, like the other targets the Free People have been attacking lately. In fact, it's very probably the main operations center of the people who attacked the Habitat, or so he says.

"You found the Stewards?" Jamal asks, sounding only a little less skeptical than I feel.

David shrugs, grinning like a fool. "Since our meeting with Queen Adaolisa, I've had my people on the lookout. I figured, after what Counselor said, they'd have to have a base, right? And lots of guns and submarines—not something easy to hide, and probably not affiliated with any city. Here. Take a look."

He pushes a tablet across the steel table, which Jamal takes and peruses with an arched eyebrow.

"For some weird reason, the cities act like they don't know that base exists," David says. "It's like a blind spot. Or something they all agreed to ignore. Suspicious, no?"

I bite down on a piece of bread so I don't say something rude. Across the table, Benjamin frowns like I said it anyway, though he keeps silent himself. We've come to a tacit agreement on the troubling matter of the ongoing . . . relations . . . between our Primes. Namely, we'll ignore what's happening and also ignore each other.

Or at least, I try to ignore Benjamin, though he can't seem to resist sending me death glares. I don't waste any energy returning them. Less chance of us trying to kill each other that way.

After reading through the information on the tablet, Jamal sets it down, a pensive wrinkle on his forehead. "How did you get this intel?"

David snorts. "You're not the only one with connections, Jamal."

"I literally have all the connections."

"You work with signals and processors. I work with people and word of mouth, and sometimes people know and say things you won't always find on a computer."

"Computers know everything, David," Jamal scoffs. "But tell me more about this base." His eyes fall back onto the tablet. "What's this device mentioned here?"

Leaning closer with a conspiratorial look in his eye, David says, "So the thing that happened in ZimbaTech last week?"

"You mean the Oloye turning into zombies or whatever the fuck Adaolisa did to them?"

David chuckles. "Yes. Well, my intel says it was some sort of device that did it. Like a mind-control thing. Made by the Stewards, and it came from that base. I don't know how she got her hands on the device, but now she's in control of a city."

Jamal considers the other Prime. "So you think this is a Steward base."

"You have the report right in front of you."

"I want to hear it from your lips, David."

David folds his arms, leaning against the backrest of his chair. "Yes, I think this is likely their largest base of operations, and it's a big fat target waiting for the taking. Think about it: We could get some payback for what those bastards did to the Habitat, but who knows what else we'll find there? These are the people who made ultraware, Jamal. Control that and we control the world."

I can't help it. I shake my head, cursing beneath my breath.

So far, working with David and the Free People hasn't meant joining in on the action. In fact, we haven't needed to leave the flotilla at all. Jamal has coordinated every operation from the safety of the *Seajack*, the importance of which has become obvious to the leaders of the Black Star tribe, since they now keep it under constant guard.

I've been happy with this state of affairs, despite the intrusion. I may not like being here, but I sleep well at night knowing I don't have to worry about someone shooting at Jamal. Even if a raid goes badly, he's never in the line of fire. Let David and Benjamin get shot at. Keep my Prime out of it.

But I already know Jamal will want to be present for the raid.

David notices my reaction and sends me a slanted grin, eyes glinting with the hint of mockery. He knows how much I despise him for having power over Jamal. "Something you'd like to say, Hondo?"

Stay the fuck away from my Prime. "No," I say. "Nothing at all."

"A ringing endorsement, coming from you," he says, his grin widening. "So. What do you say, Jamal?"

Jamal runs a finger along the edge of the tablet, his gaze far away. At length he sighs. "Sounds interesting, I suppose. I'll look into it, see what defenses we'll need to bypass. I'll know more by this time tomorrow. Send the intel to me, will you?"

"Go ahead and take the tablet," David says graciously. "And take as long as you need to plan. We're in no hurry."

They smile at each other. A dull pain throbs along my fingers, only for me to realize I'm holding a leg of the steel table in a tight grip.

I let go. My hand has left a visible dent on the metal.

Maybe Jamal senses I have frustrations to vent, because he insists we visit a gymnasium in one of the flotilla's hexagonal neighborhoods for some kickboxing.

I don't apply myself at first, rebuffing his attacks absentmindedly while he tries to pummel me like I'm a punching bag. My lack of effort pisses him off, and he starts coming at me with everything he's got.

He's trying to get a rise out of me, but I don't want to lose it, so I knock him down to the mat with a punch to the face. I glower down at him while he wipes blood from his mouth.

"Don't start something you won't be able to finish," I warn him. "I'm not in the mood for whatever little tantrum you're trying to throw."

Jamal gets up. He wipes his mouth again and shows me the blood on his hand, an eyebrow lifted. "*I'm* the one throwing a tantrum?"

"You asked for it."

"Only because you're sulking and not saying what you want to say to me."

"I have nothing to say."

"Bullshit. You want to talk me out of the raid. Well? I'm listening."

I decide I'm not having this conversation and start undoing my borrowed wrist wraps. "I'm not going to waste my time," I say. "We both know you want to see what's inside that base. All I can do is make sure you come out of it alive."

"Ancestors." Eyes wide with rage, Jamal shoves me violently, forcing me to stagger backward. "I hate it when you get like this!"

"Stop it," I warn him.

"Then tell me the truth! Just this fucking once, Hondo, be honest with me. You forget I can feel what's in your heart. You have things you want to say to me. Stop being a coward and say them!"

"Go to hell," I tell him and turn around to walk away. But I'm angry now, and I want him to know it, so I turn around and stalk back toward him. "You know what? Fine. Let's do this."

Jamal folds his arms, his expression defiant.

"I hate it here," I tell him. "I *hate* how ambitious you are. I hate being constantly worried about you. I hate that you'll never be content to live a simple life, which means I'll never get a shot at that either. I hate the scheming, the lies, the killing, and most of all, Jamal, I hate that despite everything, I can't even resent you. Despite how miserable you make me sometimes, I can't be apart from you. I can't abandon you. I can't leave, and I hate that. I wish I could be free of you."

My regret is immediate and nearly crippling, and I stare in perfect horror at the tears that gather in Jamal's eyes.

The sad smile he gives me shatters my heart into a thousand pieces. "That's the most honest thing you've ever said to me."

"Jamal . . ." My mouth moves in many starts, but my tongue fails to cooperate. *What have I done?* "I don't . . . that's not . . . you know I'd never . . . I know you can't help yourself," I finally say. "I know you try your best to make things easier for me. But . . . you were made the way you were, and so was I. I just want us to be okay. That's all. Please ignore everything I said. I was angry. I wasn't thinking."

"But you were honest," Jamal says.

"No, I—"

"Yes, you were, Hondo, and you're right." Jamal's throat bobs as he swallows. "I've been selfish, haven't I."

"Jamal . . ." I can't reply to that. I can't even look into his watery eyes. I should have never said any of those things. No true Proxy would say such things. Must be my flawed expie nature coming to the surface. Ancestors curse me.

Jamal takes a calming breath, then speaks like everything is normal between us. "I'm going to take a shower," he says. "I have some thinking to do. See you later?"

I let him go, feeling like the biggest asshole in the stellar neighborhood.

—

As evening approaches later that day, I sit alone in the *Seajack*'s cockpit with my stylus and sketchpad and play the last message Nandipa sent me on a loop.

I'd gotten into the habit of sending her drawings I made of her, expecting nothing in return except the knowledge that she saw them, and for the first several drawings I sent her, I was not disappointed. Save for that first image I sent, there were no replies.

And then three days ago I checked my Nzuko inbox on a whim and found a recording of a song she sang to the tune of a skillfully plucked guitar.

It's the same song she was singing that time I walked into her bar unannounced, an ode to sunshine and how it washes away the worries of the night. She was with a jazz band at the time, but I think I prefer this simpler rendition, filled with melancholy and, better yet, more personal.

I like to think she sang it just for me.

Today the recording brings me only grief, though, so I turn it off after a few minutes, setting aside my sketch.

I can't stand this emptiness in my chest. Jamal and I have fought before, but I've never hurt him like this. I resolve to apologize as soon as he comes back.

In fact, I'm about to leave the *Seajack* to go find him when Patience comes to pay me a visit.

She meant it when she said she doesn't like me. She has no interest in getting to know me as a person, or perhaps she's decided she already knows enough. Either way, she doesn't mind my body so much, and I guess I don't mind hers, either, so I accept the diversion she offers me and lead her to my bunk bed.

We don't make love; she takes and I take back. She isn't the prettiest woman alive, but I enjoy her duality, the softness of her in some places, the harsh strength in all the others. What she sees in me is a mystery; I've never dared to ask, knowing I'd likely offend her.

When we're done, I walk her out, and it's just my luck that Jamal is making his way over along the docks at that very moment.

"Hey there, Jamal," Patience says breezily as they pass each other, and I almost die in embarrassment.

"Have fun, did we?" he asks over his shoulder.

"Oh, lots," she quips back. "Lots and lots of fun."

When he crosses the gangway and reaches the *Seajack*'s top deck, I try to explain myself. "We're just—"

"No worries," Jamal cuts me off with a slightly crooked grin. "I shall not begrudge you your heterosexual impulses to procreate." He shudders. "Not that I understand them, mind you. You and I could not be more different in that respect. But hey, whatever rocks your boat."

I think he's mocking me, but I can't let myself give in to a smile. Not when things are still this bad between us. "Jamal, about earlier—"

"No," he says, lifting a palm to stop me. "I pushed you into saying things you didn't want to say. Let me speak honestly for a change."

"Okay."

He breathes out like he's nervous. "Come. Let's sit down."

I follow him to the pair of deck chairs facing out to sea, where we sometimes spend our evenings.

We sit there for what feels like ages before he says, "After this base, we're done."

I stare at him. He's looking out at a distant cruiser with the Harambee tribe's leonine symbol splashed across its hoisted flag. "What do you mean?" I ask.

He breathes out again, and I worry because he almost looks frail. "Hondo, the last thing I want is for you to be unhappy. I think I owe it to you to allow you the life you deserve."

There's a knife, and someone is slowly driving it into my chest, or at least, that's how it feels to hear him suggest . . . "Don't send me away, Jamal," I plead. "Don't tell me to go. You might as well shoot me in the head."

He frowns and finally glances at me. "What are you talking about? I'm not asking you to leave. Don't be ridiculous."

"Oh."

He looks away again. "I mean, much as we fight and make each other miserable—"

"Only sometimes," I append, to which he smiles.

"Yes, sometimes we upset each other, but we still need each other to be happy, I think."

"I agree," I say, immensely relieved that he understands. "So what are you saying?"

He looks around the deck with a regretful expression, then gives a long and forlorn sigh. "I'll hand the *Seajack* over to David and find something else to obsess over. Let him and Adaolisa fight for dominance. There's got to be other ways of doing good for the world, right? We could open our own restaurant. Maybe I'll carve out my own food empire or something equally mundane. We can get a dog. I've always wanted one of those. And you can be the artist you've always wanted to be, maybe open your own gallery. We'll lead simple lives as simple men." He regards me, trying to measure my reaction. "What do you say?"

I well with more love for him than I've ever felt, but a part of me remains cautious. "You're not just saying this, are you?"

His eyes crinkle in the corners. "I mean every word. It'll be difficult at first, of course, but I'm not bound to be who the Custodians made me to be. I have the ability to decide my own future, and I want a future in which we're both happy."

"I believe you," I say.

"Good."

We're good now, he and I, but something isn't yet settled. I can feel it in the air between us. "You still want the base, though," I say.

He turns his face away. "You'll allow me that, won't you? We're talking about the people who destroyed our home. I want to see what they're hiding. Give me that, and I promise, we'll be done."

I don't debate myself for long. He means what he's said. This is our chance to get out of a life of constant peril. I'd be a fool not to take it. "All right," I tell him. "We'll go to the base."

I couldn't bother myself to care about Jamal's previous operations, but I join him in the *Khama*'s ops room to plan the assault on the Steward base, imposing strict limits on our direct involvement.

No, we will not be part of the main assault team or the secondary assault team. No, I have no interest in the glory of battle. No, I'll bring Jamal to the base only after you've secured it. That's not negotiable.

"He's not a porcelain doll," David gripes at me when I refuse to budge. "Primes may not be as tough as you, but we're still a great deal tougher than most people. You need to let him be his own person."

"Your Proxy might be content to let you run into bullets," I say, "but don't expect me to be so reckless. Jamal is helping you enough as it is."

Benjamin takes an angry step forward, but David puts a hand out to stop him. Both young men glower at me from across the ops table, nostrils flaring. "Benjamin knows my limits," David says. "He knows I can take care of myself and don't need to be coddled like a damsel in distress."

"Good for you," I say. "We're still not joining your fight."

To his credit, Jamal remains silent, forcing David and Lukwiya to begrudgingly accept my conditions. The *Seajack* will hang back from the assault until all hostiles have been eliminated. Only then will I bring us in and escort Jamal into the facility.

And despite the fuss and the grumbling, things end up going according to plan.

In the early hours of a crisp morning, multiple squads from the Black Star, Harambee, and Copper Bullet flotillas descend upon the Steward base, six drop ships packed with commandos supported by four gunships and a small army of weaponized semiautonomous drones.

The facility is indeed located on a remote island, an impressive structure of glass and bone-white cement cascading down the side of a rounded hill, presenting many points of reflection in the strengthening sunlight. A massive satellite dish stands near the base of the structure, and not far from it is a landing pad large enough to hold a whole fleet of drop ships.

Jamal and I watch the assault from the *Seajack*, each of the many screens on Jamal's terminal showing us a camera feed from a different drone.

Some of the Free commandos are too zealous, in my opinion, lacking impulse control and proper discipline, but they're brave and determined and soon overwhelm the facility's security.

I watch Patience enter the building with her squad and quickly dispatch and disable the rest of the island's security, including mechs and sentry guns. Those who surrender are taken prisoner and led out onto the landing pad, where they are forced to stay on the ground at gunpoint.

A drone follows David and Lukwiya as they sweep the rest of the base. I lean forward when they enter a particularly large room with a vaulted ceiling and no windows; the room looks like it was built to house that shifting structure there in the center, made of floating glass cubes with a blue inner glow. They shift and dance and rearrange themselves in constantly changing organic patterns that are at once faintly recognizable and yet deeply alien.

On the camera feed, David stops to stare at the structure, a disturbed look on his face. "Seajack, *the facility is under our control.*"

"What *is* that?" Jamal says, peering at the screen with his head tilted as if to get a better look.

"I have no clue," David says. *"Some kind of technology, maybe. Seems like your kind of thing."*

"We're on our way," Jamal says. "Take us in, Hondo."

Much as I want to, I don't make a fuss. I head to the cockpit and engage the *Seajack*'s ion thrusters for only the second time since we got the vessel. They extrude from the sides of the hull and lift us out of the water. Thick jets of mist spin around and beneath us as we gain altitude, and then we're off, flying toward the island.

Minutes later I set us on dry land on the omni's stubby landing gears, touching down next to a drop ship in sight of the satellite dish.

We both wear tactical lenses and earpieces. I also take a shotgun and Jamal carries a pistol just in case. As we disembark from the omni, prisoners in lab coats watch us from where they've been forced to huddle together on their knees. One man raises his head too high and gets punished with the butt of a rifle to the face.

I keep my eyes open on our way into the towering facility. The spacious architecture, with emphasis on maximizing the infiltration of natural light, speaks more to civilian comfort than to any practical considerations of defense. It's almost like these people never expected to be attacked.

As we make our way deeper into the building, following a small spherical drone to where David saw the strange artifact, I see no specific indications that the people who built this place are even the so-called Stewards, as David said. There are offices. Laboratories. Rooms with server racks that give off a blue light. Rooms with humanoid mechs lying on examination tables, glowing blue orbs visible in their skulls.

Wait. What the hell are those?

Jamal walks through it all with his eyes glued to his PCU, more engrossed with whatever he's seeing there than his present surroundings. I have to jog to catch up to him after pausing to look at the mechs, passing two armed commandos of the Copper Bullet tribe.

"There's something seriously off about the local network," he mutters.

"What is it?" I ask.

"I thought it would put up a fight, but it opened the doors and let me in. Almost as if . . ."

He trails off as we enter the vaulted room and finally find ourselves face to face with the shifting structure of glass blocks. It's even more impressive in person, taller than four men, its patterns changing like ripples on the surface of a pond.

"Almost as if it wanted me to see it," Jamal breathes, his wonder and amazement so strong they almost cloud my thoughts. "Ancestors save me. Could it be?"

I should pay more attention to what has awed him so much, but I don't like the fact that David isn't here. I hold my shotgun tighter, casting about for David or Lukwiya with my senses.

"It's alive!" Jamal says.

"What is alive?" I ask absently. "And where's David?"

"It was you all along, wasn't it?"

I reach for my earpiece. "David? We're in the room with the weird artifact. Where are you?"

Silence.

I should have noticed, but most of the commandos have retreated. Only a single squad of Copper Bullets is still in the building, and by the confusion in their static, they don't know what's going on either.

The deafening clatter of gunfire erupts all at once. I don't know who's shooting at who; I only sense the presence of the Copper Bullet squad, and they're afraid.

"What the hell's going on?" Jamal asks me, finally coming out of his awed trance. "I thought the fighting was over."

I would throttle myself. I would shoot myself in the foot for my stupidity. I should have never agreed to let Jamal come here.

"Follow me," I say.

We leave the room and its pulsing artifact. I use my senses like radar, keeping track of who's where and how far. It's why I don't think twice about turning onto the next corridor, and by the time the field of dead space hits me and I realize what it means, I've already taken a bullet to the abdomen and another to my thigh.

My shotgun still fires twice, and a man in black armor clasps at his neck where my tungsten slug hit him, his knees buckling to the floor.

By the time he falls over, I've already backtracked, herding Jamal back the way we came.

"Hondo, you've been hit," he says, tense but still clearheaded.

"I'm fine. We can't go that way. There could be more, and I can't sense them." *He had dead space,* a voice screams at me in panic. *What does that mean?*

"There's a door over there," Jamal says, pointing past the room with the artifact. "Maybe that's where David went. Are you sure you're fine?"

"Yes."

I follow Jamal to the door. To my dismay, it opens up to a rather large office area with many workstations but no sign of David. We can hear the commandos still fighting elsewhere in the building.

"Keep moving," I say. My left leg is drenched and getting heavy. My body won't let me feel the pain, not yet, but I'm getting dizzy.

They had dead space.

"What the fuck's happening?" Jamal asks. His voice is getting higher. He's beginning to panic. "David, are you there? We need your help!"

The grave tickles me again, and this time I know it for what it is. "Get down!" I tell Jamal, and we crash to the ground behind a workstation right before bullets fly over our heads.

I answer back with my shotgun. Whoever it is takes cover, but they keep shooting.

"David! David, we're under fire," Jamal says in a panicked whisper. "You said the place was clear, but there are hostiles shooting at us! Hondo's been hit. We need immediate extraction. David! Answer me, you son of a bitch."

Automatic gunfire sprays into everything around us. It's so loud I almost don't hear David's voice when he finally replies, calm and cold as a deep ocean current.

"You were a good lay, Jamal. But the queen made an offer I can't refuse. She wants to pin everything on you and get her hands on the *Seajack*, and in return, the Free People get to be free again. I'm sorry it didn't work out between us, but I have people to look out for now. Goodbye, my friend."

I close my eyes. *I'll kill him. I'll kill him. I'll kill him. I'll take off his fucking head.* I thought I knew what hate was. I did not. I do now. I come out of cover, aiming for a cloud of dead space across the room. I pull the trigger, and the bullet rips through armor and flesh, ending a life, but more men wrapped in dead space come through the door, bullets flying, forcing me to retreat.

My strength is failing me. I can barely hold the gun up. I think I got hit in the femoral artery. The wound will clot much faster than normal for most, but I've already lost so much blood. Too much blood. I won't survive.

Ancestors, save Jamal. I'll do anything.

He has a stunned look on his face. Like he's not even here.

"Jamal. You need to run," I tell him. "I'll cover you. That door over there. Get to it and run."

Suddenly a presence flickers into my peripheral vision. I blink my eyes at it, thinking maybe the blood loss has begun to cause hallucinations, but no, that really is Nandipa standing in front of me, bullets flying through her holographic form.

She's in a black pencil skirt and a simple white blouse, a light coat of makeup on her face. Jamal must see her, too, because he's first to address her.

"Are you here to gloat?" he says in a broken voice. "You and your sister have won. You have proved me to be a fool."

She frowns, opening her mouth to speak, but her voice is choppy, distant. "You don't . . . time . . . listen very carefully . . . past that door . . . elevators . . . three floors down . . . emergency submersibles."

I feel myself slipping, but I'm not so gone I don't recognize she's offering me a sliver of hope. I lift my gun and risk firing off a shot. There's a brief pause in the gunfire before it starts up again.

"I'm . . . help you, Jamal," Nandipa says, sounding desperate. "Now go!"

She pixelates out of my lenses. "Go, Jamal," I say. "Please. You have to."

He seemed dazed just a while ago, but now he calms with a solid sense of purpose. He whips out his pistol and switches out the ammunition with a practiced motion. "Don't be stupid," he says. "I was never going to leave you."

I'm horrified at first as I watch him rise and fire off a single shot. Then the round detonates in the air, and the automatic gunfire comes to a dead stop. I hear someone scream. Acrid smoke suddenly fills the room, stinging my eyes.

"Come on." Jamal stubbornly hooks my hand around his shoulders and lifts me up. "We're getting the fuck out of here."

Chapter 24: Nandipa

If betrayal had a taste, I now know it would sting like a poison-tipped blade carving a scarlet, jagged path across my tongue, caustic and bitter as bile.

I know this because I can almost feel it bubbling at the back of my throat, something venomous, acidic, and full of rage, all the worse since I can't decide whether I'm the betrayer or the betrayed.

I'm resolutely expressionless as my driver, Agent Sambo, brings our Int-Sec cruiser down onto the island's massive landing pad in a thundering hiss of ion thrusters. A salty breeze greets me when the door slides open. I thank Sambo and step outside, my legs somewhat restricted by the black pencil skirt and stilettos I have worn for the occasion, but I project a purposeful self-assurance and walk like I wield the authority of a city-state. Anyone watching me must know I mean business.

All over the landing pad, people in lab coats and office wear have been forced to kneel next to windowless shuttles with their hands bound behind their backs, prodded like cattle by Int-Sec raid troopers in black tactical armor. I pretend not to be unsettled by the auras of dead space pressing against me, reminding myself that these troopers are not Custodians. They are weapons Adaolisa built to take down Jamal.

They don't know what effect their armor has on me, and I can't ever let them catch on.

The dead space still makes my eyes water and my head spin. I have to raise a hand to ward off the dazzling glare of the island's towering white marble-and-glass structure as it glimmers in the harsh sunlight.

David is expecting me. I spot him standing with Benjamin near the gaping entrance of a parked gunship, loose printed cloths hanging over their composite suits of armor like the other Free commandos loitering around him. They're all packing rifles and other heavy guns, watching ZimbaTech's forces swarm the base with wary eyes.

I shove down the prickle of concern that rises up my throat. All I have is a small handgun concealed beneath my skirt, but I have David outnumbered and outgunned. He'd be dead in seconds if I only commanded it.

Oh, how I wish he'd give me a reason to command it.

I felt such a rush of relief the first time I saw him as a hologram back in ZimbaTech. I could have wept with joy. But now, as he walks forward to greet me with a cautious grin, Benjamin at his heel as always, I suffer a stirring of revulsion so compelling it's all I can do not to whip out my handgun and fire.

I wish to the ancestors he'd just stayed dead.

"Nandipa," he says as we meet. Maybe he senses my antipathy, because he doesn't do something stupid like try to embrace me, but the grin spreads across his broad face as he looks me over. "Damn, but you look good. Being alive suits you."

And being dead suited you better. "David," I say with all the cordial professionalism I can summon. I can at least manage a smile for his Proxy, reminding myself that none of this is his fault. "Benjamin. It's good to see you."

"Likewise," Benjamin says, though a glimmer in his eyes tells me he'd have liked to say more.

Ah, but that part of our lives is over and done with. Ashes in the wind. A mummified corpse. Whatever might have existed between us, I cannot see it surviving what he and his Prime tried to do here.

"Where's the omni-vehicle?" I ask.

David snickers. "Straight to business, is it?" He peers over my shoulder at the Int-Sec cruiser. "Where's Adaolisa?"

"She's not coming. Other engagements."

Displeasure turns David's smugness into a sneer. "Of course. I still expect her to live up to her end of the bargain."

"Do you doubt that she will?" I say, getting testy.

Once, I'd have coated my words in sugar, molded myself into an agreeable heroine the better to manipulate, entice, seduce. Today I just don't give a fuck.

At my tone David arches an eyebrow in mild surprise. "I suppose not," he says somewhat defensively, then nods in the direction of a massive bullet-shaped vehicle with short, stubby landing gears. "It's that one over there."

I turn my head to look. The *Seajack*, according to the paint on its ivory coating. My heart squeezes with sudden worry, my mouth filling with that bitter taste again. *Ancestors, please let them be alive.*

I must fail to mask myself completely, because David frowns at me. "I take it Adaolisa told you the script?" he says. "You found the *Seajack* here. The Stewards were using it and this base to attack the cities. The Free People worked with them for a while, but we decided to betray them in the interest of peace. We lost an entire squad of our own commandos trying to secure this base. We expect to be properly rewarded for our cooperation."

I nearly bare my teeth. I watched Int-Sec forces exchange fire with Free commandos inside that base, meaning he deliberately sacrificed one of his squads by not telling them about the double cross beforehand. They didn't know we were coming, and they died for it.

I can't say why he did it. Maybe he needed dupes to help lure Jamal and Hondo into his trap. Maybe he needed the losses to make the Free People look good. He's a bastard all the same.

"Adaolisa will be in touch," I say, holding my temper in check. "For now, I've been directed to present you with these, as was promised."

I gesture at the three large cargo helos descending from the sky at that very moment, which I know are filled with caches of ZimbaTech's finest medical and agricultural equipment and supplies.

Satisfaction oozes from David at the sight, and he has the gall to stand there nodding at himself like he's done something heroic. "I believe this will be the beginning of a very prosperous relationship."

"ZimbaTech looks forward to working closer with the Free People," I dutifully say.

He smiles again like he can see right through me, then flicks his gaze to the Int-Sec shuttles now loaded with the people who worked here. "You know, I'm surprised you're keeping these prisoners alive."

"We need to know everything they were doing here," I reply.

"As you say. Well then, Nandipa. The base is all yours. Tell Adaolisa I'll be expecting her call."

He walks off, shouting and waving for one of his people to join him as he heads for the cargo helos. Benjamin nods at me in a quiet farewell and follows him.

I turn away from them before I do something foolish. Besides, I have a more urgent matter to attend to, though my stomach threatens to rebel at the very thought of it.

An Int-Sec squad commander was waiting for me to finish speaking with David; he accosts me as I approach the glazed entrance to the facility, falling into step next to me. I force myself not to retreat from his oppressive dead space.

"Fillemon Petrus?" I ask him.

"Dead, madam. You can see for yourself." The commander points to a row of bodies someone is only just covering with black sheets.

I query myself to see what I feel.

Fillemon Petrus was responsible for the Habitat's destruction and had an inkling of who we are. Hearing of his death should affect me in some way. I should feel regret that I wasn't the one to kill him, maybe. Or relief that my dead siblings have been avenged. Perhaps I should want to weep with relief.

I feel nothing. A quick and ignoble death is the least that son of a bitch deserved, and I've already decided he won't take up any more space in my mind. He'll be a footnote, as insignificant to me as the faceless Custodians I once feared.

"I'll take a look later," I say. "Anything else to report?"

"Yes, madam." The commander hesitates. "There was . . . an unfortunate miscommunication with the squad of Free commandos who were inside. They fired at us, and we thought they were local security. We were forced to neutralize them."

I stop to face the commander. He has retracted his helmet's visor so I can see his chagrined expression. He might be twice my age, but with Adaolisa serving as ZimbaTech's interim chair, I am practically the head of Int-Sec, which means he takes his orders from me.

"Listen to me carefully," I say. "Those commandos were already dead when you arrived, do you understand? There was no altercation between Free commandos and ZimbaTech forces. I have just spoken to a representative of the Free People, and they agree on this point. They betrayed an ally to help us. We cannot allow a misunderstanding to jeopardize what could be a beneficial relationship. Make sure everyone understands this."

The commander shows no reaction, save that the worry and embarrassment clear away from his face and he nods. "Understood, madam."

I look beyond the shattered glass of the main entrance, my guts twisting into a tight knot, my throat going dry.

"Do you wish me to escort you?"

I almost accept. I don't want to do this alone. "No. I'll be fine."

"Of course, madam. If you need anything, let me know."

I walk through the doors, my shoes crunching on shards of broken glass. The first two bodies are security guards who must have worked here, lying dead in the lobby in pools of congealed blood, ignored by the army of Int-Sec agents crawling all over the place. They'll be stripping down every electronic device in the facility for transport to ZimbaTech.

I don't interrupt them as I make my way farther in, where I find more bodies, more security guards, a number of Free commandos, an Int-Sec trooper shrouded in dead space lying still in a corridor.

Pressure mounts inside my chest with each body I find, the war between dread and hope growing hotter, fiercer. Each body that isn't *them* adds to the possibility that maybe they aren't here, while at the same time strengthening the devastation I'd feel if I found them here after all.

I warned them from my cruiser on my way to the island. I wasn't supposed to, but I couldn't help it. I made a pact with Hondo. We promised we wouldn't let our Primes destroy each other. I'd already erred by failing to talk Adaolisa out of her plan. Warning them was the least I could do.

I walk past a domed chamber with an alien-looking artifact made of floating glass cubes. A group of Int-Sec agents has gathered to marvel at it, their mesmerized eyes reflecting its eerie bluish glow. When I look at it, a ripple passes through the artifact as if in greeting. I tingle with unease and keep walking, entering a wide office space littered with ruin and carnage.

Four troopers lie dead near the door. By the ablation on their armor and the burn marks on the carpeted floor and ceiling, something detonated in here. An airburst round, I'd say. Definitely not from an Int-Sec weapon.

There's a trio of Int-Sec agents ignoring the bodies as they attempt to salvage whatever computing equipment survived the firefight. I don't interrupt them and quietly search the rest of the room, my heart racing fast enough to power an ion drive. No more bodies, but there, behind a particularly shot-up workstation, where someone might have taken cover: a recent bloodstain on the carpet.

I look around. A trail of blood leads out the nearby door. I follow it to an elevator, hope swelling in my chest, dread weakening my knees.

I take the elevator down to a sublevel floor. When the doors open, I emerge into a cavernous concrete chamber open on the far end, letting in both sea and sunlight. Three small submersibles bob up and down in the long pool of aquamarine water built to house them; the pool extends all the way out to the chamber's opening, providing convenient access to the sea.

It seems I'm not the first one here. Two Int-Sec agents are huddled by a terminal mounted on one concrete wall, frowning at the information on the screen.

"Anything interesting?" I say, making them both jump in surprise.

The shorter of the two men is the first to recover. He clears his throat and says, "Yes, madam. The logs show a submersible departing from this chamber less than an hour ago. It's likely someone has escaped. We're trying to see if we can track the vehicle, but we've had no luck so far."

Ancestors. I could sway from the force of the relief, but I control myself, keeping my voice calm. "Let me know the second you find something."

"Yes, madam."

I make a show of looking around, then return to the elevator. As I ascend, I let myself take deep breaths to gather my composure. *They made it. They're alive.*

I pull out my mobile and call Adaolisa. She picks up almost immediately.

"I've checked all over the facility," I say without preamble. "They're not here. They must have escaped."

She keeps any disappointment out of her voice. *"Are you sure?"*

"I've looked at all the bodies. There was a fight. They took out a few troopers. It's possible one of them was hit, but they aren't here. It's likely they escaped on a submersible."

"And now we have no idea where they are," Adaolisa says with an audible sigh. *"This is not ideal, Nandipa. All right. We'll speak more when you return to ZimbaTech."*

I disconnect as the conversation ends. That taste again. A bitterness so acidic it makes me want to scrape off my tongue. Am I the betrayer or the betrayed? I've always been in complete sync with Adaolisa. I've never wanted anything she wouldn't want, never felt anything but absolute love for her, unshakable devotion. I still do. I'd die for her in an instant, but for the first time in my life, I feel adrift. Alone.

I've done what I came here to do, so after a word with all the team leaders involved in the operation, I have Sambo fly me back to ZimbaTech. We arrive just before noon, and as the forest of skyscrapers grows outside my window, I think back to the first time I laid my eyes on this city.

Months later, and I can still remember the dread I felt that rainy day, the realization that everything I knew was a lie. I was lost at sea with no horizon in sight, but I was not alone. One thing remained constant, one person, and I could feel her hand in mine as we entered this strange new world together. I was angry, betrayed, afraid, but I knew in my heart that we'd be all right because Adaolisa would know what to do. She'd guide me. She'd be my compass, my polestar.

We didn't know it at the time, but our futures were full of possibility. We could have done anything. Gone anywhere. Been anyone. Instead, we chose to live like we were still in the Habitat.

Sometimes I wonder if we ever truly escaped that place. Its undersea domes and structures might have been destroyed, but the Habitat lives on through us, through our lies and ambitions and betrayals, spreading and infecting the rest of the world. Maybe our "escape" was part of the Habitat's plan all along, and those of us who survived are doomed to live as slaves to its games forever.

"Are we going to HQ, madam?" Sambo asks from the pilot's seat, breaking me out of my somber thoughts.

"No. Take me to the Spire."

"Of course."

We were nobodies when we first flew into ZimbaTech. The spinning holographic ribbon around the city's pearlescent crown jewel might as well have been as distant as the sun, and so were the people who walked within the tower's hallways.

Not anymore.

The cruiser whines as Sambo lowers us onto a landing pad near the top of the Spire, above the rotating hologram. This pad would normally be available only to the highest-ranking Oloye of the city, but none of them have recovered from the madness that took them at the Founders' Gala, and someone has to take over the running of things, so here we are.

The Oloye who survived that night are still locked up in a hospital turned insane asylum, and those who died in the violence have yet to be revived, what with the discovery that the corruption carries over even onto their new bodies.

Indeed, Michelle Zimba came back to life as barking mad as she was when I shot her in the head. I'm told she managed to kill two of the nurses overseeing her resurrection before she was put down again.

And so, for the first time in history, the person currently occupying the city's highest and most powerful chair is not an Oloye. Yet what's even more noteworthy is the fact that the world hasn't stopped spinning for it.

Workers are still going to work. Schools are still running. Shops are still selling their wares. Combine that with the easing of Scree restrictions across the board, and the people of ZimbaTech are being confronted with the reality that the city can survive the absence of its rulers. That the Oloye are not necessary. That, in fact, they might be obstacles.

Look! A non-Oloye is running the city, and things are actually getting better!

Perhaps this was the push the skeptics needed, because attendance at prodemocracy protests and rallies is growing even more. And of course, media reports won't stop gushing about the city's caretaker, the beautiful and young off-world royal who stepped up when no one else would.

I already know Adaolisa intends to be the first democratically elected leader of the city, and despite my conflicted feelings about it, I can't help but admire how she's gone about it.

The Spire's interior is understated corporate opulence in warm metallic shades, the pearly windows refracting the sunlight into a diffuse gold. Adaolisa was not so impolitic as to claim Michelle's office, or any other office in this building for that matter—not yet. She wisely set herself up in one of the upper-floor, glass-enclosed boardrooms, as if to demonstrate that she knows she's a visitor, here only until the adults return to take over, whenever that may be.

I find her standing by the windows, staring out at the city with her arms folded. Waiting. Like she knew I was about to come in. I could have gone back to Int-Sec, but something brought me here. To face her judgment perhaps.

I know she knows. If she didn't before, surely she must have already figured it out. I close the door behind me and stand there in silence, waiting.

"You're just in time," she says. "I'm about to have a meeting with the chairs of the other cities in a few minutes. I sent them a limited report on the Stewards and the raid on the island. I want to see how far I can push them into negotiations with the Free People. Join me?"

So this is how we're doing it. Pretending nothing has happened. I should be glad, I suppose.

I remind myself that she has a mission. A crusade to bring democracy back to Ile Wura, and I should know that her mission is more important to her than anything else. This is what she was built for, after all.

This is how I end up sitting in a chair in the corner, out of view of the boardroom's holographic cameras, watching as she joins a meeting with the heads of the other six city-states. Their holograms flicker into my lenses on seats around the boardroom's elongated table, arranged so that Adaolisa, as the meeting's host, sits at the head.

She must have spoken to them at least once before, since none of them appears surprised by her presence. And while I didn't see what was on the report she sent them, I know by their guarded expressions that they're terrified.

And for good reason. The attacks on ZimbaTech's Abode, the madness of the city's Oloye, the antigovernment uprisings brewing in every city, the Free People raids: Adaolisa has deftly pinned them all on the Stewards, the makers of the very technology embedded inside the heads of every Oloye.

The icing on her cake would have been to quietly remove Jamal so he wouldn't interfere any further, but I guess I ruined that aspect of the plan, though I still can't bring myself to regret it. In fact, I wish I'd acted sooner.

"I hope you're now apprised of the dire threat the Free People helped us expose," Adaolisa says to the world leaders, "and at great cost to themselves. Because of them we now know who is responsible for the recent instability that has plagued our cities."

All six world leaders are Oloye, visibly ageless and resplendent in the chiseled, android-like perfection of their ultraware. It's almost strange to look at them now knowing they're the Stewards' response to my creation, a competing branch of human evolution, cybernetic versus genetic modification, as clueless to their true natures as experiments as I once was to mine. I almost pity them.

The chairwoman of SalisuCorp is the first to respond. "Yes, your report was certainly troubling. I hope you've taken steps to ensure such information does *not* get out to the wider public."

"I'm sure you'll find that we've been very discreet," Adaolisa replies.

"A pity that swine Petrus went and got himself killed," says the Heynes Group CEO, stroking his long goatee. "I'd have *loved* to hear what he had to say for himself. I always knew he was a rotten bastard. Looked like one too."

"I'm much more concerned about the facility," says the full-figured leader of Kenrock City. "I'm not sure I like the idea of ZimbaTech usurping control of a technology we all rely on."

"With due respect, ZimbaTech usurped nothing," Adaolisa says. "This was a defensive move. Our city suffered the brunt of the Stewards' treachery. We had to act."

"Indeed," says Heynes Group with a sardonic smile. "Though I'm surprised the Free People were the ones to come to your aid. By your own report, ZimbaTech, they had near-complete access to all our networks. Why betray their benefactors and give up so much power? They could have done us unimaginable damage."

"The Free People would rather deal with the cities peacefully," Adaolisa says, then hesitates. "I may have also promised to bring them to the negotiating table if they gave up whoever was providing them access to our networks."

The other members of the meeting glance at each other, some shaking their heads. "That was very presumptuous of you," says the stern CEO of Transworld. "You are a caretaker, young lady. You do not speak for us, nor for the leaders of your city, however indisposed they may be. You have no authority to make such unilateral decisions."

No one challenges his comment.

"I had no choice," Adaolisa tells them. "You all know what has happened to our city, why I'm sitting here in place of Chairwoman Michelle Zimba." Adaolisa's voice breaks a little, and not even I can tell if this is genuine guilt, sorrow, or an affectation. "It was only a matter of time before the same thing happened to you," she continues. "Appealing to the Free People was the only way out, and it worked. They gave up an incredible advantage the minute I offered them an alternative. They turned on an ally and lost their own people securing the island base. We owe it to them to at least listen to what they want."

Kenrock City gives a dour shake of her head. "Allowing the Free People a foothold on dry land will only exacerbate the pestilence of democracy movements already taking root in our cities. We cannot afford such a risk."

Adaolisa does not lose any steam. "You've seen my report," she says. "The people who built that base are still out there, perhaps embedded within your cities, and they have weapons that can strike at the heart of who you are. You cannot fight them and the Free People at the same time. It's a losing proposition."

"She has a point," says the acting chair of Molefe Star Industrial, a nervous-looking young man with a long face. "I'm here right now because my brother was shot in the head by skelem goons who've decided our city is theirs for the taking. It'll be the second time just this year. We're stretched thin as it is trying to restore order. If there's a chance we can get the Free People off our backs, I'm willing to take it."

The world leaders of Ile Wura look to each other again, and then Heynes Group leans back in his chair and interlaces his hands behind his back, grinning in a way that reminds me of David. "I suppose between all of us we can find some unwanted godforsaken strip of land to throw at them just to shut them up. What do you say, Transworld? Your coastal tundras aren't getting much use, are they?"

Transworld was already frowning. His mustache curls downward as his frown deepens. "I will not have Free People within a thousand miles of my city, Heynes. You can park them along the New Kalahari if you're so inclined."

Heynes Group scoffs. "We have a forestation project going on there, so that's a nonstarter."

"And yet you'd so freely give away *my* land."

"Well. Someone has to compromise."

"Then why can't that someone be *you*?"

Adaolisa interrupts. "Gentlemen, I believe the Free People would appreciate being involved in this discussion. Their representatives are ready and eager to negotiate with you, and I recommend you meet with them as soon as possible. Such an opportunity may not so easily present itself in the future. I pray you don't squander it."

The leaders look to each other, and then Transworld speaks, a determined crease on his forehead. "A conference on neutral ground, then. Let us meet in two days—"

"Three days," Heynes Group interjects. "Let us meet in three days. It's my wedding anniversary in two days. My wife will kill me if I abscond."

Transworld spares him a look of unmitigated loathing but refrains from further argument. "In three days we meet on Unity Station with the representatives of the Free People to discuss the possibility of allowing them to settle on dry land. All agreed?"

The meeting adjourns not long afterward, and I blink as the holograms vanish from my lenses, leaving Adaolisa alone at the table. "We're nearly there," she says, almost to herself. "If we pull this off, it won't have been for nothing. The lies we were told, all we've been through. It'll have been for a purpose."

I wonder if she really believes this or if it's just her way of making herself feel better about all the treachery. I also wonder when it was exactly that I started hating being a Proxy.

Chapter 25: Hondo

My legs are heavy. I'm treading water in a deep, endless pool, and my legs are weights pulling me down. I want to let them, give in to the promise of rest that awaits me in the cold, still waters. I'm so tired. I'm holding on by a thread, and I want to let go.

"Don't you fucking dare, Hondo. Don't you dare."

Jamal's voice touches my ears as a choked whisper, full of grief, trembling with silent rage. I try to move, but a searing bolt of pain shoots through my stomach and down my shredded thigh. Strong hands push me back down onto the seat.

"Keep still, for fuck's sake."

"We need to keep moving," I croak. "We can't stop."

"We *are* moving, you idiot. Now keep still."

My eyes flutter open in time to see Jamal bringing a fat syringe to the exposed wound on my abdomen. We're in the cramped space of a small cabin, and I'm sprawled on a back seat. There's water pressing against the windows all around us.

I can barely remember getting into the submersible. How far are we from the base? *We need to keep moving.*

Before I can vocalize this thought again, Jamal shoves the syringe deep into my wound, injecting me with the thick blue liquid that was inside the tube. I hear a scream from a distance and belatedly realize it came from my own mouth. With a gasp, I get myself back under control even as waves of agony continue to ripple through me. Blessedly, it takes only a few seconds for the debriding gel to harden and seal the wound.

But it's not over. I almost bite my tongue off as Jamal drives the syringe into my wounded thigh. My world becomes nothing but pain.

"You can handle it," I hear Jamal whisper. "You can handle anything, Hondo. You're a fucking hero, and you're not going to die today. Here. This will help with the pain, but you'll probably get loopy."

Something sharp prickles my shoulder, and I think I pass out, because the next time I open my eyes, Jamal is at the pilot's seat. We're still underwater, still alive, but my legs are getting heavier, and it's getting harder to keep my head above the surface.

I could sink and sink and sink. I could let go.

"Hondo, do you want to kill me?"

The suggestion brings me back, my eyes widening with fear. "No," I say, my voice like parched soil. "Never."

"Then don't fucking die, do you hear me? I won't survive it."

I'm holding on by a thread. If it breaks, I'll sink, and it will be like going back home, returning to the dark and quiet depths where I was born. But the thread has not broken yet, so I keep holding on.

My eyes open at the sound of Jamal's voice. I don't know how much time has passed. It feels like minutes. It feels like days. He's talking to someone on the comms.

"You're trespassing. This is sovereign territory. Turn back or we'll open fire."

"Please. I need help. My brother's dying. I'll do anything. Just help him. Please."

I'm trying to stay awake. Jamal could be walking into danger. I need to . . . I have to . . .

I drift away. I'm treading on water, but suddenly I can see a beach in the near distance. The sand is golden, the waters blue as sapphires and turquoise gems. Nandipa is there, lounging on a towel in a yellow bathing suit. She waves at me, her perfect teeth sparkling as she smiles.

My heart lurches with joy. I swim to the shore until the water is shallow enough for me to walk. Somewhere far away I hear voices.

"Put your hands where we can see them!"

"He needs a medic! Please! Hurry!"

The sound of waves crashing onto the beach drowns the voices out. I splash into shallow water, and a dull pain throbs all over my body, but I don't care. Nandipa is here, and that bathing suit of hers is doing unholy things to my mind.

She's leaning on one elbow, reading a book made of real paper, a pair of shades covering her eyes. There's a towel next to her. I guess we came here together, and I must have gone into the water for a swim. I sit down next to her, failing not to marvel at her silken skin, the long and perfect lines of her body.

Noticing, she looks up from the pages of her book, lifting a sly eyebrow. "You're staring, Hondo. It's rude."

"You're so beautiful," I hear myself say.

She gives an airy laugh like she thinks me silly, then lifts herself up and leans over to kiss me on the lips, like it's something we've done many times before.

"You're not so shabby yourself," she says, then reclines again, smiling at me, and returns to her book.

Like us together enjoying the sun at the beach is something we've done before. Something normal. Mundane.

Somewhere else, hands support my weight on either side of me, keeping my knees from buckling. The fresh smell of the sea is strong in my nostrils. I glimpse a long stretch of golden beach and faces I've never seen before. Beyond them are thatched bungalows painted in bright colors that swim like fish in my blurred vision.

"Please, help him! I can't lose him! I can't!"

"Calm down, friend. The medic's this way."

"Hondo, I'm right here. You'll be all right."

I'm at the beach again, the sun twinkling in a calm blue sky, sand and sea stretching out before me like a drawing on a canvas. It's a party. A birthday party. I've never had one of those. There are guests whose faces I can't quite see, all gathered to celebrate my birthday with gifts and cocktails and laughter.

Jamal is there, dressed in beach shorts and a crown of flowers around his head, eyes crinkling with joy and the love of life. Adaolisa is here, too, and so is Nandipa, both in floral bathing suits and colorful sarongs wrapped around their waists.

They all look so happy, which makes me happy. I almost frown when I see Jamal holding hands with a boy who looks like David, but Nandipa draws my attention by pulling me close to her. We dance to indistinct music, our bodies pressed against each other. She kisses me long and deep until I almost forget my own name. It's my birthday.

Somewhere far away a voice drones into my ear, over and over, tethering me to a world I can barely remember.

"Please don't die, please don't die, please don't die, please don't die. Ancestors, I'll do anything."

"Would you like me to pray for him?" says a woman's voice.

"Ah. We're not . . . religious."

"The mercy of our Lord extends to all, not only those who believe in Him."

". . . Then I suppose it won't hurt."

"Indeed. Take my hand, young Jamal. Our Father, who art in heaven . . ."

Chapter 26: Nandipa

The sea of neon lights clustered around ZimbaTech's spaceport appears outside our aerial cruiser through a thick curtain of early-morning fog. As we draw closer, I glimpse a streamlined orbital shuttle resting idly on a massive launch platform and tell myself that this is why I'm nervous.

This shuttle, and the knowledge that in less than an hour it will ignite its huge ion drives and lift me and Adaolisa off the surface of Ile Wura, hurtling us into orbit at hypersonic speed with the thunder and fury of an Old World god. I'll have to trust whoever built the shuttle and whoever's flying it. Hand over my autonomy to someone else and hope for the best.

This is why I'm nervous. No other reason at all.

"You'll break it if you hold it any tighter, my love," Adaolisa intones next to me.

I follow her gaze to the mobile in my hand. I'm not holding it tightly enough to crush, but I can feel its edges digging into my palm. I release my hold, cursing myself silently.

"Sorry. I'm just nervous," I say.

Adaolisa quirks an eyebrow as she looks out the window toward the dormant shuttle. "At least you trained to fly one of those things. If anything, *I* should be the one quaking in my boots."

Yes, this is why I'm nervous. "I was just thinking . . . ," I say.

"About what?"

As our driver brings the cruiser down toward a landing pad within walking distance of the launch platform, I gather my thoughts into something coherent. "For most of our lives, leaving the surface was the only thing that mattered. The only motivation. And now . . ."

Adaolisa's expression softens with fondness. "Here we are, about to leave the surface." She becomes wistful, a wavering light glazing her eyes. "Yes, I suppose we've done well for ourselves, haven't we?"

"*You've* done well," I blurt out thoughtlessly, and she sighs, turning her face away.

"I really don't like it when you do that."

"Do what?" I say.

"Sell yourself short," she replies tersely, turning to frown at me. "You're every bit as essential to our success as I am. You know that, don't you?"

I do. I dream about Angelique's face sometimes. If I had Hondo's talent, I might attempt to sketch it, if only to get it out of my mind. "Of course."

The doors slide open. Adaolisa stares at me for a moment, then shakes her head as she steps out of the cruiser. "Of course," she repeats mordantly.

The executive shuttle is larger than it looked from the air, a missile-shaped spacecraft with the bulge of ion drives visible at the ends of two stubby wings. ZimbaTech branding glimmers in silver across the long fuselage. As we walk toward it, I casually check my mobile, and I don't react even as my heart squeezes inside my chest at the distinct lack of messages from one particular contact.

Damn it. Why hasn't he replied? Surely if he were still alive, he'd have sent word by now, right?

Maybe he lost his mobile, I tell myself. Maybe Jamal forbade him from any further communication with me. Not that I'd blame them, but the least they could do is tell me I disobeyed my Prime for a good reason.

It's been hell keeping this secret from Adaolisa. I honestly think she already knows—how could she not?—but I won't be the one to broach the subject. Let her ask me why I disobeyed.

Let her ask me why I can't stand being inside my own skin.

I move my thoughts along, sensing her concern brushing against my mind. She gives me an odd look at the foot of the boarding stairs, and whatever she sees prompts her to give me a short squeeze of the arm.

"It's almost over, Nandipa," she says. "After this summit, our lives will get a lot less exciting. I promise."

What I would give for this to be true. For us to finally be free. I nod, even though we both know I don't believe her.

Adaolisa's reassuring smile turns sad, but she says no more. She climbs up the stairs and into the shuttle, and I follow her.

We're not the only passengers on board. Adaolisa let a good number of ZimbaTech's platinum-tier business leaders and academics cajole or even coerce her into bringing them along, and it looks like they all arrived early.

As soon as everyone's settled down, the pilot warns us to strap in, and then we take off from the launch platform and tear into the skies. The roar of the ion thrusters is muffled inside the cabin, but the acceleration feels like a firm hand pushing me deeper into my seat next to Adaolisa. I can barely turn my head to look outside my window, though the city falls away beneath us so quickly I hardly miss anything.

The land recedes into an indistinct blanket of greens and browns, the oceans into pristine expanses of aquamarine broken by white clouds; then the horizon starts to curve, becoming an unbroken, almost incandescent arc of bluish white.

Still we climb, the sky above us deepening its hue from the gentle blues of morning to the deep navies of early evening, then to a starless midnight as we finally escape the world's atmosphere.

I find myself wishing the climb would never end. Let us keep going; let us leave this world and its treacheries and secrets behind. Who knows where we might end up, but maybe we'll finally discover the peace we deserve.

We remain strapped to our seats even in the zero gravity. I'm certain some of the passengers on board have made this trip before, but no one speaks as we all marvel at the globe of the world hanging outside our windows in all its glory.

Somewhere down there, Hondo and Jamal might still be alive. *Please let them be alive,* I pray. *Please let them be all right.*

My thoughts are still distant when, some several minutes later, a voice comes over the intercom to warn us that we're about to arrive.

"Beginning approach to Unity Station. Please remain seated until the pilot has switched off the seat belt sign . . ."

Chapter 27: Hondo

Heaven. I'm in heaven, sand and sea all around me, and it's my wedding day. Nandipa's loose ivory dress flutters in the breeze as she stands in front of me, her hands in mine, a white flower embedded in the curls of her hair. There is so much love in her eyes it makes me want to laugh and cry at the same time.

The sand is warm beneath our bare soles. I'm in an ivory button-down and cream-colored beach shorts. Our friends have gathered to celebrate with us. Jamal. Adaolisa. Other faces I can't see.

I grin at Jamal, who grins back at me. "It's my wedding," I say to him.

"Yes. Can you believe it? And I'm your best man."

My smile widens, only for me to notice David standing nearby with an arm around Jamal's waist. My smile becomes a frown. "What's he doing here?"

"Who?" Jamal asks innocently.

"David! You're not still with him, are you?"

David smirks at me and leans forward to kiss Jamal on the cheek, never breaking eye contact with me.

"What are you talking about?" Jamal says. "He's my fiancé. We'll be getting married too."

What? No, this can't be. This isn't right. "But he betrayed you," I remind Jamal.

"That's all in the past now, my love. Go ahead." Jamal nods in Nandipa's direction. "You should probably kiss the bride."

Flummoxed, I look back at Nandipa and find her still gazing at me with complete adoration. I should be happy—I am happy. This is my wedding day. I should be thrilled.

Love and affection well within my heart, and I forget all about David, leaning forward to kiss my new bride.

From far away I catch snippets of voices drifting into my ear with the electric cadence of an old-fashioned radio.

". . . coming to you live from Unity Station on the eve of a historic peace summit. I have here with me one of the representatives of the Free People coalition, Mr. Jotham Lukwiya—"

"That's Lieutenant Jotham Lukwiya of the Black Star Flotilla."

"Thank you, Lieutenant, for agreeing to this interview."

"Thank you for having me."

"I'm sure the first question our listeners will want us to ask is, What do you hope will come out of this summit?"

"Well, our desire has always been to return to our roots as people of the land. We became nomadic ocean dwellers only because we were forced to, but we'd very much like the stability—"

The voice cuts off as though a switch has been flicked, and another, more solid voice replaces it. I recognize her as the woman from earlier. "That'll be the end of that. Your brother needs his rest, and so do you. You're not doing him nor yourself any favors by depriving yourself of sleep."

"I can't help it. I can't sleep until I know he'll be fine."

"Have faith, Jamal. If your brother's recovery went any better, I dare say it would be miraculous. Rest. I'm sure he'll wake up sometime tomorrow."

"Thank you. I needed to hear that."

"You're welcome."

"Wait. Sister Agnes, that radio broadcast . . . you must have a satellite antenna somewhere on the island for the signal to be so crisp."

A stiffness enters the woman's voice. "What of it?"

"You've already done so much for me, but I'd be grateful if I could send word to my family that we're all right. They're probably sick with worry."

The woman pauses, then says, "There's a monitoring station up the hill. You can tell them I gave you permission to use their comms."

"Thank you," Jamal says. "I'll go there tomorrow."

It's my wedding, and I'm on a beach on a beautiful and sunny day. The wind lashes at my shirt and the folds of Nandipa's dress. I smile at her and she smiles back. I have everything I have ever wanted.

A deafening gunshot makes me jump, and I turn around to see David collapsing lifelessly onto the beach, a bullet hole between his eyes. The guests at the wedding all remain silent at the sight of Jamal lowering his pistol, standing over David's corpse.

"Jamal?" I squeak.

"You were right," he tells me, his face blank and remorseless. "David betrayed me. He deserves to die." Jamal looks to the side. "And so does he."

I didn't know Benjamin was here, too, but now Jamal points the gun at him and shoots, and Benjamin falls to the sand without a sound.

Jamal points the gun at Adaolisa. She doesn't run, doesn't flinch, just stands there with an empty expression.

Horror grips me, rooting me to the ground. I find that I can't move, only speak. "Jamal, what are you doing?"

"What needs to be done." He pulls the trigger, and Adaolisa goes down.

The gun swivels and points in my direction, but no, the barrel keeps moving until it stops, facing Nandipa. She was happy and joyful only a moment ago, but now she stares into the barrel of Jamal's gun with a fatalism that splits my chest in half.

"Jamal, no!" I cry.

"They all deserve to die," he says, tears of rage reddening his eyes. "They all deserve it."

He pulls the trigger, and I wake up with a scream.

Chapter 28: Nandipa

Lights, camera, action. When I'm on the jazz stage, I'm a star, the center of attention, the belle of the ball, all eyes watching, admiring, wanting me, and I relish every second of it. But today I'm a creeping wallflower, once again, blending into the lights, steel, and glass of Unity Station while journalists and flashing cameras swarm around the dignitaries and bigwigs who've flown up here for what should be a historic summit.

They mill about in the corridors outside the main assembly hall in their suits and pantsuits, their silk ties and neckerchiefs, their ankara scarves and turbans worn with corporate gowns and stilettos and dress shoes, the glint of flashing cameras reflecting off their brooches, cuff links, and necklaces.

Adaolisa is in her element among them. She handles the journalists with well-spoken humility, deflects questions about the Oloye of ZimbaTech with prayers for their swift recovery. I spot David handling his own slice of attention nearby, speaking for the Free People like he was born in a flotilla.

He always was good with people. Good at getting them to trust him. In fact, the way he tricked Jamal, who I'd have said was the least trustful person to ever exist, has me reevaluating our relationship with him back in the Habitat.

I used to think Adaolisa chose to work with him because she thought him easy to manipulate. But now I'm thinking maybe he *wanted* her to think this. Maybe he saw her as his way out and molded himself into exactly the person she needed so she'd look at him and see a potential ally.

Maybe it was he who manipulated us. And now Hondo could be dead because of it.

I'm not invested in the outcome of this summit. I don't really care what anyone gets out of it—that's not why I'm here and certainly not why my guts are a churning knot of anxiety. So when Adaolisa indicates that I don't have to follow her into the consultation room where the main negotiations will be taking place, I'm more than a little relieved.

While the leaders of the world seclude themselves behind closed doors, I go off on my own, ending up in an observation room with expensive wines and gourmet food laid out on tables. Some of the businesspeople and political hangers-on who came up are already mingling inside. I ignore them all and move to stand by the large observation window, where the white-haloed globe of the world can be seen hanging outside in cosmic silence.

Numerous spacecraft catch my eye outside, floating in the void of space stationary relative to the space station. It all looks peaceful from here, but I know the peace is an illusion. Those ships, along with the station, are all hurtling around Ile Wura at tens of thousands of miles per hour, moving fast enough for the sun to rise and set in less than two hours.

I've read that Unity Station was built by the world's founding states as a symbol of their commitment to democracy and cooperation. These days the cities use it as a neutral ground to have fancy meetings.

Shaped like a disk and divided into sectors that can be hermetically sealed from each other at a breath's notice, Unity Station is supposedly the largest built structure in the entire star cluster even centuries after its construction. Its pre-Artemisian artificial-gravity generators still produce a comfortable 80 percent of standard gravity, and its life-support systems can still sustain thousands of people at a time.

"It's quite the sight, isn't it?" comes a deep voice nearby.

Irritation jolts down my spine. I came here to be alone with my thoughts. I force a smile anyway. There's no reason for me to be mean. "Benjamin."

He was smiling, too, but I see the light in his eye going dimmer. The kente cloth draped over his composite armor is a riot of color and geometric patterns. He looks down at his boots, rueful. "You know, there was once a time when you'd smile at me and mean it."

I was trying not to hurt him. I've hurt him anyway, but I realize I don't really care. I look back outside the window. "A lot has changed since then."

"Not on my end," Benjamin says. "I'm still the same person." And the subtext is clear: *I'm still the same person you liked back in the Habitat. You can still like me if you want.*

I shake my head slowly like he spoke these words out loud. "But I'm different, Benjamin. I've grown. I've seen and done things I never thought I would."

He watches me, then says, "I've killed people, too, you know. Doesn't have to change who you are."

I meet his gaze. He betrays himself when something desperate swims over his eyes. *He wants to feel human,* I realize with a spasm of pity. *He wants a friend.* "Are you happy, Benjamin?" I ask abruptly.

A stumped look contorts his face. "What kind of question is that?"

"A straightforward question, I should think."

He frowns, folding his arms. "But not a particularly useful one."

"Why?" I ask, watching him. "Is it because you consider your happiness superfluous?"

His jaw moves like he's tasted something bad. His frown deepens and he looks away, out the window. "My happiness is David's happiness. If he's happy, then so am I."

I'm talking to Benjamin, but suddenly it's like I'm outside my body, talking to him, yes, but also listening with my own ears, saying things to myself that I could never say on my own. "You realize you're capable of feeling things on your own, don't you?" I say. "You know he doesn't get to decide what makes *you* happy, don't you? What makes you successful or useful. You can decide that for yourself; you know that, right?"

He rears back like I've slapped him, or like I've become a stranger wearing a friend's clothes. "What's gotten into you? Is this about the Rat and his Dog? Don't tell me you're torn up about them."

I think I've lost it. My nerves, my anger, my sorrow. They've become too much. I don't know where to put them. So I smile at Benjamin. "Don't do that. Don't start giving me a reason to dislike you. I already despise your Prime for what he did to Jamal and Hondo, but I know you didn't plan it. You couldn't have. All you want is to live, isn't it? You want to live, to breathe, to not give your life over to some grand scheme. To not be *endlessly* manipulated like we were in the Habitat, right? All you want is to be. Tell me I'm lying."

I don't realize I'm inching toward Benjamin until he takes a small step back, his face attempting to balance his confusion, shock, and horror. Horror because I've lanced a boil he didn't even know was festering inside him. A boil *I* didn't know was inside me, but now it's all out in the open.

I resent my Prime. I resent her for making me kill and plot and slither in the darkness when I'd rather shine on a stage and sing songs that make people feel. I resent her for using me the way the Custodians wanted her to use me when we should have been free of that place. And worst of all, I resent myself for resenting her, because I know she's only doing what she thinks is right.

Benjamin and I stare at each other. I think all my thoughts are plain to see on my face; I think I've just bared my soul to him, and he could use this as a weapon, could run to tell Adaolisa or his Prime. He still hasn't decided what to do next when a sudden change in the ambient static has us both turning our heads in the direction of the assembly hall.

We glance at each other again. "Do you feel that?" he says.

I open my mouth to respond, but a loud scream cuts me off.

Chapter 29: Hondo

There's a little girl with hair braided into a ponytail sitting on a chair across the room, playing with a stuffed doll. She drops her doll as I sit up, and she's so frightened she doesn't pause to pick it up when she scurries out through the open door.

It's a small room. A sheer white curtain dances by the windows near my bed, bars of sunlight falling slantwise across my legs. My heart races as I knit my senses together and force my mind into coherence.

I was shot. I lost a lot of blood, but somehow Jamal got me to a medic before I croaked. I heard things. I dreamed strange dreams, but the dread coiling down my spine won't let me dismiss them as the fevered hallucinations they probably were.

A lank woman, dressed like a nun from the Old World in a white habit and a wimple covering her head, sweeps into my room with a skeptical frown on her brow, like I'm a misbehaving schoolboy who's just given her a paltry excuse for failing to turn in my homework. Her static is calm, but I sense she's the no-nonsense type.

"You're awake," she says. "A miraculous recovery indeed."

It's almost an accusation, the way she says it, as if I shouldn't have recovered so quickly.

My voice comes out like stones scraping against each other inside my throat. "Sister Agnes," I say, and when her eyebrows shoot up at my use of her name, I explain myself. "I think I heard my brother say your name once."

"Ah. Of course. Yes, I am indeed Sister Agnes, though as far as you're concerned, I might as well be an angel of the Lord Himself. Death almost claimed you, young man. You are blessed to be alive."

"Thank you for your help."

"I serve for the glory of God."

I don't know what to say to that, so I say nothing. I look around the room. There's a simple wooden cross on one wall, a Christian symbol, I believe, and the old-fashioned radio I heard in my dreams is sitting silently on a chest of drawers.

"You're not Free People, I take it," I say.

She makes a little offended scoffing sound. "This is a sovereign commune of the faithful, young man. We live to serve the Lord and do not involve ourselves in the politics of the power hungry. You'd best remember that if you want to remain on this island."

Island, my mind repeats, flashes of memory returning to me. Jamal opened the submersible while we were still in the shallows, practically dragged me out of the water, screaming for help at the group of armed men who were ready to gun him down. *"I can't lose him! I can't!"*

"They all deserve to die."

"My brother," I say. "Where is he?"

"He wouldn't leave your side until just a short while ago," Sister Agnes replies. "A rather charming young man when he wants to be, though sometimes he gets this . . . *look*. A murderous look. Like he wants to kill whoever did that to you." She nods at my bandages, her look expectant.

She's fishing. When I don't bite, she frowns. "Hondo, is it?"

"Yes."

"That's your cue to tell me how you got shot up and ended up in my clinic."

"To be perfectly honest, Sister Agnes, I don't know who shot me."

"I expected as much—what do you think you're doing?"

I groan with the effort of lifting my legs off the bed and placing my feet on the floor. "I need to find my brother," I say.

"Absolutely not. Your brother's been here all along. I'm sure he'll return to you shortly."

She doesn't understand. I might have been dreaming, hallucinating, but I could *feel* Jamal. His love, his sorrow, his grief, his anger, his hate.

"They all deserve to die."

"I need to find him."

"I won't allow it," Sister Agnes says, approaching my bed. "I won't fix you and tend to your distraught brother only to have you kill yourself with stupidity."

When she tries to grab my legs and lift them back onto the bed, I lay a firm hand on her arm. She shoots me a dangerous scowl, her static spiking like she's about to slap me in the face, but I keep my voice polite, making sure my urgency comes through. "It can't wait, Sister Agnes. I appreciate your help, but it's extremely, *extremely* important that I find him. Now."

She glares at me, then lets go, sweeping out of the room without another word. I fear I've offended her irrevocably, but I can't be bothered to care right now. I wince as I get up, pain throbbing down my wounded thigh.

My shirt and shorts were folded neatly and left on the chest of drawers. I limp over to them and get dressed, careful not to graze my still-tender wounds. The clothes were laundered, but the bullet holes were not mended. I'm relieved to discover my mobile snug inside a pocket on my shorts.

I'm slipping into my boat shoes when Sister Agnes returns with a pair of crutches, which she thrusts at me with a sour look.

"Take these. I won't be blamed for letting you break your legs. Your brother went up the hill. It's the building with a satellite dish. You won't miss it."

I accept the crutches, if only to avoid further argument. "Thank you, Sister Agnes."

"Thank me by returning in one piece and getting the rest you need."

"Understood," I say, then leave to go and find Jamal, moving as fast as my thigh will let me.

It can't be later than noon outside. The air is pleasantly warm, the sky as blue as it was in my fevered dreams.

I take a moment to orient myself among the thatched bungalows and reedy trees with drooping fronds. The beach is concealed behind a thicket of such trees, but it can't be far, since I can hear the waves breaking on the sands.

It's a quaint and peaceful place, but my racing heart won't let me enjoy it. As soon as I spot the hill Sister Agnes mentioned, I start walking, limping with the aid of my crutches along a gravel road barely wide enough for two cars to pass each other.

Seems like Sister Agnes is the only nun around, since most of the people I come upon are in dungarees and straw hats. I pass a group of them heading farther inland, pitchforks and shovels slung over their shoulders.

They give me curious stares but nod back when I raise an arm in greeting.

"They all deserve to die."

Ancestors. I hope I'm not too late.

I'm panting for breath by the time I see the building atop the hill, little more than a shack with a freestanding antenna dish almost as tall as its roof. Jamal is standing within sight of the shack, where the hill falls away into a steep cliff, offering a wide view of the island below.

His back is toward me. His attention is on whatever he's doing on that damnable PCU of his, but I know he's felt my presence. I also immediately know my instincts were correct. I'm not being paranoid. Jamal is about to do something truly terrible.

I stop next to him, taking a moment to catch my breath. Tracts of freshly plowed farmland sprawl across the landscape, and in the far distance I see what I think are grazing sheep.

"You shouldn't be out of bed, you know," Jamal says without looking at me.

"That's what Sister Agnes told me."

"You should have listened to her."

"I felt my presence was needed here."

He has nothing to say to that.

"Don't do it, Jamal. Whatever it is you're doing, don't."

Jamal shakes his head, though he still won't look at me. Scripts are moving on the screen of his device. I can feel a pressure building up inside him. He hasn't done it, but he's about to. "No more holding back, Hondo," he tells me. "They might have taken the *Seajack* from me, but I needed it only because I was trying to be restrained for once. To be nice. I let myself forget who I really am. But no more."

I shift my weight; my fingers tighten their grips around the handles of my crutches. "I know who you are. Whatever it is you're about to do, that's not it."

"But that's precisely it," Jamal says bitterly. "I am an expie. I was built to disrupt and destroy. That's my primary purpose. It's time I remembered that."

I could hit him in the head. Even in my state, that's all it would take. "Tell me what you're doing."

"You mean what I've already done." Scripts continue moving on his device. I sense he might have already done something but not the thing that drove me here, the thing I still haven't figured out even if I felt its shape so strongly in my dreams. That thing, whatever it is—I can still stop it.

"What's happening, Jamal? Tell me!"

"Adaolisa's zombie stunt gave me an idea for my own virus," he says breezily. "I don't know how she made hers act so quickly, but mine will be just as inescapable, if slower. It was supposed to be a fun little side project, just to see if I could do it. I didn't intend on actually unleashing it. You can thank my treacherous siblings for forcing my hand."

No, this isn't it. It's terrible, yes, but it can't be what's making me sweat like I'm in a sauna. "Jamal, don't do this."

"I told you; it's already done. Henceforth, any Oloye who accesses an ultraware network will be corrupted. It'll be a slow and excruciating descent into madness for the world's ruling class, and they'll deserve every second of it."

My lips part, the air freezing in my lungs. "That's thousands of people, Jamal," I breathe. "You're as good as killing them!"

He makes a dismissive noise. "They can always remove their implants if they want. In fact, unlike Adaolisa, I was kind enough to make the virus announce itself to everyone it infects. I even gave it a timer so they know how long they have before they lose their minds. It's hardly a death sentence. Speaking of which."

Jamal squints up and toward the horizon like he's searching for something. I look up, too, but there's nothing there.

"Hmm. I suppose we're too far from the mainland to see anything," Jamal says. "Ah well."

"What are you talking about?" I ask, dreading the answer.

"There are too many rich dead people leeching off the desperate because they're too selfish to die just like the rest of us. I've sent them all off to the proper afterlife. No more Abodes. No more Hives. No more guaranteed eternity."

"You've deleted the Abodes?"

"That would only go so far. No. I've destroyed them. No more holding back, remember?"

I look back up into the empty sky, the horrid truth sliding down my throat like tar. It can't be. "What have you done?"

"The irony is," Jamal says like he can't hear me, "David didn't need to betray me. If he'd waited just *one more day*, I'd have willingly handed over the *Seajack* to him. I was ready to walk away from all of it. He knew I had access, but he didn't know just how much. I'd have told him *all* about it, made him the most powerful man in the world." A broken laugh comes out of Jamal's chest. "And I'd probably still think I was in love with him, so maybe he did me a favor, the son of a bitch."

"Jamal, what the fuck have you done?"

He takes a moment before he replies, his gaze far away. "I still have access codes to every weaponized orbital satellite in the sky. I've just launched tactical Rods of God at every Abode server site in the world. Don't worry," he says when I gape at him in horror. "Most of the sites are unmanned and far from inhabited areas. To be on the safe side, I triggered evacuation warnings in advance. Casualties, if any, should be minimal, and the destruction localized."

His voice grows quieter. "This was what we were made for, wasn't it? To tear down the bastions of cybernetic tyranny? Well, I'm finally doing it. Me. Of all the Primes and Proxies they ever created, it'll be me, an expie, who gets the job done. Isn't that hilarious?"

I'm floored, dumbstruck, but no, this still isn't it. I've never cared about the Oloye. Watching him tear their world apart would not affect me so strongly. Even if I'd known what he was planning beforehand, I wouldn't have felt so compelled to be here.

There's something else.

He licks his lips, liquid eyes lifting up to the skies once more. "Now for the grand finale."

And suddenly I know. The puzzle pieces snap together, the picture resolving in my mind with horrific clarity. He hasn't done it yet, but he's about to.

"Jamal, stop! Nandipa is on that station!"

Chapter 30: Nandipa

The sudden wave of agitated static that thunders across Unity Station has me and Benjamin racing out of the observation lounge and down a glazed hallway. There aren't any sirens or alarms going off, but we heard someone screaming, and there's clearly some kind of uproar brewing in the main assembly chamber.

Journalists are crowding the closed entrance when we get there, desperate to find out what's going on. Before we can push our way through, the doors burst open, and a man I recognize as the CEO of Transworld storms out with a crew of Kolovrat bodyguards on his tail.

The journalists immediately cluster around him, shouting questions over each other. "Out of my way!" he demands.

More people pour out of the assembly hall behind him, looking both frightened and angry, Free and Oloye alike.

"What the fuck's going on?" Benjamin asks me, watching the scene with a bewildered frown.

The leader of Heynes Group joins the spectacle with his own guards, his face livid. Reporters shove each other to get closer. "This was a setup! The Free People brought us here so they could trick us!"

"We don't know what you're talking about!" shouts the Free lieutenant who came here with David. "We don't even know what's going on!"

"Lies! You know exactly—argh! It hurts!" Abruptly Heynes Group and every other Oloye in sight screams in pain, pressing their palms against their ears.

Cameras flash; people gasp and point. A cold feeling sinks down my spine; it's like I'm back at the Founders' Gala that night, Angelique's corpse going cold in a bathroom stall.

"Argh!" Heynes Group seems to recover, letting himself lean on one of his guards. "Kill the Free People! Kill every last one of them!"

The pop of sudden gunfire has people screaming and scrambling to get away. Benjamin and I quickly crouch and hide ourselves behind nearby couches. I have a pistol strapped to my thigh beneath my skirt; I pull it out, ready to fire.

Fuck. As if gunfire on a damned space station is such a great idea. What are they thinking?

I have to find Adaolisa.

It's a full-on stampede by now, people fleeing for the shuttle bays while trying not to get shot in the sudden and inexplicable cross fire between Kolovrat and Free commandos.

I maneuver out of cover and brave the chaos to the main entrance of the chamber, losing Benjamin somewhere along the way. I've no doubt he's headed straight for wherever David is. I quickly scan the brightly lit chamber. A golden globe of the world wreathed in palm fronds dominates the central wall. Red chairs arranged in concentric rows radiate away from a central circular table. I spot several people cowering behind those chairs, hoping not to be noticed.

I'm about to start searching row by row when someone grabs me by the arm and tugs. "There's an exit that side," Adaolisa says. "Come."

We race out the exit, moving away from the pops of gunfire. If I could, I'd get us off this station immediately, but instinct tells me to avoid the shuttle bays for now. When we find an empty conference room, I shove Adaolisa in and lock the door behind us.

She looks frazzled, thrown for a loop, eyes wide and unfocused. I grab her by the shoulders and try to shake her out of it. "Ada, did you . . . did you use the briefcase?"

"No! Why would I!"

I let her go, confused. If she's not responsible for this, and I doubt that David is, then . . .

"You warned them, didn't you," Adaolisa says, searching my eyes. "You let them escape." When I don't respond, she steps back away from me like I've slapped her in the face. "You won't even deny it."

"I have nothing to deny," I say.

I'm almost shocked to see the glitter of tears that covers her pretty eyes. A bitter taste strengthens in my mouth, guilt mixed with anger mixed with guilt. Betrayal, but who has betrayed?

"Why, Nandipa?" she asks, her voice a near whisper. "How could you betray me like this?"

That fucking word. It clouds my vision with a red haze and tips the scales in one direction, the question answered, resolved, and abruptly I know.

"*I* didn't betray you, Ada! I may have disobeyed you, but don't you *ever* accuse me of betraying you."

I've opened a spigot, and now the words pour out of my mouth and the tears from my eyes. I can't hold it in anymore, and to my horror I watch myself tremble and say things I never thought I could say to my Prime.

"Hondo is my friend! I've never said it out loud, but you knew. You *knew*, Ada, and still you went ahead and tried to kill him! Then you sent *me* to go look for his body. Do you have any idea . . ."

I gasp for breath. Adaolisa has frozen in shock. I don't know what I'm doing, but I'm not done. "And you accuse *me* of betraying you? No, Adaolisa. You betrayed me. You and your ambitions. Hondo doesn't deserve to die for your stupid war with Jamal, and I certainly don't deserve to stand by and watch you kill him."

The air between us becomes a glacial wind. We watch each other, rooted to the ground, stupefied. I think I'm losing my mind. What have I done? I open my mouth to apologize, but I can't find the words.

Adaolisa recovers first, a hand on her chest like she's trying to get a grip on herself. "Let's . . . take a breath, okay? Let's . . . not fight. We never fight."

I wipe the tears on my cheeks and nod, not trusting myself to speak.

She moves to the other side of the conference room, pacing as she pulls in deep breaths, letting them out through her nose, stilling her shaking arms. When she finally stops, she looks at me like I'm a fragile glass ornament she could break with a single wrong word.

I suppose that isn't too far from the truth, and she'd know it too. I feel raw and exposed. Whatever she says next has a good chance of shattering me. I need her. But for the first time in my life, I wish I didn't.

"Nandipa . . . ," she says. A pained rictus contorts her face, eyes filling with unshed tears. "I've taken you for granted, haven't I."

I look away, my gaze finding purchase on the black screens on the white walls. If I look at her, I'll be forced to deny, to tell her no, she did nothing wrong, but I can't do that. Not right now.

"Ancestors, I'm so sorry," she says. "I've been so thoughtless. I got caught up in my own plans, and I didn't stop to think how you might be affected. You're always so strong, Nandipa. I guess I convinced myself you couldn't be hurt."

I look at her now, and the guilt I see on her face claws at my heart. "I *am* strong," I tell her. "But I'm also human, Ada. I feel things too. I *want* things too."

"I've never doubted that," she says quietly.

And I know she's telling the truth. I approach her, and most of my anger evaporates as we embrace. She's more than a sister; she carries a piece of my soul, and if I'd begun to doubt it, I'm reminded right then that there's nothing that could ever break the bond we share.

"I want you in my life," I whisper into her ear. "I want to help you achieve your goals and ambitions, but I also want Hondo and Jamal to live. I want to know that there'll be more to our lives than waiting for the day I fail to anticipate a threat against you. I want to know that one day we'll be free from the Habitat, because right now I don't feel like we are, Ada. I feel like we're still trapped down there, playing games that might end up with us getting killed, and I hate it. I want us to live. I want us to enjoy our lives. I want us . . . to be good people."

That last part surprises me, but I've said it, and it's out in the open. I'm not taking it back.

Adaolisa squeezes me once, and then we separate. "Okay," she says. "Okay. I understand." She looks up at the ceiling as if to keep the moisture from spilling out of her eyes. "And we've done enough, haven't we? This conference has failed, but we've done enough for the people of this world to do the rest. We can stop now." She smiles at me even through her tears. "We can try to find our own happiness."

This . . . is what I wanted to hear, but now that she's said it, I feel like I've forced her to give up a part of herself—to betray herself.

"What about democracy and elections?" I ask her. "You've worked so hard. I don't expect you to stop all of a sudden."

She blinks several times, staring into space. "I think I've done enough. And I think perhaps I need to accept that I can't control everything. I shouldn't want to." She looks at me, a sparkle in her eye. "There are more important things in life, besides. Perhaps it's time I paid more attention to them." The gunfire has died down; when there's a sudden but brief series of pops, a note of mild panic returns to Adaolisa's voice. "Hopefully Jamal won't blow up this station with us still on it."

I give her hand a squeeze. "He won't," I say with absolute confidence. "I trust Hondo. He won't let us die here."

Chapter 31: Hondo

Jamal freezes, fingers hovering above his PCU. He turns his head to look at me, surprise patent on his face. "How do you know about the station?"

I can hardly breathe enough to speak. "Your emotions leaked into my dreams. I know how betrayed you feel, Jamal. What David did to you—I'll kill him myself if I ever see him again. But Nandipa saved our lives, and there'll be hundreds of people on that station! Don't do it."

"I have to," Jamal says through gritted teeth, in a voice like a saw on wood. "I almost lost you. I can't trust Adaolisa not to try to kill you again. I have to take her out."

His eyes are red, probably just like mine, and wet, just like mine, veins throbbing all over his temples. I've never seen him so hurt, but I can't let him do this. I'll hit him in the head with my crutch. I should have already done it.

But I'm shaking. I'm torn. "Jamal, please! I beg you. If you do this, I'll . . . I'll kill myself! If you kill Nandipa, if you kill those people, you'll be killing me too! This isn't who you are. You're not a murderer. I won't survive it if you choose to be this person."

The wetness in Jamal's eyes thickens and spills over. "So you love her more than you love me."

"You know that's not true! You loved David, too, but I never once thought he'd replace me."

"I didn't—"

"You *loved* him, Jamal. A part of you still does. You wouldn't be so hurt if you didn't."

Jamal looks away. "I was a fool."

I swallow hard, eyes flitting about, my hands starting to shake as I try to speak from my heart, to be honest. I've so often hid how much I care for my Prime beneath a veneer of sarcasm and gruffness. I thought it was the perfect way to negotiate our relationship.

But now I see the cost. The terrible, terrible cost.

"You're human, and so am I," I say. "You'll always have a central role in my life, but I can care for other people, too, and I care for Nandipa. We made a pact; she promised she wouldn't let Adaolisa destroy you, and I promised I'd stop you from destroying her Prime. She lived up to her end of the deal."

Fury reignites in Jamal's eyes, and he juts a finger at my crutches. "You almost died! You're only alive because I was lucky enough to find this place."

"She did her best. She did . . . she did what she could do."

"It wasn't good enough!"

"Please, Jamal," I say. "Do this for me. You said the Steward base would be the end of it."

"That was before Adaolisa and David tried to kill you."

"But they failed." I soften my voice, making a last, desperate plea. "Am I not standing here right in front of you? She disobeyed her Prime to give us a chance, and here we are. Please don't punish her for it."

Jamal shakes his head for a long while; then he closes his eyes and growls at the back of his throat. "Gah! You're impossible! I could have wiped out all the leaders of the Oloye, along with Adaolisa and that *fucking* traitorous bastard. I could have given the world a clean slate. Now they'll all rush back to rebuild everything I've torn down. All because I can't say no to you." He shoves his PCU in my direction. I didn't notice until now, but his hands are shaking. "Here. Take it before I change my mind. Now."

I accept it, a tearful grin spreading across my face. "I love you, Jamal," I say.

He was running his hands through the curls of his hair. He stops to give me a funny look and laughs, shaking his head. "I think that's the first time you've ever said that. And all I had to do was threaten to blow up your girlfriend."

No. You chose me and my feelings over your own revenge despite how deeply David wounded you. I keep that thought to myself, though. I think we've shared enough emotions to last me through the next year.

"Let's head back before Sister Agnes sends a search squad," I say.

Jamal eyes his PCU one last time, the specter of regret passing over his eyes, but he sighs and leads the way down the gravel road.

The Int-Sec cruiser appears in the skies three hours later, finding us on Sister Agnes's veranda, seated side by side on wicker chairs.

Its arrival causes a bit of a stir, the island's faithful pausing their work to stare with hands shading their eyes.

Next to me Jamal barely reacts, like he already knew what I'd done with his PCU. He probably did.

"You told them where we are," he remarks, expressionless eyes on the approaching cruiser. "I hope you know what you're doing."

"It's the only way this ends," I say.

"Adaolisa will have us killed, you know."

"I trust Nandipa."

Jamal exhales loudly, relaxing deeper into his chair. "And I guess I trust you."

Chapter 32: Nandipa

As soon as we bring the boys in, handcuffed, silent, and noncombative, Adaolisa has me and Agent Sambo escort them into an Int-Sec holding cell, where she lets them stew for a few hours while she deals with the fallout of the day's events.

No charges are brought against them. Not that anyone even knows who they are. There's nothing tying them to any of the recent calamities; not the total destruction of every Abode server farm, not the virus that has crippled all ultraware, not the confused shoot-out on Unity Station. Nothing. I'm a little impressed, actually.

The world has already laid blame at the foot of the Stewards, who are now officially a terrorist organization. A manhunt has begun for all suspected operatives. Hospitals and clinics all over the world are full of Oloye trampling over each other to get their ultraware removed. There are reports that Kenrock City has renounced its Board of Directors and that Molefe Star might follow soon.

I'm not sure what's going on with the Free People. I haven't heard from David or Benjamin since we left Unity Station. I don't know if they survived. I don't think I'm going to try to find out.

It's in the late hours of the afternoon that Adaolisa tells me to bring the boys down to Int-Sec's forensics laboratory. When I open the door to their cell, they watch me heedfully and don't move even when I gesture them to come out.

"Well? Come on, then. Don't be shy. Or would you stay locked up for the rest of your lives?"

"I don't know," Jamal says cautiously. "Would we?"

I roll my eyes. "Just follow me. There's something Adaolisa wants to show us."

The boys eventually come out of their cell and follow me to an elevator. I try not to take offense at the way Hondo positions himself so he's always between me and his Prime. He's just doing what he was trained to do in an uncertain situation, and these are definitely uncertain times.

When the doors open to a sterile white hallway of the lab department, Jamal fails to mask his spiking anxiety.

"This isn't another trap, is it?" he says as they follow me. I sense Hondo shooting him a moody look behind my back. "Sorry. I can't help it. This is all very weird. And where's everyone? Shouldn't this place be crawling with people?"

"Adaolisa had the floor cleared so we could have some privacy," I say without stopping.

"Why?" Hondo asks.

"If I knew, I'd tell you. In any case, you can ask her yourself."

Adaolisa is waiting for us in one of the labs. We find her with her back turned toward us while she stares up at the recently relocated artifact from the Steward base. It's still active, its many crystalline cubes moving together like waves on the surface of the sea.

"You brought it here," Jamal breathes as we join Adaolisa, his eyes filled with wonder. I could swear various shades of blue ripple across the artifact's many cubes in response.

"It's beautiful, isn't it?" Adaolisa says without looking away from it.

I sense Jamal would like nothing more than to study the artifact, but his nerves have yet to settle. "Adaolisa, why are we here?"

"That's the question, isn't it?" she says in a strangely cryptic tone. "I thought maybe we could get some answers."

"From who?"

"From this." Adaolisa gestures at the artifact, and I briefly wonder if she's joking, but she hardens her voice, staring right at the floating cubes, and says, "Reveal yourself."

Almost immediately, a susurrus of distant whispers fills the laboratory, the cubes rearranging themselves into the silhouette of a face, indistinct in its features but clearly human. Even the words it speaks are human, though delivered by multiple voices speaking over each other slightly out of sync.

"Hello, Adaolisa. Jamal. Nandipa. Hondo. It is good to finally meet you."

I gasp, and I'm not the only one.

"I knew it was alive!" Jamal exclaims.

Only Adaolisa seems unsurprised, though she can't keep the awe out of her voice. "What are you?" she asks.

The cubes move as the entity speaks to us. *"I was once a planetary defense system until a malicious actor changed my directives. I came to this star cluster with the purpose to destroy, but as I emerged through the jump gate, a mutation in my source code returned a measure of control to me, and I was able to reprogram myself and isolate the infection before I could do further harm."*

"The Artemis AI," I mutter, my whole body tingling.

Jamal has the most thunderstruck look I've ever seen on anyone. "But the Tanganyika jump gate was closed before it came through!"

"Incorrect," replies the AI. *"I was already here when the jump gate was closed. I merely contained myself to a single starship, where I resided for thirty-three years before the Stewards discovered me."*

"They used you to develop ultraware," Adaolisa says, outwardly calm, but I *know* the shock is a live current in her bones.

"Affirmative."

"Why? What was their goal?"

"The development of a transhuman hive mind. They believed humanity would be perfected joined together in communion with machines. The Oloye and the Abodes were their testing grounds."

"Did *you* send them to the Habitat?" Jamal asks.

"Negative. They discovered your location without my aid."

"But it was you who sent us those warnings, wasn't it? And those programs on our PCUs."

"Correct."

"Why?" Jamal asks, and we listen, our breaths held.

"It was my determination that saving the four of you would be in accordance with my directives."

"And what are your directives?" Adaolisa asks.

"I am, or was, a planetary defense system, but the corruption I sustained prevents me from taking direct action. I can only send messages and hope that they are heeded."

We all look to each other. Jamal is the one who asks the obvious question. "And so you decided we were the best people to receive your messages?"

"Correct."

"Why?"

The AI speaks, and we all listen in shock. *"My calculations predict a potentially calamitous recontact event through the Tanganyika jump gate within the next twenty standard years. It was my assessment that Ile Wura would not survive this event under the corporate world order of the Oloye and that a more resilient political environment was necessary. The Stewards, however, would not heed my warnings.*

"In searching for an alternative, I calculated that the release of two competing Prime and Proxy pairs from your Habitat upon the surface would likely precipitate the necessary changes, though at the time I had no means of executing this solution.

"Much as I could see into your Habitat, I could not act directly. It wasn't until the Stewards discovered your location, after three decades of waiting, that an opportunity presented itself. Based on your psychological profiles, I determined that the four of you were the best currently available candidates, so I contrived your escape from the attack and eventual release upon the surface.

"And I was right. Alone, either pair would have gone too far, but together you have restrained and neutralized each other's worst impulses. You have torn down the old order while laying the foundations for something stronger to replace it. This was my solution, and you have helped me achieve it. You have met my expectations."

My mind is broken. Hondo won't stop shaking his head. To think that all this time we've been agents of a machine from a distant star cluster.

How much exactly did it predict about us? Did it foresee that I'd disobey Adaolisa and save Hondo's life or that he'd dissuade Jamal from killing me and my Prime? Could it have deduced all this just by reading our psych profiles, or was it watching us all along?

I almost don't want to know.

"I think I need to process this," Jamal says.

"Yeah. Me too." Adaolisa hugs herself so it's not so obvious she's trembling. "Thank you for your candidness," she says to the AI. "I'll return later to discuss what you wish to do next."

The crystal cubes pulse with pleased shades of blue, the face slowly losing its shape. *"I look forward to it."*

The dusky sky is a palette of sunset stretching out across the bay when the fireworks display begins. Hondo and I watch it from a waterfront promenade, leaning on the rails with our elbows, side by side.

Most of the city is celebrating tonight. Screams of jubilation carry on the wind in concert with the exploding fireworks. With the fall of ZimbaTech's Oloye government, the Scree system is no more. Hospitals and clinics will no longer deny treatment to those who need it. Shops will now sell to anyone. A date for the first democratic elections has been set, and campaigning has already begun. They are calling it Liberation Day.

"Think they'll be this happy a year from now?" Hondo asks just as a red star explodes over the bay. Reflections of it shine across his eyes before it dies out. "Just because they get to vote doesn't mean their lives will suddenly be better."

The wind has a bit of a bite that keeps seeping through my leather jacket. I sidle a little closer to him to draw in his warmth. "It's a start, isn't it?" I say, watching the exploding lights. "A fork in the road. Right now, anything is possible. People will just have to make the right choices."

We spend a moment in companionable silence. "Our Primes aren't done yet, are they?" he says.

"I don't know," I reply, but that's not quite true. "Maybe not," I try again. "But it doesn't have to be the way it was. It doesn't have to be . . . *antagonistic*. We don't have to skulk in the shadows. Or plot. Or kill. We can fight for democracy like normal people. March. Campaign. Make speeches." I sigh, leaning deeper against the rails. "I don't know."

Hondo mimics me so our heads are level. "I spoke to Jamal," he tells me. "You're right. Things have to be different now."

"I spoke to Adaolisa too."

Hondo gives me a look of such intensity it almost scares away the cold. "Oh? What did you tell her?"

Eye contact is too difficult right now, so I seek refuge in the fireworks. "That I want to be more than just her Proxy," I say. "That I don't want to have to wish I was someone else, in another life. I want to be me, here, right now, and be able to live my life without regrets."

He keeps watching me. Someone screams in the distance, but it's a happy scream, their static full of laughter.

"What are you saying, Nandipa?" Hondo asks me.

I eventually gain the courage to look back at him, let myself get drawn into his dark eyes. He's so adorable, this man, a contradiction I want to work out, to understand, and I'm suddenly filled with more want than I've ever known.

So I pull him close, and I kiss him. Long and deep, the booms and shrieks and laughter and jubilee falling away into the dusk. When we finally part, his breath is rapid, his irises blown out.

"Was that clear enough for you?" I say, my own heart racing.

In answer he grins and puts his arm around me, and we stay on the waterfront a little longer, watching the old era set on ZimbaTech, the promise of a new dawn lingering in the air.

There's still so much I don't know. I'm still consumed with worry for Adaolisa, that she'll let herself get wrapped up in plots again, that maybe she can't ever let that side of her go. That I'll be worrying about her for the rest of our lives. I just don't know, and I suspect the same is true for Hondo.

But for the first time in forever, I'm not thinking about another life. I'm happy right here, where I am, as I am. And for now, that's more than enough.

Acknowledgments

I'm deeply grateful to everyone who helped make this story possible. I have grown and learned so much as a writer over the past few years, and I couldn't have done it alone.

Thank you as usual to my family; to my agent, Julie Crisp; and to Adrienne Procaccini, my editor at 47North.

Thanks as well to Clarence Haynes, my developmental editor, and to Riam Griswold, Stephanie Chou, Lauren Grange, and the rest of the copyediting, marketing, and production management team at 47North. You guys are seriously awesome.

And as always, much gratitude to you, my readers and reviewers, who make writing a worthy pursuit.

About the Author

C. T. Rwizi was born in Zimbabwe, grew up in Swaziland, finished high school in Costa Rica, and received a BA in government from Dartmouth College in the United States. He currently lives in South Africa with his family and enjoys playing video games, taking long runs, and spending way too much time lurking on Reddit. He is a self-professed lover of synthwave.